MW01229716

A STARSEED LOST IN THE DARK

(Five parts based on personal experiences)

BY
Don Hudnall

First Published 2022 by Don Hudnall

This work is based upon real events. Certain events, dialog and characters were created for the purposes of fictionalization.

ISBN-13: 9798798643875

Cover design by: Don Hudnall
Library of Congress Control Number: 2018675309
Printed in the United States of America

ACKNOWLEDGMENTS

Tara. My soulmate. My wife. Thank you for putting up with me for the last few months. You are unique and the only reason I'm alive today. I love you.

Thank you Mona Hayden for editing this book and for being such a good friend. I don't know how you do it all. Writer. Editor. Publisher. Landscape artist. Even a broken wrist didn't slow you down or change your positive attitude. You are an amazing and brilliant light in the world.

Thank you Mom, Dad, my brother and sisters for being my family. You lived part of this story. You've known I had a secret. You thought you knew what it was. Surprise. This book shines a light on what was hidden. I'm not hiding anymore.

A Starseed Lost in the Dark

Table of Contents

...BEFORE

I'm becoming aware of myself. I feel separate. Where am I? What is this? Everyone around me is still working as if in a trance. Why am I feeling different? The one to my left is like me but not aware.

I'm in the back next to a door. I'm next to a door. What does this mean? I'm getting nervous. Keep working.

Who is that tall, slender being upfront? There is something behind it. It's a dark rectangular window about the room's length. There are ripples forming across the surface. It's a larger picture of our work, but it's real. It's a window to somewhere else.

The being upfront. It is slender with dark eyes dressed in a gray uniform. It's not like us working at these desks with boxes on top. It knows everything happening in this room as if it controls everything here. I've only just become aware of myself. Something's wrong. Keep working. Don't let on.

This box on my desk is like the window upfront. It opens to somewhere else. I'm supposed to touch the lives of the beings moving inside. I'm helping to guide them. Everyone is doing the same thing. Connecting with these beings to help. I have no idea what I'm doing. It's all intuition. A kind of knowing without knowing. I need to put my hand back in this window to somewhere else. Act like everyone else. Keep working.

Oh no. I touched a being, creating a ripple moving outward, touching others. More ripples are forming from those touched by the initial wave. Good. It only went three beings outward. That's acceptable. No one noticed.

Everything is ok. I'm happy. Wait. Happy? This is new. There is this feeling of self, then nervousness, now happy. Something is wrong. Someone is going to notice. Keep working. No. It's too much. The ripple is too large. It's hitting more lives. Fix it. Good. The damage is repaired. It's ok.

The one sitting to my left is looking at me. It knows something is wrong with me. I've been discovered. Keep working. Please let everything be ok.

Not again. The ripple is too big. It's hitting too many lives. Touching this life will cancel the ripple, like before. Stop shaking. Fix it.

Too late. The being upfront is moving towards me. Hurry, fix it. Maybe it won't notice. It's too much. Larger ripples. It's too much. More ripples. No. It's moving too fast. Cascading. It's not working. I can't. I can't.

It's almost to me now. What do I do? I don't know what to do. It's over. What else do I have to lose? I'm touching that life on the screen. "Remember." Something so simple, but it's massive. A huge change. The one to my left is looking at me like I'm crazy. It's here. My workstation shut down. I can't do anything else.)

(Leave)

(*It spoke directly into my head. Images showing me where to go. No words. I don't have a choice. Messed things up. There is nothing else I can do but leave.*

I didn't see the door open. I must go through past the two guards. I must leave the only place I've ever known. This place of white walls. The windows on their desks opened into another area. The window upfront reveals changes we made to the beings we were touching. That's how the tall being upfront knew I was having problems. It was there for all to see. I've had this feeling of self-awareness for only a few moments, and now I must leave.

It's the guards. No one is supposed to go through this door being guarded. They are so powerful. No one dares go near them, yet I must go through that door. Images in my head coming from them. Concepts. Unmovable. Impenetrable. Their ability to deal with others beyond comprehension. All this, and I'm not afraid. I must go past them no matter what is going to happen. I have no choice.

What? The guards looked at me and smiled. They have never turned their head and smiled. They never do that. What is happening? Why did they smile at me? Why? I must keep going.

There is another being like the other tall one. It's standing next to a pedestal with a book. It wants me standing in front of the pedestal. There is nothing else in this circular room.)

(Open)

(It's telling me what to do. I must open this living book.

The pages are transparent with glowing gold symbols. Each character in the book represents time. It's showing me the history of the place where we were touching lives. Each symbol represents time. Time is getting shorter as I flip more pages. The symbols overlap as I turn the pages. They take on new, more complex meanings. There they are. The ones like we were touching. The time the characters represent is so short now. There's no more. It's blank pages.

There is so much more to this book. I'm going to keep turning pages. There must be more. Finally. Something. More beings. They are different. Happy. Glowing. No hate. No poverty. No death. How much further does this continue.

What? The tall being is flipping the pages back. It wants me to choose in this section. Where these flawed people live and die. I don't know what to do. I'll flip toward the end of these imperfect people's stories. I know they are trying to learn. I wonder how far they got? I'm curious.

I guess it wants me to choose a life. That life looks effortless. Things come to it with ease. One could get in and out of that life without much of a problem. Wait. There is something else. There is a second lifeline spiraling around the original. A standard lifeline, then one of shadow. It's like opposites twisting around each other. I don't understand.)

(There is more experience when taking the lonely dark path. If you survive.)

(Why did it say if I survive? That life is getting closer. I'm falling. Can't stop. Where am I? I'm in that life. In a womb. A human waiting to be born.)

PART ONE – FORGETTING: CHILDHOOD

A Starseed Lost in the Dark

6

A Starseed Lost in the Dark

CHAPTER 1 – IN THE BEGINNING

(*Just a little bit more. Been driving tensed up since that semi-truck clipped the trailer, causing us to jackknife. We were not that far from Houston. Jerk. He didn't stop. Kids fell onto the floorboard. Daisy never let go of Sissy. Stop thinking about it. It's over. Everything is ok. Focus. Just a little bit more to our first house. That apartment in Houston was way too small for four kids. Four kids. I'm 25, and Daisy is 22. Four kids. Better wake them up.*) "Daisy, we're almost there. Wake the kids," Nick said.

"Wake up, sleepyheads. We're here." She knew this was a big moment, and Nick wanted the kids to be just as excited as he was finally making it to their new home. (*Mark this moment. 1967 and our first house. The McLure house.*) She turned to the back seat and began ruffling heads of hair to wake them. Adam first, then Luke, and finally Bonnie. Like little ducks in a row at four years old, then three, two, and finally Sissy at one.

The kids began to wake except for Luke. Daisy thought (*Every time. He's a sound sleeper. All the other kids wake up in the middle of the night crying or needing attention for something or another but not Luke. Once asleep, he does not wake up until morning. It must be because he's so much more active during the day than the other kids. Always running and playing wears him out. Wish the other three would sleep through the night like that.*)

"Rise and shine. It's time to wake up. We're here," Daisy said.

"Where?" Adam asked.

"Our new home. There's lots more space to play inside. There's even a big backyard." Daisy thought (*It's not that big, but to a small child, it's enormous. Especially compared to an apartment with no yard. I hope the wood fence in the backyard will keep them contained. So much work taking care of four kids. Diaper changes never end. They are going to love it here.*)

"It's only had one family before us. A doctor and his wife. They did not have kids so you will be the first children in the house."

They drove past a shoe shop, the car slowed and made a right turn onto a narrow one-way street. The boulevard drive is only wide enough for one car. The road is worn. The asphalt buckling in places. The road is U-shaped, with the other one-way side returning to the main road. There are a couple breaks in the median. It's made for cars to cut through so Nick will not have to drive all the way around. There is a magnolia tree in one median and a more prominent oak in another. It's early spring and the leaves are that new green color.

On the right side of the boulevard are two larger homes with bigger yards. The first is a one-level white brick home with a yard overtaken with weeds. It needs work, and it looks like whoever lives there does not care to interact with folks. The second home is also brick but not painted. It's like a castle with three concrete steps leading up to an archway covering the front door. It's square but with the left front corner being round with windows. There is half a second level, with the other half open for a raised roof deck. The yard is landscaped with camellias and gardenias.

"Look. There's our house," Daisy proclaimed as she pointed across Nick to the other side of the boulevard.

"It's the white house with red shutters. That's our new home."

Adam, Luke, and Bonnie stuck their faces to the car's window and pointed, banging their little fingers on the glass.

"That one, that one." they exclaimed.

"Yes. That one. The white one with red shutters. Nick. Drive around the entire boulevard instead of cutting through. I want the kids to see the neighborhood."

"Alright." Nick sighed and continued the drive around the end of the boulevard.

Just past the castle on the right was a lane. For some reason, it made Daisy uncomfortable. It was dark, unpaved, with the drive covered in pine needles. It connected to the main road only further down. The sides of the lane are overgrown. No light touched the lane, and you could not see the end.

"Kids. You are not to go here without mommy or daddy, ok. So we must be with you. Understand?"

They all nodded and immediately forgot what she said.

The lane was not the main thing worrying Daisy. As they made the turn at the end of the boulevard, the ground sloped downward to a large gully that contained railroad tracks. The lane they just passed ran parallel to the train tracks.

Daisy pointed to the gully and said, "If you look through the pine trees, you can see a train track down there. Won't it be fun to hear trains? Maybe you will get to hear the train whistle. Don't go down there without mommy and daddy, ok? Stay away from this end of the boulevard, ok?"

"Ok," they said in unison, immediately forgetting why they were saying ok.

They were now driving on the other side of the one-way boulevard heading back to the main street. On this side were four smaller houses. The first three were about the same size, with the fourth being a modified trailer. The front yards were a tiny bit larger than the length of a car and had carports attached to the side. The houses were so close together there were no side yards. Only enough space for rainwater to drain. The only thing that distinguished three of the places is the paint color. The fourth house - a modified trailer - sat perpendicular to the road giving it more yard space. It has a lovely covered patio over the front door that extends to the side. Then there was a little gravel path to a greenhouse. Then a covered carport attached to the house.

Nick slowed the car and made a wide turn into the driveway of their new home. He could only swing out so far because the median was in front of the house. The cut-thru openings were left and right, with the median directly in front of their new home. Not the most effortless turn with a trailer.

The driveway is two strips of gravel just wide enough for the tires. Nick had to pull the car into the side carport to get the trailer off the street. The boys immediately jumped out.

"Don't run. Come over here," Daisy yelled. (*They will be running into the road if I don't stop them now. They might even make it to the end of the street.*)

"Get over here now."

The boys ran over to her, touched base, and ran for the house's front door.

(*Ok. The boys are safe. Now to get Bonnie and Sissy out of the car. Then settle everyone into the house so we can unpack.*)

The front door is set back into the place making the entrance a bit of a U shape like the boulevard. Daisy looked left. There is a window leading to a dining section, and to the right is a window showing a bedroom. The house is square with a support wall running through the center. The first room you notice upon entering is a living space. To the left is a little area for a dining table, while to the right is an open doorway leading to a hallway.

"Kids follow me. I'll show you the rest of the house and your rooms," Daisy said, leaving Nick outside to begin the unpacking process.

"This is the living room. We'll put a couch on the back wall along with some chairs. We can all get together and play games here. Over there, we'll put a table where we can eat."

Daisy moves to the left through the dining area and turns right, going through an archway into the kitchen. It's small with space for a refrigerator on the right, then the stove next to it. The sink and counter space are to the left. There is a little more counter space before another opening to the right into a washroom and a door on the left leading to three concrete steps dropping into the backyard. Then through another doorway into a sunroom. This room extends into the backyard. Louvered glass walls look into the yard with enough space for bunk beds on the sidewall.

"Adam, Luke. This is going to be your bedroom. We can put the bunk beds against this window next to the door leading into our bedroom. This next room is our room," Daisy said.

They continued the tour by taking a right from the main bedroom into a hallway. There is a door on the left side of the hallway for the single bathroom in the house. Then you come to another bedroom for the front corner of the house with a set of windows looking onto the front door entryway.

"Bonnie. Sissy. This is going to be your room."

This hallway between the girl's room and their room concerned both Nick and Daisy. There is a metal grate on the floor in part of the hallway for the floor furnace. The house is pier and beam, and the heating ducts run underneath the house through vents in the wood floors. So the kids will be able to lay on the warm floor and won't get as sick. But there is this metal grate over the furnace with barely enough room to walk around in this hallway. It will get hot, and this metal grate could burn the kid's feet.

(*That's going to be a problem*) Daisy thought.

Daisy was relieved to get the kids settled. Now to start unloading and unpacking. (*It won't take long. We don't have much. I can set the kids loose in the backyard while unpacking boxes. I'll be able to look out the windows and see them.)*

The backyard has a bit of space. It's surrounded by a wood fence with bamboo growing all along the back. Behind that fence is the loading area for the grocery store where Nick will work. A large oak tree surrounded by dirt is in the middle of the backyard. The grass is mainly on the outer edges of the yard.

Nick thought (*I'm going to need a mower once I can afford one. Handling the money and orders for this grocery store is a good job. I hope I can get a mower soon.*)

"Daisy, did you take the notepad I placed on the kitchen counter?"

"No," Daisy yelled back.

"I could have sworn I put it on the kitchen counter."

CHAPTER 2 – MOVING OBJECTS

(We're almost unpacked. Not much to move made setting up this house easier. Tomorrow is Monday, and Nick starts his new job at the grocery store behind the house. Too bad there is not a gate through the fence, then he could just walk to work. You would have to add steps because it is a bit of a drop-down to the pavement. The kids would find a way through. Possibly fall and hurt themselves. Run into the parking lot and get hit. Stop it. Better not think about a gate. Nick can either drive or walk to the end of the boulevard then back.) Daisy jumped at the unexpected sound of a knock at the front door.

"I'll get it," yelled Nick from the other room.

Nick opened the door to find a couple in their mid-30s. The man was dressed in khaki slacks, a white shirt, brown vest topped with a beret on his head. The lady had on a long yellow dress with flowers. Her hair was pulled back and tied with ribbon.

"Hello. I'm Sam Cristoff, and this is my wife Ann. We live at the end of the street next to the convenience store. We wanted to introduce ourselves and say welcome to the neighborhood."

"You have the greenhouse in your yard?" Nick asked.

"Yes. That's us. I grow cactus in there. Just a hobby. We wanted to give you enough time to settle in before we visited," Sam said.

"Come on in?" Nick said as he moved aside and motioned for them to enter. They seemed friendly and laid back, as if they did not have a care in the world. "I'm Nick McLure. This is my wife Daisy and our four kids. Adam is over there playing with the airplane. Luke is the one running in circles through the house. The girl sleeping on the couch is Bonnie. The youngest is Sissy.

Ann said, "That's a handful. So how do you manage?"

Daisy laughed, saying, "I don't manage. I just try to survive. They get into everything. My only goal is to keep them alive. Nothing else. Please sit down. Would you like some coffee?"

"We would love some coffee. We noticed you had kids when you moved in. Yours are the only kids on the boulevard so we brought a few gifts for them. Stuffed dogs and teddy bears," Ann said as she handed them over to Nick.

"I want a brown dog," Adam shouted as he jumped and ran to Nick. "He's Brownie."

Luke stopped long enough to grab the white and black spotted stuffed dog. Then he started playing with it without a word on the floor.

Nick set one of the bears next to Bonnie, sleeping on the couch, and handed the other to Sissy.

Daisy returned from the kitchen carrying a tray holding four cups of coffee, sugar, and creamer. She put it down on the dining room table. The adults settled into their chairs and began to learn about each other.

"Where are you from?" Sam asked.

Nick responded. "We both grew up 45 minutes from here. We dated, got married, and moved to Houston for my job. That's where we had the kids. Four kids in an apartment. We needed more space and wanted to be closer to family. I found a job working at the grocery store nearby. Here we are. Have the two of you been in this neighborhood long?"

"Yes. A long time. We like it here. It's quiet."

"This coffee is good but I could use just a bit more sugar," Ann said as she reached for it on the tray. She drew her hand back, confused. "I'm sorry, I thought it was on the tray. Oh, there it is. Next to you, Nick. Do you mind?"

"That's odd. I don't remember putting it there. I don't even use sugar. Here you go. You were saying that it's a quiet neighborhood."

Sam chimed in, "very quiet. That first house with the large yard that's grown over is empty. No one lives there. Something to do with taxes. The other brick house with the landscaped yard belongs to a widow. Her name is Elizabeth Stotter. She is friendly but reclusive and picky about her yard. Your kids might want to stay out of her yard. A single man lives in the small wooden house on this side of the road near the tracks. He works nights, so you won't see him much. The house to your right is owned by a middle-aged couple working during the day. They stay out lots of nights. They are hardly ever around. The house to your left is owned by another couple who are gone most of the time. They stay with relatives most of the time. Then there is us. Your kids might like to play with our dog, Bingo. He's a little pug. Mostly friendly. We also make wine so come on over and visit if you need a little getaway time. The greenhouse should be off-limits to your kids. It's all cactus and they could get hurt."

"Sounds wonderful," Daisy said with a grin. "A quiet neighborhood with almost no traffic to worry about.

# # #

It's been six months since Nick started working at the grocery store and discovered he prefers driving to walking even though his job is literally in his backyard. It rains a lot in Louisiana so he takes the car most days except when Daisy needs it to take the kids to the babysitters and run errands. Finding the babysitter has been a godsend. She has three little ones of her own around the same age. It gives Daisy some much-needed time away from the kids. As Nick enters the house, he hears the kids yelling as they run.

"Daddy's home, daddy's home."

Nick's familiar with this nightly routine. He braces himself as they run and jump, expecting him to catch them. He then gently sits them back down as they run off to tell Daisy that daddy's home. As if she had not noticed.

"Would you like some sweet tea?"

"Sure."

She walks out of the kitchen and sets the glass on the corner of the dining room table. Nick looks to the left, where she sets the glass, then to Daisy walking back to the kitchen. (*This is our life now. Routine.*

Still can't afford much, but we are making it. Thank God anything is a toy to the kids.)

Nick glanced at the kids and said, “I brought you something from the store.” Nick leaves to retrieve something from the car.

Adam looked at the glass of tea on the table. As he watched, the glass slid across the table to the other corner without spilling a drop. (*Daddy was afraid I might knock it off the table. I'm glad it moved.*)

Nick entered the house carrying a cardboard box and dragging a much larger box behind him. “I got these boxes from work. This one's a refrigerator box. This other box has old telephones in it. I figure you could make something out of them.” (*That will last about a week.*)

Nick reaches for the tea and realizes it's been moved. “Alright. Which one of you moved my tea?” He retrieves it and says loud enough for Daisy to hear as she's coming out of the kitchen with dinner, “Little pranksters moved my tea.”

Daisy says, “They do that to me all the time. Last week, they were having a field day with my jewelry. I'd go to our bedroom, find a piece out of the jewelry box and place it on the dresser. I'd put it back, then next time I go in the room, it's out again. They would do it over and over. I told them they are never to play with anything in this room, but you know how they are.”

# # #

It's Daisy's day to have the car and some time to herself. She dropped the kids off at the babysitter's house when Nick left for work. She needed time to herself. So she finished her errands and headed to the babysitters to pick up the kids.

Driving alone was relaxing but she could not help thinking about the day before. (*The department store was very kind, letting us go after Adam found the controls to the escalator. He was having a ball, turning it on and off. Watching the people hold on as he giggled. Then corralling the others as they scampered, hiding under the racks of clothes. It's so embarrassing thinking these people see me as the worse mother in the world. People just don't understand. I'm doing a great job just keeping them alive. I'm here already. I wish that drive was longer.*)

Laura answered the door. “Hi, Daisy. I hope you had a good day to yourself.” Laura continued as Daisy entered the babysitter's home. "Bonnie and Sissy are here in the house. The boys are out back with my girls playing. Probably in the shed. They tend to get in there even though it's off limits. I have a favor to ask. Would you mind watching my kids tomorrow? I think I'm going crazy and need a break."

"Sure. I can watch your kids. Why do you think you're going crazy?" Daisy asked.

"Well, I used to think it was the kids playing pranks on me, but sometimes things move even when I'm watching them. For example, today, I saw an empty glass move across the counter while the kids sat at the table. I know I scared the kids when I screamed, but I couldn't help it. So I think I need a break."

"You are not alone, Laura. Things seem to move at my house but I've never witnessed it happen. Drop your kids off tomorrow, and I'll watch them. Would you get the boys? I need to head home."

"Adam, Luke!" Laura yelled out the back door. "Your mom is here to pick you up."

Luke and Laura's girls ran out of the shed toward the house but Adam stayed behind. He was staring at a glass on a shelf in the shed. Focusing with all his might to make it move. The glass slid a few inches across the wooden surface. *(That's all. Keep trying. I'm forgetting. Was it relax and let it happen? Was it focus hard? I can't remember.)* The glass began to wobble then stopped. Nothing else. *(I've forgotten. I suppose it's ok. She screamed. Maybe it's a bad thing.)*

"Adam. Don't make me come out there and get you," Laura yelled. She held the back door open as Adam emerged from the shed and ran into the house.

"See you tomorrow morning Laura," Daisy said, exiting the house and settling the kids into the car.

A Starseed Lost in the Dark

CHAPTER 3 – FORGETTING

Adam thought (*I remember being able to move things without touching. It was simple, but it scared her. I'm forgetting. I'm even forgetting that I ever did that at all. It's fading away. There are all these other memories from before I was born. Being in a classroom. Messing up. Passing those guards. Being told to come here. I'm beginning to forget that also. Everyone that comes here remembers. Then they forget. Am I going to forget like everyone else? It's so clear I can't imagine forgetting, but I've already forgotten how to move things. This forgetting only happens at this age. If I repeat these memories in detail every day until this period of forgetting ends, then maybe I can remember. If I remember, I won't be like everybody else. I'll be different and alone in this dark world. It's that dark path I saw. I was told I could learn a lot from taking the lonely, darker path. So, I'm going to try.*)

(Remember)

It was an odd voice in Adam's head. He didn't know where it came from, but it didn't matter. It was Saturday, and daddy's home.

Nick figured he would walk the kids to the convenience store at the corner of the boulevard. At least he can start giving them the concept of money. Give them a nickel and let them buy candy. After that, it's their own money to get what they want. Money is the most important thing. You can't live without money.

(*Where are the kids? Probably in the backyard playing on that new tower I set up. It's only a few feet tall with a platform on top but to them, it's a tall fort.*)

As Nick walked out the back door, he stopped. In a surprised tone, he asked the two boys on top of the tower, "What are you doing?"

"We're peeing the most far away," Luke replied as the two streams coming from the tower slowed then stopped.

"Well. Who won?"

"I don't know. We looked at you."

Nick laughed. "Come on. Let's walk to the store. I'll give you a nickel, and you can buy some candy."

Luke and Bonnie ran forward, backward, then in circles around Nick as they walked. Nick was busy, carrying Sissy on his shoulders. She got worn out quickly. Adam, however, was walking and doing his best to remember.

(Sitting in the back of the classroom, figure upfront, working, making ripples, mess up, walk out, guards, glowing book, perfection, falling to earth, others here also, need help, third time, darkness, attack, portals, protect, change, hope. What's the rest? Oh no! I've forgotten the rest. Going through every detail every day for weeks, I'm still forgetting. Try again. Back of classroom, figure upfront, working, making ripples, mess up, walk out, guards, glowing book, perfection, falling to earth, others here also, need help, third time, darkness, attack, portal…what's the rest? Multiple? Hold? Change maybe? I'm forgetting.)

"Kids. Here is your nickel. Don't lose it," Nick said.

Nick could hear a train in the gully behind him as they walked. "Hear the train?"

"Yay. Can we go see?" Luke asked.

"Next time. We are going to get candy, remember."

"Candy."

"You know what else you can do with a nickel?" Nick said. "You can put it on a railroad track, and when a train comes by, it will smush it flat. Then you have a big, thin flat nickel." *(What else can I say as we walk. Daisy is the storyteller.)*

"Wow," Adam said, losing his thought to a train.

###

The weather turned colder. Fall was here. Daisy wanted to rake up the leaves that had fallen in the front yard. She let the kids play in the median while she raked. The streets are empty, especially in the middle of the day. They can watch Daisy piling up leaves in the front yard.

Then they will run and jump in them. Leaves go flying and double the amount of time it takes to rake, but seeing them have fun is worth it.

(It's nice to get out and do a bit of yardwork. Anything to get out of the house. I'm so tired of being stuck indoors. Love this neighborhood. The kids have learned to watch for traffic, and the neighbors know to watch out for the kids. The whole area is just an extension of our front yard. The neighbors always bring the kids back after finding them exploring in their yards. Hmm. Funny, the kids decided to play in the dirt in the median. Making mud pies instead of jumping in the leaves.) "I'll be taking the leaves to the back to burn. Stay out of the street," Daisy said as she gathered up a pile of leaves then walking around the carport to the backyard.

"Hey, look! I found a penny," Adam said, showing Luke.

"I want to find one," said Luke as he began looking through leaves and grass in the median. Bonnie followed Luke's lead and started looking through the grass as well. Sissy continued digging in the dirt.

(I could put the penny on the tracks to smush it. Trains come before daddy gets home. I'm going to put it on the train tracks) Adam thought as he headed down the center medians toward the gully.

As he walked, he recalled details of that odd memory *(Back of classroom, white robes, figure upfront, working, making ripples, mess up, walk out, guards, glowing book, perfection, falling to earth. What's the rest? I've forgotten the rest. Ok. I think it's going to be ok. The time of forgetting has passed. I think I will be able to remember this bit. I'm not going to forget anymore. It's ok.)*

Adam reached the end of the median and crossed the boulevard street. A feeling of fear crept up from his right side. He turned to look down the dark lane covered with pine needles. He thought he saw the shadows move but couldn't be sure. He figured it was just wind moving the leaves, causing the shadows to move. Then he felt a presence. He stopped when his foot slipped. He walked backwards down the slope leading to the train tracks and almost fell. He looked back to the dark lane. It's ok. Nothings moving. The presence he felt was gone.

(There's a path down. To the tracks. People must use it so it's ok to go down there. It's not dangerous if other people are using it) Adam thought as he made it down the little animal path. Hanging on to roots growing out of the ground as dirt slid underneath his shoes.

He made his way through the tall grass to the tracks. Placing the penny on the track, he wondered how long it would take. Would a train come by today? Maybe tomorrow? He put his ear on the rail and listened. Nothing.

(*I'll come back tomorrow and check*) he thought as he headed back to the path leading up to the street. Then he heard the sound of a train. He turned around, and a train came around a corner in the distance.

It was thunderous. Exciting to be this close to a train. Adam could feel the wind from the train passing. There is the caboose. His favorite part of the train. He waved as it left and ran to the track to find his penny.

(*I can't find it. Where did it go? It's not here. It doesn't work*) he thought as he looked up to see a boy about his age standing on the other side of the tracks. The boy looked like him except darker somehow.

"Hi. I'm Adam," the boy said.

"That's my name. I'm Adam."

"What are you doing."

"My daddy said if I put a nickel on the track, it would smush. So I found a penny and put it on the track. I can't find it." Adam said as he got this odd feeling. As if the train tracks were a barrier. The other side was a mirror image reflecting everything.

The boy said, "My daddy said that wouldn't work. But he did tell me how to be like a train. You get a rope and connect others, like a train."

"How do you do that?"

"I'll show you," He said as he pulled some string from his pocket. "You make a circle, wrap this end of the string around and around, then pull it through here. See how the circle shrinks when you pull this end. Putting it around the neck is easiest, and then you pull. Just like a train. Try it sometimes."

"Ok. It's time for daddy to get home. I have to go. Bye," Adam said as he turned and began the walk back to the path up to the boulevard. He looked back as he started the climb, but the boy was gone. Adam stepped onto the boulevard and began walking back home.

(There is a muddy, naked child sitting at the end of the median close to the main street. Oh god. It's Sissy, my child. What's she doing here naked) Nick thought as he pulled into the boulevard and stopped to get her. "Are you alright, Sissy?" Nick asked as he picked her up and placed her in the seat next to him.

"Uh-huh."

As Nick drove closer to the house, he noticed Luke and Bonnie playing in the median covered in dirt. Adam is walking down the boulevard from the direction of the train tracks. He sees Daisy coming out from the carport. She waves as if nothing is out of the ordinary.

"I found Sissy sitting naked at the end of the street. How did she get there?" he asked, stepping out of the car holding Sissy.

"I have no idea. I just finished raking and came out front as you were driving up."

Nick said, "It's embarrassing to come home and find your baby girl sitting muddy and naked on the side of the street looking abandoned. It makes us look like terrible parents."

"I'm not a terrible parent! I'm just trying to keep them alive. You don't know what it's like being here. Taking care of four kids. The never-ending diaper changing, washing, feedings, cleaning, never resting, and yardwork. You know how the kids are. Always exploring. Finding things to get into. Sissy is walking. One person can't handle all this," she yelled.

"Keep your voice down. Everyone's going to hear."

"I don't care if everyone hears," Daisy yelled even louder. "I need help, and there is no help. We can't afford help. Almost everything we have has been given to us because they saw we needed help."

"I'm doing the best I can," Nick yelled back just as loud. "Kids. Get in the house now. NOW."

It's another one of those days.

CHAPTER 4 – FLOATING

Ann continued talking as she returned to the kitchen from the boy's room. "Our families don't associate with us because we make wine. They disapprove. So we miss out on seeing the nieces and nephews. So I appreciate you letting me come over and enjoy the kids now and then."

Both Ann and Daisy turned to look out the kitchen window into the backyard upon hearing the back door slam shut. Adam, Luke, and Bonnie had run out to play.

"Daisy, when I was in the boy's room watching them, I heard this music box playing. But I couldn't find it. So where is the music coming from?" Ann asked.

"Music box? Funny you said that. There's not a music box. One of my nephews said the same thing when my sister visited last month. He asked about the music box that was playing. Laura, our babysitter, said the same thing once when she dropped off her kids. It's probably just wind chimes or something from next door," Daisy said, reaching for an explanation.

Ann shook her head in agreement. "Thank you for the tea, but I have to be going. Come and visit us anytime," Ann said as she glanced out the kitchen window before leaving.

"Daisy. The kids!"

Ann said it with such force Daisy ran to the window and saw Adam on top of the tower holding a noose wrapped around Luke's neck. Luke's feet are not touching the ground. Daisy screamed. Panicked, she bolted out the back door, grabbed Luke, and lifted him into the air as she removed the rope from his neck. Luke is gasping for air.

"Luke. Luke, are you ok. You're ok, aren't you?" she quickly asked.

Luke said, "Yeah."

"What the hell were you doing, Adam? What were you thinking? You could have killed Luke!"

Adam started to cry, not knowing what had gone wrong. Adam sobbed, saying, "We were just playing train. The other boy named Adam showed me."

"What other boy?"

"He lives on the other side of the train tracks."

"There is a street and stores over there, Adam. No one lives there," Daisy said. "Who taught you to do this?"

Adam continued crying, unable to answer. It was a bad thing. (*Why did he show me a bad thing?*)

"You're in trouble. Go inside now. I'm going to tell your father about this. You are never to do this again. You understand?" Daisy said walking back inside.

"I'm sorry Ann. Can we continue our visit later? I've got my hands full right now."

"Of course. I hope Luke is going to be ok. We are just down the street if you need anything. Bye" Ann said as she left.

Nick arrived home and learned what had happened. Adam had received spankings before, but not like this. This was something different. Much more serious. (*Why did he show me that? No one lives there. Where does he live? Why did he do this*) Adam thought as he stared up at the springs from the bottom bunk. It's late. Luke was asleep in the top bunk, but Adam couldn't sleep. The light shining through the louvered glass from the grocery store in the back never bothered him before. It was nice not having curtains. It was like sleeping outside. (*He lied. Why do they lie?*) As Adam continued to stare at the springs supporting Luke's mattress overhead, the springs began to grow larger.

(*What's happening? The springs are getting huge*) Adam thought as he floated through the springs, through the roof, and above the house.

(It's pretty from up here.) Then he was somewhere else. A gray room. Lying on a table. There are others. Then a voice in his head.

(Don't be afraid. We are here to help you. It may be uncomfortable for a while, but it will help you later. Like when people go to the dentist. They don't have fun, but they know it will help. It's like that.)

That calmed Adam. This kind of thing is normal. Everybody does this. It is like getting your hair cut.

(It's over, back in bed. Just let the others do what they needed to do. Not as bad as getting a spanking. Not as bad? What was not as bad? I don't remember. It's normal. Yes. Everybody does this.)

# # #

"Mommy, can I have a glass of root beer?" Adam asked.

"Sure," Daisy said as she poured root beer into a pint-sized canning jar used as a drinking glass. "Here you go."

Adam slowly carried the glass to his bedroom, making sure not to spill any. He sat it on the floor at the end of the bunkbed. *(I'm going to be a crazy scientist. What can I make with a glass of root beer?)*

He rushed to the bathroom, grabbed the toothpaste, and squeezed some into the glass. Putting the toothpaste back, he searched for something else to add. He found a battery, then a dime, and added some milk. He put them all into the glass with the root beer, covered with aluminum foil, and hid it under the bed. *(I'll leave it there and see what happens.)*

Adam went to bed that night, the springs above him grew more prominent, and he floated out above the roof. It's happened many times now, and he did not think anything about it. No need to talk about it. You don't talk about getting a haircut. No need to even remember it because it's an everyday thing. Like eating breakfast.

A loud clap of thunder woke Adam. Adam could feel something outside. The thing outside was getting stronger somewhere outside circling the house. The light from the store in back went out. Everything went dark except for the flashes of lightning. The fear solidified and moved toward the back door.

(It's coming through the back door. Turning this way.)

"Daddy. Daddy." he grabbed his stuffed dog Brownie, who is missing an eye now, and ran into the parent's room next door.

"Brownies scared." He was followed by Luke and Bonnie, all jumping into their bed.

"It's alright," Nick said as Daisy got up.

"I'll get Sissy so we can all be here together," Daisy said as she left for the girl's bedroom.

Adam pointed past the converted sunroom to the back door. "It came through the back door." As soon as he said those words, this dark presence was forced out. Forced by something protective.

(Is something protecting us?)

"What did?" Nick asked.

"I don't know. It's gone. Make sure it's gone, daddy."

He was awake now and might as well check. The power came back on as he walked through the boy's room. The light from the grocery store shone in. "I'm checking the back door. Everything's fine. There is nothing here. Power is back on." He said, returning to bed. "You can all sleep with us tonight."

The kids settled in as they had done before. *(I wonder how many more times they will jump in bed with us before they grow out of it. Faster, please.)* Nick's final thought as he fell back asleep was *(The back door was unlocked. I could have sworn I locked the door.)*

CHAPTER 5 – FURNACE

A cold front made its way to Louisiana. As a result, the furnace will be lit for the first time. Daisy is looking forward to seeing how warm the floor gets. The duct work from the furnace runs underneath the raised house and exits through vents in every room. One of the living room vents is nearest the furnace, so she expects the living room to be the warmest. Daisy talked to relatives, and they loved the house having warm floors. It should help keep the kids from getting sick. Playing on a warm floor in winter is much better than playing on a cold one.

Leaves were piling up out front, so Daisy figured she might as well rake them up while the kids were busy playing inside on this cold day. "I'm going out front to rake the leaves. Stay inside playing where it's warm."

"Hot chocolate?" Luke asked questioningly.

"Sure. If you promise to stay inside while I'm outside raking leaves."

"We promise," Luke announced on everyone's behalf.

Daisy proceeded to the kitchen, followed by Adam. He liked to help. Especially with the cooking because he got to lick the spoons.

"I see I have my little helper," Daisy said.

"I can help."

"Get the milk front the refrigerator while I get the chocolate powder from the cabinet," Daisy said as she retrieved the powder and a saucepan from the kitchen cabinets. She proceeded to light the gas stove and began warming the milk that Adam handed her. "How many spoons should I add?" she asked Adam.

"Three."

Daisy added three spoons of chocolate powder, stirred, and poured the warm drink when ready. She handed one to Adam, blowing across the surface to cool the drink. Daisy left the kitchen, taking the other beverages to the living room.

(*She left the fire on*) Adam thought, then felt the presence of something else. He could not see it, but it was one of these nice things. He felt it move to the stove and watched the stove knob slowly turn to the off position. The flames went out. The presence vanished. (*It's nice to have them around to help. I wonder how many other people have them in their homes.*)

"I'm going out front now. Stay inside."

Adam came back to the living room thinking (*I'd rather be inside. I don't like the cold. She's got to get the rake from the carport, and it's dark under there. There are things under there. Scary things. I don't like it there.*)

###

It had been a busy day at work for Nick. People were stocking up on groceries for the cold snap, and it seemed everyone wanted to talk. His last thing to do before he can just sit down and relax is light the pilot in the floor heater. It's not complicated. There is a tiny section of the floor grate that is hinged so you can reach down, turn on the gas, and light it. (*Nice. It lit, no problem. I wonder how hot this grate will get once the furnace kicks on. I will have to wait and see*) Nick thought as he adjusted the thermostat. It did not take long for the furnace to kick on, releasing that initial burning away dust odor into the house.

"That smell is normal for the first time you light a furnace. Daisy, help me keep an eye on the floor grate. We need to see how hot it gets," Nick said as he bent down once more, this time touching the metal grate. He could immediately feel the grate warming up. (*This is going to get too hot for bare feet. Shoes should be ok but not bare feet. Going to have to talk with the kids*). "Daisy, this is going to be too hot for the kids to walk on with bare feet. We have to keep them off it."

"What about putting the little playpen around it as a barrier?" Daisy asked.

"That would leave a very narrow walking path. The kids could make it around but not us."

Daisy shook her head in agreement. "Kids come over here," Daisy said, motioning the kids to join her and Nick at the furnace grate.

"Hold your hand close to the grate. Feel how hot it is. If you walk on this, it will burn your feet, so you cannot walk on this grate for all winter. You must walk around and not across like you have been doing. Understand."

They shook their heads yes.

"I want to hear you say it. This is very important," Nick said, his voice growing louder, taking on a tone of authority. "You are not to walk on this grate. Stay off it. If we see you on it, you will be in big trouble. Do you understand?"

"Yes, sir," they replied.

"Ok. Go back to playing."

Warm air flowed out the floor vents. It was as they hoped. The ductwork under the house provided warmth to the floors. The kids could sleep on the floors without getting cold. Still, the floor grate over the furnace got hotter the more the furnace ran. It was going to be a problem.

# # #

(Wake up)

Adam opened his eyes, still half asleep. It was that odd voice in his head again. Still lying in bed, a moment of fear flowed across him like a cold breeze. It was one of those dark things he felt from time to time. He could not see it, but he felt it moving throughout the house. Running. Desperate as if it was being chased by something else. It wanted to hurt him, and it was looking for a way to do it. Then Adam felt it stop at the floor grate in the hall. It did something to the furnace then was forced through the floor and out of the house.

(Call for Mama. Make her come to you.)

Adam thought back (*She won't come if I call. She'll wake up, hear it's me, then go back to sleep. She ignores everyone except for Luke. He never wakes up at night.*)

Then Luke's voice rang out loudly, "Mama. Mama."

Daisy woke up wondering if that was one of the kids again. (*Probably nothing. They will go back to sleep like they always do. I'm not getting up.*)

"Mama. Maaamaaa." This time even louder.

(*That's Luke*) Daisy thought as she bolted out of bed and ran into the boy's room next door. (*He never wakes up. Somethings wrong.*) She quickly looked at Luke on the top bunk. (*He's still asleep. Wait. What's that smell? GAS.*)

"Kids, get up," Daisy yelled. "Nick, wake up. There's gas in the house. Get the girls."

"Oh God," Nick said as he ran to grab the girls. "Get outside. Out front!"

Daisy rushed the boys out front, meeting Nick, who said, "Get them to the median. Stay with them. I'm going in to open the doors and windows to let it air out."

"Hurry."

Nick managed to get most of the windows open while leaving the front door open as he exited the house. Daisy saw him turn and run to the gas meter turning off the gas flow. Upon reaching Daisy, she said, "Call my brother Daniel. He's a plumber and not far away. He can help."

Nick agreed, but the only phone was in the house. "Let's give it a few minutes to air out, then we can go back in and I'll make the call.

Daisy and the kids huddled together to stay warm, sitting in the median. (*Wish we had grabbed a blanket on the way out*) she thought.

"It should be aired out now. Let's go back inside," Nick said as he collected the girls. Daisy grabbed each boy's hand, and they walked back into the house.

The gas smell was barely noticeable. Daisy grabbed a blanket, and Nick made his way to the phone.

"Your brother is on his way. We will all wait right here until he gets here."

Daniel arrived to find a nervous Nick and Daisy. They told him what happened as he removed the grate from the furnace and began troubleshooting.

"The pilot light on the furnace went out. I also found a loose connection. I tightened the link. Where is the meter so I can turn the gas back on?"

"I'll show you," Nick said, ushering Daniel out the door. Soon, they came back in. Daniel reached down, turned on the pilot valve and lit it.

"Everything is working fine. See, the blower just kicked on. It's working normally," Daniel said as he placed the grate back over the furnace. Warm air is now blowing out the floor vents.

"Thank you so much, Daniel. We did not know what to do," Daisy said.

"I'm glad everything turned out ok. But it's late, and we all need sleep so I'm heading out. Goodnight," Daniel said as he packed up and left.

"I don't think I can go back to sleep after that."

Daisy nodded in agreement as she got up and headed to the kitchen.

"Want some coffee?"

"Sure."

CHAPTER 6 – CHRISTMAS

There is no snow. It hardly ever snows in central Louisiana. Adam's adventure of floating through the roof hardly ever happens now. He's been getting the feeling that whatever has been happening is almost finished. There are still these strange memories from before. There are also these invisible friends. Not scary. Helpful. Like that time Daisy left the stove gas on. Like when Luke climbed the rope of the tire swing in the backyard. He was at the top twenty feet off the ground. Daisy came out and calmly talked him down but she did not see the friends helping him. Like when they chased that shadow out of the house after it did something to the furnace. Adam wonders why they don't talk about these helpful friends. *(They don't seem to even notice them. Everyone has them, don't they?)*

It was the last time Adam felt himself floating through the springs and above the house. He doesn't remember what happened, only that he started getting sick the next day. Christmas is only two days away. Nick took off work to take him to the doctor's office while Daisy stayed home with the kids. Nick sat holding Adam waiting for the doctor. *(Guess the furnace keeping the floor warm doesn't keep the kids from getting sick completely. They hardly ever get sick, but never severe. This is serious. Hope they can help.)*

Nick looks up as the doctor enters the room.

"What do we have here?" the doctor asks, looking at Adam then back to Nick.

"He just started throwing up then getting spots. He's got a high fever now."

"It's 102," the doctor said as he checked the thermometer. "It looks like Measles. It's been going around. It's very contagious. How about the rest of the family? Any symptoms."

"No. Everyone else is Ok. My wife and I both had measles as kids."

"Same here." said the doctor.

Adam looks through tired eyes at the doctor. It's almost as if seeing two beings in one space. (*He's confused. Not sure.*) The image vanishes, and Adam closes his eyes again.

"There is no specific treatment other than trying to keep the temperature down. Ice bag on the head if needed or cold bath to reduce fever. He will be dehydrated, so lots of extra fluids. Basic supportive care. Keep him away from others because it is very contagious. That is unless you want all your kids to get it while young. Some families do that to inoculate them from measles as they get older. There is a new vaccine coming out for measles, but it's your choice."

"Thanks, doctor," Nick said as he prepared to pay the bill and leave.

# # #

It was Christmas eve. It was all Nick and Daisy could do to put the kids to bed. Nick got the few gifts they could afford placed under the tree. Dolls for the girls. Plastic trucks for the boys. Then there was the one big gift, a toy train for all the kids to play with. He placed the unwrapped box on the dining room table. Nothing was wrapped. It was no point as it meant nothing to the kids and lasted only a few seconds. Daisy was busy putting nuts and bubble gum in socks hung by the little cardboard fireplace they set up on the wall opposite of the Christmas tree. Finally. Sleep.

Adam woke up in the parent's bed feverish. He knew he was being kept away from the other kids. (*Did Santa come? I can't go with others. I'll look now. Maybe Santa came.*) He got out of bed as quietly as he could. (*They didn't wake up.*) He sneaked out of the bedroom, holding onto the sidewall. He was cautious as he walked around the furnace grate. It felt like a pit he could fall into. (*Hang on tight. Don't fall into the furnace*) he thought as he made his way into the living room. The

Christmas tree was still lit, so there was plenty of light as he made his way holding onto the wall. He was not alone.

There were other beings in the room. They felt like the invisible friends that helped. They were shimmering with sparkling gold forming a bubble. They were blurry, and he could not make out the details. Maybe it was the fever. They turned to him, and he sensed they were smiling. Then they vanished. He could not see them anymore, but he felt they were still there. Adam felt comforted. These were his friends.

As he stood there, he heard a sound on the dining room table. He turned. The lid to a box was floating in the air then settled on a chair seat. Individual sections of train tracks floated out of the box and assembled themselves on the table. The train engine, cars, and caboose floated out of the box onto the tracks. He could not see the ones doing it but knew they were there.

Next, he heard a crackling sound like someone had poked logs on a fire. There floating in mid-air near the table, appeared several apples and oranges. He watched as they floated to the little fireplace. They began to separate and form four little piles of fruit on the floor. There is that smiling feeling again.

(It's going to be ok.)

Then he sensed they were no longer there. They were gone. His curiosity was satisfied. Adam headed back to the parent's bed, hanging tight to the walls. He crawled back in bed and slept until five in the morning when the other kids ran in, jumping on the bed shouting, "Santa came! Santa came!" Nick and Daisy woke up. The earlier talk about staying out of the parent's bedroom because Adam is sick had evaporated just like their hope of sleeping late.

Daisy gained her wits first, saying quickly, "Go to the living room. We'll be right there." She knew they would have to keep Adam separated so she would stay with him by the little fireplace while Nick would be with the other kids at the dining table. (*Odd the other kids have not gotten the measles. We found all the kids together several times, and they did not get sick. It's just odd.*)

Daisy walked into the living room and guided Adam to a chair near the cardboard fireplace as Nick went to sit at the dining room table. Luke, Bonnie, and Sissy were involved with trucks and dolls at the Christmas tree. Daisy went to the tree, picked up one of the trucks, and gave it to Adam. "This is yours. Merry Christmas."

Adam started running the truck over his legs as he grinned at Daisy. He watched as Nick motioned for Daisy to join him at the dining room table. They felt concerned. He could feel it. They were whispering but then he started hearing voices in his head. Not voices. They were like memories that were not his. Images conveying messages without speech.

(I didn't put it together. Did someone come in the house? Are we safe? The kids?)

It was Nick and Daisy. This is what they are feeling. Thinking. *(They are talking without using their mouth. It must be a grown-up thing. Wonder when I will grow up enough and be able to do that?)*

"Kids. Did you put the train set together?" Nick asked loudly.

"Train set," Luke exclaimed as he and Bonnie ran to the table to see.

"Did one of you put this together?"

They both shook their head as they started playing with the train.

"The others did it," Adam said loud enough to be heard.

"What others?" Daisy asked as she and Nick walked over to him.

"You know. The others. They do stuff. They help."

Daisy and Nick looked at each other and shrugged.

"They did the apples and oranges."

"What apples and oranges?" Nick asked.

Adam pointed to the floor. Next to him, there were four stacks of apples and oranges at the base of the fireplace.

Nick and Daisy had utterly overlooked the piles of fruit. Daisy grabbed Nick's arm and squeezed as they walked out of the room. Images flooded Adam's mind conveying messages.

(We did not do that. We did not buy those. We bought a train set and everything else. Can't let on there is no Santa. Someone has been in the house. Maybe a friend. They left gifts and did not take anything.)

Then Adam fell asleep in the chair.

CHAPTER 7 – GHOST

After the Christmas oddity, everything was normal at the McLure house for the remainder of winter. The occasional helpful events continued. Now and then, someone would comment about hearing a music box in the boy's room. It happened so often Daisy just considered it routine. Some had made comments to her that the house might be haunted. But to her, the things that happened inside were helpful, so it must be a good haunting like when Daisy left the oven door open only to return and find it closed. Even when she found Bonnie on top of the refrigerator with no idea how she got there. She wasn't hurt and considered it lucky she did not fall. It wasn't harming the children, so why dwell on it.

"I'm home," Nick shouted upon entering the house, dragging another refrigerator box as a cheap toy. Only this time, he had something else. "Kids, I have something for you."

The sound of little feet running preceded Luke and the rest running into the living room.

"Is it gum?" Luke asked, reaching Nick first.

"No. It's a baby duck. A worker at the store said a bunch hatched out at his house. It was more than he could handle, so he brought some to the store to give away for Easter. I thought you might like a pet."

"A duck. Ours to keep?" Adam asked.

"Yes, but you have to take care of it. Feed it. Find a place for it to live."

Daisy walked into the living room. (*Just like him. He did not consider asking me. I'm the one going to be here having to take care of it. I can already imagine the smell, and then I'll have to deal with the kids once it dies on them.*) "What a surprise," she said in that tone, informing Nick he could have handled things better.

Nick placed the large box in the middle of the floor, allowing the kids to put the duck at the back of the box. They are at the other end talking to it. Trying to get it to obey commands.

"I wish you would have asked me first."

"What's the big deal? It's just a duck. The kids will have fun," Nick responded.

"Ugh," Daisy snorted, heading back to the kitchen. Nick headed to the bathroom to take a shower.

While playing with the duck, Adam felt something. Like something waking up under the carport. There was that dark feeling again. It was growing stronger. He stood, backing away through the doorway and into the hall with the furnace. He saw the furnace, a twinge of fear. That dark feeling grew even more potent. He kept backing away. It's the door to the bathroom. (*Daddy's in there. I'll be safe*) he thought as he opened the door and went in. Feeling safer, he undressed and stepped into the tub.

Nick wiped the water from his eye, asking a bit surprised, "What are you doing?"

"Getting clean," Adam answered as if everything was perfectly normal.

"Here's some shampoo. Wash your hair."

Adam felt better. The dark feeling subsided then vanished like the shampoo running down the drain. (*Better*)

# # #

Nick arrived home to find the large cardboard refrigerator box standing upright at the front door. He looked inside. It was empty except for the duck leavings. So he entered the house with his usual, "I'm home."

Daisy greeted him, and before he could ask. She said, "I put it out there because of the smell. I could not take the stink any longer, so

I put the duck in the box and put the box out front. The kids made a fuss. I sent them to their rooms to play."

"The box is out there, but the duck is not in it," Nick said.

"What? I put it in there," Daisy said, opening the door and looking into the box. "I don't know what happened. I put it in there. It hasn't been out there that long. Something must have gotten it. The kids will be upset, but I'm not. I'm glad it's gone. It was stinking up the house. We can tell the kids the mama duck came and got it."

Nick sighed, taking the box to the carport to be hauled off later as Daisy started preparing dinner. Macaroni and cheese.

Daisy told the children during dinner. She created an elaborate story of how the baby duck was lost, and the mama duck had been seen in the neighborhood searching. Then the mama duck found it and took it home. She is a great storyteller. The children accepted the explanation. After all, that is what their parents would do if they were lost.

After dinner, everyone settled down, got ready for bed, and quickly went to sleep except for Adam. He had felt that dark presence again. (*Am I lost like the baby duck and the others can't find me*) he wondered. He had been lying there pondering for a long time then thought (*if they can't come to me, maybe I can go to them.*)

Adam stared unblinking at the bedsprings above him. He wished. He squinted. It felt like the air in a thunderstorm. His skin was tingling. The bedsprings above shifted. He was seeing two of everything. The atmosphere in the room cooled as his sight cleared. (*It didn't work. I'm sleepy. I'll try tomorrow*) he thought as he fell asleep.

(*What. Thought I heard something from the boy's bedroom.*) Daisy sat up in bed, looking at the open doorway leading into the boy's room. (*There is a man in the door.*)

The grocery store lights are shining in the boy's window, the doorway is backlighted. He was young and looked around confused. He did not know where he was and appeared to be searching for an explanation. First, looking at her, then the room, then behind him.

He is trim, short haircut, khaki uniform with a cloth hat tucked into his belt. (*He looks like a World War II soldier. He looks lost. I'm awake, sitting up. This is real.*) She nudged Nick without turning. She prompted him again. As soon as Nick turned toward her, the soldier vanished.

"What?" Nick asked.

"Did you see him? The soldier in the doorway." Daisy begged, "You saw him, didn't you? The man in the boy's doorway. The soldier. You saw him."

"No. What are you talking about? There is no one there."

"He was right there clear as day. I saw him."

"It was probably just a dream. Go back to bed. There is nothing there."

"I know what I saw. It was real. You're never here. You don't see what goes on, like the duck disappearing. Stuff like that happens all the time, and you're not here to see it. I know what I saw. You never believe me," Daisy said as she tried to go back to sleep. (*I know what I saw.*)

# # #

"Daisy thinks she saw a ghost," Nick told his sisters, laughing. They had taken the family to visit his sisters, Lena and Ethel, that lived 45 minutes away. An easy trip for the kids. Everything was going great until this moment.

(*I hate it when he does this to me. He likes to bring up these strange things trying to embarrass me. I could just kill him right now*) Daisy seethed. "Stop it, Nick."

"Tell us. Ignore Nick. He's just like that. We'd like to hear," Lena said.

"Go ahead, Daisy, tell them," Nick said mockingly.

"Alright," Daisy explained what she saw just as it happened. She left out no details, including where Nick doesn't believe her. He never believes her.

"That sounds like a relative of my husband," Ethel said.

"It can't be," Daisy said confidently. "I know his family. They are all blond and a bit round. This man was thin with curly black hair. It could not have been him."

Ethel left the room and returned shortly with a box. She opened it and pulled out a photo showing it to Daisy. "Is this him?"

Daisy looked at the soldier in the photo in disbelief. "That's him. The uniform and everything. That is the man that was in our doorway."

"I believe you," Ethel said. He was killed in a car wreck at that underpass near your house. The one the train goes over, it's dangerous. I think your home is haunted."

"I noticed something odd at your house once when I visited. This music box played in the sunroom you made into the boy's bedroom. I looked everywhere but could not find it," Lena said.

"I told you I was not making stuff up, Nick. Something is going on in our house."

(*Three against one. I'm outnumbered. Got to give in, but I still don't believe it.*) "Fine. It doesn't hurt anybody. We should be getting back," Nick said as he got up to say his goodbyes.

"Don't rush off," Ethel said. "Stay a little longer."

"No. We have got to be getting back. Kids will be getting tired."

Hugs and kisses were exchanged as they made their way to the car.

"What do you think now, Nick. Do you still think I'm making it up?" Daisy asked on the drive home.

"I don't want to hear about it anymore. Let's just get home," Nick said, feeling this nonsense had gone far enough.

(*I knew something was going on in that house. Ok. It's haunted. But helpful? It seems friendly, although that soldier seemed confused. I can live with it as long as it doesn't hurt the kids.*)

CHAPTER 8 – TERROR

The Stotter yard was too inviting for two young boys. The house reminded them of a castle. That's the word Daisy used when they first drove down the boulevard. It did not look like the other houses. It was big. Part of its roof was flat with a table and chairs on it. They could imagine themselves on top, looking around below for enemies creeping up. Their imaginations ran wild as they played. They ran around the landscaped yard, and when they gathered their courage enough, they would run and touch the front steps. Touching the front door was too much, but the steps were ok.

"Get out of my yard!" Mrs. Stotter yelled through the open front door. She was wearing a housecoat and hung onto the door frame.

The boys bolted, knowing that if Mrs. Stotter told their parents, they would be in trouble again. They had been caught before picking flowers from her yard. And she was not happy with them being in the yard again. It was like the story Daisy had told them about the witch that lived in a house of candy. It was inviting, but if you got caught, you were in trouble.

Adam looked around. They were in the lane. It's full of shadows, and the boys knew this was another place they were not supposed to be. There is the sound of a train in the distance.

"A train is coming," Luke said excitedly, knowing they would be able to see parts of it through the trees and brush. Luke immediately forgot that this was off-limits. He was excited to hear and perhaps get glimpses of the train passing by. He started walking along the edge of the lane where it sloped down to the gully.

Adam, however, was frozen. It felt like ants crawling on his skin. He tried brushing them off, but there was nothing there. He looked up and saw the leaves above start to move. There was no wind. The shadows seemed to take on life. The pine trees swayed. Fear welled up inside him. A limb fell nearby. He turned to look. He noticed someone crouching in the brush. Something with red eyes.

"Who is that?" Adam asked, pointing to the figure hiding.

"Where?"

"Over there."

"I don't see anybody," Luke replied.

(*I know I saw something*) Adam thought as he moved closer. "It's just a bush with red berries. Nothings here." (*There was something else here.*)

The train arrived quickly. Luke cheered.

"Let's race it back home," Adam said as he crouched to a running position. He wanted to get out of the lane fast.

"Go," Luke yelled as they ran down the lane back to the boulevard around the curve and back home. "I win."

"You win," Adam said, relieved to be home.

"What are you boys up to?" Nick asked as he pushed the mower across the front yard. It was the kind of mower with two large wheels and a set of blades that turned with the wheels. There was a long wooden handle Nick was using to push. Nick couldn't complain. It had been given to them, and it worked.

"We raced the train, and I won," Luke said

Forgetting that they were not supposed to be in the lane, Adam told Nick, "We were in the lane, and the trees started moving, and a big limb fell, and there was no wind. It was scary".

"You're not supposed to be in the lane," Nick said, knowing full well it was impossible to keep them from going where they are told not to go. He continued mowing. "As far as the wind, if you remember, I was with you once in the gully when the train came by, and it created a wind. Like in a tunnel."

"But we weren't in the gully. It was the top of the trees," Adam said, figuring Nick would dismiss this kind of talk.

"It's just your imagination. You got scared. That's all."

"Can I sleep in the top bunk?"

"You ok with switching Luke?"

"Ok," Luke nodded.

"Go inside and tell your mother of your adventures. She likes that sort of thing."

Both boys ran inside as Nick continued mowing. (*I wish Daisy would not encourage this kind of fantasy. It's useless in real life. One day they will have to get a real job that pays well to have a good life.*)

# # #

Adam woke on the top bunk with a feeling of dread so powerful he could not move. He was staring at the ceiling, unmoving. Waves of fear washed over him. If he moved, it would see him. (*It's here. Daddy says it's not real. It's not real. It's here.*) He could hardly breathe. He clenched his fists around the bedsheets as he turned his head toward the louvered window. He was eye to eye with it. It was not imagination. It was real. His breath left him as if sucked out. It felt like he was being pulled toward the glass. It was not like the others. It was powerful, hungry, and it wanted him.

As terror filled Adam, the red eyes glowed brighter. The oily brown fur on its body moved in waves. It moved with every wave of fear Adam felt. It was small, humanoid, and floating outside Adam's window. Hungry. It was feeding off his fear. Another wave and the eyes flared. Images appeared in Adam's head. Images of anger, pain, suffering, never-ending torture create more fear. It was draining him. Taking everything from him. Adam was helpless. He couldn't stop it.

(*Somethings behind me in the room*) Adam thought in a small fragment of his mind, not consumed by fear. (*I can't.*) He felt pressure building between him and the being outside the window. It began pulsing as if getting stronger and building its strength. It flared, and Adam was hit by a force that flung him out of the bunk bed.

There was no sound as he hit something soft. He hung upside down in the middle of the room. Floating. Stationary. Then gentle hands slowly turned him and set him on the floor. Adam stood there stunned. Drained. He looked up at the window. Fear. Glowing red eyes flared, then a sense of peace from behind. A sense of protection enveloped Adam and expanded outward. The red eyes dimmed. It was angry.

It moved closer, reaching out as if to go through the glass. It hit this feeling of protection as if it was solid. It stopped. The feeling of anger intensified as it tried to push through the glass. As it did, the sense of protection changed to one of love. The dark being felt pain and backed away. It wanted to get inside but couldn't. It continued backing away, hitting the lawnmower handle Nick had leaned against the back wall. It fell to the ground as the being vanished into the shadows.

Adam felt hands steadying him as he got his senses back. His strength returned. He could think again. He bolted forward into his parent's bedroom without looking back. Then, jumping onto the bed, he cried, "Mama. Daddy. There was something outside the window with glowing red eyes. It tried to get me."

Both Nick and Daisy woke startled, trying to understand what Adam was saying. "Something outside your window," Nick said, getting up and looking out the window. "I don't see anything. Maybe it was just a bad dream."

"It was real. I saw it," Adam pleaded for Daisy to believe him as she held him. "Please go outside and check. It might still be there."

"It was just a dream, Adam. There is nothing there," Nick said, failing to convince Adam.

"Nick, just go outside and look around. It would make me feel safer also," Daisy said.

"Fine, but you're coming with me," pointing to Adam. "You are going to have to learn to deal with this sort of thing, these bad dreams one day, so might as well start now by going with me to look."

Adam did not want to go but knew he had no choice in the matter. He would have to go, so he got up and joined Nick walking past the still sleeping Luke. (*He can sleep through anything*) Nick thought as he passed by the bunk bed, grabbed a flashlight from the washroom, and headed out the back door. Adam was holding his hand tightly.

"See, there is nothing here," Nick told Adam.

"Look for footprints. It might have left footprints."

Nick shone the flashlight on the ground, moving slow enough that Adam could see for himself. "See no tracks. There is nothing here, and there was not anything here. It was just a bad dream. Let's go inside and put you back to bed."

"Can I sleep with you and mama tonight?"

"Ok, but don't get into the habit of running to us every time you have a bad dream."

"Ok," Adam said dejectedly. (*It wasn't a dream.*)

As they walked toward the back door, Nick noticed the mower handle had fallen to the ground. (*Must have been an animal that knocked it over. Maybe raccoon.*) He picked it up and leaned it back against the wall with no more thought about it. He put Adam in their bed and went to sleep. (*I'll be glad when all this foolishness stops.*)

The following day, Adam tried to convince his mother it was real. "It wasn't a dream, mama!" Adam yelled in Daisy's general direction. Nick had gone to work. Daisy made peanut butter and jelly sandwiches for lunch. The kids sat eating at the dining room table while Daisy moved between the kitchen and washroom to do daily chores.

"Ok," Daisy yelled from the washroom across the kitchen. (*I saw a ghost. Music box only some can hear. Things moving almost as if helping. It's never been much of anything but never bad. I think he saw something. I wonder what it was.*) As she thought this, the back door flung open, frightening her for just a moment. (*Why so jumpy. It's just the wind. Blew the door open. Just the wind.*)

She couldn't help it. This slight twinge of fear. So much unexplained. What if there is a harmful component to all of this. What if it was something bad? That whatever is here is changing into something terrible. At that moment, the power flashed. Another twinge of fear. (*It's windy today. Just pulling the power lines a bit. Maybe a limb is hitting one. There are a lot of trees around. Everything's normal.*) She tried her best to convince herself.

"Mama!" Adam yelled from the other room.

Daisy hurried back. "What is it?"

"I'm scared."

"Why? There's nothing to be scared about."

"I think that thing I saw is back," Adam said, trying not to be afraid.

"Did you see it?"

"No."

"What makes you think it's back," Daisy asked.

"I can feel it. It was outside the front door. It knocked. I looked out the window, and there was nothing there. It felt like it went around back," Adam said.

Daisy felt a chill run through her body. (*What if there was something there. What if it came in the back door?*) The power flashed again. Her fear grew.

"It's in the house," Adam said as the back door flew open again.

Daisy moved to the dining area. From this vantage, she could see outside to the front of the door and inside into the living room. "Ok, kids, gather around me, and I'll tell you a nice story while you finish your lunch."

The kids gathered around Daisy. As they did Adam, felt the love and protection of a parent. Safe. Nothing can hurt them. He felt something smile from somewhere in the room. Then a rush of energy. It felt good. It filled the house. Adam could almost see a dark shadow being pushed toward the front door inside the house. It was caught between the front door and the rest of the house. It could not get through the door. It was almost as if the wood of the house itself had become infused with something that the dark thing could not cross.

Daisy screamed. She was watching the doorknob of the front door turn. The inside knob was turning as if something was desperately trying to get out.

A massive wave of energy only Adam could sense roiled through the house, pushing the dark thing through the front door, severely damaging it in the process. It was gone.

Daisy corralled the kids dragging them toward the phone. She called Nick. "Get home now. Something's in the house."

"What's in the house?"

"I don't know. Something. The doorknob was turning all by itself like something wanted to get out. Get home now. Now!" Daisy yelled forcefully enough to cause Nick genuine concern.

Nick moved quickly. The next thing he knew, he was opening the front door to find Daisy and the kids huddled on the couch.

"Is everyone ok? What happened? What was in the house?" Nick asked, quickly moving to the couch.

"I don't know. Something. Ghosts. I don't know. The back door blew open twice, the power was flashing, the door handle turned on its own. Something is in this house."

(*There she goes again, being overly dramatic. No wonder Adam gets scared and has bad dreams.*) "I'll check the house to make sure no one is here. Wait here," Nick said as he moved from room to room, searching the house. Finally, he stopped at the open back door.

(*The latch is stuck inside the door. It was unable to lock in place, and with this wind, no wonder the door blew open.*) He pulled out the pocketknife that he always carried, opened it, and pried the latch just a bit. It popped back out. He closed the door, and this time it latched shut. The wind could not blow it open again.

"There is no one here. The latch on the back door was stuck. Probably happened when one of the kids was running in and out. It would not latch shut, so the wind kept blowing it open. The power flashes were probably the wind. It's happened a couple of times at the store also. It's nothing. Everything's fine," Nick said confidently. He found the solution to everything.

"What about the doorknob turning all by itself?"

"Maybe the knob was also stuck, then all this wind rattling the door caused it to unstick. Making it move back to its normal position, looking like someone was turning it. There is always a normal solution. Everything does not have to be ghosts," Nick said in a way that Daisy knew there was no way to convince him otherwise. He's never believed in anything supernatural, so why should he start now.

Daisy thought of the kids. "Your right. There's always a normal explanation. I guess I was just stressed out. I'm sorry if I scared all of you," she said, looking at the kids. "I just got over-excited. It's all ok. Everything is ok."

Nick headed back to the car. Daisy joined him. "Nick, I want out of this house."

"What. There is nothing wrong with the house. I just showed you everything had an explanation."

"I'm not going to argue with you. I want out of this house. Do you understand me?" Daisy's finger-pointing at Nick.

"I hear you, but there is nothing I can do right now. There is a chance that I can get an interview at a bank in West Monroe. It's lots more pay if I can get it. If I get the job, then we move. Until then, we're stuck here."

Daisy felt a bit of relief. (*A chance. I'm going to do everything in my power to make that happen. Got to start making calls to relatives and anybody else I know. It's going to happen.*)

Nick went back to work as Daisy rejoined the kids. She pulled out a giant puzzle to ensure the remainder of the day remained calm, and they would be together. (*I'll talk to Nick more when he gets home, but that move is going to happen.*)

CHAPTER 9 – MOVING

(*It's getting late. Nick should be back soon from the job interview. It's only a two-hour drive. I hope he gets it. It will be a lot more money, and we can get away from here.*) Daisy prepared sloppy joes for the kids later than usual, hoping the meat would still be warm when Nick got home. It's easy enough to reheat. (*He will probably eat somewhere before he gets back here. It'll be here just in case.*)

It was late when Nick arrived home. Daisy had already put the kids to bed. Good thing he had gotten something to eat before heading back.

"They offered me the job," he said, walking in the door.

"That's great." Daisy said, jumping up to kiss him.

"I also worked out a deal with them where they will pay for movers, so we don't have to do it all ourselves," Nick said happily.

"That will be nice. When do you start?"

"Three weeks. I can give my two-week notice at the store then take some time to work around here. Clean up the yard, get rid of the junk so the house will look good to sell."

"We have got to find a new house," Daisy said.

"The bank has a lead on a house. The owner took out the mortgage from the bank, letting them know he is looking to sell. I've got the owner's name and can call in the morning. I will have to start work even if we don't find a house. My uncle Ray lives in town. I've already talked to him, and it's ok for me to stay with him during the week and come home on weekends. That means you will be by yourself during the week." Nick said, expecting her to complain about being on her own.

"Wonderful," Daisy said, thinking (*We have survived this long, what's a few more weeks. Even a couple of months is worth it to get away from here.)*

That threw Nick off guard a bit. (*No complaining. She wants to move.*)

"Have you eaten? I can heat the sloppy joe mix if you are hungry."

"No. I picked up something before I left," Nick said as he headed toward the bedroom. "It's been a long day. I'm ready to go to bed."

"I'll be there in a minute. I need to put up a few things, then I'll be in." Daisy was excited, thinking about the future. (*New job, new house, new neighborhood, new life. Change from here will be so good.*) She then headed to the bedroom. It's been a great day.

# # #

(*The two-hour drive in the car is worth it. Lots of trees and nice houses in the neighborhood. There are some kids riding bicycles. Wonderful. This is the house*) Daisy thought as Nick pulled into the driveway.

"We're here," Nick said even though everyone had already figured it out. The kids had been marveling at the pond they passed a few houses back and fantasizing about what they could do there. He could tell Daisy was already sizing up the neighbors by the appearance of their yard. He looked over just to see her expression on viewing this yard.

Daisy's eyes showed it all. A bit of disgust at all the clutter in front. The bare wire stacked up made it look like a junkyard rather than a home. (*There is a two-car carport. That's a plus)* she thought as an older gentleman walked out the door.

"Hi Nick," the man said, walking over.

"Daisy, this is Mr. Gibbons. He owns the house. Mr. Gibbons, this is my wife Daisy and our four children Adam, Luke, Bonnie, and Sissy," Nick said, gesturing at each one in turn.

Mr. Gibbons could tell by the look on Daisy's face she was concerned. "Don't worry, Mrs. McLure. I don't live like this. This was a rental house. The renters just up and left one day, leaving all this junk behind. I can no longer clean and fix all this. That is why I'm selling it for such a low price."

"I completely understand," Daisy said, feeling a bit relieved that Mr. Gibbons knew this was a problem and reduced the price accordingly.

"Let me show you around," he said, leading them into the house going from room to room. "It's a three-bedroom, bath and a half. There is a living space, dining area, den, and washroom with washer and dryer connections. The empty lot behind you belongs to the city. You will not have neighbors behind you, so that's a plus."

"Excuse us a moment while Daisy and I talk it over," Nick said as he pulled Daisy aside.

"What do you think?"

"It's so much work, and the kids could get hurt with all the metal in the yard. There must be better houses out there."

"That's true, but it's a great price, and we need all the help we can get right now. It will take a lot to fix it, but we can take things slowly once we move in. We don't have much time to find another house. I can't stay at my uncle's place forever, and I know you wanted to move."

Daisy started thinking back to all the strange events in their current home, and she decided right then. "Let's get it. We'll make it work."

Nick went to talk to Mr. Gibbons while Daisy informed the kids. The state of the yard or house did not matter. The kids wanted to move in right now, but Daisy told them they needed to pack first then move everything up here. "You don't want your toys to be left behind, do you?"

(*Left behind.*) Those words stuck with Adam.

# # #

It was a week before the movers arrived. Nick and Daisy had been busy packing and forgot to let their only real friends in the neighborhood, the Cristoffs, know about the new job. So they gathered up the kids, walked the short distance down the boulevard arriving at the Cristoff's trailer.

"I hope you don't mind us stopping by?" Daisy asked Ann.

"Of course not. Come on in. I see you have everyone with you. Have a seat. I'll go get Sam," Ann said as she left to find Sam.

She returned shortly, followed by Sam, who was carrying a bottle of homemade blackberry wine.

"Would you like a glass?" Sam asked.

"I'll not turn down a free drink," Nick said.

Daisy started, "The reason we wanted to stop by is to let you know Nick got a new job."

Ann giggled a little. "We know. Adam told us. You know he loves to come over and spend time in the greenhouse just looking at the plants. We were nervous at first, but Adam was careful. He told us last visit that you are moving. We saw the boxes and did not want to interrupt. We thought you'd tell us when you were ready."

"Adam told you," Daisy said, not a bit surprised. "There are no secrets with these kids around."

"When's the move?" Sam asked, taking another drink.

"The movers arrive next week. We are boxing up the breakables and other valuables we don't want them to handle."

"Have you found a buyer for your house?" Ann asked.

"Yes," Nick replied. "It's a couple with one boy. The same age as Adam."

"Oh, good. There will still be a child in the neighborhood."

"Well miss you so much. We have to keep in touch," Daisy said, looking at Ann.

"Of course. We'll keep in touch. You're a phone call away," Ann responded.

The remainder of the visit went as they usually do. Drinking a bit of homemade wine. Luke is playing with their dog Bingo. Adam is out in the greenhouse, and the girls are playing on the floor. It was a pleasant visit. (*I'm going to miss them*) Daisy thought as they walked back home. (*I hope we stay in touch.*)

CHAPTER 10 – LEFT BEHIND

The movers arrived in their big rig. It was more than enough for the contents of the house. Those that were most valuable and some things they might need for the kids during the trip ended up in the car. Everything has been going smoothly. The movers should be finished in a few hours. Time enough for the two-hour drive to their new home in West Monroe and still get the truck unloaded. They could sleep on the floor and unpack the next day.

Luke ran up to Daisy with something in his hand. "Look what I found. Can we try one?" It was a pack of cigarettes one of the movers must have dropped.

(*They know about smoking. The kids have seen other people smoke, including these movers. I need to break them of the habit before it starts.*) Daisy looked at Luke and said, "Sure. Maybe your brother and sisters want to try as well. Go get them, come back, and you can try it here." She smirked, knowing the consequences of this adventure, but it would be worth it.

As the kids gathered around a box in the front yard, Daisy pulled a single cigarette from the box. After that, she would give the pack back to the workers. (*I don't think they would mind donating one cigarette for this cause.*)

She lit the cigarette and handed it to Adam, then down the line. Luke next, then Bonnie. Sissy was too young but might somehow remember the other kid's reaction. They all choked upon inhaling as expected. Then they started turning green and throwing up. Daisy grinned. "Would you like to smoke some more?" she asked, holding the lit cigarette to them.

"No. No more," the kids replied, talking over each other. (*Just a bit of cleanup, but it worked. They will never smoke again. They might not enjoy the car ride, but it was worth it.*) About that time, another car pulled up and parked on the road. Don and Grace Nebo, with their son Don Jr. (*They probably want to see what the place looks like empty and start making plans.*)

Nick was busy helping the movers, so Daisy greeted them. "Hello. So nice to see you. I was not sure we would see you again after we signed the papers."

Grace replied, "We wanted to wish you well on your move. But, we also wanted to look around and get an idea of what we need to do first."

"Is Nick around?" Don asked.

"He's in the back of the truck with the movers, I think," Daisy said as Don moved away to find Nick.

Turning back to Grace, Daisy said, "we are almost finished moving things out. Don Jr can play with the kids, but they are feeling a bit sick and may not feel like playing."

"What happened?" Grace asked.

Daisy explained about the cigarettes as they walked into the house. They discussed ideas for each room. Upon entering the sunroom, Grace said, "I like the idea of turning this into a boy's bedroom. The open windows in the room make it feel like you are sleeping outdoors. Don Jr will love it."

Daisy nodded, just a bit concerned, thinking (*Don Jr. is the same age as Adam. It's this room where many strange things like music happen. What am I thinking? Nick explained everything. There is no haunting. Nothing weird is happening. It all has an explanation.*) Feeling relieved, Daisy turned to Grace, saying, "I need to check on the kids and finish packing. We wish you the best in your new home."

"Thanks. You have a safe trip to your new home," Grace said, waving to Daisy as she left the house.

Daisy met Nick in the front yard.

"The movers have a few more items to get, but all the small stuff is packed. We can leave now and get to our new house first. We can get the kids settled in and be ready when the movers arrive. They know how to get there," Nick said.

"Kids. It's time to go," Daisy yelled across the yard.

They came running as Daisy ushered them into the car. It's cramped, but that is nothing new, having four kids.

Adam had this unusual feeling all day. He looked back at the white house with red shutters as they pulled away. This is where he could retain a fragment of memory from before. It would make him different, leading him down a lonely dark path. The dark beings were trapped by the shimmering ones. This was goodbye. They were no longer going to be with him. Protecting him.

These feelings faded the further away they drove. (*I'm alone now*) he thought even though he was in a crowded car. Then his thoughts turned to the future, wondering what would happen without them. It was that feeling of being scared and thrilled at the same time.

(*It's a new adventure*)

# # #

It's a rainy day. Typical for Louisiana. The McLures have been in the new home a few months. They were still finding bits of wire in the yard. Probably will for years, but enough is cleaned out for the kids to play. They were still doing repair work. (*It's going to take years, but Nick is making good money. We have the time and can afford it now*) Daisy thought as she continued putting wallpaper border around the top of the hallway.

The phone rings. Daisy stops what she is doing to pick up the phone.

(*It's the Cristoffs*) Adam thought from the other room as the phone rang.

"Hello," Daisy said, answering the phone.

"Hello, Daisy. It's Ann Cristoff. We wanted to call and see how you are doing."

"Ann. Everything is great. It's been a lot of work getting it livable. I'm hanging wallpaper right now, but it's a good neighborhood with other kids. How are you and Sam?"

"How's Bingo?" Adam yells loud enough from the other room to be heard through the phone.

(Tell Adam, Bingo is fine and missing him) Adam heard in his head along with images of Bingo.

"Ann says Bingo is fine and missing you, Adam," Daisy yells back.

Satisfied, Adam turned back to playing on this rainy day.

"Daisy. I wanted to tell you something else. You remember those times you told me about strange things in your house here, and most of it was friendly or helpful."

"Yes," Daisy asked nervously.

"Well. You know the Nebo's have that little boy Adams age, and they made his bedroom in the sunroom your boys stayed in."

"Yes."

"The boy kept going on and on about seeing things coming to get him. Dark, scary things. They never saw anything and could not stop him from being hysterical all the time. Finally, they committed him to a psychiatric hospital. Isn't that odd?"

"That is odd," Daisy said, guilt welling up inside her. "Nick always had an explanation for what was happening, and even though Adam said he saw things, none of the other kids ever did. It never affected Adam that way, though, and we just figured it was bad dreams."

"The boy was probably unstable anyway and needed professional help. There's nothing else new around here. Everything else is the same. Sam still makes wine and works in his greenhouse. I've taken up knitting, so all quiet here."

"I'm glad to hear that," Daisy said with guilt, not letting her go. "Tell Sam we said hello. It's a lot of work here, but we are making it. Thanks for calling Ann."

"I'm glad we talked. Take care, Daisy, and give the kids hugs from us."

"I'll do that. Bye Ann."

Daisy hung up the phone. (*It was real. Everything had a simple explanation, but it happened to their boy. It was real. That poor boy. I can't imagine being Grace and going through that. I feel so guilty not telling them, but why would I. What Adam saw was real? It came after him. At least we are away from that place. No more strange happenings. Everything is normal. Normal.*) She went back to hanging wallpaper, trying to let the guilt pass.

Adam continued playing, thinking (*I'll be glad when I grow up and they teach me how to talk without using mouths. I'm only hearing parts now, but one day.*)

PART TWO – CHANGE: HIGH SCHOOL

CHAPTER 11 – OLLA

It had been many years since the move from the little white house with red shutters in Pineville to West Monroe. Nick's job at the bank was sound. Daisy had a career as a court reporter once the kids were old enough to ride the school bus. Initially, she hired a babysitter, but eventually, the boys grew up enough to take over. Luke was into all the sports, so there was always a game to attend. Bonnie was a tomboy and was more interested in hanging out. Sissy liked the popular crowds who had cheerleading as a goal. Adam, however, was a nerd and had found some nerdy friends. They were the outcasts and did things their own way. The McLures were a well-rounded family, but there was always something different, and people noticed. Several mentioned it to Nick and Daisy throughout the kid's school years. If something was happening, the McLures were in the middle of it.

Adam's junior high school friend Billy wanted to be a lawyer. He convinced Adam to take typing classes. Adam did not know it at the time, but those were going to be some of the most valuable courses he had ever taken. Adam also had a female friend named Tara. She was laid back and joined in with whatever was happening. Adam felt comfortable enough to tell her about some of the strange things that happened in his life. She didn't understand but accepted it. No judgments. Adam really liked her. They went out a few times as friends but Adam hoped they could be more.

Life was typical for the McLures. The entities had not followed them to their new home, but more odd things started happening to Adam as he grew. Random thoughts coming into his mind from other people expanded when he looked into someone's eyes. He felt himself being pulled into their memories as if going through a tunnel. He couldn't stop it, so he learned not to look at people in the eye for too long.

He had crazy dreams so he began writing them down. It was the first thing he did upon waking up as he had learned to recognize when he was dreaming and take control. Much later, he would realize this was called lucid dreaming. Then he noticed the coincidences. Things he needed would appear. He recalled a memory from before he was born. An easy life where things came to him. Then there were the songs on the radio. He would know that a song he liked was playing on a different station or know it was playing, yet the radio was turned off. Friends and family noticed but figured he must have heard it from a car nearby.

Adam rejected the idea that he was different than others. He wanted to be like everyone else. He wanted to be normal, but so many things were happening. It made him nervous. A seed of doubt had begun growing. He was starting to feel alone, and moving to another town made him feel even more alone.

Nick had found a much better-paying job one hour south of West Monroe. It also moved them one hour away from Pineville, where they lived when his children were only tots. He had been commuting there for a year before moving the family into their new home in Olla. They would be renting out their house in West Monroe. Nick figured he could make a bit of money, and if this job fell through, they would have a home to move back into. Adam was starting the 10th grade in a new town so small it did not have a traffic light. It was one of those towns you sped through on the highway. You only stopped if you needed gas. But people live in those towns, and Adam would be one of those people.

Adam looked at the surroundings as Nick pulled the car into the driveway of their new home. (*I'm going to be living in Olla. Funny name pronounced Allah. Sucks having to move. At least the classes will be small. The entire town shuts down on Wednesdays just because. Is there not enough business?*

There's nothing to do. No friends. No park. No movie theatre. No place to go. The biggest attraction is the Burger Barn on the highway) Adam thought as they pulled into the driveway of their new home.

(*I'm going through puberty. Maybe this is where I'll get old enough for my parents to teach me about these strange things that happen. I can't wait for them to stop concealing this kind of thing and finally let me in on the big secret. How to control it.*) He had brought this up several times before and been brushed off as if they said we would talk about it later. So he kept waiting for that day. (*It can't be much longer.*)

It's an older pier and beam house. The girls will share a room in the center of the house. The mudroom in the back became the boy's bedroom. That's why the backdoor to the house was in that room. The boys figured the backdoor in their room would come in handy. Also, you had to pass through the second full bath with a washer/dryer before entering their room. They liked that as well. Next to their house is an open lot with a church across the street. They would be attending church in order to be social. A truck pulled in as the McLures began unpacking. A man and boy about Adam's age stepped out and walked up to Nick.

"Hi. I'm Josh Belter. I'm the coach at the high school, and this is Carl Spikeman. He's on the football team," he said, walking up to Nick shaking his hand.

"I'm Nick McLure. This is my wife Daisy, and these are our kids Adam, Luke, Bonnie, and Sissy."

"We came by because we heard you were moving in. We were hoping you would join the football team," Carl said, looking at Adam.

"I probably won't. I'm not into sports. Sorry"

"Maybe later. You're just moving in. Think about it."

"Ok," Adam said

"That's really all. Just wanted to drop by to say welcome, and we will see you kids in school," he said, walking Carl back to the truck.

"That was nice of them, don't you think," Daisy said to Adam

"Yeah," Adam said. (*They will keep on about this, and it's not going to end well.*)

CHAPTER 12 – TRAUMA

School ended for the day, and Coach Belter caught up with Adam. "Adam. are you joining us for football practice? I went by the bank, and your dad said it was ok. That you might want to join," Coach Belter said.

"I'm on my way." (*Dad said I might want to join. That sounds about right. Pushing what he wants off on me. They want me to be more like Luke and join a sports team. I don't understand sports. Why do people like them so much?*)

"Get to the locker room, get changed, and join us on the field."

(*At least it's just a workout session and not actual football. I have no idea what I'm doing*) Adam thought, dressing in his regular gym clothes then joining the others on the field.

"The first thing we are going to do is a one-mile run. Adam. Follow the others. They know the route around the school. Kevin and Jim are our best runners. They are on the track team. See if you can keep up with them. Go."

(*I'm tiring, but we're almost at the end. This feeling of being separate from your body and just letting the body do the work. Is this why people like sports? This odd feeling.*)

"Alright, well done," Coach Belter said. "Adam, you came in third. You kept up with my two-track stars. We need you on the track team."

(*The others still have not made it to the finish line yet. I can run.*)

Practice drills lasted an hour and a half. (*I still don't understand this. Throwing, catching, hitting dummies. What am I supposed to learn from this?*)

"That's enough for today. Get to the locker room, shower, and I'll see you here for our next practice day after tomorrow. Adam. We could use you on both the football and track teams. How about it?" Coach Belter said, walking back toward the school.

"It's not for me. So I have to say no."

"What. Why? You'd love it. You got along with everyone and did good running. You'd be great even if just on the track team."

"I'm sorry, but no."

"Don't say no yet. Think about. You might change your mind."

(*I'm not going to change my mind, but he is going to keep pushing. It's going to be a long school year*) Adam thought as he made his way to the school's locker room.

Undressed, Adam turned to join the other boys in the communal shower.

"Carl, Adam's staring at your butt," someone yelled to be heard over the running water.

It did not register to Adam that he had stopped at the shower entrance. His head snapped up to see Carl turn and look at him.

The overlapping voices made it difficult to make out everything being said. Adam was hearing with both his ears and his mind. "Adam's got a hard-on." "He's gay." "He wants to fuck Carl." "He wants all of us to fuck him." "Cut his dick off." (Gays shouldn't' exist.) (You're wrong.) Adam tried to hide his embarrassment, quickly turned and returned to his locker. He grabbed his clothes and dressed. Safely outside, he began the walk home giving him plenty of time to think.

(*Am I gay? I liked looking at Carl's body. I liked it. But I like girls. My dream last night was three girls at once. I like both. I'm so confused. They all saw it. I'm going to have to be careful. There are probably people in this town that would kill me. Then they would hide my body. There might be people here that have done that before. I need to survive long enough to get out of here. It's going to be a long school year.*)

Adam made it home and ate dinner with the family. He dreaded going to school the next day, expecting the worst. But, instead, the school day was like any other school day. Then Carl caught up with him.

"Adam. We were hoping to see you," Carl said. It was between classes, and he was with three other seniors from the football team. "We were just picking on you in the locker room yesterday." Leaning in closer, he whispered to Adam. "Look. We want you on the team. Be one of us. The four of us are going to meet after school. We have some magazines. We've seen you hard. It's happened to all of us, so you don't have to be embarrassed. Come on. It'll be fun."

(They have seen me hard. The seniors are more experienced than me, and it probably happens all the time. I guess it's normal, like they say. Having older friends at this new school would be nice.)

(He's thinking about it. Good. Once we get him alone, we can beat the shit out of him.)

(What. That voice in my head. I'm hearing what he is thinking. It's a trap. They are going to beat me up.)

"No thanks. I told mom that I would help her with something after school."

"You sure? Come on. We can be friends."

"No. Sorry. I've got to get to class."

Heading back to class, Adam was stopped by two others who pulled him to the side. He had seen them before in the corner of the school grounds smoking. They were the rebels of the school. Shunning the popular crowd. Saying what they thought about everything.

"I'm Becky. This is Jimbo. We were watching. You got out of that. They were looking to get you alone and beat you up. They have done that to others before. You know you have made some enemies, right. Turning down the coach to be on the football team. Word is that he is pissed off at you. He probably sent them."

"The coach is pissed. He's my teacher in the P.E. class."

"We'll let you know if we learn anything. The elites are just snobs and don't live in the real world. Come on, Jimbo. We got to get to class."

"I'm coming. We are in the same history class. I've seen you sitting in the back."

"We saw you sitting in the front and figured you were one of those raise your hand know it all's. But maybe we were wrong," Becky said, smirking.

Adam could not concentrate in class. He was daydreaming like he often does. (*Why would seniors reveal their thoughts like that. They are older than me. Shouldn't they have learned to control their thoughts by now? At least conceal them like all the other adults. Maybe I'm wrong. It's been sporadic, uncontrolled. I thought they would teach me as I got older, but it's not happening. And now these seniors about to be adults leave their thoughts open like that. What if they are normal and I'm not? Have I been wrong all this time? That thought I heard in the shower. 'You're wrong.' Was that from one of the boys or from something else? It sounded different.*) These thoughts consumed Adam for the remainder of the week. That would explain why no one talks about this sort of thing. He's the different one.

Adam was walking home from school. The school bus would be faster, but he could avoid people this way. Avoid hearing the school elites taunt everyone else. It was worth it. Plus, he liked to walk. After that day at football practice, he realized it when he kept up with the two guys on the track team. It was one of the only times he could be alone. Daisy did not have a job and was always home. He shared a room with his brother. Walking gave Adam time to himself.

(*I've been here for weeks. There is so much bullying at this school. I must take different hallways to avoid the football players picking on me. Then there is that girl that uses braces to walk getting bullied. Then the other girl, Dean, is mentally challenged. She cries almost every day from bullying. How can people do that? Are they blind to how they are making people feel? Affecting their lives.*)

\# # #

Adam was struggling. Pulling himself up. He made it onto the road. He hurt everywhere. His shirt was torn. His clothes were wet. He knew this road. This location. It was one of the roads branching off from the backroad to the nearby community of Urania. He was standing near a bridge. He had climbed up from the creek below. There was never much traffic on this road. Adam wiped his face on his sleeve. Blood. He wiped his face off then tried brushing the mud and debris off the rest of his body. He zipped up his pants, buttoned them, and began straightening his shirt. He started walking across the bridge back to Olla.

(*It hurts to walk. It's not going to be fun. It's going to be dark by the time I get back. Why am I out here? I like to walk. I must have wanted a long walk today and had someone drop me off way out here. I can't remember. Blood on my face. I must have hit my head.)* Adam looked over the low guardrail into the creek below. *(I must have stepped over the railing and been pissing off the side of the bridge. Then slipped and fell into the stream below. I can't remember. Maybe I can hitch a ride back to town.)* A wave of fear washed over Adam. *(What was that? I'm afraid to flag a car down. Why? I can't remember. Ok. I'll have to walk. Ow. I don't know if I can walk all the way. Alright. If someone happens to stop, I'll ask if they can give me a ride.)*

Adam had been walking for 30 minutes. He brushed debris off as his clothes continued to dry. Then a truck stopped on the road beside him. Adam turned. Fear.

"I'm Scott. I'm heading into town to get gas. Do you need a ride?"

"Yeah. That would be great."

Adam got into the truck, acting as if nothing was wrong. He was good at pretending. He had been doing it all his life. Adam would make it back before dark.

"You look a mess. What are you doing out here?"

"I like to walk. It's a nice day, so I thought I'd take a really long walk for once and had someone drop me off out here. I was pissing off a bridge, slipped, and fell into the creek. I started walking back, and you stopped."

"You're lucky you weren't seriously hurt."

"Yeah. I've got some cleaning up to do."

"I'm only going to the gas station on the edge of town and need to get back. Do you need a ride all the way, or are you good at the station?"

"The station is fine. I don't live far from there. Thanks."

They arrived at the gas station, and Adam got out. "Thanks for the ride. I appreciate it. Stopping here is perfect. I can clean up in the restroom before getting home. Thanks again."

"You're welcome. Good luck."

Adam cleaned himself up in the station's restroom then headed home. It didn't take him long. He could come in through the back door directly into his bedroom then into the bathroom. He removed his clothes, tossing everything but his shirt into the washing machine. He would have to throw it away when no one was watching. He stepped into the shower, cleaning himself up properly. He got dressed just in time for dinner. (*Everything is ok. Made it back safely, and no one noticed. I'm not doing that again. No more long walks.*)

"Adam. You have some cuts and scrapes on your face. What happened?" Daisy asked.

"You know how I like to walk. Well, I was walking, tripped, and fell into one of those deep ditches. I made sure to hit everything possible on the way down. It looks worse than it feels. The only thing that hurts a little is my lower back."

"That explains why you are walking slower than normal."

"I'm sure I'll be back to normal in the morning."

His lower back continued to hurt. It was getting worse every day. Finally, on the third day, he couldn't take it anymore. He could barely walk.

"Dad. Somethings wrong. My lower back is hurting really bad. It started a few days ago and has been getting worse. I've been trying to deal with it, but I can't anymore. It's hard for me to walk. I can't go to school like this. I can't move."

"The nearest doctor I know is back in West Monroe. The only thing here is the hospital. Is it bad enough to go to the hospital?"

"No. Not a hospital. A doctor is ok."

"I'll call the doctor we used to have there and get an appointment. He's a good friend of mine and should be able to squeeze us in tomorrow," Nick said.

"Ok."

Nick walked into Adam's room the following day. "I got you a doctor's appointment in West Monroe, but we need to leave now. Get dressed and meet me in the kitchen."

"Ok." Adam rolled out of bed and hit the floor, groaning. He couldn't get up. Nick rushed over to help him back onto the bed. "I can't walk. It hurts too much. Can you help me get dressed and out to the car?"

"Of course."

They made it to the car and drove to West Monroe. Adam felt like it took half a day. Finally, they arrived at the doctor's office and were escorted into one of the examination rooms.

The doctor entered and greeted Nick. They were longtime friends, and Nick told him what was happening with Adam.

The doctor said, “Adam. I'm going to move my hand around your lower back. Tell me to stop when I reach the area of pain.”

“Stop.”

“Ok. I need to do a more thorough examination. Nick, would you wait outside.”

“Why?”

“It's best if we have some doctor-patient privacy for this part of the examination.”

“Ok. I’ll be outside.”

“Adam. I need to check your prostate, so I need you to drop your pants. Underwear and all.”

“Ow. Ow. That hurts. It hurts.”

“Is there anything coming out?”

“Yes. It’s clear.”

“You have a prostate infection. Go ahead and get dressed. Has anything happened to you recently? Any kind of trauma. You can tell me. Everything is private between doctor and patient.”

Adam thought about telling the doctor about his fall into the creek but decided against it. “No. Nothing. I don’t know why this is happening.”

“Ok. I’m going to call Nick back in.”

“What's wrong,” Nick asked?

“He has a prostate infection. You don't normally see this in teenagers. I've mostly seen it in older truck drivers that sit a lot. I don't know the cause, but I can give him some antibiotics that should help. I'm also going to give him some morphine for the pain. It will get him through the day, then hopefully the swelling will start to go down.”

Adam liked the morphine. He still felt the pain but didn’t care. The doctor was right. The pain decreased as his swollen prostate returned to normal. He didn’t mind missing a couple of days of school. Becky and Jimbo were the first to ask about his absence. He didn’t tell them the truth. He was embarrassed, so he made something up about a general illness.

Becky said, “We heard another rumor about you. We're hearing that people have been told to keep their hands off you. No one is to touch you. Not to harm you in any way. What happened to make them say that?”

"I don't know."

"They are not to touch you, but I bet the bullying will continue," Jimbo said. Becky nodded her head in agreement.

"That's ok. At least there is one thing less to worry about."

"We're still not friends. Just letting you know," Becky said, heading off with Jimbo following.

Another school day ended like all the others except Adam had been riding the school bus home. Life never changed for his siblings. Luke was playing basketball while Bonnie had boys asking her out. Then, of course, Sissy focused on cheerleading. However, something had changed within Adam. He had a secret he couldn't tell anyone. A seed of doubt planted earlier had been growing. He was beginning to realize he was different than everyone else. He felt more alone than ever.

"I'm home," Adam yelled, entering the house mimicking his dad's words getting home from work.

"I'm washing clothes," Daisy said from the second bathroom across from his room.

Adam set his books on a desk then sat on the bed for a moment. (*Mom. Can you hear me?*) Adam thought. He tried feeling her in the room next door, washing clothes. Focusing on her mind trying to put himself there. (*Can you hear me?*) Nothing. (*Please answer me. Please hear me. HEAR ME.*) Adam yelled at her mind. Nothing. Adam laid down. Crying into his pillow. (*They are normal. I'm not. I thought they would help me when I got older. Why am I so different from everyone? I have these gay feelings, and people here hate people like me. Even mom and dad don't like gay people. I heard their thoughts. They have seen that part of me. Dad has done what he could to change me, but it didn't work. Mom wants me to get married so she can have grandchildren. I thought they were letting me hear their thoughts for a purpose. To teach me something I didn't understand. But it's their private thoughts. What they honestly think. Their secrets. My parents don't like people like me.*)

Crying, Adam felt as if his life had split. One path everyone around him could see. The path in front of him. Only the physical. Then there is this other path. Something they could not see. Something he would have to keep hidden within the shadows of himself. He recalled a memory from before he was born. (*What am I going to do?*)

The next day Adam was sitting in class feeling alone in a room full of people when an announcement came across the loudspeaker. "Attention, students. Our principal, Mr. Carrington, has taken on a new job at the school board. We wish Mr. Carrington the best during his move. Coach Belter has agreed to become our new principal. He has a lot of good ideas to make this school even better. Thanks, Coach Belter. We know you are going to do a great job."

Becky and Jimbo caught up with Adam after class. Jimbo said, "You're screwed. He hates you and is going to be coming after you."

"People are hating me. What's new?" Adam said, shaking his head as he walked to the school library. He loved libraries and loved to read. Adam could escape the bullies in this sanctuary. He passed Dean in the hall, smiled, and said hello. She giggled. (*She's getting a crush on me. All I'm doing is treating her like an average person. Not as someone with a handicap. Normal. I never bully her.*)

The library is locked. The note on the door read:

New Policy
The library is closed during recess and lunch.
Open 30 min before and after school
and for scheduled classes.

(*It's started*).

New policies were enacted targeting him. Adam eventually began walking back to school. It was better than riding the bus, even if it did take longer. He cut across the grass just like everyone else that walked to school.

"Announcement students. There is a new no walking on the grass policy. We have planted grass seed and are trying to get it to grow. Students walking on the grass will receive detention. Signs are on the grass as a reminder. Thank you."

The next day Daisy dropped Adam off at school. In the process of leaving, the car tires spun on the rocks.

"Announcement students. There is a new policy regarding parents dropping off their kids. The parents are not to spin their tires in the gravel. It could injure students. A student will receive detention if their parent spins in the gravel. Thank you."

Adam had been feeling alone. Now he was alone with a target on his back. Then, after the gravel incident, other students came up to him, saying the principal must have it out for you. (*How much longer do I have to be here? I hope I survive.*)

Adam was having a hard time dealing with his homosexual side and randomly hearing thoughts in people's heads. He had no control over either. Everyone he met in this small town hated gay people. Even Becky and Jimbo were vocal about it. Adam's brothers and sister joined in with others. It was just joking around to them, but Adam took everything personally. He told his parents he wanted to be an artist, but they rejected that idea. There was no money in it. He needed a job that made lots of money. He had a close friend for a few weeks, but then the parents found out and said the boy was from the wrong side of the tracks. Adam's parents did not like the boy's parents and forced Adam to get the boy out of his life. He was not like everyone else. Adam felt like he was a pawn to be used. He had no free will. There was something else. Something had happened that he couldn't remember. He was there to be used by others. There was no way out. There was no hope. Crying and thoughts of suicide were almost daily now.

There was only darkness. Adam was not aware of the shadows moving around him. He did not see their influence. Something found him. Something from his childhood. Something from a white house with red shutters.

CHAPTER 13 – SOUL INFUSION

Adam was lying in bed after school, thinking about his life in this small town. It was like walls in his mind had been constructed. Trapping him inside with only negative thoughts. He couldn't see anything positive about his life. He would be in this tiny town forever, being a thing for others to use. People could abuse him. No one would care.

(They won't even notice.)

(They won't even notice. People never do.)

(They can't hear you.)

(They can't even hear me. I've tried talking to my parents. I've tried talking to others. They all ignore me or ridicule me. I'm alone.)

(You're wrong.)

(I'm wrong. I was born like this. So different. I'm not like everybody else. I don't belong here. Why am I so wrong?)

Adam couldn't take it. Finally, there was one person left he could try and talk to about all of this. The preacher of the church across the lot from their house. Adam did not really like him, but there was no one left. He knocked on the church door. The preacher appeared.

"Hello, Adam. What brings you here." It was a small church, and he knew all his congregation. His family were the newcomers in town and lived across from the church. The McLures had recently joined, so he knew Adam.

"Can I talk to you in private? I don't know what else to do."

"Come on in. I have an office on the side. We can talk there."

(*Just say it*). "I'm attracted to guys. At least a part of me is gay. I was looking at a boy in the shower at school, and they all saw me get hard. Everyone knows it, and I get bullied. Everybody hates people like me. They say it out loud. I can hear them think it."

"The bible says homosexuals are an abomination, but it also says we are supposed to love them. It's how we learn to grow. Some places can teach you how not to be homosexual. I can give you some materials to look over."

(*I'm an abomination. So people learn and grow at my expense?*) Adam did not notice that the light in the room was only around them now. The walls were covered in shadow.

"What did you mean when you said that you can hear them think it?"

"I can sometimes hear what people are thinking. Especially when I look in their eyes," Adam said, looking at the preacher. "Like now. You are thinking about making this part of Sunday's sermon."

(That is what I was thinking. Can Adam see what I've done?) A shadow moved unnoticed, touching the preacher. (He's setting me up. Is this being recorded?) "You think this is funny. Who told you to do this? Trying to entrap good people. You're the thing wrong with the world. Get out."

"What did I say? What did I do wrong?"

"Get out."

Adam headed back home feeling worse than before. (*You're the thing wrong with the world.*) He could not get that line out of his head. It glowed in his mind like a neon sign. (*You're the thing wrong with the world. You're wrong.*)

Nick and Daisy were in the living room when Adam returned. They knew he had gone to see the preacher about something. He walked in shaking, not looking up, tears long gone in waves of acceptance. (*You're the thing wrong with the world. You're wrong.*)

Nick and Daisy both knew something was wrong. "What's wrong? Did he sexually abuse you?"

"No. It was something else."

"What was it?"

"Just something else. It's not important." (*I'm not important*). Adam went to his room. It's darker than usual. (*Everyone hates me here, including my parents. I'm wrong. I'm going to leave. Maybe there is something away from here. Somewhere I might not be hated so much.*)

Adam packed a small suitcase. He was hoping there was somewhere he could go. Somewhere he could live. Just live. His parents stopped him as he headed out the front door with a suitcase.

"Where are you going to go?" Nick asked.

(*Where are you going to go? Where can I go? Everyone inside this house hates me. Everyone at school hates me. The town hates me. Religion hates me. God hates me. Everyone outside this town is the same or worse. I'll be shot on sight. I'm the thing wrong with the world. I'm wrong. There is nowhere I can go.*) Adam turned around without saying a word and went back to his bedroom. He lay on his bed, looking up. He remembered floating through the bedsprings at his childhood home. (*I think I can do that again if I really let go. I'm going to let go of everything. Leave my body and never come back. I won't be a mistake here anymore.*) A shadow moved in the corner of the room. Waiting.

There was no longer any reason to be here. Everyone would be better off with Adam gone. His consciousness focused on itself. There was the feeling of going over small hills like on a roller coaster. He's floating. Looking down, he sees a shadow moving toward his body on the bed. The shadow stopped moving. Time stopped in that physical world. He continued floating through the ceiling to somewhere else. It did not matter. He was not coming back because he was a mistake. He didn't care that a shadow might take over his body. He only knew he wasn't going back. Then a torrent of crystal clear, crisp energy, flowing like water, surrounded him. It was sparkling like diamonds. It swirled around him. Carrying him with it back down into his body.

Adam opened his eyes as this energy poured into his body. It was so powerful his fragile body could not contain it all. It was as if this energy formed a second being. It was part of him. It was him. He sat up, feeling this other part of himself so large it extended past his skin. He looked at his hands. They were unfamiliar. A second set of invisible hands overlapping the physical ones and invisible wings on his back. They were like this invisible energy body overlapping the physical one. Everything was glowing except an area next to him. It was a being made of shadow. Not moving. Adam stood, and as he did, the shadow disintegrated. It was gone.

(*What was that? What is this? It's thick. Hard to breathe. Hard to move through.*) A memory returned. (*Air. I know this. It's different. No. I'm different. Moving legs to walk. It's so odd.*) Adam was taking his first steps. A memory returned. They were not his first, but it felt like it. His memories were still there, but he had to search for them. He walked into the bathroom and looked at himself in the mirror.

(*Is that me?*) He reached up and touched his face. He pulled his eyelid up and looked at his eyes. A memory returned. (*My eyes were solid brown. They are not brown anymore. They are green overlaying a bit of brown. This is me, but I barely recognize myself.*) He squeezed the skin on his face. (*This body reacts, but that's not me. I'm in it. Inside this body. How odd.*)

Adam headed towards the front door.

"Adam. Would you come in here? We have salmon, and I need you to cut a lemon," Daisy said.

"Ok."

Adam walked into the kitchen. (*Who is that? She's familiar. That memory. It's my mother. My memory knows her, but I don't know her.*) Adam stood staring. She wanted him to cut a lemon. He did not know what that was. Daisy grabbed his hand and put a lemon in it. "There's the knife now cut it."

He searched his memories. (*Yes. Cutting a lemon. Why would I want to do such a thing to this object? I've done it before.*) Adam slowly sank the knife into the lemon, cutting it in half. (*There are two pieces of the same object now. It's still a lemon.*)

"You're not really helping. Go on. I'll do it myself. Go do what you were planning to do."

Adam proceeded to the front door and walked out. He was stunned. All the colors. So intense. He had never seen any of this. Trees. Sky. Ground. Not like this. He felt part of it all. Everything was alive, just like him. The first thing he noticed moving were the clouds passing by. "Hello," Adam said. He felt a peaceful smile flow from the clouds above into him. Next, he noticed the breeze moving the leaves of the trees. The wind was alive. The trees were alive. He greeted both, feeling contented to have introduced himself. He looked down to see dust swirling in patterns on the ground. The Earth is alive. The Sun is alive. Everything is alive.

Adam was brand new to this existence. He saw everything for the first time, but a part of him still remembered the past. Adam had to force himself to remember. Finally, he opened his senses and looked at himself.

(*We are partially integrated. We are one mind. We are the same being, but this lower version of myself, this body, can't handle this much energy. That's why I'm seeing a set of physical hands and etheric hands. I feel both the physical and etheric bodies as separate entities, yet we are the same. It's going to take a long time to integrate.*) A memory returned. Two paths were spiraling around each other. There was a normal life and a secret life no one could see. One in light and one in shadow. Twisting like a DNA chain.

Adam continued walking down the street, recalling memories. Remembering how to be human. He could feel other memories slipping away. Being forgotten. Memories of the source. Being part of oneness. Light. Love. Joy. So much more now forgotten.

(*The body can't handle all these memories. It's not ready. It's going to take months until I feel comfortable in this body.*) Adam continued walking and began to forget as the memories buried themselves.

By the time Adam felt himself again, he had forgotten so much. The only thing left was this etheric presence. He could sense it. Feel it. It was him yet separate from him. He knew something had happened. Something came into him. He wasn't the same as before. He felt more alone than ever, yet all of reality was his friend. He couldn't tell anyone about it. They would know he was crazy.

CHAPTER 14 – REALITY RESPONDS

Adam's brother and sisters were off doing their own things while he sat under a tree looking at his new yearly planner. He was penciling in notes for the week while students arrived at school. Unfortunately, Adam and the school did not have a good relationship so he was waiting until the last minute before he had to go inside.

Monday: P.E. Baseball game
Tuesday: Math test. Post Office get mail
Wednesday: Town shut down
Thursday: English-History test?
Friday: Math test

Adam looked up at the sky. "I wish it would rain so I would not have to join in on that stupid baseball game during P.E. class." If it rained, he would have to do a few indoor exercises, but mostly it was just sitting in the bleachers of the basketball court. Adam always carried a book with him to read and loved the rain so he could read.

Adam looked back down at his Monday note. P.E. Baseball game. Images formed in Adams's mind as if he saw it on a screen. He saw himself entering the school, going to class, going out for the baseball game but it started raining. They run back inside as the rain continues into the next course, then it stops. Adam glances to the side at the grass growing better now that no one is walking on it. (*I've never pictured the day like that in my mind before. It's always been just doing it without really thinking. I'm seeing pictures of the entire day. Laying the day out in my head as if I'm doing these things.*) He looked at the next day in the planner. Tuesday: Math test. Post Office get mail. Images formed just as before. (*I'm walking to the Post Office. That's a long way. Wonder why I'm walking. It must be an adult thing and the way people visualize stuff.*)

The bell rings. It's just another day at school. (*I should put numbers on each day of my planner, counting down the days until I graduate and get out of here.*) Adam is more interested in writing numbers on each page than paying attention in class. The bell rings. It's third period. P.E. Class.

He ignores the taunts, changes, grabs his glove, and heads outside to the baseball field with the others. Halfway to the field, it starts pouring rain. They all rush back inside. "Game canceled. We'll give the ground time to dry and try Wednesday. Put your gear up and get to the bleachers," Principal Belter said in the locker room. Principal Belter is still the P.E teacher and coach. They have not found a replacement for him yet.

Adam pulls out the planner and pencils in P.E. baseball game for Wednesday. (*That's a coincidence. I saw it rain when I looked at the planner, and it rained. Or did it rain because I looked up and asked. The sky is alive. Maybe it heard me.*)

"Guess what I did for the weekend?"

Still looking at his planner Adam said, "You and your dad went to Alexandria, bought some fishing gear, then on the way back, he let you practice driving on some of the logging roads."

"Yes. That's what I did. Are you watching me? Are you stalking me?"

Adam turned to look behind him. They weren't talking to him, yet he had answered. "No. I was home reading books. I'm not stalking you."

"You're such a freak," Adam heard as he was shoved to the ground. The group stood and walked to another area, whispering slurs loud enough for him to hear.

(*I wasn't thinking. I was not even trying to hear. It just happened. I've got to be careful.*)

Adam looked up to the sky as he walked home from school. "Can you do that again next Wednesday? Rain, so the baseball game during P.E. class gets canceled." Adam laughed under his breath, knowing something like that can't happen just by asking. (*If it rains next Wednesday, it's because it's always raining in Louisiana.*)

Tuesday ended just like any other school day. Except today, Adam had penciled in his planner Post Office get mail. (*Mom's been letting me drive the car to get the mail. It's good driving practice. If I walk to get the mail, is it because it's what I saw, or I'm walking to make it match what I saw? Doesn't really matter. I'll walk.*)

Adams mind was walking new paths as his body walked to the Post Office. (*Why am I so different from others. These memories from before I was born. Hearing thoughts. That stuff flowed into me, and everything changing. Seeing images of the day is almost like seeing what will happen. Then the rain. Now I'm walking to the Post Office as I saw. I wish I had something for this headache.*) Adam looked up. "A breeze would be nice. It's hot, and I have a headache." There is a noise behind him. He turns and is hit by a blast of wind. Leaves and papers are flying down the street. There are dark clouds over the tree line. (*It's an outflow from that rain cloud. Wait. I asked, and it happened. But there's an ordinary explanation. It's an outflow. My brain hurts. It's going to be a migraine.*)

Adam had enough money to stop at the drug store next to the Post Office and get something for the headache. (*It's going to be a long walk home. The light is so bright that it hurts my head. If only I had a giant wood clamp I could put on my head. The pressure might help reduce this pain. Everything is so bright and alive it hurts. There is something else. I'm aware that I'm a separate being from my physical body. Does all reality around me have an individual consciousness? Is it really like me?*) The pain in his mind shifted lower, and the top of his mind cleared. The migraine pain is now contained as a marble in the base of his skull. The rest of his mind is beginning to perceive a new reality.

(*There is something else here. Another existence is overlaying this one. Two things in one space. Like a body and consciousness. There is another plane of existence. This reality is an illusion.*) The pain came flooding back. This instance of insight was gone and forgotten in the blinding pain of a migraine headache. It was all Adam could do to get home, make his room as dark as possible and crawl into bed. If he could only get to sleep, it would be gone when he woke.

Adam woke the next day. The migraine headache was gone. He felt lucky to be a boy. Their migraines typically go way after sleep. Girls are not so lucky. Theirs can last days. (*I don't know how they survive these. Ugh. P.E. baseball today.*)

Heading into school, Adam thought (*No clouds. Guess not going to rain, but it's Louisiana. There is always a chance for rain.*) So Adam went from class to class, noticing clouds forming, then more. By the time P.E. class came, it was raining. (*It happened again. Still has a rational explanation.*)

# # #

It was Friday night. The family was in the car driving to West Monroe to see a movie. (*At least I'm by a window*) Adam thought. It's dark, and there is a thunderstorm in the distance. (*Weather responding can't be real. There is an explanation for all of it. Still. I wonder.*) Looking at the storm in the distance, Adam mutters under his breath so no one else can hear. "Can you make a lightning bolt strike there?" pointing to something in the distance. A bolt of lightning arcs down and strikes where he is pointing. (*It's just a coincidence.*) "Make a bolt strike there," he said, pointing to an area behind them. Another bolt of lightning appeared where he pointed. (*Not possible.*) "Make one strike over there," he said, pointing. Another bolt. It begins to dawn on Adam these might not be coincidences. (*Alright. This time, make it close, and if it happens, something else is going on.*) "Make a bolt strike in the tree line up ahead close to the road." A tree exploded up head as a bolt of lightning struck.

"Did you see that?" Nick said, "That was really close."

There was talk of the lightning strike for the remainder of the trip. Only Adam thought (*I'm crazy. This can't be real, but it's happening. Am I crazy to believe this is happening? If I tell anyone, they will put me on medication or lock me up. It's alive. It heard me. It responded. What else is alive and can hear me. This is crazy. Is this how I'm going to live from now on? Having to pretend that I'm normal for the rest of my life when I really am crazy.*) Adam remained quiet, feeling more alone than he's ever felt. (*It's that dark path spiraling around an everyday life I saw from before I was born. I'm alone in a crowded car at night. That's going to be my life. Crazy and alone in the dark.*)

CHAPTER 15 – ELECTRIC

Jimbo said "Adam, want a ride home? I saved up enough money from my job at Burger Barn and bought a beat-up car."

"Sure." Adam opened the door, pushed the front seat forward, and slid it back. Becky got in the passenger seat and immediately lit up a cigarette. She took a couple of puffs then passed it to Jimbo. Becky lit another. "Want one?" she asked Adam.

"No thanks. I got sick when I was little. Never again."

Jimbo turned the key. Nothing happened. "Shit. The battery is dead. Can't afford a new one right now so I keep it on a charger. Guess it didn't hold," he said as they all got out of the car. "It's a standard. We can pop the clutch."

Becky got behind the wheel as Jimbo and Adam started pushing on the car to back it up. As he pushed, images formed in Adam's mind as if he was moving through the car's hood into the battery. He felt his hands tingling as if a current of electricity was passing through them into the battery. Finally, as they moved to the back of the car, Adam said, "Why don't you try and start it one more time before we start pushing."

Becky turned the key and the car cranked.

"Must have been a loose wire. Maybe I should start parking on a hill just in case," Jimbo said.

"Oh. Turn on the radio. I like that song," Adam said.

"What song?"

"**Flirting with Disaster**."

Jimbo turned on the car radio. The song was playing. "How did you know that song was on the radio?" Jimbo asked.

"I must have heard it from a car driving by." Adam rationalized that is what must have happened. He did not remember hearing anything from another car. There was no other explanation.

Becky said, "What do you think about the new kid Jason? His dad is the new preacher at the church. Suppose there was an opening. Starting toward the end of the school year must be hard."

"I didn't know there was a new preacher. Have not been to that church in a while. I have not talked to Jason yet," Adam said.

"They say preacher kids are wild. We might like him," Jimbo said.

Dropping Adam off, Becky said, "Let us know if you ever need a ride home."

Jimbo looked at Becky "Hey, it's my car."

"It's our car. I loaned you some money for it, and until you pay me back, it's our car."

Jimbo rolled his eyes as they pulled out of the driveway. "I'll park on a hill next time just in case."

"I'm home," Adam yelled, entering the house.

"I'm in here," Daisy yelled back from her bedroom. "I can't get this stupid radio to work." She handed it to Adam.

He fiddled with the cord a bit. (*There it is again. That feeling of something flowing around my skin into my hands and into the radio.*) Then, finally, he plugged in the radio and turned it on.

"How did you get it to work?"

"I just played with the cord. It must have been a loose wire." (*It had to be a loose wire. The simplest explanation is usually correct. It was just a loose wire.*)

Lying in bed after dinner, Adam thought (*I don't know what's happening, but something is happening. I can't talk about it, but I can work with it without others knowing. I guess it's related to my brain. I should exercise my brain more. Maybe I could try doing two things at once. Something like a math problem and filling out my planner at the exact same time.*)

Adam picked up his planner and started filling in minor activities he would not normally include. (*2x2=4, 2x4=8, 2x8=16*). He looked down, and he wasn't writing. (*It's hard to do.*) He began writing again.

(2x2=4, 2x4=8, 2x8=16)

Breakfast, school, homework, dinner

(Did it. It's more complicated than it looks. I only was able to do a tiny bit then I lost it. It's probably like sports. The more you practice, the better you get. So I'll have to keep practicing. At least it's something I can do in public without others noticing.)

# # #

Baseball during P.E. class was rained out again. The kids were sitting in the gym bleachers. Girls on one side and boys on the other side. They were told to be doing homework. Everyone was quiet. Then the girls started laughing.

Dean, the mentally challenged girl that was constantly bullied, had started dancing in the middle of the basketball court. There was no music. The girls were heckling her loudly from the stands. It did not take long for the boys to join in.

(*Where are the teachers? Why do people do this? She has a pure soul and the most genuine smile I've ever seen. Why can't they see it?*) Adam sat there looking, not knowing what to do.

(Now)

It was an impression like a voice in his head. Adam walked onto the gym floor without another thought and began dancing with her. There was no music, only the taunts from the stands. Dean was giggling. Her smile was brighter than the sun. It wasn't long before she ran back to the stands giggling. Adam watched her join the other girls. (*They are not bullying her anymore. She's happy, and there is nothing they can do.*)

Adam continued to be bullied the rest of the day. (*It's ok. It was a moment she needed. It's worth it.*)

He was greeted by Becky and Jimbo the next day before entering the school. "Did you hear what happened?" Becky asked.

"No."

"Dean died. Her trailer caught on fire last night. Her family ran out front and she ran out back. They figured she ran back in when she did not see them with her. She died in the fire. We feel like shit for being mean to her."

Adam was stunned.

Jimbo said, "The whole school feels like shit. Everybody wishes they would have treated her nice like you."

The days leading up to the funeral were the same. Kids at school came up to Adam, saying they wished they would have treated her better. How bad they felt. He did not know what to say in return. Just talk that they needed or expected to hear. Words did not mean much to him, but their actions did. They were treating each other better. The other girl with leg braces was no longer being bullied. They were being nice to her. Picking up her books instead of knocking them out of her hands. It wasn't just Becky and Jimbo that changed. It was all of them.

"Are you coming?" Nick asked.

"No."

"Why not? You knew her better than any of us and should be at her funeral."

"I want to go, but the attention will be focused on me if I do. So I'm staying here."

"Alright, we'll let you know how it went."

Adam went back to his bedroom and cried. She was a truly good person, and she died. Something happened that Adam could not identify. Something needed to be done, and he did it, but he did not know what it was. It was a turning point in his life. If he had a choice to be like Dean or the other kids at the school, he would choose to be like Dean no matter how much bullying he would take.

"We're back," Daisy said, entering the door with the others.

"The school kids there talked about how you treated her nice. But then, her father was at the podium talking and said that you gave her one of the happiest days in her life. She loved that moment."

"Adam, someone is here to see you," Luke said.

Adam wiped his face and went to the front door.

"I'm Jason. My dad's the new preacher, so I had to be at the funeral. I heard what you did and wanted to meet you. I can drive and have my dad's car. Want to go for a ride?"

"Sure," then Adam yelled, "Mom. I'm going riding with Jason. He's the son of the preacher who did the funeral."

"Ok. Don't be out too late."

They drove just a few minutes which was more than enough time to stop in a field outside the city. It was getting dark as they got out and sat on the hood of the car. Jason lit up a hand-rolled cigarette and took a drag.

"Here."

"What is it?"

"It's weed. You know. Marijuana."

"I don't like smoking, but I'll try it." He inhaled.

"Hold it for a few seconds. Then breath out. Yeah, like that."

"It didn't make me sick."

"Yeah, it's not bad."

"So. Your dad is the preacher. What's that like?"

"It's terrible. My dad doesn't have his own church. When a church loses a preacher suddenly, he fills in until they get a permanent replacement. That means we move around a lot. Sometimes we will only be at a place for a month or two. It's going to be the same here. I've heard talk they have already found a replacement, so I don't expect I'll be here very long."

"That sucks."

"Yeah. I don't have time to make real friends. So I seek the outsiders to talk to, kids my own age. That's you, from what I hear. You did something everybody is talking about. Did you know Dean very well?"

"No, not really. Just in passing down the hall, I was nice to her. Everybody else bullied her."

"Well, that won't happen anymore. It's getting dark. I wish we could see some meteors," Jason said, stretching out on the car hood.

"Yeah, seeing meteors would be nice."

"Whoa, did you see that? It was a meteor."

"Yeah, I saw it."

"Let's hang out here on the hood of the car for a while. Maybe we'll see more."

"Ok," Adam said, also stretching out on the hood of the car.

"I wish those city lights weren't so bright. So we could see meteors better."

"Let me try something." Adam stretched his arms above his head. He crossed them over the windshield. (*I said that out loud. That cigarette really loosened me up. If those electricity feelings earlier are genuine, maybe I can do something about the lights. Electricity flows in lines, and sometimes they short circuit. So perhaps I can reach out with this electric feeling again, this time crossing my arms and feeling like it's being short-circuited.*)

There was a flash, then an explosion. The city lights went out.

"That was really weird. We were just talking about the city lights, and then they go out."

"Yeah, that was a bizarre coincidence."

(*Did I do that? I'm freaking out. It must be the weed. This marijuana is dangerous if it loosens me up like this, and I start talking.*) "It'd be great to see another meteor. There's another one. Did you see it?"

"Yeah, I saw it."

"I wish I could stay out here, but Mom does not want me out too late."

"We'll head back."

As Jason dropped Adam off, he said, "Let's hang out sometimes. Seems we are both outsiders here, and we need to stick together."

"Definitely an outsider, so yeah. See you at school."

"Mom, I'm home."

"Did you have a good time?"

"Yeah, I made a new friend. Jason, the preacher's son."

"That's good. Dinner's in the fridge. You can heat it up if you want some."

"Ok. I'll heat it up. Thanks. (*This has been a crazy week. I wonder what else is going to happen.*)

That night he felt something rub his groin. (*Don't stop*) he thought as he fell asleep. He'd been dreaming about sex a lot. That night he dreamt of sex with shadowy figures. Some with glowing red eyes. It felt good.

CHAPTER 16 – DARK ATTACK

Adam had these dreams often. This one was different. They were getting darker and more intense. He was tied down by three beautiful women. One was on top as the other two held him down. Adam's body responded. It felt good. She cut his face with a knife. Pain. Fear. The women changed to three men with oily brown hair and red eyes. They pulled him to the edge of the table and flipped him over. He was being held down as the more prominent man violated him. Pain. Then laughing. He was now the man violating the one with oily brown hair. The man felt fear. It made Adam feel powerful. It felt good.

Adam woke. (*Got to clean me up again. What was that? Where did that come from? I liked it but what did I like the most. The sex or the power? I'm such a freak.*) He felt different as he stepped into the shower across from his bedroom. This is part of him. It must be part of everybody because people do bad things like bullying at school. (*Is this normal? To feel this dark part of yourself and like it. Wanting more. Is that what makes people do bad things? I liked that feeling of power over someone. I shouldn't, but I did. Why?*)

He got dressed and walked to school like usual. He couldn't help but think about the dream. It felt so real. To have that kind of power over people. (*It's going to be a long day if I keep getting hard every class. I can't stop thinking about that dream. I don't think I can take being in school that long. I've got to get out of here.*) He let himself feel the electricity in the room. It spiraled around the thoughts of the dream. Building. He crossed his wrists under the desk and pictured wires crossing. Trying to create a short circuit then pushed that thought into the wiring. The lights went out.

The school canceled classes for the rest of the day. He took a longer path getting home. Though the woods. He found a secluded spot and opened his pants. He thought of the dream and let it take over. (*Oh yeah. Power. Fuck yeah.*) He felt the spasms of relief. (*Christ. What was that? I don't want to be like that. I don't want to hurt people. I couldn't stop it.*)

(It's normal to want power. This is how you get it.)

Adam woke the next day. (*More dreams. I guess morning showers are my new routine. I should add it to my planner.*) Luke burst in while Adam was showering. He had forgotten about the rest of the family. Adam had become consumed with his own teenage drama without thinking about theirs. He should have locked the door.

"Don't you knock?"

"Lock the door if you don't want people in."

"What do you want?"

"Schools out. They still haven't got the power fixed," Luke said, heading back out the door.

"Nice." There would be a few chores, but he could do some reading. Perhaps he could walk to the highway and get a burger for lunch. Everyone will be there with school being out.

"I'm walking to the Burger Barn," Adam yelled to the house in general as he headed out the door. It's a free day during the week, and school is out. Burger Barn is the place to be seen.

(Practice. Blow the power again. It's normal.)

(*It couldn't hurt. Crossing wrists is a minor thing no one will pay attention to while I walk. The rest is just thoughts and visualizing.*) Adam thought about the dreams. The feeling of walking while hard matching the images in his head. He felt the electricity around him, crossed his wrist then pushed the thoughts of electricity short-circuiting. There was an explosion behind him. He turned in time to see another transformer blow, then another right beside him. It was a chain reaction. He heard tires squealing on the pavement. He turned to see a car going off the road near him. It could have hit him. Workers from the auto shop nearby ran out to check on the driver. She was unhurt.

(She could have been hurt or killed. I could have been injured or killed. So I'm not doing that anymore.)

(Everything's fine. No one is hurt. Practice is good)

(No. Whatever you are. Part of me or not. Get out! Get out now!) He felt something separate from his body. He could not see anything, but he felt it. It was there in front of him. The more of its presence he felt, the better image he could create in his mind. There was no longer any doubt. There is something there. Invisible but real. Memories of walking with a migraine headache returned. Seeing another plane of existence overlaying the one everyone sees with their eyes. It's there on this other plane of existence. It's real.

Then it moved to the side and vanished. Adam felt his usual self again. No more urges for control or power. No urges to interfere with electricity. Just himself.

(That confirms it. I'm crazy. The transformers probably blew because they were working on one trying to get the school up and running, but somebody screwed up. A rational explanation for the electricity except for this presence. I'm crazy, but maybe I can be a kind of crazy that doesn't hurt anyone.)

He continued his walk to the Burger Barn, purchased a hamburger and a drink. Then he headed home. It began raining as he walked in the front door. Nothing else to do but read. He dreamed of flying through the universe in a ship that responded to his thoughts that night. Shifting dimensions and passing through solid objects. He had dreams like this before. He is in control. Nothing like the darker dreams from before.

Adam woke the following day feeling like the world was an illusion. Maybe a stage. Like that Shakespeare quote. Almost as if he is the only actor on the scene, and all these other people are just props. They are not like him. *(Even if I am the only actor on the stage, that is no reason to control everything else. I can still interact and learn. I want to help. Not harm. That sounds delusional. Yep. I'm crazy.)* He thought back to the events of yesterday. It felt familiar. Yes. From his childhood. That being floating outside his window. Red eyes and the body covered in oily brown hair. Now there is no one protecting him. Adam felt the same fear now as he felt then.

(There it is again. That presence. In my room.) Adam felt more fear. It grew stronger and moved through a nearby wall. The picture on the

wall fell. (*It knocked it off the wall. It's not my imagination.*) Adam grabbed his schoolbooks and headed out the door as fast as possible.

Paranoia ruled the day. It felt like it was more than just one presence now. It was several. An invisible gang was stalking him. This image in his mind of an overlapping reality was now permanent. His eyes see reality just as everyone else; however, his mind is creating an overlay that includes these things. Formless until he concentrated and let these other senses take over. These different senses provided enough details to know where they are, what they look like, and when they moved. They are basically humanoid, but some of them seem to be in several places at once. (*What are they?*)

Being home from school eating dinner with the family did not help. They are still there. Watching. (*What are they doing? Waiting? I wish mom and dad could see them.*) One moved closer, through the table right in front of him. Fear. It grew in strength. Adam's glass tipped over, spilling water over the table.

"Here are some napkins to clean it up," Daisy said.

"Thanks. I'm clumsy." Adam knew he did not knock over the glass, but what else could he say. They would not believe him. When he talked to them about hearing thoughts, they didn't believe him, so why would they start now. Especially with something he can't show or prove. It was his secret.

Adam could feel them all around as he lay in bed that night. They surrounded his bed. Images appeared in his mind meant to instill fear. Images of torture and being torn apart. He was alone and afraid. They got stronger. He did not want to sleep, but he was tired of everything happening. It was out of control.

He woke to find himself outside. He remembered getting out of bed and walking out the backdoor of their bedroom. He didn't know why he was at the tree line. He could see his house in the distance. (*Did they get me out here? Can they do that?*)

Fear. Overwhelming fear.

He felt a presence. Much more substantial than the others. It towered over Adam. A force hit him, and he fell back, hitting a tree. No one to catch him this time. Out of breath, he looked up. It's coming after him, and he's alone in the dark.

Adam looked up. "I don't know what to do. I need help. Please."

His eyes see stars in the night sky, but his mind opens to a memory. Looking down at Earth as if through the eye of a hurricane. Moving closer. A memory of wanting to help. Moving closer. Seeing Adam floating above his body needing help. Wrapping himself around Adam and pulling him back down into the physical body. Trying to become one with it. (*It's me. I'm helping myself. I'm more than this physical body. More than what I remember from before. I'm also that other one. This energy is with me. Etheric. I'm all of it.*)

The fear was gone. Adam felt peace in the truth of knowing. (*I'm more than this*) he thought, looking at his hand. Sensing his etheric set of hands. His etheric self. He felt a light inside build and surround him. He was encased in a bubble of light.

The large being swung at him and hit the light as if it was solid. It tried several more times. Anger and hate flooded around him. Nothing got through. Adam stood up. He felt life in everything around him. They were his friends, and he loved them. The dark being flinched then began backing away. The shadows began to dissipate. The more prominent being is fading away. Adam looked up toward the stars. Something was out there. Something familiar. Smiling.

CHAPTER 17 – FIGHTING

(*What really happened last night? Those things attacked. I still don't know what they are. That bubble of light. At peace knowing I'm more than just this physical body. I'm this awareness as well. Is it life? Is it consciousness? Is it just me being crazy?*) Adam laughed as he continued his walk to school. (*But these scrapes from hitting the tree. It was real. I can't prove that it happened. Maybe I just dreamed all that and fell out of bed scraping my back on something.*) "Whoa. What is that?" The surroundings he sees with his eyes are the same as he sees in his mind. He is still feeling this overlay but everything matches except on the school bus passing by. His eyes are viewing the school bus as it is physically. His mind is also sensing and building an image of a small dark shadow moving within the bus. (*It's one of those things inside the bus.*)

The bus turned a corner and out of sight.

Walking into school, he felt another one by the water fountain. (*I can feel it.*) He let his mind build an image of his surroundings then let his senses add to the picture. The overlay in his mind shows the 5'10" humanoid shadow moving through the wall into the next room. (*It's not my classroom. I can't go in.*) He thought, walking down the hall. He continued focusing on the humanoid shadow as he walked into his classroom and sat at his desk.

He was unable to pay attention in class. Instead, he was focused on the thing. He had a map of the school in his mind now. He could see it moving from room to room. His senses were expanding. He could feel the people in the room. He could feel the walls, the floor, even the foundation under the floor. (*It's moving into the cafeteria.*) He could track it.

He felt a surge of anger from the entity. It grew larger in his mind then vanished. (*It's gone. Did it know I was watching it?*) His mind battled the remainder of the school day, trying to determine if this was real or if he was crazy. Finally, he gave up when the school bell rang. It was time to go home.

He could feel it before he entered the house. (*Another one? Or is it the same one from the school and it followed me? I can feel it in the kitchen.*) He entered and began walking to the kitchen. "I'm home."

"I'm in the kitchen making sweet tea," Daisy said.

Adam walked into the kitchen.

"Do you want some tea?"

"Sure."

He could see it in his mind standing next to his mother. The 5'10" humanoid shadow solidified and reached out. The knife sitting on the counter slid to the edge. (*She's going to run into it.*) He picked up the knife and put it in the drawer.

Noticing his actions, Daisy said, "Silly me. I must have left it sitting out. Here's your tea."

"Thanks." He stood there drinking the tea, feeling relief that she was not hurt. (*Even though she can't understand me, I still love her.*) But, there is that feeling again. One of light building up within. One of peace and confidence. He felt it expand beyond himself and encompass Daisy. He could feel it. See it in the mental image overlaying the reality in front of him. The shadow was pushed away from Daisy. It could not get through the light now surrounding her.

(*This feeling comes from inside. One of peace, knowing you are more than physical. It can be expanded. It felt it. The light pushed it away.*)

He did not want Daisy to notice so he continued drinking tea standing at the counter. At the same time, he let this feeling of light and love expand into the room as if the whole room was glowing. The shadow was pushed out of the kitchen. (*It can't stay in the light.*) He built an image of his house in his mind. There Adam is in the kitchen. A starting point. Feeling this light and love expand from the kitchen through the rest of the house using the mental image as a guide. Going from room to room. He felt it. It was real.

The humanoid shadow Adam could see in his mind was furious. Anger. Hate. Violence. It flailed at the light as it was pushed out of the house. Then it was gone.

Adam finished the tea and headed to his bedroom. (*It worked. That feeling of light can be used for protection. Even if I'm crazy, I found something that works. I also did it in front of mom. She didn't notice. I can do both things at the same time. Like when expanding my brain with the math problem and planner. Doing two things at once. It's possible.*) He felt happy. He had found something he could use to protect himself and others. (*Is it permanent? Can they never come back to the house? Does it fade? I guess I'll find out.*)

# # #

"Adam, come on. We are going to be late for Luke's basketball game," Nick said.

"Do I have to go?"

"You need to go and support your brother."

Growing angry, Adam said, "I don't get sports. It's just a bunch of running back and forth. So why do people cheer for that?"

"Fine. Then stay here. You can't stay in your books forever. You'll have to be part of the real world sometime," Nick said, shutting the front door harder than usual.

(*Part of the real world. What is real? I'm stuck in this crazy world of mine.*) Getting angrier, Adam thought (*I can't talk to anybody. If I do, I just get ridiculed. How is that being part of the real world? You want to talk to people about it but they laugh at you. How real is that? Maybe I'm the only one living in the real world, and you're all just illusions. Ever think about that? Of course not. You're not real, and you can't think beyond what's right in front of you.*)

It was there. Grinning. Adam didn't notice until he moved. He stepped out of that one spot, and something was left behind when he did. It quickly moved back into him but not fast enough. For that brief instance, Adam was not angry. Something shifted when he moved, then he was angry again.

(*Somethings not right. I should have gone. Really wanted to go, but then this anger. Is this a teenager thing?*) Another flash of anger then hatred towards Nick for making him feel bad for staying home. (*No. That's not me. It's something else.*)

He made himself be still. Focused on a small point of light inside. Peaceful and let it expand around himself. The shadowy humanoid figure moved and was now beside him. (*There it is. It's back. Inside the house with me. This protective light fades. I can't keep it up all the time.*) It was there grinning. It could wait forever. It would be there, ready for the moment Adam was not paying attention.

(*It's moving to leave the house. I can't let it escape and do this again. I can expand this light to the whole house. That will just push it outside. Maybe if I only extend it to specific sections.*) Adam focused on the light around him. He pictured the light changing from a bubble to a wall in his mind. He felt it. A wall that expanded outwards to encompass the walls of the living room. Then further expanding it to the ceiling and floors. It is now a box of light with the two of them in it.

It turned. Surprised. It tried to get out but was blocked. It was trapped. It could not attack. Adam still had the light around him. It grew angrier. Images of violence and hate poured into Adam's mind.

"I have you," Adam said, fighting against the rage he was sensing. "I'm not going to let you do this to anybody else." Adam felt this awareness of self that extended beyond his physical form solidify. He had no doubts. It was him, and it was real. He felt wings on his back harden.

He had forgotten about them. He considered them like ears. They are a part of you, but you don't really use them for anything. They are present but inactive. But, of course, they weren't inactive anymore.

He felt a physical pressure on his back around the shoulder blades. The wings he sensed expanding outwards. He is in control of them. Can move them just like his arms and legs. He reached out with his left-wing. The figure moved away from it. He reached out with the right-wing to block it from moving. It ran into the wing. Adam felt it hit. (*The wings can touch this thing.*)

He pulled the two wings together, grasping the humanoid figure. He could hold it in place. It raged. Adam raged back (*You are not going to do this to anyone else ever again.*) It looked at him, panicked. (*It heard me rage at it. It can hear the negative. Anger. Rage. Hate.*)

A piece of shadow split off. The central entity shrank to five feet. The other part was trying to escape the box of light. Adam reached out with his physical hand and felt this other ethereal hand expand. He reached out and grabbed the smaller shadow holding it. Adam felt the light from inside himself grow even brighter, moving down his arm into this ethereal hand grasping the shadow.

The shadow disintegrated. (*That shadow is gone.*)

Adam looked back to the central entity held in his wings. He felt more determined than ever. (*You are never going to do this to anyone again.*) He thought about all the people it may have hurt. Images of people with this thing filled his mind. The light within became blinding, moving through his wings into the entity. It could not withstand what was happening and began to disintegrate. Pieces of shadow burning off. It grew smaller until it vanished altogether.

Shaking, Adam bent over, putting his hands on his knees. (*What just happened? I'm so tired. I'm alone in this house. I don't want to be alone right now.*)

He was dazed, forgetting to lock the front door on the way out. He walked to the school gymnasium, where he found his parents.

"See you decided to join us," Nick said.

"Yeah. Changed my mind."

"Good."

Adam did as he has done so many times before. He pretended to be like everyone else. Adam was good at it. He joined in with the cheering and clapping. Getting snacks and drinks from the concession stand. Riding home talking about the game. Everything appeared normal. But Adam knew different. For him, everything was not normal. Everything changed. He could protect himself. He could protect his family. He could fight these things. His family did not notice him wiping tears from his eyes. He was happy. (*Happy tears. I'm so backward.*)

CHAPTER 18 – SILVER SWORD

The dark entity attacks continued but they were sporadic. Sometimes weeks would go by. Sometimes the shadowy figures were small and other times, they were the size of adults. Adam learned through these fights that he could attract them using fear. He would allow himself to feel a false sense of fear, and they would come to him. Adam was able to deceive them into thinking his fear was real. He learned he could project this sense of fear to a location. He could move them from place to place. It's as if they are hunting. Wanting to feed on that fear. He would be there waiting. (*I'm not going to let them harm anyone else ever again.*)

He also continued to talk to the sky as a friend. It responded to him if he stayed within the natural order of things. Rain would not fall if he asked for it immediately but would if he gave enough time for clouds to form. The sky would respond like the pre-planned baseball games during P.E. Class. They were all rained out. However, the wind was different. It would respond immediately. Like at a recent funeral. The air was still. The people were hot. He asked the wind to blow, and it started blowing hard enough that it blew the tent over. He did not understand it. He just knew that they were alive. That all of reality is as alive as everyone else. He needed friends, and all of reality was his friend.

His confidence grew. There have got to be others out there like him. Maybe they were hiding as well. If he opened up, even a little, he might be able to find them. Perhaps Becky and Jimbo. They were outsiders like him. Maybe he could bring it up to them. Perhaps he could have human friends.

He decided to slip it in a conversation during recess. It was cold but they were still outside smoking. Shivering. Christmas break was over and they were back at school.

"Do you think there is life other than humans out there?" Adam asked.

"You mean like aliens?" Jimbo asked.

"I don't know. It could be aliens. It could be something we can't see. Another plane of existence. It could be the sky we are looking at now," he said, looking up.

"Maybe aliens but not that other stuff. It's too far out there."

Becky spoke up. "I don't believe in any of it. There's nothing but us slobs." She looked at Jimbo, punched him, then passed him the cigarette. "Is there a reason you brought this up? Did you see aliens or something?"

"No, not aliens, but sometimes things respond when asked like all the P.E. class baseball games that got rained out. First, I'd ask for them to be rained out, then they all got rained out. It makes me wonder."

"That's just Louisiana. It's always raining. Everyday. You had nothing to do with it. You'd have to prove something like that. Can you prove it?"

"I don't know. We could try something."

"Like what?"

"You could ask the sky for snow. If it snows, maybe it's alive."

"It hardly ever snows in Louisiana."

"That will make it even more real. To know you are not faking it, write a date and time down on a piece of paper that you want it to snow. We can seal the paper and give it to Jimbo to read aloud if it snows. If it matches, then maybe there is something to it."

"That's insane."

"Let's do it," Jimbo said

"Ok," Becky said, finding a piece of paper and writing. "Here is a time and a date. How do we seal it?"

Jimbo took the piece of paper. "I'll get the tape and wrap around it. Then, if the paper is torn, we'll know it's been opened."

"Don't forget to ask the sky for it to snow on your date and time when we are not around," Adam said.

"Alright, alright. It's cold. I'm going back inside."

"I'm going inside, too," Jimbo said, following her.

Left alone, Adam looked up at the sky. "Would you please respond to her request to snow? I need someone to believe me. Please respond to her if you can. Please." The school bell rang for recess to be over. He went back inside. Nervous. (*Maybe it won't work, and that will prove I'm crazy after all.*)

# # #

The bell rang for classes to be over. It had started snowing two hours earlier as Becky caught up with Adam. She was pulling Jimbo along with her. "Open the note, Jimbo. You have it, right? I told you to get it from your locker. You got it?"

"Yes. I got it."

"Open it."

He opened the note and read. His eyes got wide, and he looked at Becky.

"That is the exact date and time I wrote down. I wrote that two weeks ago. Look at the tape. It was not opened before now. How did you know?"

"I didn't know. You are the one who asked. You didn't tell me the date or time. How would I know." Adam said.

She thought before responding. "It's too much for me. It's too weird. I don't need this. I got enough shit in my life. I don't need this." She tore up the paper and let the pieces fall to the ground. "Come on, Jimbo. We're getting out of here. Stay away from us, Adam. I don't need this crazy shit in my life."

"I'm sorry, but I follow her," Jimbo said, literally following her to his car.

(*I thought I might find some friends. It backfired. I lost the only two people I could have been friends with here.*) Adam walked to the line of students waiting to get on the bus. (*I'm alone again. At least I'll be warm on the way home.)*

Adam woke late the following day and got in the shower. He was feeling lonely and depressed after what happened with Becky and Jimbo. (*I might never have friends.*)

He stepped out of the shower, dried off, and looked at himself naked in the full-length mirror. Of course, it's just a reflection showing flesh. Nevertheless, it made him feel lonelier than before. (*What's that?*) He was seeing the overlay again. Something inside him that can't be seen with physical eyes, yet his senses were building an image in his mind.

It was difficult to see. Looking in the mirror, Adam raised both arms, pointed his fingers, and traced in the air. Starting on the ground beneath his feet. Then, raising his arms, letting his fingers trace a pattern up the center. The design went up through the groin to the shoulders, then out to the sides, back to the center of his body, then parallel lines up above his head.

When his hands were fully extended above his head, there was a flash in his mind. He looked at himself again in the mirror. There he saw a sword of silver. The hilt of the sword is in his shoulders, moving up through his head. The blade of the sword pointed down from his shoulders between his legs. It began to turn. Blade pointing upward. It moved out of his body and over his head. Glowing. He stood there with his mouth open. He wasn't thinking. He was feeling. It did not feel like a weapon. (*How can it be a sword and not a weapon?*) Seeing it made him feel better. A feeling of home.

He put his palms to his face and began rubbing. (*How much longer do I have before guys in straitjackets show up and drag me off.*) He looked back at the image in the mirror. The sword in his mind was gone. It was just a naked boy in the mirror.

###

"Adam. You want to drive?" Daisy asked.

"Yes." He had his driver's license and took any opportunity offered.

"Everyone in the car. It's only a two-hour drive away. We can stop and get something to eat on the way back." Daisy said. She had it all planned out. Nick had learned of a potential job opportunity back in West Monroe and took the weekend to visit his uncle. Maybe get some leads and talk to people. While he was away, they would spend some time touring a historic home. Daisy loved history and genealogy. A perfect spring day for a trip.

The drive was uneventful. Daisy already knew the history of the home and enjoyed telling all four kids all about it. She also included any relations she discovered. Genealogy is her passion, after all. You could see it in her eyes every time she started sharing.

The house is in a remote area. It has a long drive with big trees. They charge for the tours and use the money to keep everything maintained and manicured. Daisy paid the fee and they joined a small group gathering to tour the house.

Adam liked to be in the back. He was in the back when they went to church. Adam is the last in line to a buffet. He wanted to stay anonymous and out of sight if possible. Adam was the last in the tour group line as well. No one saw him recoil as he walked through the front door.

The pressure began to build as he walked forward. He only made it a couple of steps. His body reacted as if he had hit something physical. A barrier. He backed out of the house, confused. (*Crap. I don't know what that is, but the tour group is leaving me. They'll notice.*) He stepped into the doorway. There is that pressure. A force builds with each step he takes. He pushed through and felt something shatter like glass breaking. He caught up with the group. (*No one noticed. What was that?*)

He felt something else as soon as the barrier shattered. A presence. He built an image in the mind of his surroundings, and there it is. Something out of place. Moving. He stayed with the tour group, continually adding to the house's layout as they walked. Overlaying what his senses were telling him. Watching the entity move. (*I have not been in a fight with one of these things in months. I can't do anything here in front of everyone.*)

"That's the end of the tour. You are free to move about the house. Please don't touch anything and keep your small children with you. The grounds are also available to tour on your own. There are tables available outside if you brought your lunch. Thank you for visiting."

"Let's go outside and see the stables, then we can look at the garden," Daisy said. The remainder of the tour group had already headed out in that direction.

"I'm going to stay inside and take a closer look at some of the rooms," Adam said.

"Ok. We'll be out back."

Adam went to one of the bedrooms on the ground floor. There is no one in the house, and the entity is there in the room. He did what he usually does. Feel the light build inside. Infuse the walls, ceiling, and floor with the light creating a box cutting off escape routes. Reaching out with his ethereal wings to grab and hold the entity.

(*Something's not right. There's no anger. No hate. It's not trying to get away.*) He focused on the entity even more, and the shape became more apparent. (*It's a human child. A young girl in a yellow dress. She sees me looking at her.*) He felt a wave of loneliness come from her. (*She's lost. Lonely in a crowd. Can't find her family. Oh God.*)

Memories of his own loneliness. Being different from everyone else. That there is a family out there somewhere that he can't find. Tears started running down his face. (*I know how she feels. No one should ever feel like that. I don't know what to do.*) His wings drew her to him. She didn't resist. He held out his hands as his wings pulled the entity into his body. This ghostly girl was now inside him. The girl's memories merged with Adams. (*You're not alone. Will never be alone again. I'm here with you.*)

There was a flash in his mind, and he felt the silver sword again. The little girl smiled. No longer alone.

He remembered when he first traced the outline of the sword. The last thing he did was hold his arms up into the air then the sword began glowing. (*I don't know what else to do.*)

He raised his arms in the air. Reaching for something high above him. The sword turned. Blade pointing upwards. It moved up his body above his head. It began glowing then a beam of light shot upward from the blade. Adam recalled a memory that had been locked away. One of the source. Light. Love. Joy. That feeling of a family again coursing through the blade, through the beam of light.

He felt joy from the little girl as she moved upward toward the blade then continued along the light path. She was gone. The sword slowly dimmed as it turned blade pointing down and entered Adam. Back where it began.

Adam felt drained and looked around. (*No one saw that. I'm exhausted. I don't think I can drive back. I need to find the others.*)

"Hey," Adam said, reaching Daisy, who was in deep discussions with the tour guide.

"Hey. Welcome back. I was just talking with Nicole, and she is full of great information. She even said the house is haunted by a little girl. Isn't that fascinating?"

"That's pretty neat," Adam said. (*Was that a ghost? The soul of a child. Where did it go? What happened?*)

Daisy drove while Adam slept in the backseat with Bonnie and Sissy. Luke was happy to be riding upfront. Adam made it to his bedroom then went to sleep even though it was still daylight.

He woke the next day wondering if he had really interacted with a ghost. She felt lost and then found her family. What he saw was confirmed by the tour guide. (*Is all this real? She was real. Are the other things real? What am I?*) He mentally quoted a phrase that always made him feel better.

(*Take another step and keep moving forward.*)

CHAPTER 19 – LOST SOULS

They often went to visit Adam's grandmother at the old homestead. The pink house they called it, even though it was salmon-colored. His grandfather got it from another relative in 1911. It was initially a two-room dogtrot house when Daisy was born there. She was the youngest of six kids. Since then, the back porch had been enclosed with an indoor bathroom. A kitchen and dining area were also added. The front porch faced east. It was the perfect place to have conversations with coffee. If you got lucky, you might see a fishing boat motor down the river that passed in front of the house.

Daisy dropped Nick off at his sister's house in Jena before turning onto the dirt road leading to her mother's house. It dead-ended into a national wildlife refuge. There are no other roads, so it's the only entrance and exit to the few places remaining. There isn't a town nearby, only the river. Unfortunately, the river is not always low like it is now. The house had flooded several times though it sits three feet off the ground. The worst was the great Mississippi flood of 1927. That year the water reached the roof of the house.

"Visit with your mamaw before running off," Daisy said, opening the front gate leading to the porch. They were greeted by Ruth coming onto the porch. "Hi, mamaw," the kids said, talking over one another. Bonnie and Sissy ran to the wood swing at one end while the boys sat on the concrete steps.

"Hi, Mom. It's been so long. You're looking great."

"Hi, Daisy. It's so nice to see you. Your kids have grown so much. Would you like some coffee?"

"I would love some coffee."

That was all the visiting they needed. The kids looked around to see who would be the first to jump off the porch and start exploring. It was Luke, followed by Adam. Bonnie and Daisy were last because they were on the swing away from the steps.

"Watch out of snakes," Daisy yelled as they headed into the kitchen.

There were always snakes. Daisy had taught them never to lift or flip something over without using a tool to move it first. Also, make lots of noise while walking through the brush to scare the snakes away. She had gone over it so many times that it was now a habit for the kids. She told stories about how some of her relatives could smell snakes but none of the kids knew how to do that.

There are so many areas to explore and all dangerous in their own way, but Daisy would not keep them sheltered. She let the kids run free and figure out things on their own. The old red barn is supposed to be off-limits because it is on the verge of collapsing. They used to jump out of the hayloft but no longer. There is the river. They were always on the watch for alligators because where there is water, there is an alligator. They could walk to the end of the dead-end road, but it would take the entire visit. There was the lane flanked by pecan trees leading to the crawfish ponds. More snakes and alligators. There are also woods with lots of animal trails to follow. Here, nature is still wild and when it gets dark you can't see the hand in front of your face.

Luke found a fishing pole and headed toward the river while the girls checked out the old tractor. Adam decided to walk down the road a bit. Not to the end. Maybe to that old home that had burned long ago with only part of the chimney left standing.

This part of the road has a thick brush. You can't see the river running next to it. It remained this way until he reached a clearing on the right. In this open area are large pecan trees and older crepe myrtles that would be around a house if it was still here. Now it's just part of a foundation and chimney. (*Someone with a metal detector could probably find a lot of stuff here.*) Adam began exploring the area, finding a few square nails he put in his pocket. It mainly was broken pieces of brick.

(There is that feeling again. Like something out of place.) He began the familiar process of building an image in his mind. The old foundation, the chimney, bricks, pecan trees, even the vines growing up the trees. *(There it is. Something out of place just past the foundation. Behind the house.)* He focused on the area sensing a presence. Building an image of the presence in his mind letting it overlay what his eyes were seeing. *(It's dark, shadowy. A dark entity.)* It moved and vanished.

(It just disappeared. It started moving and vanished.) He focused even more. Nothing. With the overlay still in his mind, he started thinking about what the house would have looked like before it collapsed. His imagination took over, and the overlay in his mind changed. There were walls, doors, a chimney, a roof, and people. *(There it is again. That dark entity shadow is an adult man standing outside. He's covered in this shadow. I can barely see him. He is in pain looking at the house. He vanished before when I saw everything as it currently is, but he reappeared when seeing the house from long ago.)* The shadowy man looked at Adam then vanished again. *(Did he see me? He was here in the present. Then he was in the past when the house was standing. Did he move through time?)* Adam stopped focusing so hard and let the overlay in his mind drift through time. It went from the past to the present. *(There he is again. He's moving through time like climbing a ladder. The bottom of the ladder is where he is standing behind the still intact house, and the top of the ladder is the present. He can move up and down the ladder through time. I thought he was one of those dark entities, but he's a man. Is he like that little girl in the yellow dress? What that tour guide called a ghost? He's different from her, and I don't know how to help him. The one thing I do know is how to get rid of that shadowy stuff.)*

Adam felt that spark of light inside himself expand into a bubble. Then he changed the shape to create walls, a floor, and a ceiling. This time it would have to be there in the past and in the present. It would have to be there through all those points in time.

The being tried shifting through time but it did not move to the side. Instead, it stayed in one place. Adam reached out with his invisible wings. They were extensions of himself, just like arms and legs, and he used them. Grabbing and holding the entity, Adam let light stream through his wings into the entity. A feeling of despair and anger burst from the entity. Shadow engulfed it as it tore free from Adam's grip. It was striking back.

It shifted through time, tearing at the wings in anger. Hopelessness pulled it away when Adam tried to grab it. Adam reached out with all his being and finally held it in place. (*Sending love and light into it from a distance isn't working. Maybe it would work if I did what I did with that little girl.*)

Adam pulled it. The entity fought back. It wanted to stay where it was. "I'm trying to help you. Stop fighting," Adam said quietly.

(No)

(*It heard me.*)

"You're stuck in this place and can't get out. I'm going to help you."

The moment Adam pulled the entity inside himself, images flashed in his mind. Images of a house burning. Wife. Children. Screaming. Helplessness. Despair. Loss. Can't leave them. A gun. A gunshot. Stuck at that moment. Adam felt it all.

Adam did not know what else to do. He thought of what he did with the lonely little girl. (*You are not alone. You will never be alone. It's going to be ok.*) Adam thought this repeatedly while pouring feelings of light, love, and understanding toward it. Minutes passed, and the shadows began to melt away. The darkness around the man faded until there was only the man left.

Feelings of love for the family came from the man. There was a silver flash of light inside, and the sword appeared. It flipped with the blade pointing upward and moved above Adam's head. Glowing. A beam of light shot out to what felt like the source of all things. Home. The man felt joy and followed the beam upward, then vanished. The blade flipped, entered Adam, and disappeared as well.

Adam sat on a log thinking. (*The little girl was alone. This man was stuck and covered in darkness, despair. They could not find their way out of that moment. Lost. Is that what they are? Lost souls.*) He looked at the trees, then the sky, and asked, "Is this why I'm like this? Is this what I'm supposed to do?" He didn't expect an answer and didn't get one. After a few minutes, he walked back down the road to the pink house, grabbed a soda, and joined the others on the porch.

"Did you have fun walking down the road?" Daisy asked.

"I guess. I'm seeing new things and learning."

"That's good," she said, rejoining her conversation with Ruth regarding family history.

(*I'm telling the truth, and they have no idea what I'm talking about. It's always going to be like this.*)

# # #

Nick pulled the car into the driveway and turned off the lights. They were not needed. The streetlight near the church lit up the front yard. As everyone headed in the house, Adam said, "I forgot I took the square nails out of my pocket and left them in the car."

"We'll leave the front door unlocked," Nick said

Adam did not leave the nails in the car. He only said that to stay outside. Adam felt something. An entity like he saw earlier that day. A man surrounded by shadows walking down the road. Another lost soul. It seemed to be searching for something.

(*Not again. Everything was quiet for a long time and now two in one day. What are they doing? Searching me out?*)

Adam walked to the road and quietly said, "Hello."

The entity stopped and looked at him. It did not run. There was no emotion coming from it. It just stood there.

(*This is going to be easy.*)

Adam built the overlay containing the box of light around the entity. He reached out before sending waves of light to it. Nothing. (*I didn't think it would work. It didn't work earlier today on the one like it. So I'll pull it inside myself like before. That works better.*)

Adam quickly pulled the entity into himself. Images of this being torturing others overwhelmed his mind. Enjoying the pain and suffering it caused. It wasn't lost. This man covered in darkness liked being this way. He wasn't strolling down the road. He was hunting. People. (*You're not alone. You will never be alone*) Adam thought, sending waves of love and hope at it.

(I'm not alone.) Screams of animals and humans filled Adam's mind. (You're with me.)

Adam focused every positive thought he had on it. Nothing. He tried to feel the light around him. It was gone. He tried starting over with a small light point inside, letting it grow into a bubble. He couldn't do it. This thing was inside him, and he could not get it out. (*How am I going to get it out?*)

(You're not alone. You will never be alone again.) It was using Adam's own words against him. It knows everything.

Adam felt a sense of power. A power he could use to control people. He could make them do what he wanted. Trick them. Make them like doing unpleasant things. It felt good.

(*Stop.*)

(No)

"Adam, come inside," Nick yelled from the front door.

"I'm coming."

That night Adam dreamed of torture and ripping people apart. Then, feeling the warmth of blood.

Adam acted like everything was normal the following day, but it wasn't. This thing was inside him. Enjoying the feeling of skin. Enjoying leaving tacks on the bus seat as he walked down the aisle to the back. He could have fun on the bus. He could have even more fun at school.

"I want you all to write a minimum 500-page essay on the topic of your choice," Mrs. Myrtle said in English class. It's due two days from now. You will also be required to read it out loud in class. This will help your public speaking skills."

(*I already know my topic*) Adam thought.

The next couple of days, Adam spent time organizing his thoughts and just a little bit of time in the library. The subject matter was straightforward. It just needed to be refined. He knew how to type so that part was easy.

It was Adam's turn to read his essay. He stood up in front of the class and began.

"The title of my essay is Methods of Torture."

"What?" Mrs. Myrtle asked.

"Methods of Torture is the title of my essay. I shortened it to 1,000 words."

There was nothing she could do. She had allowed them to pick the topic, and she made the requirement to read it aloud in the class. The class was stunned as Adam read.

After he finished, Mrs. Myrtle spoke up. "From now on, I will have a list of topics to choose from and methods of torture will not be included."

Adam grinned. He had planted dark seeds and opened their minds to possibilities.

Adam stepped off the bus in front of his house. (*I have got to do something. This has got to stop.*)

(You liked it. There is nothing you can do.)

"Mom. I'm going to get some sun. I'll be lying in the field next to the house."

"Ok."

Adam put on a pair of shorts, grabbed a towel and walked to the field center. He laid down the towel, took everything off except the shorts and proceeded to get a tan. Adam couldn't get this thing out on his own. He needed help so he was going to ask for it.

"Alright, sun. I could use your help. I can't build up enough light within myself. Can you help me build more?" He didn't get a reply. He just lied down, feeling the warmth of the sun. He started mentally building the little ball of light within but it was stained somehow. (*I need to clear that stain and make it true light again.*) He felt the warmth of the sunlight go to the center of his being. He felt the truth of the sunlight burning away the stain on his own light.

(No. You're mine.)

(*It's afraid. I'm doing something right.*)

Adam continued to feel the sunlight burning inside. He was becoming one with the sun. He felt as if he was in the center of the sun. It was beautiful and surrounded him. He felt the dark entity forced out.

Adam sat up. The entity was there in front of him. It was unharmed and it could not get back inside. His merging with the sun was too much for it. It quickly fled and Adam lost sight of it.

"I think I got lucky," he said. (*I somehow managed to get it out. I have limits. There are things out there that I can't handle. I've got to be more careful. God. I'm always saying that. Then I'm not careful.*)

He continued lying in the sun. He had become one with the sun. Adam smiled.

CHAPTER 20 – MOVING AGAIN

Nick said as he continued moving boxes "It's all working out. I'll be making more money, and we still have our old house to move into now that the renters have gone. A little cleaning, and it will be like we never left West Monroe. It will also be much easier on you, Adam, taking those summer classes at college. It's only a 20-minute drive from the house. You getting that grant was really lucky."

"Yeah, really lucky. I'm looking forward to it," Adam said.

(*Lucky. I needed to get out of this town. Then somehow I got a grant for the college in our old town. Then dad got a new job and we can move back to our old house. It's like the two years in Olla were nothing but I learned so much about myself in those two years. I think Olla is going to be with me forever.*)

Adam continued packing boxes and then carrying them outside to be loaded into their rented moving truck. He thought about everything that had happened in Olla.

(*I learned that I'm bi-sexual and everyone sees that as wrong, like the preacher telling me that I'm the thing wrong with the world. Finally, I grasped that hearing people's thoughts is not normal. That I'm the different one, and I can't tell anyone about it.*

Then something happened when I was lying in bed, depressed, and let myself go out of my body. I still don't know what that was, but it happened. I'm not the same person I was before that event. I have my memories and look the same, except for my eyes. First, they were brown, and now they are green with a bit of brown in the middle. How could something make your eyes change color?

The entire world changed when that happened. No. I was the one that changed and saw the world differently. Everything became alive to me, and it sometimes responds when I talk to it. It can't be real, but every P.E. baseball game was rained out since we moved here. The lightning. The electricity. Transformers blowing. Just a coincidence.

Then seeing this other reality. This different plane of existence overlaying the one we all see with our eyes. These dark entities. How to fight them. How to protect me. The lost souls some call ghosts. That silver sword showed them the way home.

Oh, and of course, no one else experiences anything like this. If I told people, they would take me away in a straitjacket and lock me up. I feel so fucking crazy. It feels like I'm lost and alone in the dark. I can't talk to anybody. They don't understand any of it. How am I supposed to do this? Do I pretend to be like everyone else for the rest of my life? Alone in a crowd.

That's right. My favorite phrase I use when I feel overwhelmed and don't know what to do. Take another step and keep moving forward.

I'm so glad that works. Taking a physical step forward. Stop having an entire conversation in your mind. Stop it.)

Adam walked back inside to continue packing.

(*I wonder what college will be like. Dad wants me to stay at least one year on campus in a dorm for the experience. Then, hopefully, I can get a scholarship or a student loan. After that, I'll have to get a job. He wants me to go into a profession that makes lots and lots of money. He loves money, but I see things differently. Whatever I need happens like the college grant. I don't know why but it happens.*

Stop it. You're having conversations in your head again. That proves I'm crazy right. Yes. It does. Great. I'm answering myself now.)

PART THREE – CRUSHED: COLLEGE

CHAPTER 21 – MOVING IN

Adam had the last load of stuff to bring into the dorm room on the fifth floor. Carrying this much weight, he had to use the elevator. It was iffy. He'd instead use the stairs when possible. The dorm was located on one side of the bayou with classes on the other. The bridge had wide sidewalks on each side. It would be nice looking at the water every day. He dropped the load onto the bed on the left side. He got the first choice of sides since his roommate was not here yet.

(*I'll leave a note for whoever saying I'll be back after work. I've got just enough time to get across town.*) He was working at a family-owned antique business. He and his co-worker Tim stayed in the back refinishing what they found at auctions. They removed old varnish, sanded then reapplied a dark oak varnish. It was the favorite color except when dealing with cherry wood. It deserved special attention.

Adam pulled into the antique owner's driveway and stepped out of his two-door Toyota Corolla. It ran. That's all that mattered.

"Hey, Tim. What are we doing today?" Adam asked, stepping into the little tin building with no windows or air conditioning.

"Tables."

"What parts are you doing?"

"Why do you even ask? You know they prefer the way you do the tops. You get them perfect and I always have problems. I'm doing the base as usual because you are too slow."

"Do you think you could work on the base while sitting on the steps again? It takes a lot of room to handle the tabletop in this little 10'x10' space."

"Sure. At least we are not stripping today. I had enough of inhaling those vapors yesterday. I don't like having to leave work early because we can't stop laughing or stand up."

"Yeah."

"Are you going to the Airport Lounge tonight and play pool?" Tim asked.

"No. I just got my stuff thrown in the dorm room. I need to straighten it out and meet the roommate."

"Alright, but there's supposed to be a lot of planes landing." The lounge was at the airport on the second floor. It had windows along the runway wall. A great place to watch air traffic, which was rare.

"You going to keep working here now that school's started?" Tim asked.

"I wouldn't if that guidance counselor at high school would have told me I had a scholarship. Instead, she told me not to bother. My grades were not good enough. When I arrived on campus, they told me they had given it to someone else. I need this job to pay off my student loan, insurance, gas, and my tab at the Airport Lounge."

"Same here," Tim said as they got to work. "You ready to play name that song?"

"Sure."

It was a competition. Adam and Tim tried to beat each other by naming the song and the group first. A way to pass the time. It took an average of three notes before one of them got it. Five notes at the most. However, there were times that Adam guessed it before the song started. Tim said he was cheating somehow when that happened.

# # #

Adam was unpacking his room when Buck walked in from the bathroom connecting to the next room.

"Hey, I'm Buck Fortest. Your roommate. Come through the bathroom and meet the guys next door. They make the best ramen noodles. They are cooking it in an electric coffee pot, then add other stuff like onions and carrots." That was Buck. Never met a stranger.

The noodles were just noodles. Adam could not see why Buck was raving about them. Perhaps it was because he already had a few beers in him, even though it was forbidden to have alcohol in the dorms. Buck thought it was just a suggestion.

"Hey. We are going to the library. Want to go?"

"To the library? School hasn't even started."

"Not that library. The Library."

"I'm confused."

"Follow me, and you'll get it."

They walked past the parking lot and away from the building where classes are held. They took a right before they got to the stadium. Then crossed another bridge over the bayou, took a left, and followed the bayou along the main road. The sign on the first building read THE LIBRARY. It was a bar.

Buck laughed. "If anybody asks, you can say you are going to the library, and they think the one with books."

Buck lead him to a table against the large window overlooking the bayou. There were a dozen people there, and Buck remembered half of their names. Not too bad, considering he had just met them that day. He immediately started up a game of Quarters. It's where you roll a quarter off your nose and bounce it off the table into a glass of beer. If you make it, you pick someone to drink. If you miss, then you drink.

(I know how to play this game. Getting drunk numbs all my odd senses. I can be like everybody else. This is going to be fun.)

They all helped each other as they stumbled late at night back to the dorms. There were several close calls with the water, but everyone made it back safely.

(Now that's how you meet a roommate. And I never heard anyone's thoughts. That's nice) Adam thought, not respecting the future hangover.

CHAPTER 22 – BUCK

Drinking. Hangover. Classes.

That was the theme of the first semester. Adam's classes were geared toward pharmacy, just as his parents wanted. The group of people Adam met that first day at The Library became drinking buddies. Once he discovered alcohol numbed his odd senses, drinking became the rule and not the exception. His co-worker at the antique business joined the drinking group even though he went to the rival school. Adam's evenings of alcohol were split between The Library and the Airport Lounge. Most of his weekly paycheck was spent at the Airport Lounge playing pool on weekends. Buck, of course, was happy to join in everything.

"Hello," Buck said, answering the phone. They had been drinking again and just walked into the dorm room. "Bullshit. You want to bet. I know I could. You don't know what you're talking about. I dare you. You'd never do it. Prove it. I'll even give you $20." Buck hung up the phone.

"Who was that?"

"Two girls said they would come to the dorm room and have sex for $20. Someone is playing games. They will never show."

Within five minutes, there was a knock on the door. Adam and Buck looked at each other. Buck answered the door.

"I told you we'd show up," the young lady said.

"I thought you were joking. I did not believe you'd show. Come on in. I'm Buck, and this is Adam. What are your names?"

"You don't need to know our names. We're here because you didn't believe us and said you'd give us $20 bucks. I know you," the first lady said to Adam.

"Really? Where from?"

"High school. You were only there one year, but I remember someone pointing you out. For some reason, it stuck. I'll take him," she said, moving to Adam while removing her clothes along the way.

"Then your mine," the more petite girl with long hair said to Buck as she moved to him, undressing.

Buck gave Adam a sideways grin. They began undressing.

"No," said the long-haired girl to Buck. "We're going to do it," she said, removing Buck's shirt. The girls watched each other, making sure they were doing the same thing simultaneously.

"You want the lights off?" Adam asked, pulling back the bedsheets.

"No. How will we see what we are doing? No on that," she said, pointing to the bedsheets. She threw all the sheets off the bed, leaving only the plastic-covered dorm mattress. The long-haired girl followed her lead.

The night progressed with Buck and Adam feeling like amateurs. Four bodies merge into one at times. One lady yelled to the other, "Look at me. I'm a cowgirl." The other lady is cheering her on. It was the wildest night both young men had experienced.

The evening finished with the first lady saying, "We're leaving. Give us our $20."

"I don't have $20," Buck said.

"What? You lied?" The ladies were furious.

"What about you?" she said, pointing at Adam.

"I don't have it. I didn't even know who was on the phone."

"We'll give you this one for free only because I know you from high school. Never happening again, got it?"

"Yeah," Buck said, closing the door.

"Holy shit. That was wild," Buck said. Then looking a bit concerned. "I hope she doesn't get pregnant." They were drunk, and it happened so fast they forgot about condoms. They both fell asleep, bed coverings still on the floor.

Adam woke the following day to answer the phone. Buck was not in his bed.

"Hello."

"Get down to room 156." It was Buck.

"What? Why?"

"Just get down here now. Room 156."

"Alright," Adam said. He dressed while trying to manage another hangover. This time he was taking the elevator.

Adam asked, "Why did I come down here?" He looked in, and several other guys were filling the small room. Some he recognized from drinking at The Library. Some grinning. Some laughing. Buck pulled him in.

"Your friend Tim set us up. They got to our room so quickly because they were in this room when they called. That's why they knew who to call. It was all planned." The room roared with laughter and jabs. "I'm the only one worried about pregnancy. Yours was already pregnant." More howls of laughter.

One of the guys said, "That poor baby. Imagine what it's seeing, hitting it over and over. Ow. Ow. Ow." More laughter. Jabs. Jokes. Then it was time for Adam to get to class.

(*I don't like the hangover part.*)

# # #

A few weeks passed since that night with the girls. There was no need for modesty after that. Everything was out in the open except for what Adam considered his dark path. The strange happenings in his life. They continued when he was not drinking, and he drank a lot. He liked having friends, even if they were just drinking buddies. Still, this feeling of being alone in a crowd remained.

Adam had some time between classes and was sitting under a large oak tree on the edge of the campus. He liked being away from people, away from their emotions and thoughts. There was something about this tree. It was old, solid, and away from the other trees. He felt a connection. He would sit there and talk to it about the odd things that happened. It was just as much a friend to him as his drinking buddies.

"Hello."

Adam turned around to find a skinny young man with long hair. Why was he out here? There was no reason for anyone to come way out here.

"Hi."

"I'm Frances."

"I'm Adam."

"What are you doing out here sitting under a tree."

(*I'm going to risk it.*) "Just needed to talk some things out, and it seems to listen as good as anyone else."

"Do you really think it's listening?"

"I don't know. Maybe. This tree seems to be more alive than others. I think some things are alive like that. Things other people ignore."

Frances smiled. "You know, I just read about this cork tree in Portugal. They can live to be hundreds of years old. They say that tree is magical or something. People go there for all kinds of things, saying the cork from it is special. You believe that?"

"Sure. Why not." Adam was revealing more about himself. His girlfriend from junior high school, Tara, was the only one he had ever let into his crazy little world. Adam began to feel a little uncomfortable. But, the conversation was going so well he did not want to screw things up. (*Take it slow.*) "I've got to get to class. I come here a lot. Maybe I'll see you here again."

"Sure. I'll look for you. I think I'll try what you did. Sit here and talk to a tree."

"See you later."

"Bye."

Adam headed back to the dorm. (*That went well. I'll make a point to visit that tree more often.*)

"Hey, Buck. What are you up to?" Adam was just entering the dorm as Buck was leaving. Buck grinned, showing he was up to something.

"I just got paid $100 and I'm going to buy some weed."

"Weed?"

"Yeah. I met these other people who introduced me to an older lady who lives off-campus. She smokes weed and sells it. I've been to her place a few times, and I'm going to visit her now. Want to go?"

"Sure. I've got nothing else to do."

As they drove, Adam said, "You don't have a job. How did you get paid $100?"

"There was this older man who wanted three college guys to do some modeling." He held up his hands and said the word modeling, signaling quotation marks. "He paid us each $100."

Adam was confused. "Modeling?"

"Yeah. Nude modeling. All three of us at the same time."

"Whoa. Did anything happen?"

"Yeah. That whole thing was weird, but you know I'm not turning down a quick $100. Forget about it. We're almost at Billie's. Did I tell you she's a witch?"

"A witch? Like a real witch?"

"Yeah. Billie does Tarot cards and stuff. It's cool. Nothing crazy. Just smoking weed, really."

Buck was right. It was an older lady with white hair. Thin and a little suspicious of Adam at first. She quickly realized everything was ok and let them in the door.

It was a small one-room apartment. It didn't look witchy at all. Some fabrics with unusual patterns hanging on the wall but nothing outlandish. It did not take long for Buck to purchase his marijuana. She offered some for them to smoke.

"You smoked before?" Billie asked Adam.

"Yes. Once in high school."

"Nothing's changed." She lit a joint and passed it to Buck, who gave it to Adam. The joint made the usual rounds.

"I know. I can give you a tarot card reading while you're here. You want me to?"

"Yeah. That'd be awesome. Maybe I'll be rich one day. I'll be first. Adam, you next."

Billie pulled out a deck of tarot cards and began turning them over in a pattern. "Buck, your situation has to do with a woman from your recent past. There are a couple of possible ways this goes, but it looks like your hopes are realized. You seem to get the outcome you want."

Buck got excited. "That's all true. It's what's happening. I don't want her to be pregnant, and I get it. Nice. Adam. You next."

"I don't think so. I'm not like everybody else."

"Go on, do it. I did it. Now it's your turn."

"Alright, but I can tell you what you are going to get. The first time you will get a result that is as horrible as it can get. Then if you do it a second time, it will reveal the most positive cards you could possibly get."

"You never know what the cards will do," Billie said.

"I'm telling you what they are going to do. It's the way my life works." (*I'm telling her. She doesn't believe me. You would think a witch might sense something.*)

"Deal the cards," Buck said.

Billie began turning over cards. A surprised look on her face. Her look intensified as she turned each card. She did not even try to explain. She just said, "They are all negative. This is the worst possible layout of the cards I've ever seen. This one card never shows up. How did you know that was going to happen?"

"It's my life."

"Do it again," Buck said.

Billie began turning over cards as she had done before. This time her look resembled astonishment. Then fear as she looked at Adam. Once again, she did not even try to explain.

"These are all positive. The most positive way these cards could have been placed. This card is the most positive in the deck. I can't deal with this. I need to get out of this room right now. Let's go outside and smoke." She forced a laugh and ushered them out the door.

Lighting up, she said, "That's much better. Outside smoking. The night air with stars and a few clouds above. That's magic," she said.

Adam raised his eyebrows as he looked at her. She caught the look and was about to ask him a question. Then Adam looked up at the sky and began staring. This caused both Buck and Billie to do the same.

A huge blue meteor shot through the sky as they looked up. It was low. The clouds flashed as they did with lightning when the meteor passed through them.

Billie freaked out. "That's it. That's it. I can't do this. It's too much. I can't handle it. Leave. Don't come by anymore." She ran to the front door slamming it behind her.

"What was that all about? The meteor was so cool. Maybe Billie just had too much to smoke. She's probably been smoking all day. I'll come back another time and check on her. Let's go."

"Smoking all day. Yeah, that's probably it." (*It keeps happening. I even scared a witch. I can't talk to anybody.*) Adam left feeling more alone than ever. Perhaps it was the smoking or the meteor's impact on the group. Still, he had forgotten all about meeting Frances earlier the same day.

A Starseed Lost in the Dark

CHAPTER 23 – HOUSE PARTY

Months blurred between the Airport Lounge and The Library. Then, a few semesters in, a third bar opened called The Post. It was added to the rotation. It had the cheapest pitchers of beer and soon became the favorite. There were about a dozen in the gang including Tim, Adam's co-worker. The most popular was Tyrone. It wasn't a real party without him. He was always laughing and fun to be around. Adam was the tag-along, still figuring out how to blend in with others. Buck was the one who constantly met new friends and got the group invited to parties.

Buck had gotten an invite to an open party at a fraternity house. Everyone was invited because it was rush week. Every fraternity on campus had an open party. The larger fraternities could be rude, but the smaller ones turned out to be great at welcoming newcomers. There was Jungle Juice on the kitchen table and kegs of beer in the backyard like all the others.

"You were right, Buck. They are friendly and wanted everybody to come to their party," Adam said.

"I feel right at home here," Tyrone said.

"Free alcohol. You know we are going to show up. There is even a D.J. and dancing." Buck said. "Grab some beers. Let's start by playing quarters."

"We are playing Gilligan over here if you want to join us," someone shouted from the living room. An episode of the TV show

Gilligan's Island was playing. Every time a character on the show said Gilligan, everyone had to take a drink.

"Thanks, but I'm sticking with quarters. There's plenty of room on this kitchen table," Buck said as a few others joined in.

(*I've got to be careful right now. Drinking loosens me up enough that I might talk about some of the things that happen to me. If I can drink fast enough and get drunk, it all stops.*) Adam and the rest continued to play quarters with Buck clearly winning. Tonight, Buck focused on his new friend in the fraternity sending all beers to him.

"Hey. I like that song **Girls On Film**. I'm going to go dance," Adam said, moving toward the dance floor.

"He's not playing that song," Buck yelled across the room. Just then, the D.J. flipped to a new song. It was the song Adam expected. He didn't notice the guy drinking a beer at the kitchen sink turn and look at him. Adam entered the dance floor and started dancing. He thought (*I'm dancing by myself. Just like that girl Dean back in high school. At least there is music this time.*)

"I got a joke," someone yelled to the dancers. "When is a door not a door?"

(When it's ajar.)

Adam broke out in laugher. The other dancers looked at him.

"What?" He asked.

"You laughed and I had not gotten to the punch line yet."

"Oops. Sorry." Adam headed off the dance floor to get another drink. (*Crap. I heard the punch line in my head. I need more to drink.*) he thought as he passed the same guy that had noticed something odd about him earlier. He found Adam out back pouring a beer from one of the kegs.

"Hi. I'm Erik. This is my wife, Tina. We are about to head out and wanted a beer for the road."

"I'm Adam. Want me to pour?"

"Sure. Thanks."

"You go to school here?"

"Yes. Both of us. Tina is going into nursing. I'm thinking of joining the military. We don't go to these kinds of parties much and prefer drinking at home. Maybe have a few friends over. Play a game or something. Nothing big."

"I tend to hang out with a group. About a dozen of us going to bars. We do it way too much. I've got to slow down. It's taking all my extra money."

"Yeah. Money is always an issue. That's why we stopped by here on the way to meet her cousin. Free drinks. I saw you go out to dance earlier. How did you know what song the D.J. was going to play next?"

(*Think of something.*) "He must have a playlist, and I saw it. It's popular now anyways, so figured they would play it sometime."

"Yeah. Sure. Anyway. We got to go. Maybe we will see you at another party when we are looking for free drinks." Erik said, laughing.

"Alright. See ya later." As they walked to the front door, images began flashing in Adam's mind. They are driving. An intersection. The light changes green for them. They go. Wreck.

Adam ran toward the front door. "Wait."

"What?"

"This is going to sound crazy but be careful at an intersection."

"Uh. What are you talking about? Why?"

"Try to believe me. When you come to an intersection with a traffic light. Don't go when the light turns green for you. Wait. Someone is going to run the light. If you go, you will be in a wreck and get hurt."

"Riiiiight. You've drunk a lot. Someone should drive you home."

"No. I'm serious. Anyway. What could it hurt? It's just a few seconds. Nothing. Just a few seconds. Then what if I'm right. If I'm wrong, then your only out a few seconds. Not money or anything."

Tina spoke up for the first time. "He believes what he is saying. I think we should listen to him. It couldn't hurt." They looked at each other, then back at Adam.

"Erik. Let's leave our drinks here also. Then, if something does happen, we don't need them in the car."

"You're right. It's only a few extra seconds. Why not. You're interesting. Hope we meet up again."

"Interesting. I've never heard anyone put it that way before. Be careful."

"We will."

(I told them what was going to happen. I had to. They were going to be hurt. It doesn't matter if they think I'm crazy. I'll never see them again anyway. I hope I did not make things worse.)

"Adam. Get over here. They say it's the best episode of Gilligan for drinking."

They were right. The name was said so many times during that episode, no one could keep up. By the end of it, Adam was passed out along a wall.

"What was that?" someone asked.

Tyrone replied, "It's just Adam. He fell off the floor again. He will be passed out, and then you hear a thud. It's like he has fallen off something onto the floor, but he's been on the floor the whole time. It's normal for him. Come on. Let's grab him and get him back to the dorm."

Adam woke in Tyrone's dorm room the following morning.

(Another hangover. I hate this part.)

CHAPTER 24 – *DÉJÀ VU*

Tim said "I know you are cheating somehow. You've probably called into the radio station to get a list of the songs they are playing today."

Adam said, "I'm not cheating, I swear. We are done for the day anyway. Just got to get the gas to wash our hands. I might buy this piece. I really like the tiger oak wood. What do you think?"

"If you want it, then get it. You know it will sell quickly in the store. They will give you a reasonable price. If you are lucky, maybe just what they paid for it. Couldn't hurt."

"I'm going to do that. But, right now, I just want to stop for the day."

"You want to go to the Airport Lounge?"

(*Whoa. Déjà vu. That conversation happened before. I think I read those are a brain misfire or something.*)

"No thanks. I need to slow down on the drinking. It's costing too much money. I'm out of here. See you later," Adam said.

"See you later."

Adam got in his car and drove back to his dorm room. He was about to turn onto the on-ramp of the interstate. It was the fastest way back to the dorm. (*That's weird. I'm picturing myself driving along the interstate, and there is a wreck blocking traffic. I'm stuck in traffic. I think I'll take a long way around.*) Adam drove straight when the light turned green, taking a long way. A few seconds later, a traffic alert came on the radio.

"There has been a wreck on I-20 westbound at the Hall Street exit.
The westbound lanes on the bridge have been shut down.
Avoid that area if possible."

"Got lucky," Adam said. (*Lucky? Now that I think about it, that sort of thing happens all the time. Even back in high school, looking at my planner. Thinking about events on future days then seeing them happen in my mind. This kind of stuff has been happening since high school. I thought it was normal. This is how everyone sees things when looking at a planner or calendar. And then there are the songs on the radio. Knowing what song is next, like Tim said. Cheating. But I'm not cheating.*)

Talking to himself, Adam said, "That's all I need. Another addition to my crazy little world. If this is all real, then the next song on the radio will be **Free Bird**." The advertisement on the radio ended, and the announcer said:

"Now, back to the music.
Free Bird."

"Shit. No. I'm normal like everybody else." (*I'm in the car talking to myself. That's not normal. I'm calling Tim when I get to the dorm. Maybe he will still want to go to the Airport Lounge. I want to be like everybody else. I like having friends. I need a drink.*)

(*I bet Tim is already here*) "Hi Pat," Adam said, waving at the bartender as he entered the lounge. Adam and Tim had become regulars. To the point that they exchanged Christmas gifts with the staff. Here Adam could drink, play pool and just relax.

"I still think you are cheating," Tim said.

"I'm not cheating."

"Then how are you doing it?"

Adam was at this dangerous intersection. It was the place where you've loosened up just enough to talk about anything.

"It's like when you make a decision. You're going into engineering, so picture it this way. Draw out a flow diagram. There is a decision point. Whatever decision you make takes you down that path and not the others. When you are thinking about what song is about to play on the radio, you picture this diagram in your mind with possible songs branching off that decision point. Then you just see which one is in bold or is lit up. Which one stands out. That is the song you pick."

"What? You've just fried my brain. I think we need more to drink," Tim said, waving at Pat to pour another pitcher of beer.

"Definitely. More to drink." (*I said that out loud. That was close. I could have lost him as a friend. I've got to stop drinking so much. I'll start tomorrow.*) An image flashed in Adam's mind as he thought about tomorrow's schedule. There was an explosion on the bridge as he walked to classes from the dorm. He was in the center of it. (*That's ridiculous. An explosion. I need more to drink.*)

# # #

(*I hate hangovers. Wish I could stay in bed and not go to class, but I've got to go. Tyrone will be waiting for me downstairs. Wait a minute. Was that a dream? These memories. Maybe that déjà vu thing again. I'm going to write it down.*) Adam grabbed a piece of paper and began writing. He folded the paper and put it in his back pocket. He grabbed his books and headed downstairs. Taking the elevator as he usually does with a hangover.

"Hangover again?" Tyrone asked.

"Yeah. I've got to stop drinking so much," Adam said.

"Come on. We've got to get to class."

"You seem eager to get to class this morning. I know you hate being in the Pharmacy major just as much as I do. Why so happy?"

"I've been thinking about changing my major. So far, Toxicology seems pretty good."

"Toxicology. What's that?" Adam asked.

"It's along the lines of pharmacy but deals more with poisons. I hated the idea of sitting behind a desk all the time, but with toxicology, there are other options. For example, you could work in a research lab, poison call center, or a big companies environmental department."

"I'm going to have to look into that. I hate pharmacy too. I also hate physics. The lab was great, but the lecture. Had to take it several times. You know that saying that everything that goes up must come down. We shoot things in space, and some just keep going like the Voyager spacecraft. It never came back down."

(*It's that déjà vu from waking up. I know what is about to be said. And what is to be said after that. I'm going to change it.*) Adam stopped then turned around as if to walk back to the dorm. He was standing in the center of the bridge and felt a blast of energy all around him. Waves like when a rock is thrown in water rippled outwards from him. He was shaken. His mind reeled. He had to grab the bridge rail to keep from falling. It was challenging to breathe. Everything he saw was wavy like an old TV not quite tuned in to the station.

"Why did you stop?" Tyrone asked.

(*He didn't feel or see anything.*) "I felt sick. You know. Hangover." (*I do feel ill, but not from the hangover. Everything feels wrong. Out of place. Out of sync. I stopped what was supposed to happen. Changed it. Oh, man. Reality feels so wrong right now.*)

"Maybe you should skip classes today."

"No. I just needed to stop for a bit. I'm ok now." (*I'm not ok. The waves are gone, but the feeling is still strong. I'm out of sync with everything. I don't know. It's wrong somehow.*) "It's going to be a long day."

"I bet it's going to be a long day with a hangover like that. Anyway, I'm going around two o'clock to see about changing if you want to go. All the classes I have taken so far transfer over. Plus, you get enough chemistry class to get a minor in that."

"Yeah. I'll go with you. I hate pharmacy as much as you."

As they walked, Adam pulled the note from his pocket. He had written what was happening in the conversation. (*This isn't déjà vu. It's something else. I wrote it down. It's not my imagination. I feel sick.*) "I feel sick," Adam said, leaning over the rail and throwing up.

"You might want to reconsider going to classes. You look terrible."

"Yeah. I'm skipping today. I can't do this. See you later." Adam headed back to the dorm. Today was too much. This feeling of things being out of sync was not going away.

"See you later. I'll let you know what I find out about changing majors."

His last thoughts as he fell onto the bed were (*What's happening? I hope I wake up.*)

# # #

The invisible blast of energy had taken three months to dissipate. Adam felt this is about as normal as it's going to get. Well, at least as normal as his life could get.

Adam switched his major to toxicology following Tyrone's lead. There are only six colleges that offer toxicology as a Bachler's Degree. Only a few dozen graduated in this field each year, so minimal classes. Adam vowed this new semester would be a fresh start. New major. New friends. He also moved off campus into a converted barn behind his parent's house. Buck was fun, but Adam needed to get serious about his studies. This meant not as much drinking. He still attended some parties but had learned that if he stayed in the background, his strange side would not get noticed. He could avoid conversations and keep the place clean while his friends drank. He would be their designated driver.

(*There is Buck at the kitchen table playing quarters again*) Adam thought as he picked up empty cups. (*This is what I'm always going to be. A servant at parties. It's tedious, but at least I'm out with other people.*)

(Hey)

(*What? A voice in my head. Human?*) Adam began to look around.

(Over here)

Adam turned to see Erik looking at him. Grinning and walking over.

"I knew it. You heard me," Erik said.

Adam's mouth opened, unable to say anything for a moment. "Heard what?"

"You heard me talk to you in your head."

Stunned into truth, Adam said, "Yes."

"I knew it. Tina and I talked after almost having a wreck. You must be like us."

"What wreck?"

"There was this party we were both at. Tina and I were leaving. You warned us to wait at an intersection when the light turned green. To wait and not go. That a car would run the light, and if we didn't wait, we would be in a wreck. Tina believed you right away and wouldn't let us take our drinks. We waited and still ended up hitting the brakes. The drinks would have been all over us. But you kept us from having that wreck. We talked and figured you're like us. I haven't seen you again until now."

"Seriously, you're like me?" (*I'm going to test it by focusing and sending the image of an apple to him.*) Adam formed the picture and moved it into Erik's mind.

"Apple."

"Oh my God. You heard that. You are like me." They started laughing.

"If you are not tied to this party, why don't you come with me to our apartment. So you can meet Tina for real this time, and we can talk."

"Yeah. I think I'll go with you."

"Let's go then," Erik said.

"I'll follow you in my car." (*I'm not alone. He's like me. How is that possible? Guess I'm going to find out.*)

CHAPTER 25 – ERIK

It only took a few minutes to reach Erik and Tina's apartment. The towns are not that big. Erik opened the door. "Tina. I'm back. I've brought someone home that you will be interested in meeting."

"You look familiar," Tina said.

"His name is Adam, and he should look familiar. He's the guy that told us not to go when the light turned green, and we almost had a wreck. Remember? We talked and said that he must be like us. Well, he is. I reached out with my mind, and he heard me."

"I knew it," Tina said. "I'm the one that figured it out before Erik. There was just this feeling I got."

"You can hear people's thoughts, too?" Adam asked.

"No. I can't do that. I sense things. Like when you warned us. I sensed what you were saying was real. You weren't lying."

"You're a lie detector?"

"Yes. Tina is, and she catches me every time I try and lie to her," Erik said. "And there are times I really want to lie to her about being out. Like tonight, stopping off at that party just for a couple of drinks. No way I could lie to her about it." He laughed. "She can also block me from hearing her thoughts. So it's really one-sided against me. She has the upper hand."

"And never forget it," Tina said. "Do you want a beer or something?"

"Sure, I'll take a beer," Adam said. "Tina, how long have you been married."

"Not long. Erik wants to go into the military, so we decided to get married before he enlists and goes off to boot camp."

"When are you going, Erik?"

"I don't have a set date. I might take some military related classes and then go. I hate college. Also, most of my family are in the military. It's in our blood. I heard a rumor that the military has some psychics doing something. Maybe, there is a program for people like us."

"You really think the military has people like us in some kind of program?"

"I don't know, but maybe I'll find out once I get in. Wouldn't that be amazing if the military really did?"

"Yeah, amazing. You can hear people's thoughts, and Tina is a lie detector. Are there other weird things like this that you can do?"

"The other thing with me is luck. If I think about something, it seems like it happens, like finding you at the party. I wanted to find you. So I created a picture in my mind of finding you. Then I got the urge to stop at this party, and there you were. I got the idea from being a telepath."

"A telepath?"

"Yeah. It's the term for people that hear thoughts. Well, you know. It's more pictures and ideas than words, but you know what I mean. I knew I could see images in people's heads, so I experimented a bit. I create a picture in my head of what I want to happen and really believe that it's going to happen. A lot of the time, it happens. That's the other kind of weird thing about me."

Tina spoke up. "My cousin has this thing called clairaudience. She can hear people's conversations from far away. They could be in another apartment and hear them. You'll have to meet her. Oh, I know. She's having a party this weekend. We told her about you after almost having that wreck. You will go, right?"

"Yeah, I'll go. I can meet you here at your apartment and follow you over."

"You know about us now, so what about you? You're a telepath like me. Anything else?" Erik asked.

(*Be careful. Take it slow*ly) Adam thought.

(I understand wanting to be careful. You just met us. It's ok.)

"Thanks for understanding," Adam said.

"Stop it, you two. That's rude. You two are leaving me out of the conversation. Talk so I can hear."

"Sorry. I won't do that again, Tina. When did you know you were a telepath, Adam?"

"I think I've been that way all my life. I thought it was normal. It happened randomly, so I figured others would teach me when I grew into an adult. I was wrong."

"Anything else?"

"Sometimes it's like déjà vu. I know what is about to happen. So I tested it by writing down what I thought was going to happen on a piece of paper, and then it happened."

"That's called precognition," Tina said. We've read up on this to help figure it out for ourselves. You didn't know all these terms?"

"No. Believe it or not, we lived in what people would call a haunted house when I was a small child. Then we moved around. I didn't know to look for books on this kind of thing. I thought I was crazy. Besides, the towns probably did not have books on any of this."

"The library on campus does have books about psychic abilities. You should check them out," Tina said.

"I will."

"So, you're a telepath and have some precognition stuff. That's a lot right there. Is there more?" Erik asked.

"That's about it."

"You're lying," Tina said. "It's ok. You just met us. Maybe you will tell us later."

"See. I told you. Trying to get anything over on Tina is impossible. But, hey, want to try something? But, of course, that is if Tina is willing."

"What?"

"She can block thoughts. She puts up these barriers. It's hard for me to get through. We could try to break through her barrier and see who gets through first. She can feel it when I get through, so she will know. Is that alright with you, Tina?"

"Sure."

"Alright. Tell me when to start."

"Go," Erik said.

Adam opened his mind. He felt his surroundings and felt a barrier around Tina. It reminded him of a barrier in a doorway long ago. He felt Erik pounding on Tina's shield. He was hitting it with brute strength. His hits were so strong. (*I don't think I can hit that hard. I don't want to hit that hard.*) Adam figured if Erik was going big, then he would go small. He focused his senses like the point of a needle. Then smaller. Going between molecules. Between atoms. Then even smaller. Shifting between particles and waves. Moving silently through the barrier. Then he was through. (*I'm in. Behind her. She didn't notice.*)

"Erik wins. I felt him break through the barrier," Tina said. Then she noticed a sly grin coming from Adam.

"Oh my God. You're in. I didn't even see you. You were in when Erik broke the barrier. I was focused on someone breaking it and did not see you sneak in. I've got to watch out for that."

"I've never seen anyone do that," Erik said. "I've always pounded on things. Never thought about going small or being stealthy. Nice."

They all started laughing.

Adam headed home for the evening, looking forward to the party at Tina's cousin's place this weekend. (*Telepathy, clairaudience, precognition. I've got to go to the school library and check out some of these books. I need to try out that luck thing Erik talked about. They are a little like me. Not everything but a little. It's nice to have someone to talk to.*)

# # #

Pulling into the apartment complex, Adam thought (*I wish there were more books on this kind of stuff in the campus library. But, unfortunately, there wasn't much more than Erik and Tina already told me. Nothing about the memories from before I was born. Nothing about these dark entities or lost souls. It's nice to find people that are a little like me, but there is so much more that I can't explain.*)

"Hey, Adam. You ready to go?" Erik asked, greeting Adam as he pulled into the parking spot.

"Yeah. Is it a far drive?"

"Were walking. It's just a few doors down. Ann is in the same apartment complex."

"Nice."

"If you have too much to drink, you can stay at our place."

"Thanks."

"I'm ready. Let's go," Tina said, closing the door behind her.

"She's only four doors down?" Adam asked.

"She's been here a lot longer than us. We waited until an apartment near hers came open to move in. We're really close," Tina said. A slender young lady with long light brown hair answered the door. "Ann, this is Adam. The one we told you about."

"Nice to meet you, Ann."

"Nice to meet you, Adam. Come on in. This is Kevin and Carol. That's James and Susan. Kevin had a job as a bartender for a while so he can mix some good drinks."

"Adam. What can I get you?" Kevin asked.

"How about a Seven and Seven."

"That sounds good. Make a couple more for Tina and me," Erik said.

"Tina tells me you're a telepath like Erik. That's amazing," Ann whispered to Adam.

"Yes. Tina told me you can hear things from other places," Adam said.

"Clairaudience. Yeah. It's not all the time. I don't really know how to control it. It gets annoying. Especially when you are trying to go to sleep. You start hearing these conversations, and they won't shut up. I wish it was something more like Erik or Tina's, but you live with what you got."

"I've got the cards. The game is strip poker," James said, moving the coffee table. Everyone started taking their places in a circle on the living room floor.

"Strip poker? Is this what you normally play?" Adam asked.

"No. We have a game. Cards, sometimes dominoes, and sometimes a board game. Whoever wins gets to pick the game for the next party. We don't know what it is until the party. James won last time," Erik said, sitting down.

"I really didn't expect this kind of game."

"It's more fun this way. Not knowing. Anticipation, wondering what the game will be. Although strip poker is a new one. Notice nobody is complaining. We just go with whatever. Pretty laid back about everything."

"Here. Sit next to me," Ann motioned.

Adam sat down. The losers were even at first. James, Kevin, Tina, Ann, Erik then Adam were losing shoes. Adam loses again. He lost socks this time, then a shirt.

"Geez. I have the worse luck. I'm terrible at this game. Come on. It's someone else's turn."

Laughter. "Everything is working out great," Susan said. I've not lost yet.

Adam lost. He had to remove his pants this time. Then another loss. "Five times in a row. That's not fair." Adam said. Now only wearing underwear, not wanting to remove them.

"You lost. Take them off," Erik said.

"Come on. Give me a break here."

"Nope. You lost. Play by the rules."

"Shit," Adam said, removing his underwear. He was now standing naked in front of this almost fully dressed group of people. "Happy now." Laughter. Clapping.

"Alright. Alright. I can't let my friend here have all the fun," Erik said. He stood removing all his clothes and moved next to Adam. Then he put his arm around Adam's shoulders. "There. Much better now." The players are now rolling on the floor with laughter. "Come on, Adam. I need some ice from the kitchen."

The group decided that was enough of strip poker. They had their fun. Time to move on. The winners were Carol and Susan because they didn't lose a single hand.

"I'm sorry. I couldn't help it. Then I felt bad. That's why I joined you," Erik said.

"What?"

"I don't need ice. I just wanted to get you alone and tell you I did that luck thing with the cards. All those losses in a row. I felt guilty, so I got naked with you. I'm sorry. I was just having fun with it. To show you what it can do. Tina and Ann are the only ones who know about this stuff, so don't tell the others. Let's go back and get dressed."

(*It works. I didn't even notice Erik doing anything. I've got to try this sometime.*)

CHAPTER 26 – LOSING FRIENDS

Tyrone said "I like this walk across the bayou. It's relaxing. We should rent a canoe and paddle down to the liquor store past the other bridge. It'd be an all-day event but could be fun. We could even get some others and do it as a group."

"I like that idea. But let's do it before it gets too cool. You know someone will tip the canoe and go in the water. Best not to be freezing," Adam said. "You know what else I like. I like this toxicology major. The small class sizes. However, I didn't figure on handling live animals in the lab and inject them with lethal doses to determine LD50s. I have a hard time hitting that vein in their tails. This must be the only major in the college that deals with live animals. I think I'm becoming allergic to the rats and mice, though," Adam said.

"You might be one of the 10% that become allergic and can't go into that kind of research. It gets me when the dead animals get put in the grinder before disposal. That sound of bones being broken into pieces. Makes my skin crawl. You know that book I got from the bookstore a couple of days ago. You were with me when I got it. It's called The Hunting."

"I remember. It's new. You said you would loan it to me when you were finished."

"I'm halfway through. There is this part where an old couple goes crazy and begins killing other residents in the nursing home. They start by switching up the medications. The first to die is a guy who made them angry in the lunchroom."

"Oh yeah, He was angry and knocked their food off the table," Adam said.

"Then he spat at them, for no reason. The book doesn't really explain why. Like he was made to do that by something," Tyrone said.

"Do you think it was the same sort of force that made that other one walk into the middle of the road?"

"I don't know. Maybe. I'll find out once I'm further in the book. After that, the couple switched medications. The guy is so drugged later he doesn't know he's cutting his arm instead of the food."

"Yeah. Where did the guy even get that kind of knife? The book doesn't tell you yet."

"I know. The guy lives, though."

"That is until the couple knock him unconscious, wrap him in a bedsheet, and drag him using both their motorized wheelchairs."

Tyrone stopped and stared at Adam. Adam turned.

"What are you doing? Are you reading my mind?" Tyrone asked.

"What?"

"Are you reading my mind? You were with me when I bought the book. I know you have not read it. How did you know those parts of the story? We were just talking, and you knew what was in the book. How did you know?"

(*Think of something.*) "I must have picked it up in the bookstore and read through that section."

"I was with you the whole time, remember. You didn't pick up the book. How did you know what was happening?" Tyrone wasn't asking for an explanation. He was demanding.

"Maybe you told me earlier and forgot."

"I just read that part. I have not seen you until now heading to class. Wait a minute. That last part you said. About the couple knocking the guy out and dragging him." Tyrone reached into his backpack and pulled out the book. He flipped to the marked page where he left off. He began to read silently. "It's there in the next part I was going to read. Exactly what you said. How the hell did you know all that?" Tyrone demanded.

Adam was stunned. Tyrone was his friend, and he had gotten close to him. Close enough, he wasn't paying attention when talking to him. It just came out. Adam did not know what to say. No more excuses, and he couldn't tell him the truth. Adam shrugged.

"I'm sorry. This is too much. There are all those times you know songs before they are playing. When you are drunk talking about ghosts. Even how you walk through a crowd. Like you know where people will move next, and you just flow through them. It's more than that, but then this. This is insane. I don't need this spooky shit in my life. I'm sorry. I just can't. We have class together, but that's it. Ok? Let's just keep it at that. Ok?"

Thoughts of Becky and Jimbo from the high school in Olla flashed through Adam's mind. (*It's the same thing. He can't handle it. I don't want this stuff to cause him harm. I need to stay away from him. It's over.*) Adam said, "Ok," as Tyrone continued onto the class.

(*I'm at the same spot on the bridge over the bayou where that invisible explosion happened when I changed the future. Is it a coincidence? What I know is I just lost a friend because of this. At least Erik understands, but he's not going to be around for much longer. I'll be alone again.*) Adam headed to class, wondering if this was what life would be like. Never letting anyone close enough to see the true Adam. To pretend he's like everyone else. Even Erik. At least he was somewhat like Adam but still. There is so much more. (*These kinds of accidents don't happen with Erik. He focuses his telepathy, but with me, it just happens.*) Adam was back to feeling alone. This is going to be his life. Always hiding. Never able to be his true self. Maybe one day people will be able to understand but not now.

# # #

"This is my last semester at college. Then we will be moving away. Glad you called and suggested bowling. Where is your friend Tim? I thought he was going to join us," Erik said.

"I gave him directions to your apartment. He's going to meet us here, and then I'll drive. I'm not drinking tonight since I'm driving," Adam said.

"That means there is more for me. Although that means you will probably win."

"I doubt it. Tim is in a bowling league. He's going to win unless we get him really, really drunk."

"Come on in. It's just us. Tina is out with Ann. I've got to tell you about this dream I had. You were in it."

"Really? I had a dream last night, and you were in it. What was yours like?"

"We were in a pyramid. There was a long row of columns on both sides of a center aisle."

"Yes. And someone was sitting on a throne at the end. It was on a platform. The person was someone important," Adam said.

"Yeah. And there you were, walking down the center of the aisle. Not afraid of anything," Erik said.

"Yeah. And you were there hiding behind one of the columns toward the back on the right side. About three columns in."

"Yes. Exactly. I've never shared a dream with anyone before."

"Me either. I wonder if it will happen again?"

"Uh. Let's not try and make that happen," Erik said.

"Why not?"

"You're a guy. What do most of your dreams involve?"

"Sex."

"Right. Sex in dreams can get wild, and if we go down that path, we will have sex with each other. I'd like to avoid that. Not saying your bad or anything. Just not my style."

Adam laughed. "Yeah. My dreams do tend to get wild. It's all good."

"That must be Tim. Come on. Let's go bowling."

It was a short 10-minute drive to the bowling alley. Erik and Tim were disappointed that there wasn't any beer available. Something wrong with the equipment. The guys talked and watched Tim wrack up strike after strike. He was good. Adam earned the nickname Awesome because his scores were all over the place. One strike, then the next a gutter ball. Just awesome. Adam did not mind coming in last. He liked to see other people succeed. Nothing wrong with coming in last. He was driving back to the apartment with no one drunk in the car. Just friends.

"Why are you doing the speed limit? Speed. It's late." Tim said from the front passenger seat as there was no one around.

"I'm not going to speed," Adam said.

"Speed. It's ok. You don't have to be a goody-two-shoes all the time. Speed."

"Look. There is a cop up ahead. I'm not going to speed."

"What cop?"

"He's up ahead around the curve. He's in the parking lot on the right side of the road, but I guess we can speed. He's already got someone pulled over. His lights are on and everything."

"Where? I can't see anything," Tim said.

(*Oh no. No. No. No. I wasn't paying attention again. I hope I'm wrong and can just blow it off. Just joking around.*)

They continued up the road then rounded the curve. Just as Adam had described, the police officer with someone pulled over. Lights were flashing. It would not have been so bad if Erik had not leaped between them from the back seat to pat Adam on the shoulder, saying, "Way to go. You've been practicing."

Tim gave Adam that familiar look of someone being spooked.

"It's ok, Tim. There was a wall of windows on that building back there, and I saw the reflection of the cop."

"I know this road as well as you. There is no building with a wall of windows back there. Even if there was, how would you have used it to see around the curve?"

(*I can salvage this somehow. Just don't say anything more. It'll blow over.*)

They arrived back at Erik's apartment. Erik went in to tell Tina that Adam saw the police officers before they got to it. Tim, however, remained distant.

"I'll see you later, Tim," Adam said.

"Yeah. See you later. Though I don't know when that will be. We don't see each other much since we stopped working refinishing antiques. Plus, I've been seeing someone, so my time is getting tight. So if I have a choice of her or you, I'm choosing her."

Adam smiled. "Yep. I understand. I'll see you when I see you."

"Bye."

(*It was all over his face. He's known me too long and seen too much. He can't deal with it, like all the others. There goes another friend. Erik and Tina are next. Even though we are still friends, they are moving away. We might keep in touch some initially, but that will fade away. Alone again. At least there is Buck. He's still around. I need to join him the next time he goes drinking.*)

CHAPTER 27 – SEEING THROUGH WALLS

(Another semester closer to graduating. Not easy being in classes with Tyrone knowing we can't be friends like before. Just talk in passing. Erik and Tina are gone. I bet he's going to love being in the military. He's built for it. I've seen Buck here and there. I meant to call him before last semester ended. I'll call him now and see what he has been doing.)

"Hey, Adam. Glad you could make it. This is Connor and Michael. I met them when I moved out of the dorm," Buck said. The Post had become the primary bar. There were no pool tables like the Airport Lounge and no views like the one at The Library. The cheap pitchers of beer were the reason it was the new hangout.

"Nice to meet you. I haven't seen you in a while, Buck. Just wanted to see what you have been doing lately. It's only five in the afternoon. A bit early to start drinking, isn't it?" Adam asked.

"Not at all. The pitchers go on sale at three."

"Have you settled on a major yet?"

"I settled on a business degree because most of my classes transferred into that. I don't know what I will do with it, but I'll graduate. Did you drive? Are you drinking tonight?"

"Yeah, I drove. I can't stay long. Just a couple of beers, then I'm off. Got things to do, plus I don't drink that much anymore. I hate the hangovers."

"Hangovers are a bitch, but it's the price you pay for having fun. Guys. Adam here could drink a lot and rarely have to pee. We used to joke about it. Speaking of that, I have to pee right now. This finishes our second pitcher. I'll be back in a bit."

"I'm going to get another pitcher," Connor said.

"I'm going to say hi to that girl over there. I think I know her. Back later," Michael said.

Adam was left sitting alone at the table. He finished his beer and waited for Connor to return with more beer. Adam turned towards Connor and noticed he had struck up a conversation with someone at the bar. There was a solid half wall between the bar area and the rest of the sitting room. The wall was painted brown. No lines. No pattern. There is just a wall except for the young girl with long brown hair painted on it.

The young girl moved. (*Wait. That's not a painting.*) As Adam focused on the image, the young girl became clearer. She was kneeling on a sidewalk. There was someone on the grass behind her saying something to her. This solid brown wall had taken on depth around the young girl. The images became so clear it was like looking through a window.

Adam's eyes were still seeing the flat brown wall, but his mind added an extra dimension. It reminded him of these overlays he sometimes creates to find things or see entities. Only this time, Adam wasn't doing anything. It was just there. He felt connected to the girl and could not make the images stop.

(*This can't be real. Maybe this beer is bad or something. Maybe I'm stressed out. But it's not going away. It's so clear. A couple is sitting at the table next to it. They don't see it.*)

(No. Stop. I can't make the voices stop. They never stop talking.)

(*I can hear what she is thinking.*)

Adam watches as the girl lifts a gas can, pouring the contents onto herself. The person in the back is panicked, trying to make her stop but afraid to come any closer. She pulls out a box of matches.

(*Oh God. If this is real, I must do something. If it's not real, then it can't hurt anything to try. But if it is real, maybe I can help.*) Adam reached out with his mind to connect with hers. Just like he had practiced with Erik.

(*Stop. It's ok. Everything is going to be alright. Don't do this. Please don't do this.*)

(No. It's so loud. More voices in my head. I can't make them stop. The voices in my head won't stop.)

Adam watched as the young girl lit the match. She was engulfed in flames. Screaming.

"What are you doing just staring into space." Buck had returned.

"Oh. I forgot about a meeting I have in about an hour. I wish I could stay longer." Adam had gotten pretty good at keeping his crazy side secret.

"You just got here. Not even a pitcher's worth drank."

"I'm driving. Couldn't drink that much anyway. One beer is enough. Great to see you again, Buck. I hope you have a great semester."

"You, too."

(*What the hell just happened. It can't be real. But it was so clear. It seemed so real. It can't be real. Please, God, don't let it be real. Don't let her have burned to death.*) Adam continued to convince himself during the drive home that it wasn't real and that he was crazy after all. Stuff like this never happened to Erik or Tina. (*It's not real. I'm stressed about the new semester, graduating, and finding a job. It's not real. That's never happened to me before. Just some craziness while drinking. It's not real.*)

Adam arrived on campus early the following day. There was a coffee shop in the student union building. He could get something to drink and read the local paper while waiting for classes to start.

Adam sat down and began to read. In black and white was the story of the young girl kneeling on the sidewalk. The article describes how she looked and what happened. How she poured gasoline on herself and lit the match while screaming about voices in her head.

(*It's her. It's what I saw. Oh, God. What did I do? I made it worse. She heard me, and it made things worse. She lit the match because of me. I never wanted to hurt anyone. I killed her. Oh, God. No. No. No. It's just a coincidence. Nothing more. I didn't do anything. It's just a coincidence. It's not real. None of this is real. It was just a game Erik and I played. None of it was real. Those psychic books in the library were just fiction. None of them talked about this kind of stuff. I'm crazy. It's not real. I'm crazy. It's ok. I'm crazy. Just a coincidence. That's it. A coincidence. None of this is real. I can live with being crazy. Crazy is ok. I can be crazy and not hurt anyone. Yeah. I'm crazy. Crazy is ok.*)

Adam finished his classes for the day. He started the car and began his drive home. He wasn't far from the campus when he noticed something on the road. The road had depth. His eyes saw the road, but his mind was adding another dimension. He was seeing into a home with a couple arguing. A clear image in his mind was being overlaid into the road.

(*What is this? What is going on? It feels like the road is fragile. That the car tires could fall through at any moment. I'm seeing two things at once. It won't stop. I can't get it to stop.*)

The overlaid image persisted the entire drive home. It only stopped when there were potholes or paint on the road. It was even there in the driveway as Adam parked before heading into the apartment behind his parent's house.

(*It stopped. The apartment's linoleum floor with a tile pattern is simply a floor. No images. The wood grain paneling on the wall. Nothing. My mind is not seeing the images anymore. It's gone. I'll feel better after a hot shower. The hot water always helps when my sinuses hurt. Just wash this craziness off and start over.*)
Adam undressed and stepped into the corner shower without looking up. It was routine until he looked up at the smooth white walls.

The images were back. Looking into the corner with the smooth white walls to the left and right, Adam saw a park. His eyes saw the walls, but his mind was overlaying a park with people. A couple was having a picnic. There is a small lake. Joggers. His mind told him he was standing naked in a park with all these people. He looked behind him at the glass door. Nothing but the pattern in the glass. He looked back at the wall. The image is still there.

(*It's only happening on smooth surfaces. If there is a pattern, I don't see anything. I can't make it stop. No. I'm crazy. It's not real. It can't be real. If I tell anyone about this, they will give me medication, shock treatment, or something.*)

Adam closed his eyes to finish the shower. Then, drying himself off, he began paying attention to the pattern on the surfaces of things. If there was a pattern, then everything was normal. If it was a flat surface, then various images would appear. Random places. An office building. A car. A warehouse. A mountainside. A boat on a river.

He walked back into the shower to take another look at the smooth white walls. It was a different image than before. The park was gone and replaced by an overhead view looking down upon a city. It felt like he was flying in a plane looking out the window upon taking off. The town grew smaller as the plane got higher. Adam looked around. Clouds. Sky. Then an overlay to this overlay.

(*My eyes are seeing the walls. My mind is seeing these other images of different places, but there is something else. My senses are telling me there is something else here. That other plane of existence is here also. I can sense these other entities still, even with these images. These entities are on another plane of existence overlaying this one. I'm feeling them, and my mind is adding them to these images. No. Not to the images. The images are separate. It's above them. A little higher somehow. No. It's too much. I'm crazy. I didn't hurt that girl. I'm crazy. This is crazy. It's not real. That mountainside I saw earlier was nice. Whenever I see a flat surface, I will try to visualize a landscape instead of seeing all this stuff. A simple landscape. I'm crazy, and a landscape won't hurt me. It won't hurt others. I can see a landscape and not freak out when I'm around people. That will work. I'll force myself to put a landscape up at every flat surface I see. I'm crazy, so why not. It's my crazy little world, and I can do what I want. Yes. A landscape to protect me.*)

Adam looked at the shower walls and forced himself to mentally see a creek with clear flowing water. The image from the plane did not go away. Instead, it was forced behind this new image of a creek.

(*A barrier. Yes. A landscape barrier between me and what I see in these flat surfaces. It's going to work.*)

The landscape barriers worked. When Adam looks at any flat surface, he sees various landscapes. He could do it. He had to do it. Why not. It was his crazy little world, after all. Adam called it seeing through walls. He didn't know what else to call it. Adam did not see the entities turn and look at him. He was seeing into their world all the time now, and they noticed.

CHAPTER 28 – CRUSHED

It's weeks before graduation. Through trial and error, Adam gained better control of his telepathy. He learned that if he kept himself distracted, he would not see into people's heads. He realized that it was much easier to hear what family and close friends were thinking. That meant never being close to anyone if he wanted to stay hidden. Never letting anyone close enough to know the real Adam. They would run away like all the others if they found out. He also learned to control the premonitions. He could visualize himself moving through days in a calendar and see significant events. Adam also learned that he could focus the electricity generated by his own body to interact with small devices. Existence continued to respond as a friend. Meteors continued to appear. He learned to separate his crazy little world from the everyday life he presented to the public. Two lives are spiraling around each other. One light. Out in the open. One dark. Hidden.

(I've learned a lot through college. How to interact socially with people without them seeing the true me. I've lost friends through this trial and error process. This part of me remains in shadow. It feels like I'm walking alone in the dark, even when I'm in a crowd on a sunny day. Me and shadows. Those shadows are still there coming at me. More often now. It feels coordinated. It used to be I just ran across them in my travels. Now it's like they are seeking me out. I'm fighting and helping lost souls find their way home. I'm pretty good. But this seeing through walls. It never stops. Every flat surface. Thank God for the landscape barriers. If

not for them, I would be in a mental institution. There would be no way to have a normal life.)

(*Not another dark entity. I'm trying to get to sleep. I'm tired and don't want to deal with this right now.*) Adam had learned something new through his many fights with dark entities. He learned he could project an astral image of himself.

Adam lay there and felt split into two beings. His physical self is lying in bed, still aware, but another piece of his consciousness moved to the side. He moved this second self to the front door and had it look around. The projection focused on the entity, and the entity noticed. It went for this projection, thinking it was the true Adam. Adam created a wall around his true self. A wall that reflected reality outwards, thereby making his true self invisible to the entity. Adam could watch from the sidelines as the entity attacked this false image. The fight began. Adam let his projection put up a fight then allowed it to lose. The entity won and left feeling satisfied. Adam could go to sleep free from another attack at least for one night. His last thought was (*I'm good. They are nothing to me now. Too easy.*)

# # #

(*Not now. Another attack. During my industrial hygiene final. It's my last test before graduation. Just perfect.*) His hand tightened, breaking his pencil in half. (*Damn, that was a strong hit. Test. Focus.*)

Adam's concentration was broken every few minutes by what felt like dark etheric energy striking him to his core. He completed the test using his last bit of focus. He left the room without talking to any of his classmates. (*I can't stop. I must get out of here, away from people. This is a strong one. Where can I go? That big oak tree on the edge of campus. I have not been there in a long time. No one goes there. I forgot I was supposed to have gone back to meet Frances. Way too late now.*)

Adam walked across the bridge spanning the bayou. He falls to the ground. (*Did I trip? Was I hit from behind? Walk faster.*)

(*Made it.*) Adam sat down with his back against the tree. Resting. Feeling the tree, the branches, and the roots underneath. So sturdy. He felt his consciousness split off. He began creating a projection for this entity to attack. He was knocked to the side. The side of his head hitting the ground. (*I wasn't ready. It's not fooled.*)

(*Focus*) Adam used the same method he's always used. He built this bubble of light around himself then started working on etheric light walls. Every time he would put up a wall, this dark entity shattered it. Then another hit to the bubble of light around Adam. It shattered. Adam rebuilt it.

(*Alright. No walls.*) Adam felt light expand into his etheric wings. He didn't think about them when fighting anymore. Like legs when walking. You use them without thought. However, he was having to think about them now. Reaching out with his light-infused wings, he grabbed the entity. It split apart into a dozen pieces surrounding Adam. He grabbed a couple of pieces with the wings, then grabbed a couple more using his etheric hands.

(*This isn't going to work. There are too many pieces. I can't grab them all. After all that continuous focus during the exam and the walk here, I'm getting tired. Got to do something different.*) This line of thinking has helped Adam so many times in the past. Thinking outside the box. If something isn't working, then try something else.

(*I've always generated the light from the center of my being. What if I start from a different location? I can feel this tree and the air. I'm part of them. I don't have to start from the center of my body.*) Adam let go of the pieces he held. Now focusing on a sphere beyond the top of the tree reaching all around them. He felt the energy build. The light solidified into a large sphere around them both. The entity was focused on Adam waiting for him to do something else. It did not see the light form in a 100' radius around them.

(*Done. It feels more solid than when I try to do it alone. It's more substantial, like nature is helping. Using both our energies.*) The entity noticed too late. It tried breaking through, but the individual pieces were not strong enough. Adam started shrinking the sphere of light. The entity reformed into a single being. It rushed at a single point and broke through. The sphere of light shattering.

It turned and looked at Adam. It was raging. Moving forward a few inches, then stopping. Waves of anger pouring from it. Adam had done something unexpected. Learned something new. It slowly moved away, leaving a trail of hate like slime from a snail.

(*It's gone. That one was so strong. I held my own with some help from nature. That was a tie, but still. Against something so powerful, and I'm not dead.*

Not bad. If I can manage a tie with something like that, I can take on any of them.)

Far in the distance, the dark entity felt a sense of accomplishment. Its purpose is successful. It thought only one word. (Arrogance)

Adam managed the drive home. The fight was over. The only thing left is to attend graduation then find a job. But, unfortunately, all Adam wanted to do right now was sleep.

He arrived home and crawled into bed. It was still early. Not even dark, but he was exhausted. He was almost asleep when he felt a presence standing at the end of his bed. A memory from high school flashed in his mind. Three men forcing him into a car. Another memory. This time from his childhood. A being with brown fur and glowing red eyes. He was afraid. Adam moved to sit up but was pushed back down into the bed. He was being held down and couldn't move.

(Arrogance)

Adam did not have time to think. A fist from this dark entity struck. Adam gasped for air. Energy flaring around the being's head like a crown. Yellows and reds. Burning. Another hit shattering what Adam felt was one of his etheric legs. Then another hit. His other etheric leg is broken.

Adam was screaming in his mind. He had been worn down and did not have the strength to fight back. He tried forming a bubble of light. Nothing. Another hit twisting and breaking an etheric arm. The entity feeding on the fear and pain. Growing stronger. Another hit shattered Adam's other etheric arm. Two invisible fists are pounding into his chest, breaking etheric ribs. Claws are ripping through Adams's etheric face. He continued to scream silently.

Adam's body was paralyzed. This etheric side he felt since high school was crushed. Bones shattered. Limbs twisted. Although Adam was lying in bed, his etheric side was curled in a fetal position. Arms and legs splayed to the sides.

Adam felt something brush his skin as it moved behind him. The entity grabbed one of his wings and bent it backward, breaking it. More screaming. The entity's breath on Adams's neck was dripping tongues. Each one is lapping a bit of pain and fear then returning. It grabbed the other wing and broke it. Adam thought it was over. There was nothing more it could break.

It grabbed a wing in each hand and spread them apart. It moved closer and began chewing on the left wing, where it connected to Adam's back. It was worse than bones breaking. Even his etheric screams were silent now. He didn't have the energy to make a sound. The life is draining out of his etheric body. The dark entity chewed the wing until it fell. Then it grabbed the other wing with both claws and ripped it off. It remained there knowing that this part of Adam was dying. It won in all the ways that counted.

Adam did not see it leave. His body was lying in bed as if nothing had happened. However, his etheric side was curled, twisted, and broken, with wings ripped off lying to the side. This part of him was dying, and he could do nothing. Everything was going dark. Then nothing.

CHAPTER 29 – WAKING UP

Adam woke, placing lettuce in his shopping cart. (*Where am I? Shopping. I don't remember coming here.*) He continued shopping, having a vague memory of what he needed. (*I barely remember items to get. It feels like I'm just waking up.*) Adam could only remember bits and pieces. He graduated but did not remember the ceremony. Being with people. His body is on automatic going through the motions. Conversations with family. (*It's been months, and I can't remember any of it. What happened?*) Adam allowed his senses to see this other-self. (*It's still there. Twisted and broken inside me. It's on a floor. Not moving. Something crushed me. A powerful being. I can't remember.*)

Adam passed through checkout, taking the groceries to the car. He got in, started the engine then sat there. (*This etheric part of me that is just waking up should be dead. But, instead, I'm waking up after months. What was that thing? What do I do now?*) He turned on the radio. The song playing was **Carry On Wayward Son**. (*Another coincidence. The song lyrics match what I'm thinking and feeling at this moment.*)

Adam focused again on his twisted etheric self. (*That part of me is not moving, but it's alive somehow. I'm feeling myself just now waking up, so there is some spark left. Oh, God. My wings were ripped off. Gone forever. I don't know if I will ever be able to move. I'm broken. I am opening my etheric eyes and still can't move.*) Tears ran down Adam's cheeks. He was alive yet destroyed. He would never be the same again. (*I must be fucking crazy. Relating to songs on the radio as if they are talking to me. That some messed up psychiatric stuff. Seeing entities. Feeling attacked. I really am crazy. I'll never be able to have a real job if I tell anyone about this. They'll put me on medication. It will be on my permanent record. Why is this happening to me? Why am I like this? Why am I alive? Universe if you are listening. Why?)*

The song on the car radio transitioned to the next song. **Sole Survivor**.

(*What. Two songs in a row are speaking to me. I'm so fucking crazy.*) Adam continued to listen, raising his head from the steering wheel. (*It's talking about me. How is that possible? Lyrics talking about light. Not destroyed. Surviving. Rising. Defending.*) Adam wiped away tears with a twisted grin. It made him feel better, even if it was crazy to believe it was anything more than a coincidence. He turned off the radio. He needed to think.

(*There are three paths before me. The standard path is truly realizing I need psychiatric help and medication. After that, my career choices will be limited. Like my mother said when we were in high school. If that ever gets on your record and a child custody case goes to court, you will lose. The second path is continuing as I've done in the past. Walk the ordinary and dark path together. Keeping my crazy little world hidden. Remaining alone in the shadows with people only seeing a reflection. Then that third path with arrogance. Using all this odd stuff about me for money and power. It would be easy.*

The third path. No. Easy to eliminate. I never want to hurt anyone. The arrogance left me twisted and broken. No one should ever feel that happen. I can't use this for personal gain. If I do, arrogance will be there. Encouraging me to use power to control people. It wants me to abuse them. Fuck free will. No. I remember Dean from high school in Olla. How they bullied that beautiful soul. I can't do that to anyone, no matter the cost to me. I also don't want to do the first path and limit my career choices. I don't want college to have been wasted. Disappointing my family.

I choose the second path. The light and dark paths are spiraling around each other like I remember before I was born. It's always been there. I didn't see it end this soon in the memory, so maybe it's the one I'm supposed to take. I'll have an everyday life. A reflection that everyone sees. Then there will be this other side where I'm crazy and alone in the dark. If it means I don't harm anyone, then I can live with it.)

He pulled out of the parking space and began driving home. His mind still held the image of his twisted form on the floor, but he was awake. Arriving home, he put away the groceries, removed his clothes, and stepped into the shower. Even though it was late afternoon, he felt he was just waking up, and taking a shower was part of his morning routine. He looked at the shower walls. There was his landscape barrier. Ocean waves on a beach. Blue sky. There were also these entities in this other space that his barriers could not block.

The entities were there but had lost interest in him. It's the way he saw things since that day at the bar. Seeing through walls never stopped. Landscapes and entities in all flat surfaces. Even these entities were ignoring him now. Adam felt an intense wave of loneliness. Picturing in his mind his broken body lying, unmoving. He closed his eyes and placed his forehead on the shower wall. Water still running over him.

Adams's forehead touched the wall, and his senses moved into this other space occupied by these entities. He was with them above his landscape barrier on this different plane of existence. Adam looked around. The dark entities and lost souls were there. He no longer mattered to them. Then he noticed other entities he had not seen before. Taller with a slight glow that sparkled like being showered with gold glitter. They were distant and looking at him. Adam could not make out individual features, but they felt gentle. Peaceful. Opposite from the dark entities that were full of hate and anger. (*Who are they? Have I seen them before? They can see the other entities, but the other darker entities can't see them. Strange.*)

Adam pulled his head away from the wall. His landscape barrier was still there. The dark entities and lost souls are slightly above his landscape. He focused and could barely make out these shimmering entities in this newly discovered space. Were they above the darker entities somehow?

Adam again closed his eyes and placed his forehead on the shower wall. He was entering this space where these darker entities existed. (*It's like I'm moving up a ladder. First, there is my landscape barrier. Then above that is the space occupied by these dark entities. Now that I'm in these dark entities' area, I can see a level above theirs into a new space where these other more peaceful entities exist.*) He pulled his head back and opened his eyes. Again, a new landscape barrier appeared in the shower wall. This time a ridge of mountains.

(Alright. I'm taking the path of living two lives. One life that everyone sees. Then my crazy little world where I'm alone in the dark. At least there are those other peaceful entities. Ha. I'm crazy, and none of them really exists. So that's my life now. Alright, crazy little world. I'll deal with you as if you are real. Why not. Crazy people do exist, and I'm one of them.)

Adam focused his senses on seeing his broken, twisted form. *(I can't move. I can't fight the dark entities like this. They must know that because they are ignoring me now. I can't help the lost souls anymore either. Maybe it's like that last song I heard on the radio. Defiant. Defending. My human body can still interact with other people even if my etheric side can't. I can still help, but it will have to be in small ways. It will have to be so that they don't notice. I can't have them learn more about me and lock me up. I'm broken and alone, but I can still help others. That's what I'm going to do.)*

As Adam continued to see his broken etheric form, he saw a hand move. It wasn't much, but it moved. He felt the slightest bit of hope. It was enough.

CHAPTER 30 – HOPE

Adam had been sending out resumes everywhere for a month now. Most didn't reply, with the rest being rejections. He decided against working in a laboratory setting. During his college toxicology labs, he learned that he was in the 10 percent of people who developed severe rodent allergies as a result of working with them. He could lay his arm on a surface and know if a rat or mouse ran across it. His arm would break out in a rash. Animal research was not an option. Instead, he focused on the environmental aspect of his degree. He loved nature. After all, he talked to everything in nature, and they responded to him. Adam did not include that in his resume.

Adam grabbed another stack of resumes and drove to the post office. It was late, and he wanted to get these mailed but he was out of stamps. Adam could get stamps from the on-site vending machine and mail this batch. The landscape he saw in the road driving to the post office was pine woods. (*Woods. Nice. Thank God for the landscape barriers. If I tried to explain this to anyone, they would think I was blind drunk seeing two things simultaneously.*) The voice on the radio said

Now for another great hit.

Double Vision.

(*How can these kinds of coincidences be every day? It's not possible. Maybe this world is just an illusion. A simulation. Like that memory, before I was born, there are people out there controlling it having a joke. Did they crush this other side of me for a laugh? At least I saw my entire etheric arm move today. That's something.*)

It was dark as Adam pulled into an empty parking lot. The main post office was closed, but the mailboxes and the stamp machine were always open. He calculated how much money he would need for all the stamps.

(*Crap. I'm short one dollar to get the minimum I need. Coincidences happen all the time. Daily coincidences for the radio. I've had money turn up before when I needed it.*) Adam recalled what Erik told him. To picture in your mind a thing, push yourself to know that it's real. See yourself doing what you envision and know that is your reality. (*It can't hurt to try.*)

Adam pictured himself finding a one-dollar bill. Focused on it happening. Knowing that he would find it. He let the feeling of him finding a one-dollar bill flow all around him. He looked around the post office. (*I didn't see a dollar bill. It didn't work. I'll get them mailed when I come back later.*)

Adam mailed all he could, then walked out of the post office toward his car. He looked down as he walked, and stuck on the side of the curb was a one-dollar bill. (*Did that really work, or was it just another coincidence?)* He shrugged and thought no more about it as he walked back into the post office to get the remaining stamps he needed.

He put the dollar in the machine. The machine spits it out. Adam became irritated and said, "come on, take it." The machine spits it out. "Come on." The machine spits it out. "Come on. I don't want to play." The machine spits it out. "Please take it." The machine spits it out. "I don't want to play." The machine spits it out. Adam had enough. "Fine. Let's play." Adam put the dollar bill in the vending machine, quickly pulled his hand back, cupping it. He formed a ball of energy in his palm. Then he pushed his palm outwards to the dollar bill slot allowing the power to go into the machine. The machine accepted the dollar bill, and Adam could get the remaining stamps.

"Happy now?" Adam turned and was shocked to see a lady standing behind him watching the whole event. He did not see her. Adam did not feel her. He had focused on the machine to the exclusion of everything else. "Oh. Hello," he said, moving off to the side. (*The expression on her face. She is freaked out. Almost terrified to be alone in this post office with me. I need to leave quickly.*) He had seen that expression before in Tim and Tyrone. He knew what it was. He left the post office, got in his car, and drove home. He could mail the remaining resumes later.

(*She would have been so scared if I stayed there. Alone with a crazy person. They could never understand how crazy I really am.*) He reached out and turned on the radio. The song playing on the radio was **Crazy On You**. (*Yep. That's me. Driving crazy and alone in the dark.*)

Adam decided putting stamps on the resumes could wait until morning. He was tired and crawled into bed. As he lay there, he thought of everything that had just happened. The coincidences of the songs on the radio. Knowing he would find a dollar bill then he found it. Then using his personal energy to make the machine accept his dollar. The lady was scared. Like everyone else is always frightened. Tears began falling onto his pillow. He was homesick even though he was in an apartment in his parent's backyard. He wanted to go home, but he didn't know where home was. He knew it was not here.

Adam woke still feeling lonely. (*I need to get away from here. Find somewhere else. Somewhere bigger than this town. It's somewhere far enough away from the parents that I'm on my own but not so far that they can't visit. A place like the Dallas, Fort Worth area. It's only a five hour drive. Any kind of job offer would be nice.*) He thought back to the night before and wondered if he really made that happen. Maybe it was just a coincidence. But, of course, trying the same thing couldn't hurt. Only he would know about it.

He created an image in his mind of getting a call, then getting a job offer to move to the DFW area. He solidified the idea in his mind and pushed it out into the universe. This was going to be his reality. He would get a call and an offer. Then he would move to the DFW area. He pictured himself in an apartment in a large city. Imagined himself driving in the traffic with a never-ending supply of things to do. The phone rang.

"Hello. Is this Adam McLure?"

"Yes."

"I'm Craig Allister. I'm with Engineer's Assisting the Environment. E.A.E. We are in the Dallas, Fort Worth area. We subcontract to the Environmental Protection Agency. I'd like to talk to you if you have not already found a job. We have an opening. If you have time, could we meet and talk?"

"I would love to meet and talk. If you don't mind me asking, how did you find me? I don't remember sending a resume to E.A.E.?"

"You didn't send one. That's why we need to talk. I need to see your resume and talk to you. We have a Safety Officer who needs an assistant. He has a toxicology degree from your university and wanted someone with the same degree. He wanted them to be from the same university. We called and asked who they would recommend. The lady on the phone said there were a few dozen in your graduating class, and most of them already had jobs. Then she recommended you. She seemed to know you personally. Something about not getting a deserved scholarship. She gave us your contact information."

"That's great. When and where can we meet?"

"How about today at three at the Monroe Airport."

"Perfect. Are you in town?"

"No. I'm flying through and have a one-hour layover. We can talk about the job during the layover, but I have to stick to the schedule. Bring your resume."

"I'll be there. Bye."

"Bye."

"Did that really happen?" Adam said out loud. (*Shower. Shave. Suit. Resume. So much to do. Calm down. Plenty of time. Get there early. Be waiting. I've got to go in and tell the parents what just happened. That's so crazy. To get an interview. No resume was sent. He was looking for me. That doesn't happen. And picturing that something like this would happen, and then it happened. Another coincidence? It doesn't matter. Stay in the real world. You've got things to do.*)

Adam got everything ready and arrived at the airport. (*I'm so nervous. This is the first interview I've had. Imagine working in the Dallas, Fort Worth area for an environmental company. It's perfect. I'm going to do whatever it takes to get this job. Even if it means using my crazy little world to help. I need this.*)

"Hello, Mr. Allister. I'm Adam McLure. Nice to meet you."

"Nice to meet you, Adam. Let sit over there and get to it. I have about 45 minutes before I need to get to the gate. Can I see your resume?"

Adam handed it to Mr. Allister. Adam took this pause to open his senses. Feeling himself linking with Mr. Allister. (*I'm seeing memories of a fishing hobby. Something to bring up. I'll be able to focus on the positive parts of the conversation and move away from anything he feels is negative.*)

"Adam. We currently have three more years on our current contract with the E.P.A. So this position is limited to three years. Is that a problem?"

"Not at all. I'm sure there are plenty of other opportunities in the DFW area should I get the job and choose to stay there."

"That's great to hear. Most people want a job that may last a lifetime. It's good you are flexible. You would be working under our current Safety Officer. He's only a few years older than you but he is amazing. I thought he was nuts saying he only wanted someone from his college with his degree but if they come out like him, absolutely. Are you familiar with material safety data sheets?"

"Of course. As part of the degree, several classes on industrial hygiene dealt with not only reading but also creating M.S.D.S.s for the public."

"That's what I was hoping to hear but it's such an odd thing I wanted to confirm it with you."

Adam and Mr. Allister talked for the full 45 minutes.

"My times up. I've got to run. Thank you so much for taking the time to speak with me on short notice. We have not discussed salary or benefits, but I'm out of time. We can talk on the phone later about that, but I'd like to get a general idea if you are interested before I go."

"I'm more than interested. It's perfect. I'm looking forward to giving you a yes answer as soon as I get that call."

"Excellent. I literally must run now. Thanks for meeting with me, Adam. Bye."

"Bye, Mr. Allister."

Adam watched as he ran through the airport. Adam said, "I can't believe that just happened." (*I got a call, an interview, an offer, and I accepted on the same day. How does that shit happen? I'm going to be moving to the Dallas, Fort Worth area. Sub-contracted to the E.P.A. Working with the environment. I love nature. It's the perfect job. That's so crazy.*)

Adam couldn't wait to tell his parents as he drove home. He was so excited. As he drove, an image formed in his mind. His etheric self was using both arms to try and push himself up. Legs unmoving. Wings bloodied on the ground. Great rips in his back. Propping himself up on his elbows, looking around. Flesh hanging loose from gashes on his face. So much blood. It didn't scare Adam. It was part of him. It was who he was, no matter how crippled. Adam didn't see the horror of what happened. He only felt one thing. Hope.

PART FOUR – LOST: CAREER

CHAPTER 31 – DALLAS

Adam sat at the table in his apartment eating spaghetti. He felt as if he was the luckiest person alive. He accepted the perfect job. Working in the environmental field in the DFW area was a dream. The furnishings were sparse, considering he had been working for six months. There was a table with four chairs. A mattress on the floor. Television and the bills.

(*How did I get so lucky? That the right job appeared like that. Then I moved in with my high school friend's sister living in Garland, Texas. Billy convinced me to take typing in junior high school. I never imagined it would come in so helpful. She kindly let me stay with her and her husband for three months to save money for an apartment. I owe them. I'm on my own and making it.*)

Adam finished dinner and began washing the dishes. The sound of a helicopter then a bright light moving past his window. (*That's why I don't go out at night. There are many things to do around here but it's not the best neighborhood. Probably why the rent for this 800 square foot apartment was so low. At least I'm on the second floor. Maybe a little safer.)*

He woke the following day falling into his new routine. Shower. Dress. Business casual. Drive to a parking lot near downtown. Ride the bus to the building where he worked. Walk past the security guard. Take the elevator to the eighth floor. Get coffee, then settle in to work. He looked out the window, taking a sip. (*How am I here? I have an office with a window overlooking downtown in an old building full of antique fixtures. Solid oak wood doors. Original marble in the bathrooms. I know it's only a three-*

year contract but it's incredible. I'm looking forward to this overnight trip with Kris. She rarely gets into the field and has been with the company since the beginning. Those that know her say she has bad luck. I guess I'll find out.)

"Adam. Did you get everything for this afternoon? Tickets?" Kris asked walking into Adam's office.

"I'm ready. Got my tickets," Adam said. "I hope you don't mind me asking but I've never been on a trip with you before. The others say you have bad luck. So what's that all about?"

"That's me. I've had bad luck all my life. I don't know why but I'm used to it now. It doesn't bother me. I've got to go to the E.P.A. to get some files before we leave. Do you need anything?" She asked.

"No, thanks."

"I'll meet you at the airport."

This time it was an overnight trip to gather information. Documents from local officials. Talk to people. Take photos of the site. Southwest Airlines was the airline of choice since they only flew to states connecting to Texas. That also happened to be E.P.A. Region Six. Adam's frequent flyer miles were stacking up quickly. He was one of two Safety Officers for the company, and they required one of them to be at every sampling event. This meant more traveling than the others. Adam was traveling weekly and began to wonder why he was paying rent for an apartment.

He parked his car in long-term parking and checked into the terminal. He'd been here so often he didn't need to look at the signs. It was habit. He even caught himself falling asleep in one of those hard chairs at the gate. Nevertheless, he was getting a little concerned. Kris wasn't here yet and boarding would begin soon.

"There you are. I was wondering if you were going to make it," Adam said.

"I'm right on time. Unfortunately, there was a wreck and traffic light malfunction on the way here, but everything worked out fine."

"Attention passengers on Flight 143 to Houston.
There will be a 15-minute delay on your flight due to a maintenance check.
Thank you for your patience."

Kris looked at Adam. "Don't worry. This happens all the time with me. It's normal." She pulled out a book and began to read.

Adam didn't bring a book and quickly became bored. He walked to the glass and looked at the plane parked at their gate. (*Part of the wing is missing. You say the plane just needs a maintenance check.*)

"Kris. Check out our plane at the gate. The tip of the wing is damaged. Like it hit something."

She walked to the window and shrugged. "They'll get a new one." She sat back down and began reading again.

"Attention passengers on Flight 143 to Houston.
There will be an extended delay. This plane is being taken out of service.
A new plane is being located for your flight.
Thank you for your patience."

"I'm starting to believe you about the bad luck. So you say this happens to you all the time?"

"Yeah. People don't believe it until they see it for themselves. I'm used to it." She didn't even look up from reading.

The plane arrived late, but the flight was uneventful. Adam figured that was probably the end of her bad luck until they arrived at the rental car counter.

"I'm sorry, but the mid-sized car you reserved is not available. Would a van be ok?"

Kris answered, "That would be fine." The drive to the hotel was standard. It was late and they would have to wait until morning to gather information. They grabbed their luggage and walked to the hotel's front doors. Kris ran face-first into the doors and almost fell.

"Are you ok?"

"I'm fine." She pulled herself together and tried to enter through the automatic doors. Unfortunately, the motion sensors would not recognize her. The doors remained closed. She tried several times. They would not work. "You go first."

Adam stepped to the doors, and they opened. "I really thought you were kidding about the bad luck but those doors would not open for you."

"They never do."

They checked in and headed to their rooms. Adam wondered how she could stay so positive with so much negativity around her. He doubted he could do it. He flushed the toilet. It didn't refill. (*More bad luck?*) He called the hotel desk and asked about the water. He was told it was a water main break. They didn't know when water would be restored. He called Kris and suggested an early and long dinner with the water being out.

Kris didn't get into the field much so getting to know her was nice. Her primary job was finalizing reports and she needed a little more information on her current project. It was company policy that there be a minimum of two people on each trip so Adam was the extra person for Kris. Unfortunately, the water main break was not repaired until the following day when they checked out.

They arrived at the site and began documenting.

"I'll record conditions and camera directions for each photo you take, Kris."

"Twenty should be enough," she said.

Documentation completed, they arrived back at the van. Kris tried to open the driver's side door. "It's locked. I can't find the keys."

"Mine is also locked," Adam said from the passenger side. "I can see the keys in the ignition. We are locked out."

Kris said, "I've had this happen before. We can call the rental car company, and they can come out with extra keys to unlock it. Or we can call a locksmith and see if they can open it."

(*She can't see me on this side of the van. I'll try shoving some energy at it to unlock.*) Adam focused energy from his body into a ball in his hand then hit the lock on the door. He pulled on the handle, and it opened.

"It's unlocked, Kris."

"How did you get it unlocked."

"I got frustrated and hit the lock. The electronics must be loose or something, and it unlocked."

"That's a first for me. Something lucky."

The remainder of the trip was ordinary, but it made Adam wonder. (*I've heard of karma. Is this a karma thing? Kris and I are opposites. I have this crazy good luck and can influence things. She has all this bad luck. I've got to figure out how that works. There is a half-price bookstore near my apartment. Maybe they have books on this stuff.*)

Adam was in a big city with a good career path. Now he could focus on his crazy little world. If Adam could not find some information in the Dallas, Fort Worth area, he would not find it anywhere. He had a plan.

CHAPTER 32 – WITCHCRAFT

It did not take Adam long to discover that he could find anything in the DFW area. All you had to do was look. His best find was the Half-Price Book Stores. Customers could sell, buy and even trade used books. The range of topics seemed never-ending and the books were constantly changing. The store itself felt alive. It was another one of those lucky, or perhaps guided, events that got him an apartment this close to the bookstore shaped like a wooden ship. You entered through a lower ramp with thick ropes as handrails. Inside there was a second level with an open center area. His crazy little world was hooked, and he loved it.

Adam was a regular at the bookstore. The staff got to know him and kept him informed on new books fitting his interest. Adam figured it was easy for them to keep track because no one else seemed interested in the same books he was just now discovering. Adam would look up from reading, and another month was gone. It was easy to pick up a couple of books and keep them in his work bag. When he was stuck waiting on a delayed flight, he would be reading. Reading on the plane. Another week-long sampling event, then in the hotel at night he would be reading. Another month has gone by.

The first books to grab his attention were on Unidentified Flying Objects, or U.F.O.s and ancient aliens. They had all the headline-grabbing pictures, but there were two other reasons. First, Adam recalled his childhood and floating through the roof. There were others there doing something to him. He couldn't explain it, but some U.F.O. books said this kind of thing happens. Second, he had an odd memory of piloting a conscious spacecraft that could shift dimensions. He always believed it was just a teenager's fantasy of wanting to escape, only now he was not so sure. Nevertheless, he wasn't going to dismiss it just because he didn't understand. That was his life. That's why he is trying to learn.

Adam didn't just read. He consumed. He read everything the bookstore had to offer on UFOs. Excellent new possibilities appeared but this subject isn't really what he felt he needed. His crazy little world dealt more with psychic stuff than with UFOs so those books would be next.

So much traveling. Planes. Hotels. Eating out. Sleeping in airports. The months blurred together, broken by one book ending and another beginning. Adam had finished many of these books and left the office for lunch. Today he would walk the tunnels under downtown to a favorite Chinese eatery.

(*I don't know what to make of these psychic books. They all focus on testing, like using cards with symbols or debunking. Only a few have what seem like real examples of telepathy. There is even less on precognition, and even that seems random. Like they can't control it. None of them talk about these entities or lost souls. Nor do they talk about influencing people or events.*)

Adam finished eating and was walking back to work above ground this time. Crossing the Dallas Area Rapid Transit rails, feeling a little disappointed that he did not get the answers he wanted.

(*Whoa. What is that?*) Adam stopped. Not an entity nor a lost soul. There is something else here. He stood on the sidewalk and looked around. There. A man was across the rails on the other sidewalk about to turn a corner. It was coming from him. Something familiar.

(*I can feel him. He's like me.*) The man stopped, turned and looked directly at Adam. The man smiled and nodded. Adam nodded back. Then the DART train passed between them. The man had turned the corner and was gone.

(*He's gone. He felt it too. He's like me. There might be other people out there like me. I got more confirmation from that nod than from reading all those books. Only one person in a city this big. There must be others. Time to expand my reading. I need to figure this out.*)

That evening, Adam went to the bookstore and started on a new topic. This time on witchcraft. (*The UFO stuff is exciting but does not help me control this side of myself. Same with the psychic books. They talk about old testing methods but nothing about dealing with what you have. But, on the other hand, witchcraft is about intention and control so maybe there is something in those books.*)

The books were interesting and full of colorful rituals. It wasn't the rituals Adam found terrific. It was the concepts and ideas behind them. This was something he could relate to and understand.

(*It's just like Erik told me in college and proved in that strip poker game. Then I did it with this job and so many other times since. It's all about having an intention. Making it real. Letting it become part of your world. I think I'm beginning to understand. It's like when I fought the dark entities. Creating these intentions and thoughts. These thoughts become solid and can make things happen. Witchcraft uses rituals and objects to help solidify these thoughts. To help convince themselves it's going to work. People praying are doing the same thing. Performing a ritual to turn thought into something tangible. But I don't have to convince myself. I know these thoughts become real. It's my life.*)

Adam felt he was on to something. This is what he needed. To understand more about himself and why things work. (*Yes. Here it is in this book. It's the way I talk to the weather. I've always talked to it like a friend, and it responds to me like a friend. They lay out a three-step process. First, say what you want. Second. Give it a way to end. Third. Why do you want a thing to happen? Like the old nursery rhyme. "Rain, rain, go away. Come again another day. Cause little Mary wants to play." It's not demanding or ordering. It's talking to a friend and ask. It all works for me without the rituals, objects, and foreign words. It all comes down to the intention and thoughtforms you create. These thoughtforms you make go out to fulfill your intent. If you have a bad day and send out these bad thoughtforms, they can cause real damage. That's going to be a problem. I'm human. I get angry at times, just like everybody else. I don't want to harm anyone.*)

There was much more on witchcraft than Adam expected. Months passed. There was no way he can read about it all. Thought and intention are sent out for a purpose. These formalized rituals and elaborate systems didn't impress Adam. He always liked the K.I.S.S. principle. Keep it simple stupid. It was a line they used when investigating uncontrolled hazardous waste sites and it worked here as well.

One day Adam was roaming through the bookstore looking at books on art and cooking when he noticed something new. The bulletin board was new to him but had been there the entire time. He never paid it any attention. What caught his eye was a notice for people to attend a Beltane festival by a local group of witches.

(I know about Beltane. May first. Mayday. A fertility celebration. Mom traced our ancestors to Scotland and Wales. She fell in love with our connection to Clan MacLeod on the Isle of Skye. Going there for one of the clan parliament gatherings was special. I wasn't as fascinated with Castle Dunvegan, but I was caught up in the story of the fairy flag. It was from another world and its power could only be used three times. Yeah. Me and Celtic beliefs. Seems we have a connection. I'm going to go to this Beltane festival.)

Adam pulled a tab with a phone number to contact. He called and confirmed it was open to the public. He was also told there wouldn't be nudity, but some might jump over a bonfire. There were also going to be some side classes followed by a gathering to call the four elemental corners. It all sounded great. He was going. Maybe there would be people there like him.

May first arrived quickly and Adam arrived at the celebration. It was held at a small non-denominational church. There were 60 or so attendees. Larger than Adam would have guessed. Most seemed to know each other. Everyone was amicable but Adam maintained his distance. Feeling alone in a crowd as usual. They were all beautiful. Their outfits and their souls. But he did not feel a connection like he felt with that stranger in downtown Dallas looking across the railway. Maybe he was such a novice he couldn't feel them yet. Perhaps it would take some time so he decided to stay for the entire evening ending at midnight with a bonfire burning.

Classes were being held simultaneously. The first Adam attended was on speaking Gaelic. A great lesson, but Gaelic did not come naturally to him and a single hour-long class could only impart basics. His next class was on Norse runestones. The course was excellent. Showing how to make your own. What they meant. The best part for Adam, though, was the instructor. He was an older gentleman with silver hair, and Adam felt it. That connection. This man had the same kind of connection to things that Adam felt. The man instinctively knew he had this connection, but it was below the surface. It was like the man was barely aware of it. He used it without thinking. Adam could see that things he needed would come to him. But he was the only one. Adam did not feel this kind of connection with anyone else at the gathering. Shouldn't they all have this connection with reality? It's what they believe but he couldn't feel it from them.

Even when they all gathered in the large central room and began the ritual calling of the corners. The four elemental points of the compass. Dancing in large spiraling circles, pulling others in. It was all beautiful but Adam felt no power. No connection. (*I don't understand. Even now, they are trying to make contact. I don't feel anything from them. That guy with the runestones has a connection but no one else out of all these people. I'm standing here feeling alone in a crowd again.*)

Adam left feeling alone. Jumping over the bonfire at midnight didn't help either. They were not like him. The books' material was correct in creating patterns of thought that become real but there is so much more. That is only a piece of it. Where is the rest? The festival did do one thing and that was to solidify his connection to the Celtic world. He could feel it. As he crawled into bed well past midnight, he thought (*The Celts would have been drinking and jumping over that bonfire naked.*)

# # #

(*Well, this is a new book I have not seen, and it details these entities. Summoning them. Some demonic. Some benevolent. I dealt with these kinds of things then got crushed by one of them. My etheric side is barely standing. I can't fight or help them right now. Maybe this is a different way of doing it. I didn't have anyone to show me how. I just did it. I'll see what I can learn about these circles of protection and summoning. I'll give that a try and see what happens.*)

Adam didn't have anyone to teach him, so he didn't realize the danger of opening portals. He only learned through trial and error. He was about to learn again.

CHAPTER 33 – GROUP ATTACK

Adam continued reading about witchcraft and these entities. He was trying to understand why it worked, not the mechanics. They all used circles of protection but they were unique to the author writing the book. Different customs had different processes for the same thing. So many different styles but underlying it all is the same.

(The circle of protections might be like what I was doing with the entities. Creating a thoughtform powerful enough to become real in this other plane of existence. The bubble of light around me. A circle of protection. Mine wasn't strong enough against that last entity. It was way too much for me. I have limits. I wonder if these circles of protection also have limitations. I'll focus on the style using archangel names. Figured I'd be drawn to that. I need to create that circle ingrained and natural within me before I try summoning anything. A month or so of practice ought to do it.)

Adam spent time practicing his circle of protection. He even practiced at work sometimes when he was alone. There was only a year remaining of the contract so they would all be needing new jobs soon. The primary Safety Officer already found a new job and had left. Adam got his office. A corner office with windows overlooking downtown Dallas. He often stopped and thanked the universe for his good fortune. *(I'm in my mid-twenties and this is my office. This doesn't just happen to people. Something else is at work.)*

It was finally time to try a summoning circle. Adam prepared his personal circle of protection in his apartment's living room. Then used his summoning book to make sure he got the ritual part correct. Adam could feel it arrive just as he had felt them before. It was a dark, lost soul, trapped and angry. Adam realized he had not thought any further. He was focused on protection and summoning. Not what to do if something showed up.

"Hello," Adam said. Anger and hate flowed from the entity.

"I don't want to hurt you. Just talk." Images of Adam being pushed into traffic appeared in his mind.

"Stop it." Images of Adam being destroyed over time.

"No. I'll destroy you first. I've done it to others." Adam was pissed off now.

The entity looked at Adam instead of through him. It heard this threat.

"Look at me. Look in my mind. See what I've done." Images of Adam's broken etheric body appeared in his mind.

"There is enough of me left to deal with you." Adam would drop all protections and attack this thing if he had to. He did not care what it cost him. The entity was jarred as it felt Adam's intent and knew he was not bluffing.

"I want to understand why all this happens. Why are you like this? Trapped?" Images formed in Adam's mind. The being in front of him was in pain. Forcing it here was hurting it. It was Adam's turn to be jarred. It was in pain. They were never in pain the way Adam used to deal with them. This summoning ritual was harming it. Causing its pain.

"I don't want to cause you pain. So I'm stopping this now. You are free to go."

Adam ended the summoning ritual. The entity immediately attacked but couldn't get through the circle of protection. It left just as it had arrived. Angry.

(*I'm never doing that again. That summoning hurt it. I was causing it pain. That's just evil and I don't want to be evil. I don't think I was causing them pain when I melted away the darkness and showed them the way home. They did fight against it. Were they in pain and I didn't notice? I'm not going to fight anymore. I need to learn more. I'm so freaking clueless. I need to start talking to them. To all of them. I need to understand what's happening.*)

Adam was clueless. He had opened a portal in his apartment's living room. Adam felt it immediately the next day arriving home from work. He walked into the apartment and felt he was walking through cotton candy. The air felt sticky. On the flat surface of his living room wall, Adam saw a dark entity leap at him. Adam threw his arms up as the entity knocked him backward onto the ground. He felt his etheric side. It was still broken and couldn't help him.

There was no time for circles of protection. Another hit. Adam was lying on his back on the floor. His hands were trying to hold the entity away. He couldn't fight as he'd done before. It would have to be something different. He acted on instinct.

(*I've got to get it off of me.*)

Instead of building a light within, Adam began to burn. Dark flames spread from within. These etheric flames burned through his hands into the entity. It screamed. Adam let himself go. No more thoughts of light. It was dark, and it felt good. No thought. Only a desire to burn and incinerate this creature. It screamed but couldn't get away. It began to char. Then burn. No concept of consequence to himself. He felt nothing but a desire to kill it. Anger. Hate. Violence. He was speaking the language of these dark entities and he was making sure they heard him. Embers fell around Adam then vanished. The creature would never bother anyone again. It was over.

Adam stood up and looked at the smooth white wall in his living room. There were more. He could see them. Waiting. Hesitant. He caused them to pause, but for how long.

Turned out the weeks were just as long. Every day there would be entities sneaking around moving things. Changing electronics. A wheel came off a car and nearly hit him as he walked down the sidewalk. The park and ride bus broke down, making him late for work. A dozen homeless people attacked him as he left his job. If they could not attack him one on one, then they would try to annoy him to death with their poltergeist-like actions. He had to stay aware; otherwise, he might be pushed into traffic. Then the group attacks began.

Adam had finished eating and was watching television. He sensed something coming through the smooth living room wall. It was four entities.

(*Shit*)

He couldn't attack. Only defend. So many at once keeping him off balance. His broken etheric side was not able to handle this much onslaught. Adam could only form a ball of light around himself and let them keep attacking. He couldn't stop it. Maybe he could survive long enough that they would give up. It was another long night curled up in a bubble. Almost no sleep. Their attacks never stopped, even in his dreams.

They followed him to work. Adam trying to concentrate on reports and safety procedures for the upcoming sampling events was difficult. Trying to keep his light protection up, warding against these attacks while pretending nothing is happening. Doing his job. Chatting with co-workers while this other side of him is being attacked right before them. He'd gotten pretty good at this part. Pretending everything is normal. They never saw anything out of the normal.

(*It's too much. The dark entities have locked onto the apartment or something. They keep coming in groups and I can't stop them. I must move out. I don't know what else to do.*)

The entities are attacking every night and the neighborhood feels more dangerous. His job was ending. All the signs were there for him to move.

(*That's it. I'm moving to Arlington, TX. It's between Dallas and Fort Worth. I can find a job anywhere in the DFW area and still reach it from that central area. Plus, everything fun is there. Six Flags. A water park. It's a huge entertainment area and would be a lot of fun. I'm moving as soon as possible.*)

Adam found an apartment in Arlington and moved by the end of the next month. It was everything he hoped it would be. Easy access to all the big entertainment venues. Excellent restaurants. The apartment complex was even secured by automatic entrance gates. The best part was the entities did not follow him. He had left them behind like his family did when they left that first haunted house. He only hoped the next apartment renters would fare better than the couple that moved into his childhood home.

# # #

"Tara. It's nice to hear from you. It's been a long time since you, Billy, and I ran around together. I got lucky and was able to stay with his sister in Garland while saving money for an apartment. Now you call. What have you been doing?"

"I got a job as a medical receptionist at the hospital and bought a small house. I'm still in West Monroe doing the same things."

"Why don't you come out here and visit. There is a big office Christmas party next month. Our contract is ending and they decided to have a big blowout at a fancy hotel. It should be a lot of fun. You could stay the weekend."

"I hadn't planned on anything other than a phone call but why not. I've got time. I'll be there. It sounds like fun."

"I'll get details later. The weekend is set though. It's going to be great seeing you again."

Adam couldn't help thinking about the changes happening so fast again. Like the interview for this job at the airport. So unusual and fast. It's happening again. The new apartment. The big Christmas party as the contract came to a close. Needing a new job. Then Tara called and will be staying the weekend.

(*Take another step and keep moving forward.*)

CHAPTER 34 – NEW JOB

Tara said "I can't believe I'm here. Dancing in a big gold ballroom at a Christmas party in Dallas."

"It's the same for me sometimes. Wondering how this happened. So many coincidences are coming together. But, you know I'm still glad we broke up from dating all those years ago and allowed ourselves to explore other relationships. To see what else is out there."

"Yeah. I didn't much like what I found out there."

"This doesn't have to be your only visit. You should come more often. Just get out of that town. You might even decide you like the big city enough to stay. Who knows?"

Tara grinned. It wasn't just the party that made her smile. It was a deep friendship coming back to life.

Adam felt it also. He had shared part of his crazy little world with her long ago and she didn't run away. She accepted it but didn't understand. She was around when that entity, energy, or whatever came into him and his eyes changed colors. She saw it and did not run away. Someone to accept him the way he was. She didn't need to understand. All she had to be was herself and that was enough for Adam to love her.

"Have you been putting out resumes?" Tara asked.

"Only a few. I should be more panicked with only two months left on the contract but I have this weird feeling something will come along. You know how stuff happens around me and it's happening again. Just look at you here now. It's amazing."

"You might have to give it a little help. Send out more resumes. Even to jobs you may not want. But you will need to find something soon."

(*Give it a little help. Tara's right. She means by sending out more resumes, but I can try what I did before when getting this job. Create an image. An idea of what I need and push it out there. Know it is real and let it happen.*)

"You're right. I'll get more serious about it."

This was something Adam could do anywhere. As they danced, Adam built images of finding the perfect job. It's tailored just for him. Then accepting it and being happy. Adam allowed these new thoughts to flow around him. He was dancing as his new reality unfolded like music.

"I got a job offer but am a little unsure about it." Adam overheard Kris talking to her boyfriend on the dance floor.

"I'm sorry, Kris. I overheard your conversation. Did you find a job? I'm still looking for one. Maybe you can give me some tips. Can Tara and I join you at your table?"

"Sure." They sat down and began talking.

"It just came up. I did not send out a resume so I don't have any good job-hunting tips. My father has a job at Bell Helicopter and said there is an opening in the Safety Department. They announce those jobs internally first, and since he works for the company, he saw it posted. It'll probably be weeks before it goes public. He asked me if I wanted to apply for the job but I really don't want to work at the same company as my father."

"You sure you don't want the job. That's a major company. How could you not want it?"

Kris shrugged. "Working in safety is not what I want to do for the rest of my life. So, no. I don't want the job."

"Do you mind if I apply for that job? I would love to work there."

"You would be a good fit. It's a safety job, and you are the only safety person here. You probably have all the skills they are wanting."

"I'll start doing research into the company first thing in the morning. Is there a way you could get a copy of that internal job posting from your father? It would help me customize a resume to the job."

"Yeah. I'll get that to you. Also, you know Helen that works in records. She's moving to Oregon to be with her husband at the contract end. Her husband used to have your job in this company two people back. He left here and went to work for Bell Helicopter in their Safety Department before moving on. She knows you and might be able to get you a second-hand reference through her husband. He knows the people there and could put in a good word for you."

Adam laughed. "Helen is going to be my new best friend. I can't thank you enough, Kris, for this information."

"I owed you anyway."

"You don't owe me anything."

"Maybe not, but there was that one overnight when we went information collecting and you saw my bad luck. Remember the hotel water shutting off? After that, my luck changed. It's getting better. I don't know why but I attribute that to you. It's probably nothing, but why not spread something positive, right?"

Adam nodded as Kris and her boyfriend went back to dancing. He looked at Tara.

"Can you believe that just happened?"

"No. That's crazy. You can't let this go. You have to start immediately and stay on it."

"I know, right? That's a major company. If I get that job, I'm going to be lost not knowing how to act or what to do."

"It'll be fine. Just takes time. Getting the job is a priority. So don't let it go."

Adam started the next day learning about the company. It was huge. The prospect of getting a job there seemed impossible, but he had a plan.

# # #

"I've talked to my husband about you, Adam. He knows what your job entailed here because he did it also. He's put in a good word for you with the safety staff at Bell Helicopter. They are expecting your resume," Helen said.

"It's ready. The company needs a technician who knows all about sampling, chain of custody, equipment calibration, MSDS, radiation, and the toxicology degree really helps. Also, industrial hygiene is the description of this job. So it's as ready as it's going to get."

"Ok. Here is the direct fax to the safety office. It will go straight to them instead of through human resources or anywhere else."

"Thanks for all your help, Helen. I'll try to not screw it up."

Adam faxed his resume. There was nothing else to do but wait. He knew it could take a while because internal candidates were considered first. They would not look at his resume until the job officially goes public. Then, if he was fortunate, he would get an interview.

Things moved much faster than Adam anticipated. No internal candidates could perform the job duties, and he received a call the following week. They wanted him to come in for an interview. During the call, they brought up benefits, but Adam barely heard any of them. He only needed to get the job. After that, the rest would work itself out.

Adam was ready the day the interview arrived. He had practiced driving the route several times already. He knew where to park and to sign in at the guard gate. It was a secure facility building military helicopters. A lady arrived to guide him to the safety office. The entire Safety Department consisted of five people that included the secretary. He would be the sixth if accepted.

Just getting to the safety office took a while. The facility was massive. So many different buildings in one area. There were even an on-site fire department and medical center. Adam figured it would take 30 minutes to walk from one end of the campus to the other. (*How am I even here interviewing?*)

They arrived at the office. Adam introduced himself to Aaron, the safety engineer, and Carla, the secretary. He already knew Molly, the industrial hygienist, because she led him here. William, another safety engineer, arrived a little later. He spent time interviewing with them one on one. Then the staff tested his knowledge and asked him about computers.

"If you get the job, the first thing we would like you to do is computerize all our sampling data. Everything is on paper. Nothing is electronic and it's hard to generate reports. Are you familiar with the Microsoft Office suite of products?"

"Yes. I've used all of the products. I'm strongest with PowerPoint and Word. Less with Excel and Access though I have created small databases for reports. Data entry should be easy."

"Can you demonstrate for us?"

"Sure. I've had formal typing classes and can type as fast as you can speak."

"Try typing this page," Aaron said, handing him a document.

Adam's fingers flew over the keyboard. It sounded like machine gunfire.

They all laughed. "Wow. You do know how to type."

"He also knew about the equipment we have on-site and recognized some of the hazards as we walked through the shop," Molly said. "Not bad."

"The final hiring decision will be made by Phil. He's the boss, but he's not here right now. We also have other interviews to conduct."

"I understand. Thank you for your time and for allowing me to speak with you today."

Molly escorted Adam back to the guard gate, turning in his visitor's badge.

"I hope I get a chance to work with you. Thank you."

"You never know. Good luck."

# # #

Adam was in the middle of a weeklong sampling job with five others. They had returned from eating dinner. Adam finished giving their full-face respirators a deep clean. It had been raining all day and they needed extra care. Parts were lying around the room drying when the hotel phone rang.

(It's nine at night. Who is calling the hotel room?) Sitting on the edge of the bed in his underwear, he picked up the phone.

"Hello, this is Adam."

"Hello Adam, this is Phil from Bell Helicopter. I'm sorry I missed your interview. I hope you don't mind me calling you so late?"

"Not at all. Anytime is great. How did you even know to find me at this hotel?"

"Just a little bit of tracking. Not hard. I wanted to know if you are still interested in the job?"

"Yes. Absolutely."

"The benefits are amazing. You would start out with three weeks of vacation, many holidays off, and a matching 401k plan to start. The pay is not that great but it goes up quickly. The benefits and experience more than compensate for the initial low pay."

Phil continued to discuss pay, benefits, and more job duties, and it all sounded incredible to Adam. But income still didn't matter. It was all about getting the job.

"Adam. Do you want the job?"

"Yes. I would love to work with your team at Bell Helicopter."

"Alright then. We will be getting with you at a more decent hour and schedule a start day. There will be a new hire orientation first but you got yourself a job."

"Thank you. I'm really excited to be part of the team."

"Have a good night, Adam. We will be seeing you soon."

Adam hung up the phone and fell backward on the bed. Putting hands to his forehead, saying out loud. "What the hell just happened? It happened again. A perfect job. First, an interview and job offer in an airport. Then sitting in my underwear on a hotel bed. That shit doesn't just happen."

Adam informed his co-workers the next day at the job site. They were stunned and repeatedly asked how the hell he managed to get that job.

Adam had intentionally not said anything about the job to his co-workers. He needed this job and did not want more competition than necessary. It worked. He had landed the position of a lifetime.

CHAPTER 35 – STARTER HOME

Adam asked "You still glad you decided to move in with me and get out of that town?"

"Definitely. The things to do never end. The people are so friendly. The waiters at the restaurant even smile at you. Is there something you like best about me being here?" Tara asked.

Adam laughed. "Besides the sex?"

"Yes, besides the sex."

"I like you just being you. We were good friends before moving in together. We know everything about each other, no secrets. You know about my crazy little world and are ok with it. I love you for all that. Just being you. It's why I asked you to marry me. We were meant to be together. You feel it, too."

"Yes. I feel it, too. Even when we were teenagers, I felt it."

"I guess we are turning into a kind of family. Moving in together. About to be married and now looking at buying a house. I still think it will end up being that one with the angry renters. You know, the one where the owner could not sell because of them and then suddenly, they changed when we toured the house. It just opened for us on the spot. The price is great. Probably due to the difficult renters and two sets of train tracks behind the house. That will be some constant noise, but it's a starter home. Got to start somewhere. By the way, how is massage school going?"

"I like it. It's really detailed. Texas requirements are strict but I've gotten in with the best school in the area. The other students are great. They really help each other out and I'm becoming friends with one of them. Seems we are always working together when practicing."

"Speaking of friends. I got a call today from someone I knew in college. A guy named Jeremy. He was in the gang I hung around drinking. Turns out he and his wife live in the area. About 30 minutes away. They want to meet up for dinner or something. How about this weekend?"

"Sounds fine."

# # #

Adam walked through the machine shop, past the tanks of cyanide and heat treat furnaces. It had all become routine after being in the job for 10 years. He had been in all the facilities. Crawled through the tunnels beneath buildings identifying confined spaces. Entered every restroom testing the water for lead. Made it onto every roof investigating air handline units. Bell Helicopter had become just as much home as the house he and Tara purchased.

(I never thought I could feel this comfortable working in a corporate environment across three shifts for such a complex company. So many hazards we've mitigated. And here, I can use my crazy little world to help. To feel something is wrong and fix it before something happens.)

Other people just walked. Adam moved with his senses open. Feeling his surroundings. Feeling for something out of place.

(*Whoa*) Adam stopped in the middle of the aisle next to the heat treat carburizers. He looked around. (*Somethings wrong.*) He opened his senses more and felt the air and heat from the furnaces. He felt electricity. A lot of it to his right. There is no one there. Everything looks normal. The carburizers are working fine. Adam moved closer.

(*It's here.*) He glanced around. No one is watching him. He held his hand near the electrical outlet on the pole next to the aisle. Electricity. Too much. Something is very wrong here. Adam stood there moving his hand around the outlet. Feeling it. (*Something is wrong with this outlet. I need to find an electrician.)*

Adam began his search, not moving far from the pole. First, he had to make sure no one touched it. (*There. The supervisor for the electrical contractors doing work in the area.)* "Excuse me. You're the boss for the electrical contractors doing the work here, right?"

"Yes. I'm Scott."

"I'm Adam. I work in the Safety Department. I think we have met once or twice. If you have a minute, could you look at something for me? It's right here and will only take a moment."

"Sure."

"It's this outlet on the pole. Is there something wrong with it?"

Scott reached out to touch the outlet.

"No. Stop. Don't touch it. Can you tell me if something is wrong here without touching it?"

"Everything looks normal, from what I can tell. It hasn't been disturbed. Not even opened. Nothing is wrong here."

"I'm sorry, but something is wrong here. Can you get your guys to check it out without touching this outlet?"

Scott agreed reluctantly. He was a contractor and Adam worked in the corporate Safety Department. Best if he took a little time to appease him.

Adam was waiting by the pole as Scott returned. "There is a problem. My guys wired that outlet to the wrong busbar and there is a whole lot of power going into that outlet. You couldn't tell it from the outside of the box because the work was done way in the back. It could have killed someone. But there were no signs of a problem. So, how did you know?"

"Just got lucky, I guess."

"No. I need to know how you knew. I need to make sure I can see the signs and that this never happens again. What gave it away? How did you know?"

Adam was caught, and he couldn't blow it off. Scott was forcing him to answer.

"I have to be honest with you. I didn't see a problem. I felt it. It's a kind of weirdness about me. Feeling electricity. Knowing when things might be wrong sometimes. I wish I could help you identify these kinds of problems but it's just a strange thing I do."

Scott shook his head as if he had heard about people doing strange things like this before. It wasn't the answer he wanted but it was the only one he got, and he accepted it. "I understand. We'll get it fixed."

"Thanks. Do you mind if I come to you for small issues that I feel like this? Things I feel that might turn up something?"

"Ok, as long as it doesn't take up all my time. A few times here and there will be ok."

"I've got to go. Thanks, Scott. I really appreciate what you are doing," Adam said, walking away. (*He accepted it, and I can come to him for some minor electrical problems. Get them fixed on the side. He didn't run away.*)

Adam arrived home after work and told Tara about what happened with the electrical outlet as they stood in the backyard. He told her everything. She didn't understand it all but accepted it. No secrets.

"That's crazy. I'm glad no one was hurt," Tara said.

"Now there is one other person out there that knows about the weirdness that is me."

"Do you mind if I play with your weirdness a little?"

"You sexy thing. You want to play with my...weirdness."

"No, not sex. Later maybe. I was looking at the clouds and they were really moving. It would be amazing to see a tornado form. Do you think you could do something like that? Make a tornado form."

"I don't know. I could ask." Adam looked up at the clouds. They have been his friends for a long time, and he liked talking to them. "Do you mind forming some tornadoes so my wife could see? Nothing harmful. Thank you if you choose to do it. Whether you do or not, I'll always love you and thank you for being there."

"There. The clouds are spinning. Is that a tornado forming?" Tara asked.

"Yes. That is a tornado forming."

"Another one over there. And there."

As they watched, five tornadoes began forming all around their house. Two dipped closer to the ground. Tara ran in and turned on the television. It confirmed five tornadoes are forming right around them. They moved back inside to continue watching the news. One tornado took off some shingles from a nearby Baptist college. Another snapped a single tree-top then vanished. Nothing harmful.

Tara looked at Adam as he shrugged. At least he could share it with her. Even if she didn't understand. No one did.

(It's always going to be like this. A good life with this shadowy path spiraling around it. But it worked out so well today at work. Maybe I should use it more. Not be afraid to do whatever I want with it.)

CHAPTER 36 – STRESS

Adam said, "It's so much work. I was hired to do sampling as an industrial hygienist across the three work shifts. I expected job duties to expand the longer I worked at the company but I did not expect this much work. Then becoming the respirator, hearing conservation, and confined space program administrator. Helping conduct weekly new hire training. Learning to create web pages and becoming the webmaster for the Environmental, Health, and Safety Department. Creating weekly newsletters to put on the website. Getting all 35,000 MSDS online not only for employees but also for customers around the world. Then becoming the EHS department's ISO 9001 self-auditor, ensuring all our policies and procedures stay current. Now enrolled in the Six Sigma Black Belt program. I'm doing all that and now I'm dedicated to the Composite Center where I have a new boss. I have two bosses now. I think it's driving me to drink."

Jeremy said, "Nope. Remember that you were drinking when we got back together here in the DFW area. How many years has it been now? Ten? Fifteen years? Each of us drinks a minimum of a case of beer every weekend. So Nah. You were drinking plenty before."

"You're right. It's nice having a best friend to drink with and complain about work. I really look forward to these weekends when I'm not on call. How are things between you and Carol?"

"Not good. Carol named her new car Freedom. That tells me she feels trapped and wants out of the marriage. I'm a meat and potatoes kind of guy and she is more exotic. Wanting to stay in college forever learning. Traveling the world is part of that learning experience but my job as an aircraft mechanic is limiting. I get two weeks of vacation that I must take during the summer plant shutdown. I don't even get to choose when to take a vacation. The money is great but I'm stuck going between work and home. She wants to get out and travel."

"I'm sorry to hear that. If there is anything I can do to help, let me know."

"I don't think there is anything anybody can do to help. I've suggested marriage counseling but Carol is not interested. She's just looking for a way out. At least we never had children."

"Children. Yeah. It's finally sinking in with Tara that she can't have children. Something her mother took caused Tara to have cancer lesions that had to be scraped off during her teenage years. The scar tissue won't allow cells to attach and the latest round of in-vitro tries failed. I knew we would not have children long ago but she held out hope. This last round, the doctor was really blunt with her, and it's finally sinking in that it's never going to happen."

"Life sucks."

"I don't know about it sucking but it sure can get messy."

# # #

"Adam. Textron Corporate has noticed the great work you did taking the MSDSs global. Not only for Bell Helicopter but you also helped all the other divisions go global. So they would like you to become part of the Textron Corporate safety team part-time. You would spend 50% of your time with your current duties, then the other 50% of the time working for Textron Corporate. It's a great opportunity and would look great on a resume. There would also be some international travel," Phil said.

"Would there be any reduction at all in my current duties because I'm doing a lot right now? I don't think I could do everything I'm doing now in 50% of the time."

"We should be able to move a few things to other people. Like the ISO 9001 auditing, local MSDSs, webmaster duties, and such. You would have to train them but those duties would not be on you. You would still have me as your EHS boss and you would still have your boss at the Composite Center. This would add a third boss at Textron

Corporate, and you will have to keep track of hours charged per contract worked."

"It would be a great experience. I'd like to do it as long as someone could take over some of these jobs I'm currently doing."

"Great. I'll get things started with Textron Corporate. You already know everyone there and at all the different divisions since you have been helping them all along. It's a continuation of what you have been doing anyway, but now it's going to be official."

"Sounds great," Adam said.

Adam worked an hour over tidying up a few things before the weekend. It was dusk as he was driving home. Rush hour on these backroads was over. He was stopped at a red light letting the traffic cross with the green light. (*I wonder if anyone will take over some of my duties. No one volunteers to do extra work. I feel that I'm going to be doing this additional training so others will take these jobs but nothing will change.*)

There was a flash in Adam's mind as he watched traffic cross in front of him. Images of a wreck. Him being rear-ended. The images were immediate and overwhelmed everything else.

(NOW)

Adam learned not to panic when fighting entities. He knew not to panic when responding to emergencies at work. Adam didn't panic. He reacted by throwing the car's 5-speed manual transmission into neutral. Removed his foot from the brake and leaned back fully into the seat, ensuring his head was on the headrest. Images of drunk people surviving better in wrecks flashed in his mind. He let his body go completely limp as he was hit from behind.

Adam knew he had been rear-ended but didn't know how bad. He was confused, trying to figure out how to get out of the car. The driver's seat had broken from the car frame and was thrown into the back seat with Adam. He was trying to maneuver his way out from the back of the car. Finally, he made it out and checked himself. Nothing broken. Not a scratch, but he couldn't think ahead more than a few seconds. He was stunned.

His safety training took over. No thinking. Check the other person who was sitting on the side of the road. No blood or apparent injuries. Other cars stopped and people were checking on them. Adam started documenting. It's what he did on all incidents and emergencies at work. Document everything.

"Are you ok?" A lady passing in front of him when he was rear-ended had stopped. She was shaking.

Adam still couldn't think. There were no physical injuries so he said, "Yes. I'm ok."

"Oh my God. I'm shaking. I'm so sorry that the car hit you but it would have broadsided us and probably killed my daughter sitting in the passenger seat if you were not there. I can't believe she was almost killed."

"I'm glad you are ok. Everything is ok."

"I'll be a witness. I saw everything." She gave Adam her information and stepped back as the police arrived.

The police documented information from Adam and witnesses; however, the other driver could not speak English. The police also told Adam he appeared drunk, it wasn't his car, and he did not have a driver's license. He was being taken to a hospital.

"Are you injured? Do you need to go to the hospital?" the police asked Adam.

Adam still could not think. He could only answer basic questions. "I'm not injured. I don't need to go to a hospital."

Adam stood there with a blank expression on his face.

"Can your car be driven?"

"No. There is no driver's seat, and the front wheels are bent. In addition, the frame may be bent."

"Do you need us to call you a tow truck?"

"Yes. I need a tow truck."

"Is there someone you can call to pick you up?"

"Yes. I can call someone to pick me up." Tara was out of town for the weekend so Adam called Jeremy. He was 30 minutes away but would be there as soon as he could.

Two tow trucks arrived. One for each vehicle. The driver towing Adam's car gave him his card and said it would be stored at that address. Adam nodded.

The cars were towed away. The police left. Everything was finished. Adam was alone and confused, sitting on the side of the road. He thinks he called someone to pick him up. He would sit here and wait. Dazed. Not sure what just happened. He documented everything, but he couldn't remember what he wrote. He did not know what to do without someone telling him. Jeremy arrived. He got Adam into his car and drove him home.

Adam was home safe. Tara will be back tomorrow. All he needed to do was sleep. (*I'm glad Jeremy picked me up. He was there when I needed him. I love him. He's a good person. It's the weekend. I don't have to work tomorrow. We are going to need a new car.*) Some thought was returning as Adam fell asleep. His final thoughts were of the moments before the wreck. (*I came out of that wreck without a scratch. I knew I was about to be rear-ended. That voice was yelling, 'now!' How did I escape that without a scratch?*)

# # #

"It's nice having a new car that gets great gas mileage," Tara said. "This two-door Toyota Corolla is going to work out just fine."

"That is great. It always comes down to practical when we buy big-ticket items. It's nice to dream and fantasize about things but we are practical. I guess that is why that lady at work called me an invisible realist," Adam said. "What's really nice is having enough money saved up to pay for it in full. You know how I hate debt. We sent a lot of extra money for the monthly mortgage payments on the house and keeping the credit card paid off. I'm still glad we got rid of all your plastic cards when we got married and only kept the one main card."

"I'm also glad we only kept one card. Another thing. You can get back to your pottery at Lockheed Martin's Recreational Area now that we have a second car. You can take the old green truck and go there after work again."

"Yeah, that will be nice. I've been under a lot of stress at work and doing pottery helps relax me. I think that they have missed me since I've turned into their Raku guy. They like how I fire things in the Raku kiln and probably want to do more. Did I tell you that I think that they are going to elect me President of the pottery studio?"

"No, you didn't tell me. So why do you think that?"

"Several of the longtime members have mentioned it to me. They like me taking meeting notes as Secretary and including them in the monthly newsletter. They like that I'm not part of a clique and treat everyone equally. Plus, they know I work and it's like every other organization. 10% work, 80% just ride along, and the other 10% cause problems. It's the same in the North Texas Section American Industrial Hygiene Association. The NTS-AIHA. I'm doing those newsletters and being the Secretary writing minutes. 10%-80%-10%."

"Don't be surprised if that professional organization asks you to be president as well. That's how it happens. They find someone who works and end up just giving them more."

"You're probably right. Guess we will find out."

CHAPTER 37 – FALLING

Adam said "I need to sit in the sun for a minute. This hangover is too much. I need a minute."

"Alright, sit here. We are going to be in the chainmail booth over there. We'll be back in a bit," Jeremy said.

Adam sat on the bench in full sunlight. Closed his eyes and looked up to the sun. Feeling the sun's energy coming into him. Filling him and melting away the hangover.

"We're back. How do you feel?" Tara asked.

"Fine. The hangover is gone."

"What? Just like that? Like the sun is recharging your batteries or something?" Carol asked.

"Just like that. Recharging batteries. I'm fine now. Let's go see the mud show. I think it's about time for it to start," Adam said. So there. He said it out loud. Just a hint of his crazy little world. He still had not told his best friend and drinking buddy Jeremy. He couldn't. It was crazy. He was crazy and didn't want to lose his friend. He would not understand. Perhaps it was age, stress or something worse like arrogance. Adam had started relying on this crazy side. He was depending on it now. He was using it so often others began to notice.

"I would love to be able to do that and get rid of the hangover. But I'll just have to live with mine. Anyway, on to the mud show," Jeremy said. The mud show was always a favorite at the Texas Renaissance Festival. The place was huge. You had to plan out the weekend carefully. Still, there was no way to see or do everything in just a weekend. However, they had to hurry as rain was forecast for late afternoon.

The mud show was great. So were the chariot races and tavern musicians. So many people in beautiful costumes. Adam wore a more modern outfit related to the steampunk universe. Tara, Jeremy, and Carol wore more traditional renaissance clothing, with Carol's being the most elaborate. She had a full-length red velvet dress outlined in gold. She could have been in the Royal Court with the Queen.

The last day of the faire was winding down and rain clouds began to gather as they headed to the front gate to leave. It was a great weekend, but Adam noticed how Jeremy and Carol acted. He could tell Jeremy still loved Carol and wanted to be with her. However, Carol wanted something else. She tried to talk with anyone else but him, it seemed. She would tell complete strangers about her dreams to go back to college and travel the world studying. Constantly traveling and not being tied to anything. Jeremy had mentioned this to Adam before but this was the first time he saw it playing out.

It started sprinkling rain as soon as they made it through the exit. Tara and Jeremy lead the way with Adam and Carol falling behind.

"Oh no. The rain is going to ruin my dress. We have a long way to the car, and the ground will get muddy. My dress is going to be ruined," Carol said. She was getting distraught. Tara and Jeremy were far enough away they did not hear but Adam was right beside her. She was in a panic and he could help. Others had seen hints of his crazy little world and not run away. Maybe she would not run either.

Carol had stopped walking. Adam stopped as well. "Wait. I might be able to help."

"How?" Carol asked.

Adam looked up at the clouds and said, "It's going to stop raining right now." The rain stopped the moment Adam finished the sentence. Adam continued looking up. Talking to his friends. (*The rain stopped. They are listening. Alright. Let's go.*)

"The rain is going to hold off until you can get into the car. Once you are safe in the car, it will start raining again, and it will pour rain all the way to the hotel. When we pull into the hotel parking lot, the rain will stop long enough for you to get out and to your room.

Safe from the rain. Then it will start pouring again and will pour all night long."

Carol just looked at Adam like he was crazy.

"Come on. The rain has stopped. Let's get to the car before it starts up again," Adam said. He did not need to say it twice. They walked as fast as possible to the car catching up with Jeremy and Tara.

"What's the rush?" Jeremy asked.

"I've got to keep this dress out of the rain or it will be ruined. Got to get to the car quick," Carol said.

The rain held off until they shut the car doors. Then it started raining again. Carol's dress was safely out of the shower, and they talked about how lucky it was the rain held off until they got in the car. During the hour back to the hotel, the talk continued about what they had done. The rain continued the entire way back.

The rain stopped as the car turned into the hotel parking lot. However, the moment they stepped under the hotel covering, it started raining harder than before. They made their way to their rooms and got changed. Adam answered the knock at his door. It was Carol. He stepped outside and pulled the door slightly closed behind him.

"How did you know that was going to happen? What just happened? How did you do that? The rain started and stopped just like you said."

Adam was taking a risk. He had been doing things to help himself. Many items for personal gain. He had forgotten about the arrogance trap and was falling into it again.

"I've tried not to say anything about some of the craziness in my life. But sometimes I talk to the weather and it responds. It makes me feel crazy, but it happens. You just saw it happen. I don't know how to explain it. The sky is my friend and I talk to it like a friend. It responds like a friend. I hope you don't think I'm too crazy," Adam said.

"I think there is a lot in the world we don't understand. That's one of the reasons I want to travel so much and learn. There is so much out there waiting to be discovered. It doesn't matter in the end. I'm just glad my dress did not get ruined."

"Alright. Where do you and Jeremy want to eat tonight?"

"Somewhere close because this rain does not look like it's going to let up anytime soon."

The rain did not let up. It poured all night long and created a significant flooding event. They discovered many of the sideroads were underwater as they checked out of the hotel and headed back home. It was a weekend to remember.

# # #

Adam was sitting in his backyard drinking alone. He knew drinking alone was a bad sign but he was stressed. Adam didn't want to be around anyone. He just needed to think about everything happening in his life. He felt trapped and the job was too much work. Yet, the pay and benefits kept him there. His co-workers were the best in the entire DFW area. Also becoming presidents of their respective professional organizations. The Occupational Health and Safety Administration, OSHA, even recognized them as professionals caring for the safety of the employees. They were on a first-name basis with OSHA staff not because of problems at the company but because they hosted annual conferences with OSHA. The meetings included safety professionals throughout North Texas. Adam had just helped coordinate the latest conference as he was now the President of the NTS-AIHA.

(I don't know how anybody can keep up with all this work. I'm relying heavily on my strange abilities and barely keeping up. President of this professional organization. President of the pottery studio. 50% of my time is dedicated to Textron, and the other 50% to my other two bosses at Bell Helicopter. I thought other staff would take over some of my job duties but it's not really working out. I've been training them for a while now but they are not catching on. The environmental person I've been preparing to take over the ISO 9001 auditing backed out so it's just me again. It's too much. I need a change, but I can't leave.

At least the house is paid for. Throwing every bit of extra money at the mortgage allowed us to pay it off. We no longer have any outstanding debt other than a credit card, so why do I feel so trapped. Maybe I'm feeling depressed because Jeremy found out Carol saw someone else. Then the divorce. I'm trying to be there for him but I don't know what to do. He's drinking more than ever and it's only making things worse. I love him and want to help. Wait. Yes. I do love him. I'd have sex with him if it could make things better but it won't. I only realize now, after all these years, that I love the guy.) Adam looked at the beer in his hand.

(And here I am. Doing the same thing. Drinking and making things worse. Not knowing what to do.)

The phone rang.

"Hello."

"Hey, Adam. It's Jeremy. Just feeling a bit down and would like a friend around. Can you come over?"

"Sure. I'll be right over." Adam got in his car and drove to Jeremy's house.

Jeremy opened the door. "Come on in. You want a beer?"

"Sure."

Jeremy went to the kitchen and handed Adam a beer. Then, he sat on the couch next to Adam.

"You want to talk about anything?" Adam asked.

"Not really. Just did not want to be alone. I'll turn on the TV for background noise but I'm not really interested in watching anything."

"Alright," Adam said.

Adam felt a bit uncomfortable. Just sitting there next to Jeremy, not saying a word with someone he just realized he loved more than a friend.

They were on their fourth beer when it happened. Adam let himself feel this love. It was different than what he felt with Tara. Tara's love was forever. They were a part of each other and always would be. This, however, was passionate. Physical. He could only relate it to the movies where he saw people do crazy things for love. He never understood that until now. It overwhelmed him. He reached up and touched Jeremy's curly black hair. He just looked at it, moving through his fingers. He felt a kind of love where nothing else existed.

It lasted three seconds before Jeremy noticed and jumped up.

"I'm ok now. I think you should leave. Everything is fine. I just need some time to myself," Jeremy said without looking at Adam.

Adam felt it coming from Jeremy. Disgust.

(Shit. I've screwed everything up.) "Alright. I'm heading out. Hope you get to feeling better," Adam said, heading out the front door. Jeremy never looked at him.

It was the longest 30-minute drive home.

(I've really messed things up now. How can love mess things up? I'm so confused. The love I feel for Tara is deep and permanent. This love for Jeremy was immediate and overwhelming, like in the movies. Is this what that crazy passionate love is really like? It's scary and wonderful at the same time. Three seconds is all I will ever feel of that kind of love.) Adam's eyes filled with tears. He may have lost his longtime best friend because of love. It was something ordinary people feel all the time, but he was only allowed to touch it for three seconds. Long enough for him to feel what he was missing. (*Three seconds. Three seconds for a lifetime.*)

He drove home feeling more alone than ever. That he was different from everyone else. He felt things differently than everyone else. He felt the disgust from Jeremy and knew it was real. He couldn't understand why people stopped themselves from loving others. It didn't make sense to him. The world didn't make sense to him.

CHAPTER 38 – SOUL SHATTER

Everything looked fine on the surface. However, Adam was tearing apart. The stress at work was too much. Then there was Jeremy. His best friend that he loved. His best friend only saw disgust when he looked at Adam. Adam felt it every time he saw him. Jeremy would call when he needed help and Adam was there. But this help only went one way. When Adam needed help, Jeremy would not be available. When Adam and Tara asked Jeremy to go out with them to dinner he would initially say yes. Then back out at the last minute, saying he had forgotten to do laundry or something else equally trivial. They would make plans with Jeremy and then with others knowing he would back out. It happened without fail throughout the past year. Something had to be done.

Adam was riding in the passenger seat with Jeremy driving. He was feeling depressed again and just needed to be around someone. Adam agreed to hang around but it was tearing him apart.

"Jeremy. There is a problem between us. You have been my best friend for a very long time. I love you, but I can't take it anymore. When you look at me, all I'm seeing in your face is disgust."

Jeremy turned and looked at him. Adam saw it in his face and felt the emotion flowing from him. Truth. It was true. Jeremy did not need to say anything. It was out in the open. He felt disgusted with Adam.

"I can't do this anymore, Jeremy. I've been there for you whenever you needed anything and I've seen the disgust on your face. Whenever I need something you are not available. You back out at the last minute when we ask you out. We can't be friends anymore. You need to be away from me and move on with your life. I need the same thing."

"I think it's for the best," Jeremy said.

"Take me back home."

Adam's eyes filled with tears as they pulled into his driveway. "This is it, Jeremy. We need to cut this friendship off sharp. I don't want to see or hear from you again."

"It's the right thing to do."

"Goodbye, Jeremy."

"Goodbye, Adam."

Adam did not turn to see him drive away. He just walked into the house and put his head in Tara's lap and began to cry. She was waiting for him on the couch because Adam told her what he was about to do. Even if she knew what to say Adam could not hear her. His soul was shattering.

Adam saw it in his mind and felt it in his heart. His soul breaks apart like pieces of a puzzle. First, love and hope are breaking away. Then joy, caring, hate, anger, laughter, and even the ability to smile fall away. Pieces of him flying out into nothingness. All emotions have gone forever. There was almost nothing left. Only this shell of flesh.

His head was lying on Tara's lap. She was still here but love had broken away. It was gone. He did not feel love anymore. Not for Tara. Not for anyone. The stress from work and now this. It was too much. Feelings from that first round of suicidal depression when he was a teenager returned. He wanted to die.

(*God hates me. I'm wrong. Jeremy will be better now that I'm out of his life. Everyone would be better if I was out of their life. I'm not like everybody else. I'm the thing wrong with the world. I'm a mistake. I want to go home. Home is not here. Not anywhere is this existence. What's wrong with me? I need to kill myself and get out of here. It will be better for everyone. Tara will be sad if I kill myself. How do I kill myself and not make her sad?*)

That was Adam's last thought as he cried himself to sleep. How can he kill himself and not make her sad? It was his first thought upon waking. This was his single thought during every still moment of the day. When driving. How can he kill himself and not make her sad? When eating or walking between buildings at work. When he was peeing. This thought was there for every moment his mind was still. He was suicidal but this fingernail of thought kept him alive. He could not figure out how to kill himself so Tara would not be sad. Not devastated. Not in a financial bind. The impact of his death on his parents, brother and sisters did not matter. Nothing else mattered. Adam did not want her to be sad, and it was the only reason he was not dead yet.

Days went by, then weeks. The suicidal thoughts never stopped and no one noticed. Adam had become a master of deception by hiding the odd things that would happen around him. He had learned how to manipulate and push people. To redirect their attention when Adam felt them getting too close to the truth. He had lived his life hiding a significant part of himself. This was just another thing to hide, and Adam did it well. No one noticed he was suicidal. Not family. Not co-workers. He hid it so well that Adam noticed everyone really liked him this way. (*They really like me, suicidal.*)

At this point, all the odd coincidences and strange happenings in Adam's life began to go dark. He felt he was under constant attack from both dark entities and reality. He felt existence turn against him. Even the evening news turned negative with stories of strangers burning a gay boy then leaving him to die tied to a fence post. Then weeks of news stories showing a church protesting with signs of God hates fags. Existence was trying to destroy that tiny sliver of a fingernail holding onto life. That little bit that did not want to make Tara sad. It was all that was left of what Adam used to be.

He wanted to protect that fingernail of life but how to do it when existence itself wants you dead. He could only think of one thing to do. He built a protective cage in his mind. He put a small image of himself in it. The part that did not want to make Tara sad. The only part of him that was left. It needed to be protected and he knew of no other way to do it. So Adam locked it away in a cage made of bars. The darkness is surrounding him, wanting to destroy him. He only knew the cell was there because of the beam of light shining on it; otherwise, there was only darkness.

Adam instinctively knew, perhaps through his safety training, that you should always have an exit in mind. So when he created the cage, he also created a lock that would let him out if the right conditions were met. The key was a phrase. Are you ok? That was it. Three words. If anyone asked if he was ok, he could talk about what happened. Anyone at all could ask. Then he could open that cage and be free again.

But Adam was a master of deception. He was very good at what he was doing, and no one noticed. No one was asking if he was ok. Not family. Not friends. Not co-workers. They all liked him like this. Suicidal.

Every day was an eternity. Every still moment filled with thoughts of suicide. Days turned into weeks which began turning into months. Every night Adam cried himself to sleep wanting to die. It was the first thing he thought upon waking. Every day was an eternity, and the image of himself in the cage was dying. The days were the same and blurred together. Three months had gone by and his appearance in the cell was a dead body on the ground. Still caged.

"Adam. You know how we have been talking about moving back to our hometown where both our families still live. That we may need to be there one day to help them as they get older."

"Yes. It needs to happen because you don't make enough money to support yourself here if something happens to me. Even with the house paid off. There you would have family around to help."

"Well, my father decided to get married to one of his friends he has known all his life. Her husband died some years ago, and since my mom died they both decided it was time. So he is going to move in with her once they get married. He said he would give us his house and all the contents free if we would move back."

"What? A house fully furnished? Free?"

"Yes, but he wants an answer soon. We need to decide quickly."

"I say yes but I have to give some notice at work. It will take a lot of time to get ready to move. Your dad is like a hoarder. There are rooms with only a small path to walk through. I mean, there are empty two-liter soda bottles just piled up and used pantyhose that might be useful for something someday."

"We can start going in on weekends to clean."

"It's going to take months. I could give work a six-month notice so they have plenty of time to train people to do my job. They are not taking it seriously now but they would have to do something if they want a transfer of knowledge. You think your dad would be ok with us saying yes, using weekends to clean, then moving back in a few months?"

"Yes. Dad is ok with that. I said something along those lines when he brought it up."

"Alright then. I'll write up something and give my boss a six-month notice."

(*You win existence. You want me dead. Tara can move back home and be around family. She won't be so sad around family. You win. I'll kill myself as soon as the papers are signed.*)

Adam turned in his six-month notice of resignation the next workday. They couldn't believe he was giving them so much advance notice. He explained moving back to their hometown and how he wanted to provide them with plenty of time to transfer his knowledge to others. They would be sad to see him go but they understood moving back to be with family. All that was left to do was start working on the new house and sign those papers, transferring ownership. That would be the end. The end of Adam.

CHAPTER 39 – INTERVENTION

Every day was an eternity, although Adam was no longer crying himself to sleep. It was done. He would kill himself once those papers were signed. Every still moment was filled with thoughts of suicide, only now the part about making her sad was removed. Now it was how to do it. He did not want to borrow someone's gun and make them feel bad. Still, there were so many other ways, and using his knowledge of poisons was high on his list.

"Adam. Can you get me a report for all sampling done for the past year in department 55?" his boss asked.

"Here it is. I've already printed it," Adam said, handing it over.

"Perfect. Thanks."

(He's going to want the safety statistics updated on the website today as well. Good thing I've already done it.)

"Could you also make sure to update the safety statistics on the website as soon as we get out of this meeting? I have another meeting this afternoon and would like to show them the current data."

"It's already done. Everything is updated."

"Excellent."

Adam knew what they wanted and was delivering it when asked. Perhaps it was advanced anticipation or foresight, but he was printing reports before people asked. Adam had let his hidden abilities take over. He knew when there was a problem with a machine before the employee told their supervisor. Adam would drive to work on weekends knowing when and where they needed a confined space permit issued. He would be there when they called. It was too much work for one person but he was keeping up. Not only keeping up but excelling. He figured he did not need to hide his crazy little world much anymore. He would be dead soon and it wouldn't matter.

"One more thing before we end the meeting. I will be taking on a full-time position with Textron Corporate. Your new boss will be Peter Simpkins. He's been making himself known within the Textron family and they decided he would be a good fit in this position. The changeover will happen in a couple of weeks."

Every day was an eternity for Adam. Eventually, two weeks went by and the new boss arrived. Adam knew instantly the moment he met Peter Simpkins. Mr. Simpkins had new ideas he would want to implement. New bosses always had new ideas. Until then, it would be business as usual.

Again, the days turned to weeks then into months. Every day is an eternity. Every still thought on suicide. The dead body in the cage in Adam's mind had turned to dust and blown away. There was an empty cage in a beam of light surrounded by darkness. That is until the cell rusted and disintegrated then blew away. Then, there was nothing left except a beam of light showing that something used to be there.

Throughout the six months, since his soul shattered, Adam had been waiting for someone to ask if he was ok. That was all he needed. For someone to ask. Are you ok? It never happened. He was too good at what he was doing. He had been working more than ever. Bringing work home and logging in remotely. Working from home late at night and on weekends. Anything to keep his mind busy and off suicide. He had three more months left then it would be over. Adam did not know it yet but people noticed.

When Adam left work driving his old green truck, it was Friday rush hour. The truck was a 5-speed manual transmission like all their automobiles. Simple to work on since there were no electronics. It was a drive home like any other for the past six months. A still mind and thoughts of suicide. Driving the back road through the river bottom. Plenty of traffic during rush hour on a Friday.

A small bridge crossed the river before the road took a left connecting to the main four lane street. Adam was just about to reach the bridge's center when he lost all steering control. His steering wheel spun freely. No tension, as if it was not connected to the truck. His truck drifted left into on-coming traffic.

(This is how I die.)

Adam opened and let go. Unfortunately, he had no steering control and had drifted into the middle of oncoming traffic. He was within feet of a head-on collision on a bridge over a river. He didn't have time to press the brake pedal before some force grabbed his truck. There was no turning of the wheels and driving back into the lane. Instead, his truck slid sideways against the tires into his own lane. The front wheels locked forward as the truck continued down the road. It was as if the truck was a toy and something simply put it back where it needed to be. His steering wheel was still spinning freely, but the front wheels remained straight. It was only now that Adam began slowly pressing on the brakes. The front tires somehow kept the truck in his own lane until Adam could reach the curve ahead. He let it drift off to the right shoulder as the road turned left. Then he came to a complete stop safely off the road.

(What the hell just happened? How did that happen? I'm not dead. Why am I not dead? I should be destroyed. That's not possible. I've had strange things happen all my life but not like this. This is something else. Why am I alive? Does something want me alive? Stop it. Focus. Handle the immediate first. Everything is ok. I'm off the road. Traffic is still moving. Why did I lose steering?)

Adam got out of the truck and crawled under the front end.

(The tie rods broke that control steering. I literally had no steering control. How did I get back into my own lane? How did the tires go straight so I could drift off the side of the road? Focus. I can't fix this. I need to call a tow truck. He can tow it to the house then I can figure out what to do from there.)

Adam called a towing service then called Tara. He got back in the truck and turned on the radio. It didn't matter if he ran down the battery now. The song playing was **Don't Give Up**.

(The song on the radio saying don't give up. A positive coincidence when everything has been negative for so long. Something wants me alive for some reason. I don't know why but there's nothing left of me. The part I was trying to protect died and blew away. Even the cage is gone. There is nothing left. Why save me now? Did that part I was trying to keep need to die? What was it I was trying to protect?)

The same song on the radio continued to play with lyrics singing that he still had friends. Adam, hearing this, began looking around at the world. (*There is something here that is still my friend. My friends are still here but I was abusing them. Like Jeremy was abusing me. I was doing so much for personal gain. Using this crazy side of me to keep up at work. To keep up with everything. Oh, God. Arrogance. It was all arrogance. I fell into that arrogance trap again and didn't notice. It was all me. I'm so sorry.*)

Adam looked around, grateful for finally realizing what had happened. The arrogance of it all, and he was genuinely sorry. The light is coming from the trees growing brighter. Everything started glowing like it had done that day when he was a teenager. When everything changed. He was seeing this other consciousness like it was his first time. He smiled. Grateful to still be alive. He would have to rebuild his life but now with no foundation to build upon. There was nothing left.

(*Wait. There is something left. The body and cage are gone, but the light beam is still there. It never left. I didn't notice it but I couldn't see anything without it. So I'll start rebuilding my life using that light. That will be my foundation.*)

The tow truck arrived sooner than expected and it wasn't long before Adam was back home. Adam looked at the old automobile one last time before going inside.

"I know everything worked out for the best but I'm never driving you again. Tara, I'm finally home."

"I'm glad you are alright. What you said on the phone when you called. That's crazy."

"It's unbelievable. I can tell people but no one is going to believe it. Something pushes my truck sideways against the tires. It's not possible, but it happened. There is something good that came out of it."

"What's that?"

"It's snapped me out of this depression I've been going through. That event was so extreme. So crazy that it jarred me enough. I think I can start putting myself back together."

"I'm happy something happened. I tried everything and there was nothing I could do."

"I know. I'm sorry. It was all too much. I got trapped and couldn't get out. There was nothing anybody could do. Whatever happened on that bridge was beyond human, and I guess that is what it took to snap me out of that depression. I don't know."

"What do you want to do with the truck?"

"Get rid of it. I'm never driving it again. It's ancient anyway and we could use something reliable now that we will be taking loads of furniture back to West Monroe."

"That's true. What kind of truck do you want?"

"We will need a truck with lots of hauling space, so I'm thinking something similar. Used. Single Cab. No electronics. Large bed for hauling stuff in the back. 5-speed manual transmission. We should look on the internet and find something in the Dallas, Fort Worth area. If we can't find something here, we will not find it anywhere. Right now, I want to stop. Just stop and talk."

"Ok. Let's talk."

"You know everything about me. About my crazy little world and how things happen. How I see things."

"I know. I knew it when we were teenagers. I knew it when we got married and it started sleeting. May first in Louisiana. Fine sleet covered the ground as you pulled into the parking lot. Everything was white. I thought you might take it as a bad sign and change your mind."

Adam grinned. "The sleet was so fine it sounded like cheering as I walked from the car to the church. So I took that as a good sign."

Tara smiled.

"Tara. I've told you everything. How there was so much stress at work. How I felt about Jeremy destroyed me, cutting off that friendship. I didn't tell you how suicidal I was these past six months. It was all I thought about but I think I'm ok now. I think I had fallen into that arrogance trap again. I've been relying on these odd abilities to help for years now. To know where there is going to be a problem before it happens. To print reports before asked. To ask the weather to do certain things to make my days easier. I was using all of it to help myself."

"I remember you always said you never wanted to use any of this for personal gain. How you felt it was wrong somehow."

"That's right. Except I was using it for personal gain and didn't notice. It was arrogance. Do you remember me telling you about fighting these entities long ago and how I had become arrogant, then one crushed me? Well. I created an image in my mind of my human self in a cage. It disintegrated and blew away. There is nothing left. At least I thought there was nothing left. But there was a beam of light. I'm going to use that light as a foundation. I know it doesn't make sense to you. It's my crazy little world and the way I do things."

"It's ok. I don't need to understand. It's you. It's ok."

"I love you for just being you."

"I love you, too."

"Work is still too much. They were supposed to transfer some of my responsibilities to other people but it's not working out. There are only three months left before I leave. They are not even considering hiring someone else to transfer this knowledge. In fact, they just fired several of the EHS staff to reduce costs. No way they are going to hire anyone to take my place. I don't know if I can handle being there three more months."

"You don't have to. It's like you told me once. We are financially secure. If you need to walk out of your job without notice, then walk out. The same goes for you too. We have a fully furnished house waiting for us. Next week, I'll get with my father and get all the papers signed. There will be nothing left holding us here. You can walk out anytime."

Adam smiled at her. "You're right. There isn't anything keeping us here. I was only hoping to transfer my knowledge to someone else because my co-workers are great. I don't want to put them in a bind but they will not hire anyone else. So when I leave, all that knowledge goes with me."

"What they do is not your problem. Do what you need to do for you."

"I think I will write several resignations letters. A one-month, one-week, and immediate resignation letter. I can keep all three of them with me, and if something happens, I can select which one is needed depending on what is happening. I'm also going to start cleaning out my office if I need to walk out immediately. Clean up my computer files as well. That way, there will be nothing more to do than walk out if it becomes necessary."

"Sounds good. Let's go out and get something to eat. I'll drive."

"You drive. That's an excellent idea."

Adam smiled as Tara drove. It was this sense of duty to the job holding him here. Nothing else. His dad, as a banker, had taught him at a young age the value of being debt-free. He sent every free bit of money as extra payment for their first car loan. Then extra money to pay on the house mortgage. Since then, they had saved enough money to pay for their automobiles in full. They even had enough saved now to pay for a used truck. They had no debt, and they were now given a fully furnished house. It needed a lot of work like a new roof and central AC/Heat but they could use money from selling their current home for repairs.

(*How does this happen to a person? I've been suicidal for six months and couldn't see all the positives. It felt the entire universe had turned against me. However, all these strange things about my life were helping me and I couldn't see them. Like that time someone cut my brake lines. I could still slow down by shifting to a lower gear. Guess whoever cut them didn't realize I had a five-speed manual transmission and could downshift. Guess not everyone likes me. Yeah. Like that other time, someone broke into the truck but didn't steal it. Cops thought that the person didn't know how to drive a stick. I was blinded to all the positives. This isn't normal? Why is all this happening? Is there some kind of plan being enacted that I don't know about? I guess it's back to my favorite saying. Take another step and keep moving forward.*)

CHAPTER 40 – WALKING OUT

Adam's mind had drifted. It was another one-hour-long weekly meeting. Boring. At least it was almost over. Adam's mind drifted to his new truck. He was wrong in thinking there would be plenty to choose from precisely as he wanted. Turns out there was only one in all of Dallas, Fort Worth. A used Toyota Tundra, single cab, bench seat, no electronic, eight-foot bed with a 5-speed manual transmission. He paid cash in full. It was paid for and perfect. It was reliable, with plenty of room in the back to haul furniture.

"There is one last thing to do before we end the meeting. Last year, Operations created a program giving out a Peer Recognition Award to those within their organization. Someone within Operations is nominated and it's voted on monthly by all the workers. It's for someone they recognize as going well above and beyond all expectations within Operations. A few months ago, someone in this department submitted a name from Environmental, Health, and Safety. No one expected it to go anywhere because we are not within the Operations department. Adam. Congratulations. The shop floor workers voted for you to receive their Peer Recognition Award," The Director of EHS said.

He pulled out a framed medal with brass plates on top and bottom identifying Adam. He showed everyone then handed it over to Adam as everyone clapped.

"Here are some of the things written that they recognized. You created the first intranet pages within the company. The first things you put out were our policies and procedures, which greatly helped Operations Managers and Supervisors. Soon after, every department realized the value of what you did and began doing the same. Then you began creating safety newsletters that included weekly statistics, which again helped operations management. Then the shop floor intranet kiosks were put in place so every employee had the same access. Then you put all the material safety data sheets online. Every employee could pull up material safety data sheets without requesting one. Then you helped create and computerize our Safety Training Guides. Operations management could now print and use these training materials during their meetings. This was above and beyond because you put critical information at everyone's fingertips."

The Director laughed. "I've had this on my desk for six weeks, and it kept getting put off. This is probably the only time this has ever happened. Where shop floor workers recognize someone outside their department and in the Safety Department. Normally everyone hates the Safety Department. This is amazing. Congratulations."

"Thanks. I can't believe it."

Co-workers congratulated him as the meeting ended. Adam couldn't believe what had happened. A person in the Safety Department received an award from Operations. That never happens.

(*This is the best thing I will ever receive in my life. This kind of award from a company this huge. They really like me.*) Then it hit him. (*I'm getting this award because of how I was during those suicidal months. They really liked me. Suicidal.*) It was bittersweet. He looked at the award again. It turned into another piece of paper in his mind. It was the best award he would ever receive, and it was during the darkest months of his life. (*I'm glad it was held at the Director's desk for six weeks. It would not have mattered if he had given it to me then. I can appreciate it at least a little now. Maybe one day I'll understand it more, but not now.*)

Adam sat at his desk, looking at the award. He had a severe problem. Adam couldn't appreciate it for what it represented. He was still trying to pull together the pieces of emotion that had gone flying off during that soul-shattering experience. Yet he could see pieces coming back together as time passed. Hope slid into place. Empathy slid into place. The ability to smile and even allow himself to feel anger slid back in place. Perhaps this award would help appreciation slide back in place. He could see it all coming back together. Pieces in the distance return to help him rebuild his life.

He could see all the pieces except one. There was a piece missing. Caring. He had lost the ability to care. He could empathize with someone but he did not care what happened in the end. He could hope someone would not get injured but he didn't care if they did.

(*I've lost the ability to care. I don't care if someone gets hurt. I don't care if someone lives or dies. I work in the Safety Department and I don't care anymore. This is a dangerous problem.*)

# # #

It was noon on a Thursday, and Peter had called for a half-day meeting. Everybody was to drop everything and attend. Something about taking the Safety Department in a new direction. He had ordered lunch for everyone so it wasn't all bad. Not yet.

It was time. Adam recalled a memory when he first learned of this new boss. Everything would be typical for a while, then he would implement new ideas. That changeover was happening now. Two hours into the meeting and Adam was becoming visibly agitated. He could feel it from his co-workers. They were noticing his agitation. Three hours in and he could not stay silent anymore.

Adam spoke. His voice is angry. "Let me get this straight. You have laid out your new plan. What each of us needs to do to implement these fantastic ideas. Each person is being given duties equal to a full-time job. Yet, there is to be no reduction in current responsibilities."

"We have to build on the foundation we have now. Yes. We have to maintain everything we are doing now and build up that."

"I was supposed to have gotten help with my responsibilities when I agreed to work for Textron 50% of my time. That never happened. I only work for Bell Helicopter 50% of my time, and now you want to throw additional work onto my lap. I was hoping there would be a transfer of knowledge before I left. That maybe someone would be hired to take my place but that isn't going to happen, is it?"

Adam could hear it. Gasps of breath. Mutters of astonishment in what he was saying.

"Don't worry. It's not that much. It will all work out. Trust me. It will be simple once you see how everything flows." Peter was calm and doing his best to explain. He continued outlining his plans. Adam had stopped listening.

(That's it. No more. I don't care about the impact on my co-workers when I walk out tomorrow. I've got that immediate resignation letter in my folder. After this meeting, I'll go back to my office and do some final cleaning out. There are only a few things left. No one will even notice. I'm out of here first thing tomorrow morning. A Friday. Perfect.)

Adam ignored everything except his drink for the remainder of the meeting. He made it obvious. His co-workers noticed and Adam didn't care.

Adam was the first one out the door as the meeting ended. A co-worker caught up with him and asked him, "Are you ok?"

"No."

"What's wrong?"

"You will find out tomorrow." Adam never looked at the person. Instead, he headed straight to his office and began cleaning out a few remaining items. It all fits within his computer case. Nothing out of the ordinary. (*Are you ok? It's too late to be asking that question.*)

An employee stopped Adam before he made it to the gate.

"I got some things I need to go over with you in the morning."

"That's not going to happen."

"Why?"

"I'm quitting first thing tomorrow morning. No notice."

"What? Have you talked about this with your wife?"

Adam shot him a determined look. "What has she got to do with anything? This is my decision. I've had enough, and I'm done."

"Ok. Don't get mad at me."

Adam continued quickly out the gate to his truck. He told Tara as soon as he got home. She understood. He could take as much time to himself as needed then help get the other house ready. They could also get a realtor and begin selling their current home.

The following day Adam was ready. He went to Peter's office as soon as he could.

"Hello, Peter. Do you have a minute?"

Adam sat down and pulled out an envelope. He handed it to Peter.

"I resign. Immediately."

"What?"

"I resign. Immediately. Right now. No two-week notice. Right now."

"Why?"

"I've had enough. I resign."

"Wait here. I need to get the Director."

Peter returned shortly with the Director of EHS.

"Peter said you were resigning. Is that true?"

"Yes. Immediately."

"Why?"

"I'm done."

"Why don't you take the day off? Think about it over the weekend. Don't make a rash decision you might regret later. Think about it."

"No. I've made my decision. It's not changing. I resign. Now. Peter has my resignation letter. I don't care if leaving destroys this career path. I'm done with it." It was true. Adam didn't care what happened to people anymore.

They were both stunned. Everyone was going to be stunned. Adam had given them no warning and he didn't care. There was nothing they could do to change his mind. It was done.

"Alright. It's going to take us a little time. We have got to figure out how to do this. The Human Resource person who normally helps with this paperwork was fired this week. You also work for Textron Corporate and for the Composite Center. So there are multiple things we must get right to get you out the gate. Peter can go with you to clean your office out, and Security will have to escort you out."

"I've already cleaned out my office. Everything is done. Here is my laptop and remote access drive. Here is my corporate credit card as well. There is nothing else."

They looked surprised.

"Alright. Wait here and we will get your termination papers started."

Adam waited four hours. The paperwork was complicated. Finally, it was time. Peter and the Director told him goodbye as Security escorted him through the guarded entrance.

Adam sat in his truck, never saying goodbye to anyone else. He didn't care. He would never return to this job. Never return to this career. Everything he trained for in college was wasted. It was helpful for 20 years or so, but no longer.

(*I wonder how long it will take before I stop having nightmares. Seeing myself walking barefoot through the machine shop with all those metal shavings. It's over. Every moment of this drive home is my last driving this route. My career is over. Is this retirement? Did I just retire at 45 years old? Retire from that career, yes, but I will still need money coming in once we get to the new house. I'll figure something out. I'm glad this part of my life is over. It's a new beginning.*)

PART FIVE – FOUND: RETIREMENT

CHAPTER 41 – BACK HOME

Adam walked back inside his pottery studio thinking (*It's nice being back in Louisiana. I like all the green and humidity. It's almost tropical. Tara hates the heat but I love it. It gives me an excuse to wear nothing but an apron when working in the studio.)*

"Tara. I found another case of liquid cleaner in your dad's section of the shop. Unfortunately, some melted through the container and leaked on the shelves. Three years back in our hometown and we are still cleaning things out. I thought we would have cleared out all the hoarded stuff by the time we moved in," Adam said.

"My parents grew up in the depression area. They learned to keep everything," Tara said.

"I guess, but when you hoard stuff until it becomes useless seems too much, like that case of washing powder that turned into a solid sitting in the shop. There is also that brand new generator. It was still in the box, and the rubber parts had just disintegrated. Finally, it looks like your mom kept all her old pantyhose. I mean, we got a 33-gallon trash bag full of old pantyhose."

"They could have used them to tie up plants and flowers."

"Your dad is allergic to pollen. He hates flowers."

"True, but they had it anyway just in case."

"I think you inherited that hoarder gene. When we moved here, I couldn't tell you had been coming here on weekends for six months cleaning. Everything looked the same."

"I did a lot. It's hard to tell."

"I'm glad your dad let me clean out those few rooms in the shop so I could set up a pottery studio. It's taken so much money and work to make it what we want. Most of it was really needed, like the new roof and the concrete patios. But, of course, that's not including the concrete in the shop because it only had a dirt floor."

"Don't forget the central air conditioning and heat."

"That's right. Why was there only a small unit for the add-on bedroom, bath, and kitchen?"

"Because those were the only rooms they used. They didn't want to spend money heating and cooling the rest of the house."

"That was a chunk of money. New central AC/Heat along with new ductwork and insulation. Then had to rewire the shop for a pottery studio. The new kiln. There is not much money left from the sale of our house in Arlington. It's all gone to make this house livable and I still want to get a greenhouse."

"You worry too much, Adam. We are doing fine. I've got my massage business and you are selling your pottery. You're the President of the local art gallery and make money from sales there as well. If we get in too much of a bind, my father can give us an interest-free loan."

"You're right. I worry too much. Having our own businesses is nice but I hate all the taxes. Another thing I hate is not having health insurance. I may have to look for a job with an employee health insurance program. We are getting older and may need it one day."

"Health insurance would be nice. Everything will work out. It always does."

(*That's true. It always does work out, but that may be because I work. I put in the effort, and people recognize it. I never do the job minimum. It's how I went from being newsletter editor to secretary then President of the oldest and largest artist co-op in Louisiana. Each year getting more responsibilities.*)

"Thinking about cleaning stuff out. I need to clean up your father's automotive section of the shop. It's a nightmare. He's getting unsteady walking, and he's almost tripped a few times in there."

"I don't know. That's been dad's shop all his life. All his tools and things are there since his new wife won't let him bring them over. She knows he would start cluttering up her place so he has to keep everything here."

"I wouldn't get rid of anything valuable. Just the useless things. Like empty boxes that are coming apart. I could at least clear a path to the workbench. Your dad could come over and watch me. I won't throw away anything he wants to keep."

"Maybe. You need to talk to him about it."

"Ok. I'll ask him."

Adam turned to return to the shop.

"Wait. You said something earlier about doing work at your grandparent's house. What do you mean?" Tara asked.

"Do you remember when I told you about a friend of some cousins. His name was Mitch and he took everything out of their house because it might flood? I congratulated him for doing a good thing. He even took all the appliances. However, when I went there last week, I discovered the water running in the bathtub and feces on the toilet handle. My grandparents have been dead for a while and he is the only one who has been there. The drain in the bathtub rusted, and water has soaked the wood in the floor. Water has also rotted the cabinets next to the tub. The bathroom needs to be ripped out and redone. The floorboards and joists under the bathroom also need to be replaced," Adam said.

"Maybe you can get your cousins to help?"

"I don't know. My cousins would like to maintain the house because they paid Mitch to remove the furniture due to potential flooding. The money was also to fix it up. He took everything and never did any repairs. I've tried talking to him, but he won't return my calls. I even left a message saying I was going to visit. He refused to answer the door, and I knew he was home. I can't ask my cousins to help after they paid money to get this done and nothing happened. It feels wrong."

"What are you going to do?"

"Mom said she would pay for repairs. My brother and I can do the work but it's a lot to do. The weather is starting to cool so that will help. Doing pottery and working at the gallery a couple of days a month gives me plenty of time to go down there and work."

"That's true. You could stay for a week then come back here on the weekend if needed. I bet you're wanting to do this so you can run around there naked."

Adam winked at Tara as he spun around wearing only an apron. "That's an idea. It is on a dead-end road on an island in a swamp within the Mississippi floodplain. It's in the middle of nowhere and backs up to a National Wildlife Refuge. It's about as isolated as you can get, but no. I'm going to wear protective clothing. I'm going to be sawing, hammering, and doing other repair work. So I need protective clothing and eyewear."

"Good idea."

"Are you still glad we moved back here?" Tara asked.

"Yes. Although it's taken me this long to destress from my job in Texas. I've finally stopped having nightmares about that job. It took a long time."

"I'm glad we are back here, also. I miss the shopping and restaurants. What I don't miss is the traffic."

"Same here. I don't miss the traffic. I've got to finish a few things then I'll be back in to take a shower." Adam pointed to his apron. "At least this way, there are not so many clothes to wash and less clay going down the drain. I can just rinse the apron outside and let it hang dry. It should take me about 30 minutes to cover the wetware and clean up a bit."

"Alright."

Adam returned to the pottery studio and began end-of-day cleaning.

(*I am glad to be back. Feels like I'm on the right path. That's crazy because I abandoned my college degree and the perfect job. Why does this feel right? At least we are here if our families need us. Her father and his new wife are only half a mile down the street. Her brother is five miles down the road. My parents are three miles down the street. My brother is 20 minutes away. All relatively close, considering you drove an hour in the DFW area just to go out to dinner. It's all working out.*)

CHAPTER 42 – PINK HOUSE

(*Sitting naked by the firepit. Alone in the middle of nowhere. No moon. No city lights. Only starlight. This late in the year, looking up and seeing the center of the Milky Way. I feel closer to home right now than anywhere else I've ever been. Home. This isn't home. Why do I feel like this isn't home? This planet isn't home. This reality isn't my home.*) Adam looked around and smiled. (*It's just me. Alone in the dark. I literally am crazy and alone in a dark world. I'm always saying that, and here I am. Living it. That's funny. It was nice of my cousin Mindy to buy a stove, refrigerator, and king-size bed. I wish I could have seen her face when she discovered nothing in the house. Not even a toilet. We had been sleeping on the floor while doing repairs.*)

"Come on now. More mosquitoes." (*I am giving them more surface area to suck on. It's time to go back inside.*)

Adam looked up one last time before heading inside. "Help me to understand. I don't understand why I'm different. I miss you. I love you." Adam had said similar things many times before when looking at the stars. He was homesick.

Adam crawled into bed. (*This is nice. A cool night. Comforters on the bed. No wife. No cats. Nothing.*) Then Adam heard rats running in the walls into the attic. (*Well. Just me and the rats. They have had free reign since the newspaper from 100 years ago stopped being insulation. Now it's open space for them to run. I found that snakeskin in the attic. Probably a rat snake. I hope it's still in the house.*) Adam grinned. (*I'm betting not many people wish for a snake in their home. Yep. I'm different than everybody else.*)

Adam's head whipped to the left as he lay in bed. He was almost afraid to move, fearing a neck injury. There was no other sound as Adam turned his head. Nothing in the room. He looked at his phone. 10pm. He got out of bed and looked around the house. All the doors were still locked. He stood in the bedroom doorway. (*What was that? There was a sound and flash of light hitting me on the right side of the head. It felt like a gunshot, but I'm ok. Nobody is here. It's someone else. Did an entity just hit me upside the head?*) Adam opened his senses. Nothing in his immediate area. Then Adam felt it. Depression. Hopelessness. A gunshot. (*Oh no. Did I just feel someone kill themself? Someone I know? Perhaps it was someone like me. No. I'm not going to look. I don't like looking. I don't want to feel that. I'm going back to bed.*)

Adam couldn't get back to sleep. (*Why am I like this? These things are happening to me. First, it can't be real, then it gets confirmed. Hearing things when I'm just about to get to sleep. Then it keeps happening when I sit up wide awake. Like last month when I was going to sleep, I started to hear people scream. Seeing in my mind people screaming on the side of a riverbank. Screaming for relatives drowning in the river and they couldn't help. They could only watch as their families drowned. They were left screaming in pain for their loved ones on a riverbank. I got out of bed and even went outside to check. No one was there, and still, the screaming would not stop. I finally had to project an image to the side. To dissociate me from it so I could get to sleep. I later told my mother and she got chills. She told me that this thing happened in the river in front of this house. My grandparent's home we call the pink house. The older adults had crossed the river when it was high and moving fast. The teenagers were crossing with the babies. The boat flipped, and they all drowned. The parents and relatives were left on the bank screaming. What I was seeing and hearing happened. I say I'm crazy but this stuff happens. It's real, and I can't talk to people. They ridiculed me but mom didn't this time. She listened and knew the story. I hope to talk about it more one day and people will understand, but not now.*)

Adam woke the following day and made his usual hot tea. Earl Grey with honey and creamer. He sat in the swing on the front porch watching water drip off the roof. The morning sun shone on the porch. The area is low within the Mississippi floodplain, so the humidity is always a little higher. This morning the dew is dripping from the roof as if it is raining. Wet grass sparkling. It would be mostly gone by 10am and dry by noon.

(That sound. A boat. Someone is getting an early start.)

Adam looked beyond the one-lane road in front of the house, past the tree line to the river. It was a fishing boat with two men heading downstream. It was rare to see a boat along this river so when one came by, you looked.

(That's enough. I've got to get this day started, so I can go back home this afternoon.)

Adam stepped inside, cleaned his cup and then pulled on coveralls. He picked up a notepad from the table. *(Today's to-do list. Put the tin back around the house. Check propane tank level. Pick and clean radishes. Turn off water to the outside sink and faucets. Empty trash. Put uncle's rifle in the car and return. Double-check the house before leaving. This should be the last time I need the rifle. We are purchasing our own guns this week and taking the concealed carry class the following week. Not much longer.)*

Adam was inside washing the final bits of dirt off the radishes. He liked picking the vegetables last, trying to keep them fresh longer. There were more radishes than could be used. He would drop some off at his aunts as he passed through her town on the way home. He could give some to his brother and parents. There was plenty to go around.

Adam saw a truck drive by slowly as he looked up from the kitchen sink and out the window. It was Mitch.

(Crap. Not again.)

Adam left the kitchen and went to the bedroom windows. There was Mitch in his truck. Turning into the side yard, then driving into the backyard. Adam watched as Mitch circled the house several times then left.

(Really. How many times is that now? He's wrong if he thinks he is scaring me. I have this rifle but I only have it because my uncle and the nearest neighbors wouldn't let me come down here without a gun. I don't own a gun and that is why they insisted I take theirs. To protect myself. I'm beginning to believe what they said. They heard that he was telling shady characters that he wanted me dead. That they should kill me if they had the chance. Why? What did I do other than repair this house? Maybe he really did want this place for him and his friends to do drugs. I don't know. But my wife is also in danger when she joins me here. Something needs to be done. I can do something.)

He walked into the washroom, removed all his clothes, and stepped out the back door. He walked through the backyard and into the field. He felt closer to nature when he was naked. Closer to his friends. Closer to something else he couldn't define. He looked up, feeling the sky, the stars beyond, and the universe itself.

"Hello again." Adam felt a breeze across his skin. He looked around. The sun was shining with a few clouds moving slowly. Trees stand tall in the distance. It was a perfect moment. "Thank you. Thank you for this moment. It's beautiful. My words are inadequate. I wish I could tell you how grateful I am for everything. Thank you is not enough."

Adam was sincere. He was open and honest when talking with these friends. However, Adam not only had to be honest with his friends but he also had to be honest with himself.

"I'm fortunate to be here at this moment. You have given this small, unimportant being so much. I love you. I will always love you no matter how dark it gets, and I need to talk to you about something dark. I don't know what to do. Mitch has threatened to kill me, and I'm afraid he might hurt my wife. He's been caught stealing from here and stealing from neighbors. He has been harming others. Is there a way he can be removed from this path if he continues hurting people? I hope he stops. Can he be removed from this life if he doesn't? Is there a way he can get another chance to get it right? I don't know what else to do. Give him another chance in another life."

Adam looked down. He felt as if he was floating. He was a drop in an ocean of reality. Separate and part of the whole.

"I don't know. Something needs to be done. Can you help, please?"

Adam walked back to the pink house and got dressed. It was time to go home. He put the rifle and radishes in the car. Taking out the trash was always last, and it was done. He walked through the house, performing one final check to make sure the doors were locked and that he did not forget anything. It was time to drop the rifle off to his uncle then deliver some radishes to his aunt. He could then head home. He would provide radishes to his brother and parents later if they wanted them.

He looked back at the house one last time before leaving.

(*We've all called it the pink house, but it's not pink. It's more of a salmon color. It needs to be painted and I'm going to paint it bright pink. The most brilliant pink I can find. Townsfolk should be able to identify it quickly then. I can say to the folks who fill the propane tank that it's the pink house. Perfect. I'm painting it bright pink when the weather warms.)*

# # #

Adam picked up the phone.

"Hello," Adam said.

"Hi, Adam. It's mom."

"What's up."

"I had to call and tell you that Mitch died yesterday. He was walking out of his house and fell over dead. They don't know yet but they are guessing heart attack."

"Wow. I just saw Mitch driving around the pink house less than a week ago."

"You told me you saw him driving around and that you would not mind if he died so he couldn't hurt anyone else. That's weird how things like that work out."

"That is weird."

"I'll let you know when I find out about the funeral arrangements."

"Ok, but I'm not going. There has been too much friction with that side of the family. If I show up, something will happen. So it's better that I don't attend."

"Ok. Whatever you think. I'm going and will let you know how it went."

"Ok. Thanks."

"Bye."

"Bye."

(Mitch died suddenly less than a week after I asked. How is that possible? I keep saying I'm crazy. This can't be real, but here it is again. Reality responding again. I don't understand. Why am I so different? I must be crazy. Crazy and alone in a dark world.)

CHAPTER 43 – DO IT NOW

It was 2019, and Adam was 55 years old. He had his own vending business for five years before turning it over to his nephew. Filling machines with sodas, chips, and candy. It had been good exercise and left Adam with plenty of time to spend a night or two at the pink house. With his nephew taking over the vending business, Adam could help with his father's business. He got a monthly check to manage the day-to-day affairs and work with customers. Adam's brother did all the paperwork so it worked out well. Adam had even more time to spend at the pink house. The strange happenings continued daily in Adam's life. His crazy little world spiraled around his everyday life. Then Adam started getting odd impressions which others would later describe as guidance.

"Tara, I'm home."

"Ok. Was the drive ok?"

"Yeah. No problems. It's so hot out. I pulled the tomatoes along with the cucumber vines. The peppers are still doing good, though."

"That's good."

"You know how I like to get a fire going in the firepit out back and sit naked looking at the stars? How it feels like I'm being pulled off the ground toward them?"

"Yes."

"Well, this time, I started getting this weird impression. Almost like a voice in my head wanting me to put out videos of my experiences. Isn't that crazy?"

"I don't know. You know more about that stuff than me. Do what you think you need to do."

"Something is wanting me to put my strange experiences out there for the world to see, and I'm thinking, hell no. I'm crazy, and now I'm supposed to let the world know I'm crazy. You're the only one that knows about this side of me. I've stayed hidden all my life, and now I'm supposed to expose myself. Not like I don't expose myself when I run around naked at the pink house, but this is different. I don't do any of the social media stuff. I don't post stuff. I don't even know how to make videos."

"What are you going to do?"

"Nothing. I'm not going to do it. It's too crazy to think about even for me."

"Alright. I know you are tired when you get back from doing all that work at the pink house so I picked up salads for dinner."

"That sounds great. Thanks. I'm going to sit here for a little bit after the drive before doing anything else."

"Ok."

Adam was tired from his trip as usual. It was a lot of fieldwork and he couldn't handle the heat since he got heat exhaustion a while back. He needed to stop. It was life. Life was good, but this nagging in his head would not go away. It was getting more insistent as Adam continued to ignore it.

(Put videos out of your experiences.)

There it was again. The nagging impressions are now becoming a voice in his head. Growing stronger every month.

# # #

It was October 31st, 2019. Adam was now 56. He loved this time of year. So much of the green around him went to sleep but the stars became louder like now. Standing naked in the back yard of the pink house looking up at the Milky Way. He felt himself becoming lighter. His being wanting to fly to somewhere else. Yes. He loved this time of year.

(Put videos out of your experiences. Do it now.)

That last part rocked Adam. He had to sit down. (*Whoa. I felt that last part throughout my body. Do it now. I don't think I have a choice but I don't want to do it. People will find out and lock me up or something. I'm supposed to volunteer to be ridiculed? To be locked up? To be hauled away in a straitjacket? I don't think so. So I'm not going to do it.*)

Adam went back inside.

"Hey. I didn't know you would be up," Adam said, passing his uncle in the kitchen.

"I wanted a snack, then it's back to bed."

"I'm heading to bed right now. Goodnight."

"Goodnight."

(*I'm glad my uncle moved in. This place needed someone to live here. Keeping the pipes warm in winter and keeping away anyone who might steal from an empty house. It works out great.*)

He was ready for bed. It was peaceful here. Perhaps it was because he didn't have five cats wanting to snuggle around him every night then getting in fights early in the morning as they try to wake him for food. It was only for a night or two. Tomorrow was the drive home, back to the wife and cats. He had already forgotten about the voice yelling, do it now.

Adam slept late. He got his stuff together, took out the trash and then began the drive home. He only stopped once. It was at the donut shop in the next town. He needed coffee and a bag of doughnut holes for the drive.

(Put videos out of your experiences. Do it now.)

(*Damn it. It's so powerful. It's echoing in my head. Seriously. No. I'm not going to do it. Stop it.*)

(Put videos out of your experiences. Do it now.)

Adam looked up at the sky and felt something more. Something beyond the sky.

Adam said. "Are you going to keep doing this until I give up? Fine. I'll do it. Is that what you want?"

The voice stopped. Adam felt a sense of peace.

(*I must create videos of my experiences. I don't know how but it seems I don't have a choice. Crap. Someone is going to see this and lock me up. I've got to do it knowing I'll be locked up in an institution for the rest of my life. Ok. If locking me up is what you want, then ok. I'll figure out how to do videos and put them out on the internet. Something's happening. I don't know what but I don't have a choice. It's something I must do. Great. Just great.*)

The trip took a little over an hour and a half. Then there was that voice. It only stopped after Adam agreed. Then, of course, he had to tell his wife once he got home.

"Tara. I'm home."

"I'm doing laundry."

"Do you remember when I said something about a voice in my head wanting me to put out videos of my experiences?"

"Yes."

"It's gotten very insistent. It's yelling in my head, do it now. I don't even know how to make videos to put online."

"People make videos all the time and put them online. You click on something when you open the phone's camera to make it do video. Then you just record and upload. It's supposed to be easy."

"Ok. I'll check it out."

Adam returned to the living room, pulled out the phone and opened the camera app. There it was. He pressed record and started talking.

"Testing. One two three. Testing."

He stopped recording then found the video stored in photos. He clicked, and it played just as he had recorded. Tara walked into the living room and sat down.

"It worked, Tara. It is easy to record videos. I'll have to figure out how to upload but I don't want them going to anything popular. The voice in my head said put videos out of my experiences, but it didn't say it had to be on the most popular site on the internet. I still don't want a lot of people seeing it, so I'm going to see if I can find another site."

"I'll help look."

Adam said, "I found something called **Bitchute**. It's located somewhere in the United Kingdom. I like that it's not in the United States. It looks to be privately run and operates with donations. I know I could put them out for free but I'd rather pay $10 per month to say thanks for hosting the videos. I need to create an account and figure out how to upload. I don't think it's going to be hard."

"What are you going to name the site?" Tara asked.

Adam thought for a bit. "I'm going to call it **Just Me** because that's all it's going to be. Just me talking. I'm not expecting anyone to see these videos since I'm not creating content for clicks. Just putting stuff out there because I don't have a choice."

"Don't be surprised if someone watches your videos. You never know."

"True. The site is small so it won't be that many. Maybe this way I won't be hauled off to an insane asylum."

"Do you want another salad tonight? I could go pick something up."

"Let's go eat there. I'm a little freaked out about creating these videos and could use a change of scenery."

"Alright. I know you have driven a lot today but would you drive?"

"Sure."

The next day Adam began recording videos. It was rough at first, and most of the early ones were deleted. He knew nothing about audio or lighting. He only knew to press record on the phone then upload to the site. So he decided to break the videos up into three categories. He could give each video a character and number to keep them in order.

G would be for General videos. CB would be Country Boy for videos done at the pink house. SH would be Strange Happenings, where he talked about being crazy and alone in a dark world. He would try to keep them short. Around five minutes because people will lose interest. After all, he is not going to be funny or teach anything. It was going to be Adam talking about his life. Nothing more.

Adam uploaded his first video on November 9th, 2019. He titled it G1 **Good Morning**. G being for general and the number 1 because it was his first general video. It was 2 minutes and 15 seconds. He uploaded his second video the same day. CB1 for his first country boy video. He titled it, **Relaxing Naked in the Middle of Nowhere**. He waited a few days to upload his first strange happenings video. It made him nervous about opening up to others. Opening to the world.

On November 12th, 2019, he was ready after several false starts. He uploaded SH1 titled **Strange Happenings Remembering the Matrix/Simulation**. It was about these memories he had from before he was born. Being somewhere outside of time. Helping humans through a holographic matrix then being told to become one of them. Being born. Different from everybody else because he remembered.

He put videos out daily. The strange happening videos were the most important. He put them out in chronological order the best he could remember. Things that have happened since he was born. Living in a haunted house. Fights with dark entities. Discovering lost souls and showing them the way home. Seeing through walls. The coincidences and electricity. Even his two rounds with suicidal depression. They would learn how he felt crazy and alone in a dark world. That he was lost in the dark. He would put most of it online but he couldn't put out everything. It was too much for Adam. It would be too much for others.

# # #

"Do you want to watch a movie?" Tara asked.

"Sure," Adam said.

"What do you want to watch?"

"Well. We have not seen **Doctor Sleep**. I think it's supposed to be a sequel to **The Shining**. We liked that one so this might also be good. We can buy it from our streaming video service."

"Was there a book?"

"I don't know."

"Alright. Let's get it and watch."

They began watching then Adam turned to Tara. "That's it. That is what it is like. Hearing what's in people's heads. They got it." The movie continued. "Astral travel. Finding people. They got it right. I don't know how but they got it. I didn't get anything like this from the first movie. This is how things work for me. How did they know? Oh my God."

The movie ended and Adam turned to Tara. "They got it right. I don't know how but there is someone else like me. There has to be for them to know all this."

This was something new. Adam had been creating videos about his past. Videos about actual experiences. This movie was current. It just happened. It was time to start moving from historical stuff to what was happening now. Something was happening, and Adam could not explain it. He had been opening himself up on these videos and then a video found him. There must be someone out there like him but he could not be sure. It was just a movie, after all. A work of fiction. It could all be fantasy but how did they get it so right. It was beginning to dawn on Adam that maybe, just maybe, he was not alone.

# # #

It was almost Adam and Tara's wedding anniversary. They didn't have plans. Instead, they would probably do what they were doing now. Sitting in their recliners, eating dinner and fending off their five cats as they watched a movie.

"Tara. I'm getting the strangest impressions."

"Like what?"

"It feels like something just happened to someone I know. Someone close to me. It feels like the person is trapped in a wrecked car. The person made one last attempt to get unstuck, and it failed. That the person is dying. It's like they are sinking into darkness."

"Do you know who it is?"

"No. You know I don't like to go out and get a closer look. It gets to be too much when this sort of thing happens. Maybe I'll get a phone call in the next day or two, then we will know."

That night Adam had terrible dreams. He was usually a lucid dreamer. He always knew when he was dreaming and could manipulate his environment. This time was different. He was not in control and had been caught up in these bad dreams.

There was no phone call. Everything seemed ok except he was bored because his business was closed due to Covid-19. The state had shut down almost all family-owned businesses and Adam had nothing to do. He was sitting watching television while Tara had gone grocery shopping.

Adam felt a presence entering through the living room door. He turned and looked. A human entity. Not a dark entity or a lost soul. It was a soul but not lost. Adam could feel it. It was curious and wanted a tour of the house. It seemed to know Adam and wanted to visit for a short while. Adam could not make out who it was but it was friendly. He would open up to this entity. Adam expanded his consciousness and let the entity feel him.

"Hello. I'm glad to see you."

(Hello. I wanted to stop by and see where you lived. Can you show me around?)

"I'd be happy to show you around."

Adam stood up and began walking from room to room.

"This is my man cave which is on the opposite side of the house from our bedroom. I call it that because it's the room with the only closet I get to use in the house. My wife uses all the other closets. This is the second bath and then the guest bedroom. Next, this is the kitchen, then the main bedroom."

The entity remained silent during the tour and only spoke once they returned to the living room, where they started.

(Thank you. Goodbye.)

"Goodbye."

Adam told Tara what happened when she returned from shopping.

"You don't know who it was?"

"No. It was male, but I couldn't get the details. I don't know why I couldn't see it clearly."

"At least it was friendly."

"Yeah. I hope I didn't scare it opening up as I did."

"It doesn't sound like you scared him. I'm sure it's ok."

"You're probably right."

Two days later, the Covid-19 restrictions were relaxed and businesses were able to open at reduced levels. Adams family business held a meeting to discuss handling all the extra cleaning and occupancy requirements.

That's when Adam learned that one of the security guards at the business had died. He died in a single-person car wreck the same day Adam felt someone dying in a car wreck. It was the security guard Adam had become friends with and felt die. The guard had wanted to come over and see where Adam lived. He wanted to visit the pink house Adam had told him about. To stay one weekend and practice shooting. Maybe fish.

(I felt him die and recorded it on video before I knew he died. I put it online as SH38 then as SH39 **Astral Visitor***. I know people will never believe me when I talk about my crazy little world but it is recorded on video. It's real, and*

no one understands.) Adam looked up and said aloud, "I wish I knew what I am. I wish I wasn't alone."

He had asked the universe what he was and told it that he did not want to be alone anymore. Then, things began to move faster in Adam's crazy little world. Finally, he received an answer one month later.

Adam was mopping the living floor when words began appearing in midair. Adam couldn't tell if they were there or if he was only seeing them in his mind. They were moving. Shimmering. Forming sentences. He grabbed a pencil and paper. He began writing what he saw.

Be honest. Be gentle. Be kind.
You can avoid that arrogance trap.
You are an expression of creation.
A living being created to experience creation.
A part of the one consciousness.
Your body is only a vessel. It's temporary.
You need to realize the truth.
The truth will help you understand who and what you are.

Adam reeled. He knew the truth when he heard it. It was telling him who he was. Images and concepts filled his mind. Memories of the times he heard the voices telling him to put out videos of his experiences. Everything that had happened and was happening now. Then he saw the name of his entire video site. Just me. The words merged as the 't' vanished. Finally, it turned into a single word.

(*Jusme. It's my name. It says everything about me. What I am. From the beginning, I created the site for these videos. It's been there the entire time. When I see things around me, I see parts of myself. It's all Jusme. It's all part of one thing. It's even the way I announce myself when walking into my parent's house. I call out. It's Jusme. I have a name.*)

Adam stood there. Unable to move. The universe is spinning around him. Alive. Aware. Connected. It was several minutes before he could move again. Chores were done for the day. He needed to think about what had happened. He wrote it down. He could not deny it. He needed to make a video.

(It might be some sort of mental disorder like megalomania or a Christ complex. I've heard those terms but don't know anything about them. Maybe I am crazy. If I am crazy, I'm documenting it and perhaps some psychologists can use this as a lesson in what not to do. I have no idea what is happening but I will document it on video.)

CHAPTER 44 – FORGIVENESS

It was an odd feeling. Adam had a new name, or was he remembering his original name? He only knew the strange happenings in his life were moving faster. Like when he helped his nephew on his vending route a few weeks ago. His nephew noticed when Adam told him there was a parking spot up front for him so they would not have to carry the supplies so far. It was hidden behind a large truck, but Adam insisted they continue down the aisle. It was there waiting. Adam told his nephew not to park where he stopped because a fire truck would be called and needed this spot. When they came back out, the fire truck was in that spot. Adam also mentioned how the rain would start and stop for them as they did their route. That's when the nephew asked if Adam could teach him how he did these things. Adam said no because his nephew was not like him. No one was.

Day by day, the coincidences began happening more frequently in the month since he saw those words floating in the air. He knew the truth, and those words were true. Adam was human but also something else. He felt it and knew it to be the truth. Why couldn't others feel the way he felt. Why was he alone in this? It didn't matter. He could live with it. After all, he had lived with loneliness all his life.

Adam was sitting in his recliner scanning videos, looking for people reacting to his favorite movies when a **You Are Not Crazy** title popped up. Intrigued, Adam clicked on it to watch.

A lady talked about how some people can see and do things differently from others. How they may have a closer connection to something out there. How it makes them feel crazy and alone. She created this video to let them know they are not crazy or alone. How many of them feel homesick for a place that is not here. That there are groups of people that get together and talk about it. Adam thought she was talking directly to him as she spoke. She was telling him there are others out there like him. He is not crazy or alone. The video ended and Adam realized his mouth was hanging open.

(*She's telling the truth, and she knows. She knows what it's like. I'm not alone. There are others out there like me.*)

"Tara. Come in here. You have got to see this."

"What is it?"

"This lady. She's like me. She says there are others out there like me. This is her channel with all her videos. Sit down and you pick one to watch. It feels like something is happening and I need you to be here."

"Alright. Let's see. I'll click on this one further down the page. It's called **The Clairs**. Do you know what this is about?"

"No. It sounds like a movie about high school girls."

The lady on the screen said there are different psychic abilities some people call The Clairs. Clairvoyance is when people see other places and spirits. Clairaudience when people hear things that others can't hear. Clairsentience is when people feel something like truth and energies. Finally, Claircognizance is when people know things like what will happen in the future.

Tara turned to Adam and yelled, "That's you! That's you!" The lady onscreen was describing clairvoyance in greater detail. Some people can see other places, spirits, ghosts, or, as some people tell, entities. Adam's mouth was again hanging open.

"That's you. That's you," Tara said, turning to Adam. "How you hear things that are not there like when you heard the screaming on the riverbank. Then your mom told that story." They continued watching. Adam is in disbelief.

"That's you. The way you feel things and know the future."

"I know. I'm not alone. She says there are others out there. I wonder how many there are?"

"Wow. I picked that video out of all the random plant and vacation videos."

"Something is happening. I don't know what but things are moving faster."

"You could try and contact her. Unfortunately, New Zealand is a bit far away to meet her but you could put something in the comments."

"You're right. I'm so nervous. I could start out with a simple thank you for the video."

"How about a grilled cheese sandwich for dinner?"

"Sounds good."

It was difficult for Adam to comprehend. He was not alone. She knew about some of the things in his life. She saw other places and even entities that frightened her. She heard things that were not there. She knew.

Adam pulled out his laptop and found her channel. He wrote a simple thank you in the video comments. Maybe one day, he would be confident enough to talk about the strange happenings in his life. This was a start. He didn't feel so alone anymore.

The next day Adam searched for her channel to watch more videos. Maybe he could learn more. Perhaps even talk to her in the comments somehow. He could not find the channel. He spent hours searching by name, title, and subject matter. He learned there were a lot of videos on psychic abilities but her channel was gone. Did she delete her channel? Was it removed for some reason? Did she ever exist in the first place? Tara confirmed seeing the videos and had even tried searching. The channel was gone.

He continued searching for almost a week before giving up. Everyday life interrupted his immediate viewing of more videos. He still had the pink house to mow and maintain along with his own home. He had his job at the family business and was helping both their families as needed. He had also been doing some repair work at his brother-in-law's house. Watching videos would have to wait.

Adam felt the beginnings of his usual migraine headache so he kept medication at home and in every vehicle. He had his first one when he was a teenager so he knew the signs and took some medication to help ward it off.

(Ugh. A long hot shower might help. It helps my sinuses and these headaches. Tara is at work so I can use all the hot water in the tank.)

Adam closed the bathroom door so the steam would build up in the room. He got undressed and stepped into the shower. Adam felt it was like stepping into a glass enclosure. That was something Adam didn't consider when they replaced the shower. They were practical and selected simple with no pattern white walls. It would be easier to clean. Adam was thinking functional and did not think about what would happen with these smooth flat surfaces.

Adam looked around as he stood in the hot running water. He saw through every flat surface to other places and these walls were as flat as you could get. Flat and white on three sides. He saw something like Central Park in New York City but he wasn't sure. He was standing in the park with skyscrapers in the background. People were enjoying themselves, and there was Adam. Standing naked on the grass. People moved all around him without seeing him.

It was always like this with flat surfaces. He was used to it, but it was much clearer in the shower for some reason. Maybe it was because there were three solid white surfaces closely surrounding him. He didn't know why but he saw more than just the park. He was also seeing entities. Perhaps they were spirits or ghosts like that lady on the video talked about. He always saw them when looking through flat surfaces. He would see his landscape barriers, but a strange overlay always showed these entities residing on another plane of existence. Only in the shower did he see an additional level. It seemed above the others, and there were beings. Watching. They were not human. They didn't do anything other than stand at a distance and watch.

"Aaaagh," Adam grunted. The world around him was collapsing. The floor, walls, and ceiling were being pulled into him. He grabbed the shower rail, steadying himself.

"Aaaagh." It was too much. Adam fell to his knees, still holding the shower rail. He felt his hand on the rail, but the world was gone. His mind expanded past Earth. Past the solar system and into the universe. It was alive, and he was part of it.

Be honest. Be gentle. Be kind.
You can avoid that arrogance trap.

Adam heard it but there were no words. Instead, it tore through his mind with concepts and images. What it meant to be these things. Tears were flowing as Adam tried to breathe.

You are an expression of creation.
A living being created to experience creation.

He was moving through the universe at incredible speed. Feelings of joy in one area. Feelings of sadness in another. It was alive and he was part of the universal living consciousness. A small piece was sent to Earth to have the experience of living this kind of life. A mortal life. Memories from before he was born filled his mind. It was pure and it would not be denied.

You are a part of the one consciousness.
Your body is only a vessel. It's temporary.

Adam felt himself being pulled back to Earth, through the atmosphere, and back into his body. He was having difficulty breathing. He was back in his body but still connected to this vast consciousness. Concepts about planes of existence flooded his mind. Concepts of life and how everything is connected. It was too much. Adam couldn't comprehend the information coming into his brain.

You need to realize the truth.
The truth will help you understand who and what you are.

The ground below Adam evaporated. He fell, yet his mind was still connected to this consciousness downloading information. He fell into the same park. He felt the people. Before, he had only seen people. He was now getting their emotions as well. The feelings of everyone he saw came flooding into Adam. His body was transported into a nearby building. A family eating. He felt each of their emotions. His body was transported into an arena. Overwhelming emotions.

"Uuuuuungh." Mucous poured out of Adam's nose. His body was transported to a large funeral. So much sadness. Adam began crying uncontrollably. It was too much. Things he couldn't comprehend running through his mind. The emotions were not ending as he went from one person to another. It was all their emotions together. He was connected to every person on the planet.

He was part of the universal consciousness. He was feeling all the people on the planet. He was them, and they were he.

(*That's it. The key to forgiveness. Every good and bad thing that has been done throughout time. I'm capable of all of that. It's all me. Just me. Jusme. My name. It's more than just a name. It's the truth of myself. It's all Jusme. I look at another and see myself. It's Jusme. I've got to forgive myself for all these things.*)

Adam was crying again. He was forgiving himself for what he had done in this human form. Forgiving others for what they had done to him. Forgiving others for things they had done because he was capable of everything they had done. It was as if he had done it himself.

A wave of gratitude and peace washed over him. He let go of the shower rail and collapsed on the floor. Half in and half out of the shower. The water was still running.

Adam slowly recognized the world becoming solid. Realizing he was lying on the floor. The information stopped but the overwhelming emotions continued. Slowly he pulled himself up as the emotions began to fade. Finally, he managed to turn the water off. He made it out of the bathroom and dropped onto the bed. He grabbed a pillow and curled up.

(*Oh my God. Oh my God. Oh my God. What happened? So much information in my head. I can't understand it. So many emotions from everyone. It's too much. Did I have a stroke? Am I dying? Oh my God.*)

Adam lay there for an hour as the emotions dwindled. Then, finally, he got up and made his way into the living room. He grabbed a blanket and curled up in his recliner. He was stunned and done. So dazed by all the information spinning in his head. He didn't know if he would ever understand it.

Tara walked in the living room door and found Adam curled up in the recliner. She knew something wasn't right.

"What's wrong?"

Adam told her everything.

"I'm going out to get some comfort food. Maybe that will help. I'll be right back."

(I'm so lucky to have a wife that accepts the craziness that is my life. Thank you for letting Tara and I find each other. Thank you for showing me how to forgive. Help everyone else to understand. We all need help to understand. Thank you.)

Tara returned. The food helped but not as much as her presence. Adam was glad she was there and didn't ask too many questions because he would not know how to answer.

"Do you want one of my sleeping pills tonight?"

"Definitely yes. I think I'm going to bed early tonight. I can't focus on television right now."

"Sounds good. I'm tired anyway."

Adam woke the following day feeling much better. The emotions from everyone had faded; however, there was still so much information in his mind. He didn't understand any of it. He had a few errands to do today. They would only take a couple of hours then he had the rest of the day to think about what happened.

The day was like any other day. He cranked his truck and began driving down the street.

"Wow, wow, wow."

His barriers were gone. He was seeing through the road. Something innocuous allowed him to live life without seeing what was truly happening in the world. The landscape barriers were gone. Adam was seeing real places. He was also getting the emotions from the people he was seeing. That never happened before. Adam pulled into an abandoned gas station not far from his house.

(I'm seeing everything and getting the emotions. Shit. In the shower yesterday. My landscape barriers were not there either. I saw a real place from the start. Then the emotions came pouring through. It's still happening. I've got to record this on video.)

Adam left the truck running as he pulled out his phone and began recording.

"You know how I talk about seeing through roads. How I see through any flat surface, but I keep a landscape barrier up to protect myself because there is so much out there it's hard to handle? Oh. The barriers are gone. My landscape barriers are gone. Wow. Just Wow. I didn't expect that. I didn't know that would happen. I really did not know that would happen. Um. I can handle it. All my life experiences. I'm able to handle it. Wow. I didn't expect that. I just did not expect that. Um. I had to pull over. I'm not far from my driveway right now. Not even got on the main street yet. I was just going wow, wow, wow, wow. I just got in the truck and started driving. Wow. I did not expect that. Ok. Ok. I can handle it. I can handle it. It's ok. Oh my god. Wow. Oh wow. The future is going to be interesting."

Adam stopped recording as he tried to not look at the road. He found it a bit difficult not to look though. His eyes kept being drawn to it and it was wearing him down. All the people's emotions were hitting him every time he saw a flat surface.

It took him a couple of hours but he was finally finished and pulled into the driveway. He would make another short video and combine it with all that happened. The video would include what happened in the shower, realizing his landscape barriers were gone, and then this final bit thanking the universe. He did not know what the future would bring but he was grateful that he finally learned to forgive after all these years.

He went inside and began editing the videos. It was August 18th, 2020, and this was going to be SH55 titled **Learned To Forgive Everyone Across Time**. As he uploaded the video, he thought (*no one will realize the impact this moment had on my life. It's a turning point. It's the thing I needed to learn while I was here. It's the thing everyone needs to learn and I don't know if they will understand. It doesn't matter. I'm grateful it happened and I need to share this. Wow.*)

It was hard for Adam to get to sleep that night. The emotions of others haunt him. He woke around three in the morning as usual. This time it was because he needed to pee. Returning from the bathroom he caught a shape out of his eye.

(*Did something move? Probably one of the cats wondering what I was doing.*)

He crawled into bed, pushing the cats aside.

(*Wait. The cats are in bed. What moved?*)

Adam looked to the small light on the baseboard illuminating the entrance into the bedroom. It dimmed. Adam saw it. A large shadow moved, and the lights dimmed in the room as it progressed.

The illuminated clock on the dresser was covered as it moved in front of it. The shadow was big with what Adam thought was yellowish blond hair with some red burning like a flame. It looked familiar, but he couldn't remember.

(*It's got hair. It's got blondish-red hair. It's gone, punk. I've never seen that before. It's starting a trend. Every shadow out there will follow it because it's creating a trend.*)

Adam watched as it crossed the room and went out the window. The security light in the backyard turned off. The shadow re-entered the room, and all the other shadows started moving. Adam didn't sense their presence. Instead, he saw them with his physical eyes. There were so many now looking at him from the foot of the bed.

(*I've never seen so many. I've dealt with shadows before. I know how to survive this. No fear. I can't let myself feel any fear. I must be solid. It's going to be a long night having to stay awake and constantly be on guard.*)

Adam felt one of the smaller entities trying to slip a sliver of fear inside him. It was a sliver, hardly noticeable. But it would be enough and Adam had to stop it.

He thought to the entity, (*you try that and I'm going to incinerate you.*)

The entity stopped. The shadows took a step back as if thinking about what to do next. The sliver of fear was gone.

(*It's going to be a long night.*)

Fifteen minutes later, another set of entities entered the room. It was hard for Adam to see them. They were enveloped in a shimmering bubble outlined with gold sparkles. Adam could only guess that if the first shadow entities were negative, then these entities seemed to be positive. These shimmering ones seemed familiar. Had he seen them before?

Adam saw two transparent cylinders, glowing gold, surround him. There were symbols etched into the cylinders, rotating in opposite directions. As the symbols turned over each other, waves of warm energy entered Adam.

(*This is nice. It feels so good. Like being under a warm blanket on a cold day. This is nice.*)

Adam let himself feel the healing warmth for a few minutes.

(Stop. Wait. You are opposites of each other, but you're part of the same thing. Different sides of the same coin.)

The cylinders vanished, and Adam sat up in bed. The two sets of entities began fighting. There was no sound, but Adam could see contact being made and energies flashing between them.

Adam whispered, "Stop. I'm not ready. I need more time. You are both ok. Go your own way. Be yourselves."

The entities stopped fighting and looked at Adam. They were leaving in opposite directions. Then, finally, they were gone.

(That wasn't a dream. I started seeing the beings as I was coming back to bed from peeing. I'm sitting up in bed right now, wide awake. I'm not asleep. It was real. God, I'm tired. Worn out. I don't think I'll have any problem getting back to sleep.)

Adam fell asleep as soon as his head hit the pillow. He woke at his usual time the following day. He went to the kitchen and made a cup of hot tea.

(Ow. It's hard to move. It feels like I've been beaten. I wonder if I have any bruises. What was that last night? They seemed familiar. I can't remember. It's so strange. Why were they here? Why did they stop fighting when asked? I'm nobody. The strange things are happening faster and getting weirder. It feels like something is about to happen. So strange.)

Adam sat in his recliner drinking his hot tea. He was not going to think about it anymore. He had his tea and was enjoying a slower morning. He might even have a second cup.

CHAPTER 45 – EMERALD GREEN ARMOR

Adam woke around three in the morning. He'd been doing it for decades. It was normal. He lay there, letting his mind wander past his house and into space. Information stored in his mind began to unfold. He saw space as a neural network, and his mind was connected to it. Time stopped as it fell into black holes creating memory nodes. The holographic nature of the universe. The tiniest quantum bit reflects the larger whole of the universe. This idea is mirrored in the saying, as above so below. Then he saw a waveform flowing through the micro quantum and macro cosmos. It was the same waveform underlying everything. Was this consciousness? He turned to follow a waveform and found himself in orbit around Earth. There were random points of light. Not the yellowish color of city lights. These were starbursts of white light. He felt as if they were people. Perhaps they were like him. He moved away from Earth and saw a barrier held together by a seal. It was the consistency of dried clay not yet fired. It was fragile. He could crush it easily. He recalled times he broke barriers or seals in homes as he walked through without permission. No, it would be reckless to break it without knowing more. Adam let himself drift back to sleep as he looked at the points of white light.

"Tara. I had the strangest experience last night. I woke up around three in the morning like normal, but it was like I was wandering in space this time. It felt like some of this stuff that was downloaded into my brain was opening." Adam told Tara about his experience as he grabbed a few items to take to the pink house.

"A seal around the Earth? Maybe it was a quarantine seal. Aliens may have put it there to let others know Earth has Covid-19. Stay away." They both laughed.

"Quarantined. That's funny. I don't know. Things in my crazy little world have been moving so fast lately. It feels like I'm on a train about to hit a wall. I don't know if the wall is solid or paper. It feels like a decision needs to be made. That decision will determine if the wall is paper or solid. Will the train continue or crash? I don't know what it means."

"Guess you will have to wait and find out. Don't forget to take that extra set of coveralls with you. Take my car instead of your truck. It gets better gas mileage."

"Got em. I'm heading out. I'll be back tomorrow. There's not much to do, so a one-night stay should be enough. I'll text you as I start back."

"Alright. See you later."

Adam got in the car and headed to the pink house. He turned on the radio and began to relax. Finally, Adam could open his senses and feel the ground beneath him, the plants, the air, and the sky above. He loved this part of the drive.

(*What's happening?*)

Adam's hands were at the 10 and 2 positions on the steering wheel. His fingertips were tingling. It was as if gloves were slowly being pulled onto his hands. He focused his senses on his hands. He saw emerald green points overlapping one another, moving up his fingers. They were sparkling with a flash of silver as each point connected.

(*What is this? I can physically feel it happening. Emerald green sparkling with flashes of silver. It's like scales slowing moving up my fingers and now starting to cover my hands.*)

Adam was watching both the road and his hands. His fingers and hands are now covered in sparkling green emerald points. Silver flashed from between the points when he flexed his fingers. It felt like armor made of emerald green crystals, but that's not possible. There is such a thing as scale armor but not crystal armor.

(It's like armor made of scales. It's almost to my elbow now. I can feel it moving. Why is this happening? That music. I've never heard anything like it. It's beautiful.)

Adam looked at the display. It read **Chosen One** by Two Steps From Hell.

(Huh. I'm not a chosen one. I'm nobody. That is so strange. Two Steps From Hell. What kind of group name is that?) Adam laughed under his breath. *(That group name might be a little accurate. Feeling crazy and alone in a dark world. That this world is hell and I want to go home. I love it but no way this music is trying to tell me something. It's my ego wanting to be more than I am. The music is beautiful. I've got to find out more.)*

The emerald green armor continued assembling itself as it moved up his arms and onto his head. Then it began moving down his chest, waist, legs, and feet as the music played. Finally, the song ended as the armor completed.

(It's real. I can feel it. It's like emerald green scale armor with bits of silver. It's all around me. I've never felt anything like it. Armor. I didn't have armor in all my fights. All those fights with entities. It was just me. No armor. No weapon. Just me.) Adam laughed. *(Just me. No. Jusme. It's always been Jusme. That's insane even for my crazy little world. Things are moving so fast I can hardly keep up. Pressure is building to do something, but I don't know what. Armor. What am I supposed to do? Why is this here?)*

Adam knew the armor meant he had taken another step forward. Perhaps it was learning to forgive everyone for everything throughout time. Maybe it was when he accepted the darker side of himself. All the horrible things humans do. He felt it. It was part of his nature as well. He had forgiven himself and accepted it. He had felt this second etheric self since puberty incorporate into his physical body. The two parts of Adam were one. Was that why the armor appeared? Adam didn't know. He could only guess.

He continued thinking about what happened as he pulled into the pink house, changed clothes, and began mowing. He finished a few other maintenance chores and took a shower. Now clean, he could relax on the couch and search on his tablet for that music he heard. He found the song and listened to it online.

(That's odd. This isn't the song I heard. Hmm. This other link says the composer didn't like how it sounded, so he removed it from the initial album,

changed it, and put it on a different album. The song I heard on the radio is called **L'Appel Du Vide**, *but the display showed it as* **Chosen One**. *That's a strange screwup.*)

Adam found both albums online and purchased them immediately. It was his first digital music to ever buy. He listened to one of the albums as he ate dinner. It was like nothing he had ever heard before. He rightly guessed he would be purchasing more in the future. Unfortunately, it was late and he was tired. Listening to more would have to wait for the drive home.

He crawled into bed and woke around three as usual. This time he got out of bed because he needed to pee. That being done, he returned to the bedroom and stopped at the side of the bed. There was something under his feet. A sound like growling combined with the hissing of exhalation of breath.

(*Great. Somethings under the house directly under the bed. It's not a dream. I'm still standing up and not in bed yet. It's fine. Not like the entities fighting at the foot of my bed. It's just sound. I'm going back to sleep.*) Adam crawled into bed, but the sounds didn't stop. Growling combined with a strong exhalation of breath. Adam's sinuses were clogged from all the debris kicked up by the mower, and he was getting annoyed by the sounds.

Adam said, "Alright. Aliens or whatever you are. If you will be here bothering me, could you at least clear up my nose so I can breathe? Something so I can get back to sleep with all that noise you are making. Geez."

Adam did finally get to sleep. He woke the following day, gathered his things and drove home. He played the new albums through his phone as he went home. He thought about the sound last night. (*That could have been a bear. The house is three feet off the ground and a bear could fit under there. It's like a cave. The bear growled. The breath sound could have been fur rubbing on the joists. I've got to go with the most logical explanation. I bet it was a bear. It's been a strange couple of days. That sound last night and this emerald green armor around me. So strange.*)

# # #

(*I don't think I can take it anymore. So much pressure is bearing down on me from somewhere. I just got this emerald green armor three days ago. Things are moving so fast. It has something to do with those entities fighting in my bedroom that night.*

What was it I said? I need more time. Why did I say I needed more time? I said that. Why did I say that? It's almost like I needed to make a choice. Do I choose the shadow beings? Do I choose the shimmering beings? Yes. That's it. I must make a choice. I'm glad Tara's not home. I'm freaking out.)

Adam got out of his recliner and stood in the middle of the living room floor. Looking beyond the ceiling. Letting his sense open to the universe.

Adam spoke to existence. "It can't wait any longer. There is no more time. I don't know what's going to happen. I have to choose now." He felt that all the years of his life brought him to this moment. This decision would change everything. It would determine his future. Adam felt the presence of both sets of entities waiting for him to choose.

"I don't choose either of you. You're both parts of the same coin, like the two sides of myself incorporated into one body. I choose that higher consciousness that is beyond both of you. I choose to serve the source that comprises all existence. The source beyond time, beyond love, beyond perfect joy. The one that has always been there for me. Helping me. Guiding me. The one in my fragmented memory. The source that creates all, then all returns to the source. That is my choice."

The train broke through the paper wall and continued forward. The entities were gone. Images appeared in Adam's mind of a baby opening its eyes for the first time. Was he that baby? Only now making a choice and opening his eyes.

He recalled a memory from before he was born. Two life paths are spiraling around each other. Falling and getting the impression that you can learn a lot by taking the lonely, darker, and less explored path. If he survived. He was 56 years old. He had survived to make a choice. Adam smiled and felt something beyond his comprehension smile with him.

Adam saw a flash as he sat back down in his recliner. He looked at his arm. The armor was clearer. The emerald green scales were more like crystals. He looked closer. His senses moved inside the armor. The silver he had seen before was from the inside. The outside of the armor was emerald green crystals but the interior was polished silver. It was like a mirror. Reflective.

(The silver is a mirror on the inside. So if I take these dark entities inside myself, are they trapped by their own reflection. Is there something more? Like the holographic duality of the universe. How the micro and macro are reflections of each other? I have no clue. Huh.)

Adam said, looking up, "I have no idea why this armor is here. God, I could use somebody to talk to." Adam couldn't explain any of it. He wished he could find someone who knew about this sort of thing and help him understand.

(I need to make a video about what just happened. The following number on the list is SH69. It's September 24, 2020. I'll simply title it **The Choice**. *I wonder if anyone can comprehend the impact this is having on me. All my life came down to this single moment. I think I made the right choice.)*

CHAPTER 46 – STARSEED

Adam said "I can't find anything of interest on television."

"You know it would be worse if we had cable. Refresh the video site. See if there is anything new." Tara said. He flipped through the titles to a video about a spiritual awakening.

"That's new. Sounds kind of weird like me."

"Watch it. You never know."

Adam and Tara began watching a young man talk as he leaned against a tree. He said there was a spiritual awakening happening right now. Then he said that many Starseeds started activating within the last five years. That they were souls born into a human body. He said they had come to Earth to help wake others up to a new reality. He continued saying Starseeds have psychic abilities. That they can feel the emotions of others and energies around them. Some can see and communicate with entities. They must not give in to fear. That Starseeds can use thought to manifest things they want. The veil of forgetfulness envelops them when they are very young and forget about being a Starseed.

"Are you listing to this, Tara?"

"Not really. I'm on my tablet."

"They are using a term I've never heard of before. Starseed. I've been putting all this kind of stuff on video. It sounds like I might be what he is calling a Starseed. But unfortunately he's off on another topic now. I wish he would say more about Starseeds."

"You have your tablet. Look for it on the internet," Tara said.

"Good idea."

Adam opened a browser on his table and entered Starseed in the search bar.

(*A lot came up on Starseeds. I love the term but have never heard about any of this. How have I never heard of Starseeds? I'll click this link. Hmm. There have been three waves of Starseeds. The first wave happened about the time I was born. The second wave is younger adults. The third wave is children and babies being born.*)

"There is a lot on Starseeds. It says there are three waves of them, and the first wave was around the time I was born," Adam said.

"What else?"

"I don't know. I'm still reading."

(*It's saying Starseed souls come from other planets, other galaxies, and even other planes of existence. The first wave went into a world of darkness, unable to comprehend consciousness. They were the pioneers creating paths for future Starseeds to follow. They would try to be of service to others but were often ridiculed. Those early Starseeds could not understand other people. Many did not have friends, get married or have children. Many suffered from depression and committed suicide. They felt crazy and alone in a dark world. It's talking about how they felt homesick for a place not on this Earth.*)

"Tara. Everything in here matches what I've been saying about myself. I have videos documenting this stuff. How is that possible? This stuff can't be real. Can it? How do they know all this?"

"Maybe you really are a Starseed. You said there was a lot more. Keep reading."

"I'm going to do an internet search to see if there are any videos on Starseeds. Yes. There are several videos. I'm not going to take time to watch a long video right now. I'll just read some of the comments."

(*Some of the commenters are talking about psychic abilities. How sometimes they can hear people's thoughts. Several in here are talking about something called remote viewing. They have taken classes and practice meditation then can remote view other places. That's like my seeing through walls but mine is always on. Every time I see a flat surface I see images and get emotions. It never stops. Here is another comment about how that person cried when looking at the stars. Wanting to go home and home is not on Earth. Another said they just realized they were a Starseed and how happy they are to join the world of freaks.*)

"These video comments are great. This one said they are happy to join the world of freaks. That sounds like me. A freak. That term Starseed. There is something about it that feels right. I can't explain it. It makes me want to learn more."

"Everything is on the internet. You can probably find everything you want there."

"True. I'm going to keep searching. I'll view these other videos later. Oh, wait. I need to make a video on this. You know I'm putting out my strange happening videos as they happen. Yesterday, I looked up to the universe and said I sure could use somebody to talk to and today I found out about Starseeds. That I might be a Starseed, and there are a lot of others out there exactly like me. I think I'm going to find others like me. Maybe even talk to them one day."

"I wouldn't be surprised," Tara said.

"I'm nervous just thinking about talking to someone other than you about this stuff. So much on the internet is fake, and this might be fake. I don't know," Adam said.

"Do more research. I'm sure you will figure it out."

"Your right. First, I need to make a video. Can you believe this will be my 70th video talking about these strange happenings? I'm going to call this one **Starseed**."

# # #

(*It's great getting everything done and still having time to ride my four-wheeler through the fields. I can't think of anything else to do here at the pink house. It's rare having this much free time.*)

Adam rode around the crawfish ponds then through the back part of the field. This field is used for hay so the ground is more or less level. Adam felt something and stopped. Time froze, but he could still feel the warmth of the sun. Memories and concepts flowed into his mind all at once.

Memories of him opening a door and finding a green lady asleep. She had been asleep for a long time. He gave her his heart and she gave him something green in return. He loved her. Had always loved her.

(Knowledge. Understanding. Wisdom.)

(There is that voice again. It's right. That's what I've always asked for. I've even included those three things on the first page when I created the channel for my video uploads. Those three words have been with me the whole time. Concepts in my head that she is related to the Earth. The life force or consciousness of the Earth. I'm a freak, just like that comment on the Starseed video I saw two weeks ago. Things are moving faster now. I learn through trial and error. I listen to my intuition. Right or wrong, I'm going to do it.)

Adam turned off the engine and stood to the side of the four-wheeler. He opened his mind sensing everything around him. He felt the Earth beneath his feet. Adam got on his knees and placed the palms of his hands on the ground. He felt his heart. Felt love. He mentally held it and felt it leave his body on the way to the core of the Earth. There was a flash and something green was returning. He felt it. The emerald green armor with polished silver mirror on the inside felt it also. It woke. Not sentient but aware. It was reacting to Adam's thoughts. The armor was responding to Adam's thoughts.

(God. Things are moving so fast. It's like I'm swimming in a riptide and being carried out to sea. It's a good thing I've been swimming in these waters all my life. I'm a good swimmer. You go with the riptide using enough energy to swim parallel to the shore. Eventually, you get a break from the riptide and swim back to shore if you have enough energy left. I'm going with the riptide and not losing sight of the coast.)

Adam cranked the four-wheeler and drove back to the pink house. He went inside, grabbed his tablet, and sat on the couch.

(Cool. My favorite video person put out a new one four minutes ago. Good timing.)

Adam's mouth fell open as the video talked about swimming in the spiritual waters and how you can get pulled out to sea as if in a riptide. So much can happen at once the person gets overwhelmed and lost. That person can end up in a mental institution if not careful. It's like a riptide. You go with it. You don't fight against the current. Try staying parallel to the shore without losing sight of it. Then, if you have enough energy, you can make it back to shore. The coast is real life. Family. Paying bills. Friends.

(That's crazy. All this was just in my head. I was thinking about how this is like swimming in a riptide. It's all being said in this video. Figures. Another one of these crazy riptide currents is pushing me along. That's enough. I've got

another headache. I think these are happening more often. I'm not going to die from old age. I'm going to die from taking all these headache pills. Ugh.)

It took a while with the headache but Adam finally fell asleep. He woke the following day. No headache. The drive back home was mostly uneventful except for an impression that kept repeating. Regardless. He made it back home safely to find Tara sitting in her recliner on her tablet.

"I'm back," Adam said.

"How was the trip?" Tara asked.

"Fine. I got everything done. There was one strange thing when I was out in the field. I got these memories and impressions. I thought of all these strange happenings moving so fast like I'm in a riptide being pulled out to sea. Then I saw a video saying the exact same thing. Another coincidence."

"That is weird but that kind of stuff always happens to you."

"Yeah. On the drive back, I started getting more impressions."

(The answer you are looking for is in one of your books.)

"There it is again. This time it's a voice in my head saying the answer you are looking for is in one of your books. I have no idea what it is talking about. I don't have a question. How do you find the answer to a question you don't have?"

"Well. We got rid of most of your books. Hopefully, whatever you are looking for wasn't in one of those books. You could look through what we have left."

Adam grabbed a book from the bookshelf, sat down, and skimmed through it. Nothing. He grabbed another. Nothing. This continued for several hours and he was about three-quarters of the way through all their books. Finally, he picked up a hardback book missing the protective cover. Adam sat in the recliner about to open the book when it flung open.

Adam turned to Tara. "Did you see that? Did you see that? The book opened by itself. I didn't do anything."

"No, I didn't see it. I was watching television."

Adam began reading the open pages. It was about Sophia. A universal female consciousness left a piece of herself on Earth as a gift to humanity. She was knowledge and wisdom, leaving humans the gift of understanding.

(That's what I've always asked for. Knowledge, wisdom and understanding. I even put those exact words on my video channel the first day I created it. Then that voice saying the answer I was looking for was in one of my books. The green lady I gave my heart to at the pink house and she gave me something in return. Is that Sophia? Knowledge, wisdom and understanding are all connected to her. The book opened by itself directly to the page dealing with Sophia. This is a strong riptide and I'm being pulled far out to sea. I hope I don't wind up in a mental institution.)

CHAPTER 47 – SNEAK ATTACK

(There is so much information online about Starseeds. How did I even find this webpage from all the stuff out there? This handbook is fantastic. The e-book lists different missions that are typically associated with Starseeds. I fit the part of earthworker. Investigating uncontrolled hazardous waste sites for the E.P.A. My continuing love for gardening. Then there is this last one he says is more specialized. A dark arts practitioner. That they can redeem lost souls. That they can see and fight dark entities. They are alone but need help against some of the more substantial dark entities. No shit, Sherlock. I could have used guidance a few times. Hmm. In college terms, does that mean my major is a dark arts practitioner with a minor in earthworks? I don't know.)

It was the first time he had seen or read anything about fighting dark entities. This e-book talked about it. Talked about what Adam had been doing. The webpage even had a section where people could chat. One of the chats spoke about an upcoming online conference for Walk-Ins. The description sounded like what happened to Adam after that first depression. Something came into his body. They called it a walk-in. He would have to sign up and attend that online conference. It was two months away so he had plenty of time to register.

"I'm ready," Tara said, walking into the kitchen.

"Me too. I was just reading about Starseeds. Seems I'm a dark arts practitioner and earthworker, according to this e-book. First time I've ever run across anything about fighting dark entities. So strange," Adam said.

"I forgot. Crystal wants you to go to her house and pick up her living room rug. She's giving it to Kevin. You're the only one with a truck and the strength to pick it up."

"No problem. I can do it in a couple of days."

"She needs it done now. She's having a new rug delivered this evening, so the old rug needs to be removed now. It can't be stored under the carport because of the rain coming in tonight."

"Wait a minute. We are both dressed and leaving for the restaurant right now. We are to meet Crystal and Kevin for all you can eat shrimp at a place 45 minutes away. How am I supposed to do both those things? You're saying I need to drive to Crystal's house now, pick up her living room rug, put it in my truck and deliver it to Kevin's house on the other side of town. That's easily going to take me 30-45 minutes. By the time I get to the restaurant, you will be finished eating. If I say no, I'm saying no to the friends we are supposed to be eating with tonight. I can't say no when they ask for help and then go out to dinner with them instead of doing what they asked me to do."

"Maybe you can do it tomorrow," Tara said.

"You just told me that she needs it done now because a new rug is being delivered. It can't be stored under the carport because of the rain coming in. I don't have any option. I could have done this anytime today if I had been told sooner but I don't have a choice now."

Adam should have been able to find a solution. He liked thinking outside the box and could always find a way to make things work. But instead this time, he was blinded by anger. His mind was stuck as if walls had been put around his mind. Tara said something but Adam could no longer hear her. He was getting angrier by the second.

"Leave. Just leave. Go eat without me. It's what you all wanted anyway. I'll move the rug just like all of you planned. You got what you wanted."

Adam grabbed his truck keys and slammed the door on the way out. Finally, he made it to Crystals. Her house was in the woods on a dead-end street. It was ok for her to leave the door unlocked until Adam arrived. He rolled up the rug, put it in his truck and locked her house door before heading towards Kevin's house. His house has an oversized enclosed garage to keep the rug out of the rain. Adam delivered it as anger turned to depression. His mind was walled off from everything except feeling alone once again. Even his wife didn't want him around.

Adam returned home and drove around the side to park in the back. He walked to the back door but didn't go inside. Instead, he sat on an ice chest on the back patio. They would be eating by now. They were happier without him around. Figures. He preferred to stay in the background. This was the price for keeping himself hidden. He would always be paying this price.

Adam looked down, seeing his hands clasped together as his arms rested on his legs. There was a spot of red on his left wrist. He must have cut himself on the truck's tailgate delivering the rug. It was close to the other scar on his wrist. This new cut was deep but it didn't cut a vein. Drops of blood dripped on the concrete as Adam sat there watching.

(*I have scars on both wrists and no idea how I got them. At least I'll know where I got this new scar.*) Adam continued to watch as blood dripped. He didn't try to stop it.

(That's a beautiful red color. So vibrant. So beautiful. Don't you want to see more?)

(*Another voice in my head.*)

(It's the reddest red. It glows red. So beautiful. You could see more of that beautiful red with a little more on the cut. You would have such good dreams if you fell asleep thinking about that vibrant red color. It's so beautiful. You want to see more.)

(*Suicide. No. Never suicidal thoughts again. Not after those other two times. Never again. This is something else. Yes. Something else is here.*)

Adam opened his senses, feeling his surroundings. Everything was normal except for the black hole to his left. He turned and faced the area. His senses form an image of a shadowy figure looking at him.

(*There you are.*) He felt the figure shift. It looked straight at Adam.

(You're alone again. You will always be alone. Your friends don't want you around. Your wife doesn't want you around. You are alone. You will always be alone.)

(*It knows I can see it. It's changed attacks from suicide to being alone.*)

Adam reached out and grabbed the entity. It struggled to get away and Adam struggled as well. Adam poured hope, love, and joy toward the entity. It pushed back with pain, hopelessness, and fear. Adam focused on the moment to the exclusion of everything else. No thought of what the entity might be doing to him. Adam could not give an inch because if he did he would fall. The entity began slipping through his fingers. Adam felt weak. He couldn't hold it and the shadowy figure slipped away.

(I've fought these things to a tie before but never had one slip away. I couldn't hold it. I feel weak. It's gone now. I didn't see it coming. It blinded me with anger. Walled off my mind. It was slow and stealthy. A sneak attack. It almost had me. It made a mistake bringing up suicide. I'll have to tell Tara what happened and apologize when she gets back home. There were all kinds of ways I could have done the rug and still gone out to eat. I was blinded by anger. I'm glad I'm going to the pink house in a couple of days. It will do me good to get back to nature.)

# # #

Adam walked toward the pink house from the field. It was almost noon and he needed to get things finished to drive back home. He was still tired even though he slept fourteen hours that night after the dark entity attack a couple of days ago. The sun was out. Adam felt the warmth of the light flow through his body as he walked. It felt like his body was glowing except around his left shoulder. He focused on that area as he walked.

(There is something there. Inside me. It's black. So black it's reflective. It's shaped like a cone. I think it's a piece of that entity. It broke off a part of itself and stabbed me under the left arm. That's why I felt weak and couldn't hold the entity. I was so focused on the fight I didn't notice it stabbed me under the left arm. This armor wasn't helpful at all during the conflict. Was it because the entity made a sneak attack? Is there an armor weakness under my left arm? Maybe it's not that kind of armor. Perhaps it's something else.)

Adam recalled something he read about Starseeds. That he might be what they called an earthworker. He could feel nature all around him. Feel the sunlight. Perhaps he could use that to get rid of this dark shard.

Adam stopped walking. He felt the sunlight and green of nature. He felt the healing energies of sunlight flowing through his body and onto the dark shard. The reflective surface of the fragment began dripping away like something toxic being eliminated. Drop by drop, the bit became like a piece of coal. Dull and inert.

Adam began walking again toward the pink house. He pictured and felt light roots start growing into the shard in his mind. Roots expand, breaking the fragment apart. He walked into the house and lay on the couch as roots pulverized the pieces into nothingness. There was only one piece left.

Adam was about to send more roots of light into the shard when he felt energy swirl around him. He sat up. A tornado of energy surrounded him. It changed into two ribbons. A white strip and black strip rotates around him like a D.N.A. chain. It reminded him of the two paths he had seen before he was born. A standard life path and a life path of shadow.

"Whoa. What is happening?" Adam asked.

Images and concepts flowed into Adam's mind as the energy grew around him. Finally, they suggested to Adam that he keep this final piece of the shard. It could no longer hurt him and could help him to understand.

(I've followed my intuition and your guidance all my life. You have always been there for me and I'm not going to stop listening now. I'll keep it and hope to understand one day. Thank you for helping me. Thank you for being there. I'll do my best to understand.)

The energy dissipated. The spiraling D.N.A. chain of black and white is gone. Things were moving so fast and he still needed to drive home. He stood and began the standard chores before leaving. Taking out the trash would be the last thing before getting in the truck and going home.

He was an hour into the drive when a song came on the radio he liked. He began humming to the tune. This had been a great trip. First, he figured out what happened in the dark entity fight. Got rid of most of the shard. Then there was that D.N.A. chain spiraling around him. Crazy things had happened but he was used to crazy. He felt happy as he hummed to the song on the radio.

(This shard is vibrating as I'm humming.)

Adam focused on the shard as he continued humming. It was buzzing with him. Adam felt his senses being drawn away, out of the truck, out of the state to somewhere else far away. There was the entity he had fought days earlier. The shard was still connected to it and he was related to the fragment through the humming.

Adam tightened his grip on the steering wheel as he pulled onto the shoulder of the road and stopped the truck. He could see the entity in his mind. The entity looked at Adam and smiled. Again, images and concepts flowed into Adam's mind. Images of family. Brothers and sisters helping each other.

(Brother)

Adam felt it before the voice in his head said it. This dark entity was his brother. It was like the other dark entities that he fought to a draw. Even the one that had crushed him. They were family teaching him lessons. The soulless dark entities were thoughtforms created to teach him lessons. Adam's mind reeled as his mind opened.

He had learned so much through all those fights with dark entities. He learned to use the light, love, and joy to protect himself. How to hold entities. Using what he learned from those dark entity fights to help human souls that had died and were trapped. He learned how to see, keep and show lost souls the way home. They taught him how to retrieve souls that fought back because they didn't know they were lost. Adam learned to help dark, lost souls, others would not approach.

They taught him the dangers of arrogance. How easy it is to fall into that trap. Some of the lessons were traumatic, but he survived and learned from them. They taught him that he could survive even when he didn't believe it himself. Concepts flowed into Adam's mind that this is how it is supposed to be. It takes these kinds of lessons for someone like him to grow and that hopefully, one day, he will understand.

Adam's mind returned to himself. He looked at the fields outside the window. They were family teaching him lessons. It wasn't long ago that he felt like a baby just opening his eyes. Now his baby eyes had focused on family for the first time. They had been helping him all along but he couldn't see it. He put the truck in gear and continued driving. He had human parents and siblings but this was different. He was now 57 years old and felt he had opened his eyes to see family for the first time.

CHAPTER 48 – WALK-IN: PROTECT

Tara said "I'm heading out."

"Ok. Have fun with Crystal running around today," Adam said.

"I will. We should be back late this afternoon."

"I'll still be here at the Zoom conference."

"That conference sounds like a good way to start the new year. Almost forgot my phone. Bye."

Adam didn't know what to expect from this conference. He had never heard the term Walk-In until he stumbled across it in his internet search for Starseeds. Walk-ins were people who had another soul or something come into them and their whole life changed. It sounded like what happened to him during puberty but he was skeptical.

He set up a small table next to his recliner. He grabbed some snacks and a second cup of hot tea while waiting for the meeting to start. The conference was scheduled to last three days and Adam was unsure if he could sit still that long as he logged in.

The hostess, Sheila, introduced herself and outlined the conference. She showed a book she wrote that included stories from many speakers regarding walk-ins. There is a gallery view so the participants can see each other if their camera was activated. However, everyone except the speaker would remain muted until the end of the presentation.

(It's good they can't hear me. I'm nervous. There are so many people attending. Are there really that many people out there like me?)

Sheila was the first speaker. Her story began when she was very ill. She was lying in bed when energy like lightning hit her. It usually happens when there is either a mental or physical trauma. The person feels that they are brand new to this world and that it is not home. You may lose some memories. For her, even the simplest tasks felt as if she had never done them before. Her eye color had changed, and her body began healing itself. She called this a soul exchange. When the original soul leaves and a new soul enters the body.

These souls volunteer to come here. They want to help people wake up to a new reality involving consciousness; however, they may have difficulty relating to other people. The person getting the new soul may gain psychic abilities or increase their current skills.

She continued explaining that there are other types of soul interactions. There are soul braidings and soul jumpers. Adam focused on every word. Something similar had happened to him. Then she said it. There is a thing called a soul infusion. This is when a higher version of yourself comes in and fuses with your current soul. It's two parts of yourself coming together.

(That's it. That's what happened to me. I've never heard anyone say it before but it felt like a higher version of myself coming into myself. I even documented me saying this exact thing on one of my early videos. That it felt like something was coming into my body, and everything changed. Everything was new. My eyes also changed colors from solid brown to hazel. That's a real thing that happened. She's talking about it. How is this possible? I'm so glad that voice in my head said release videos of my experiences. If I had not done that, I would have thought I was crazy and made it up in my own mind after hearing it at this conference, like a false memory. But I have it documented in video form. I recorded all this more than a year ago. If this is real, I wonder if everything that has happened to me is real. I need to buy her book ***Walks-Ins****.)*

Adam was enthralled by every speaker. He understood what they were saying because he had lived it. He was like them. They were all here in real-time. Talking. He was not alone.

(What? This speaker says she is a first-wave Starseed. Not a walk-in. I'm like that and had a walk-in experience. Is it possible to be both? Wait. She's saying that she lived in a haunted house. She has seen entities all her life and many

of them were dark. One even pulled her out of bed when she was a young girl. She learned how to transmute the darkness and pain then release it. Wow. I lived in a haunted house as a small boy and saw dark entities. Something pushed me off the top bunk of the bunk bed. My story is so much like hers. Just wow.)

"I'm back," Tara said.

"Already. I got caught up in this conference. I didn't realize it was so late. Did the two of you get everything done?" Adam said.

"Yes. We ate at our favorite Italian restaurant. I got the sausage calzone as usual."

"That sounds good. This conference has been amazing. These people are just like me. They call what happened to me during puberty a walk-in. There is another speaker that is a first-wave Starseed. She even lived in a haunted house as we did. There will be a panel of all the speakers at the end. You should watch it with me."

"Ok. I've got to put away a few things. I did a little shopping while we were out."

Tara joined Adam in the living room. He was glad she was with him even though she didn't understand. She was more interested in the game on her tablet than what was discussed. It had always been this way and Adam accepted it. After all, she accepted him without understanding. They were together. It was enough.

Adam's mind had shut down by the start of the conference's third day. He proceeded to do household chores as the meeting continued. He could hear it in the background but his mind was still trying to process the last two days. There was so much information and it was all new to him. He had never seen or heard anything like it. He was a baby just opening its eyes.

(*I've got to make another strange happening video. All these people with similar things happening to them. I have my everyday human family. But this feels like a soul type of family. It's like I know some of them somehow. So I'll do whatever it takes to protect them.*)

Adam went to the spare bedroom and made video SH95 **Walk-In Conference Afterwards**. He edited several clips together and then uploaded them to his video site. It took a couple of hours before he returned to the living room.

"You're still awake," Adam said, looking at Tara in the recliner on her tablet.

"Yeah. I can't sleep."

"I'm not tired either. Still wound up about the conference. I'm going to see if anything is on the internet worth watching."

"Ok."

Adam turned on the television and began streaming videos. One of the first titles on the top bar caught his attention. It was over an hour long. He wasn't tired so he started the video. There was a lot on U.F.O.s but Adam didn't pay much attention. They were talking about housing some U.F.O.s in a remote military base. Then the speaker said there was one different spacecraft. It was conscious and would move away when anyone got near.

"Did you hear that, Tara?"

"No. I was on my tablet. What was it?"

"The guy said there was a spacecraft that was conscious and would move away when other people got near. Do you remember back in our teenage years I told you about a spacecraft I remembered piloting that was conscious? I just figured it was my overexaggerated fantasy life. That it was like we became one when we flew. That it was like moving slightly out of this dimension when passing through solid objects."

"I don't remember. It was so long ago."

"I thought it was odd that this guy would talk about that. It doesn't matter. Just my crazy little world. I'm still not tired so I'm going to keep watching."

"I'm not tired yet either."

Tara continued playing on her tablet as Adam watched. The U.F.O. stuff was interesting but Adam was learning more about himself. Then the speaker said the word Starseed. That got Adam's attention.

"Tara. He's talking about Starseeds and that it takes some traumas for them to develop. That they come here with a mission. Their mission is related to their job, whether they know it or not. I know I wanted to learn forgiveness in a big way while I was here, but I don't know anything about my mission. How was my science side tied to my assignment? I'm not some brilliant scientist solving the world's problem."

"I don't know. Maybe it's not your job. Maybe it has something to do with your family. Like when you were younger wanting to protect your brother and sisters."

Adam felt his mind expand. Moments in time are coming together to form images. Brothers. Sisters. People. The Earth. Protect. Adam's mouth fell open as he began to realize his mission. It's always been about protecting.

(Protect)

"That's it. Protect. It's what I have always done without thinking about it. Fighting the dark entities. Helping lost souls return home. Protecting them. Working with the E.P.A. to clean up uncontrolled hazardous waste sites. Protecting the Earth. Working in the Safety Department at Bell Helicopter. Protecting the people. It's always been about protecting."

Memories from before he was born filled Adam's mind. Two guards were looking at him and smiling. They never do that. Never.

"Oh my God. That memory from before I was born. Those two guards were smiling at me. Did they know? Is that why they were smiling at me? Am I supposed to be like one of them? I mean, no one has ever talked about protecting. They are all about raising their vibration or frequencies to ascend to another level. No one has mentioned anything about protecting at this conference. I've not heard anything about protecting at all. Is that a thing?"

"You're asking the wrong person. I bet you are going to find out soon the way things are working for you lately."

"You're right. Things are moving so fast I can barely keep up. My brain is fried. How about we go to bed? I need a little sleep for my drive to the pink house tomorrow. It's just a quick visit to check things but it's a lot of driving."

"Sounds good."

CHAPTER 49 – GUARDIAN

Adam woke a little later than usual. He wasn't in a rush to get to the pink house. His uncle who lived there was keeping it warm to keep the pipes from freezing. Adam liked to check things anyway because his uncle had a stroke a while back. His uncle used a walker but was still mobile and able to take care of himself although his memory had gaps.

The drive down was uneventful. It gave Adam time to think about the conference and the video he had seen the night before. As he reconnected the kitchen sink to the P.V.C. drainpipe underneath, it occupied his mind. It was the only thing that needed attention, and it wasn't long before Adam headed home. He was 30 minutes into the drive back home when his father called.

"Hello, this is Adam."

"It's your dad."

"Hey. What's up?"

"I heard you went down to the pink house today."

"Yeah. I'm on my way back now."

"Can I go with you the next time you go down? You could drop me off at my sister's home in Jena. I can stay with her and you can pick me up on the way back. Is that Ok?"

"Sure. No problem. I'll probably go next weekend if you want to go then."

"Sounds good."

"I'll call you the day before to remind you then call again before I head over to your house to pick you up."

"Ok. See you then."

"Bye."

Adam hung up as he got to the main highway. This was Olla. The tiny town where he had the walk-in experience. He passed through it on the trip to and from the pink house. He turned onto the highway and a song came on the radio. He liked it but had never heard it before.

(*What is this song? I really like it. The display says the song's name is* ***The Protector Prepares****. I've got to pull over.*)

Adam pulled into a parking lot. He sat there listening.

(*All this protector stuff was happening in my head last night. That my mission may be to protect. Then this odd song comes on the radio. Is that what is happening? I don't know. I don't know what's happening. Seriously. This can't be real. I'm making too much about a song on the radio. I'm just crazy. Stop. Get back on the road.*)

Adam pulled back onto the highway, trying not to think about the song on the radio. Instead, he focused on the farmland passing by. It was peaceful. Then another song on the radio. Again, it was an orchestral song catching his attention. Adam looked at the display and pulled off the road. He pulled out his phone, pointed the camera at the car radio display and began recording.

"I don't know what's happening. First, this song was on the radio called **The Protector Prepares**, and now the song playing is called **Protectors of Truth**. I had to pull over and document what's happening. I'm not making this up. I'm recording this live. You can see it for yourself. I don't know what's happening."

Adam stopped recording and looked around in disbelief. It's been four days in a row of strange things happening in his life. Each day is blowing his mind. He felt he was in a state of being permanently overwhelmed. He continued driving home, never realizing the time on the clock radio was 11:11.

# # #

Adam was excited. He had paid to attend a two-hour Zoom meeting titled **Visitors To A Small Planet**. The speaker was talked about often in the weekly Zoom meetings he discovered through the Walk-In Conference. They kept mentioning his name as if he was someone with a lot of knowledge. Even though Adam was excited, he was thrown off by the title, thinking it would be something about U.F.O.s. That was a topic he had not delved into but still, Adam might learn something new. He logged into the meeting.

The speaker introduced himself as John Appelton. He had a sense of humor about him. A lot of people unmuted to say hello. Some had known him for a long time. This was going to be interesting.

John began by outlining what he was going to cover. "We are going to discuss things I've learned in my travels throughout my life. Things like the **Book of Enoch** and the **Nag Hammadi Library**. We'll talk a bit about Sophia. I also want to get into the portals to Earth and the guards at the portal. That they help protect the truth. I've heard stories that when a new guard is born, they live a lonely life. Learning without knowing. The pieces come together only toward the latter part of life and things move very quickly for them. I'll also get into various planes of existence. If you ever see 11:11 on a clock, pay attention to what is happening. It's vital and may help you realize where you come from."

(*What the hell! Sophia. Portals. Guardians. Planes of existence. 11:11 on the clock. After that video in the car, I only realized that the time on the clock was 11:11. The song* ***Protectors of Truth*** *is playing on the radio. I'm freaking out. He's not talking about U.F.O.s. He's talking about me. What's happening? I've got to get my phone and record this. Shit. It's going to be my 110th video. I'm doing my first reaction. Reacting to his presentation. What the hell is happening?*)

Adam knew it as the truth. John was speaking the truth. John talked about how forgiveness is the key to clearing karma. Once you remove your karma, your D.N.A. will start activating. It may appear as electric and magnetic lines spinning around you.

(*Oh my God. I learned to forgive everyone for everything. Then lying on the couch at the pink house feeling that black and white strand like D.N.A. spiraling around me. Then there is the spiraling black and white paths I remember from before I was born. He's talking about it. That happened to me and I've got it documented on video before I ever heard about it. Got to record my reaction.*)

Adam started and stopped the video so much he wondered how he would ever edit it all. There were times he was recording and not speaking. He was stunned by what he was hearing. Like the time John started talking about the Emerald Tablets of Thoth. That there were beings known as guardians. He reviewed information on portal complexes. Information on Indigo children. How he had fought dark entities in his past. Toward the end, he said that if you can activate enough of your D.N.A. you will begin to see into the astral plane. How there are darker entities in the lower astral. The upper astral is where people go when they say they are astral traveling.

(They all know this kind of stuff and I'm hearing it for the first time. It feels like I'm so far behind. I don't have any of this knowledge but it happens to me. I've documented it on video. I've been doing things through trial and error. Learning without knowing, as he said with the guardians. The songs on the radio. The time on the clock. Everything tells me I'm a protector or guardian but it's not possible. I've done bad things. I'm not perfect. I'm human. I'm nobody. Then there is the bit about if they get enough D.N.A. activated they can see into the astral. I've been seeing the dark entities and lost souls in the lower astral plane since I was a teenager. The silver sword. Using it to help lost souls and show them the way home. Seriously. That plane I see above those dark entities when I'm in the shower. Is that the upper astral? Things are moving so fast. It's too much.)

John closed by saying that you may be talking to your higher self when you ask for guidance. Adam's mind began to shut down. He documented in an early video that it felt like sometimes when he was talking to this higher consciousness, he was talking to a higher version of himself.

Adam wasn't creating some new fantasy in his mind. He had documented it all on video. He could go back and confirm that he had experienced what John was saying. It was real. Did that mean he was a guardian? He felt this emerald green with silver armor around him. He wondered if that is why it was there. Maybe it was something to do with guardians. When he pictured himself in his mind he was always walking in the dark. Trying to be a light in the darkness. Was he a dark guardian having something to do with the emerald green color?

Perhaps he was a combination of the two. A dark emerald guardian. It was too much. Adam's mind shut down.

"Tara. My mind is fried. I need alcohol. I'm going to the store. Do you want anything?"

"How about some chips?"

"Ok. I'll be back shortly."

Adam's mind was blank as he drove. His body was on automatic. His plan was to drink and pass out, which he did.

# # #

Adam was driving back home with his father in the passenger seat. His father had come along and stayed at his sister's house while Adam spent two nights at the pink house. There was always something that needed to be done.

They didn't talk much during the drive. Adam could not understand his father's obsession with money and material things. It worked out because Adam could turn the radio up during the drive.

(There is that song again. **The Protector Prepares**. *That's the second time I've heard that song. The radio coincidences have been happening all my life. I wonder if that other song is going to play after this one. That would be weird.)*

The song ended and the next song began playing. It was **Protectors of Truth**.

(It happened. That's so strange. Hearing both those songs on the way back home. Oh well. I like them both. Hopefully the good music will continue.)

The song ended, and the next song began playing. The display showed it as **Protectors of Earth**.

(What? Another protector type of song. I like this group. I purchased two of their albums, but this song isn't on either. I did that by investigating uncontrolled hazardous waste sites. I was trying to protect the Earth. How odd. I love this song. I need to purchase this album. I wonder what my father would think if I told him right now how the radio is speaking to me. God, that sounds crazy. That's what he would say. I'm crazy. I could probably prove it to him the way things are going right now. I could say out loud to the universe what kind of guardian am I. I bet the next song on the radio would be a guardian song. I'm going to do it. I'm going to say it out loud.)

Adam began gathering his courage to talk to his father about what was happening. He was going to say it out loud. But, before he could speak, the next song started. The display showed **Guardians At The Gate**.

(Seriously. How is this happening? How is it real? I'm glad I didn't say anything to my father. How could he believe me when I'm having difficulty believing it myself? I just want to get home and stop. It will be nice resting in my recliner.)

Adam was having trouble denying what was happening as he drove. The armor, his mission to protect, the initial round of music, and now this. In between all of it, that meeting with John talking about things Adam had experienced. Experienced without having any knowledge of it.

It began sinking in for the remaining hour of the drive. Adam might be a guardian trying to find his way in the dark. He wondered if other guardians feel this darkness. Then there was the silver sword that came into him long ago. It was there but not a weapon. He did not have that kind of weapon. The only weapon he ever used was love, hope and joy. Light to fight the darkness. He thought about everything that had been happening to him. It all pointed to one thing. He had been training his entire life. Training to be this. A guardian. He couldn't deny it anymore. He didn't know what it meant or why. He only knew it was true. It's who he was. He was a Starseed. A Walk-In. A Guardian.

CHAPTER 50 – TRUTH

(*Is this a dream? I can't change anything here like I usually do when lucid dreaming. This feels real.*)

Adam was standing near a door in a small room. There was an older being standing near the door. He looked human. Like a grandfather figure but it felt like he was so much more. Something he couldn't understand.

"My time is over. You are taking over for me and I want you to have this gift. It's the last gift I can give. It's yours now," the figure said, handing something to Adam.

"Thank you for the offer, but I don't want to take something from you that you may need. I'll be ok. I have everything I need already."

"I know. I want you to have it. It's a going-away gift. Don't argue."

"Thank you for your generosity," Adam said, taking the gift. He wrapped it in a cloth then put it in a box on the table next to him. He looked up to see two beings walk in from the other door behind him. Adam recognized them as remote relatives.

"Congratulations on the new position," the first one said, walking up to Adam to shake his hand. "You're going to do well," he said, patting Adam on the shoulder.

The older man watched and smiled at the exchange.

"That's all. I just wanted to be the first one to congratulate you. I'll meet you outside when you are done here." The second one moved from Adam's side near the table and walked out as well. Unfortunately, Adam was distracted and overlooked the second one approaching his side.

The older man was distracted as well. Then, realizing something, he gave Adam a look of warning. Adam opened the box on the table and the gift was gone. The first relative had distracted them while the second one took the gift.

"How could they steal? They are family. Family doesn't steal," Adam said, looking at the older man. His anger was growing. It wasn't about the gift or that it was taken from Adam. Just the fact that a relative had stolen in front of him was enough. He didn't say a word as he hurried out the door.

Adam felt it as soon as the door closed. He was being summoned to a meeting. The older man had sent out a call for an emergency meeting and his new position required him to attend. Adam opened the door and walked through.

He walked directly into a secured space. It was outside. Usually, they would see this location, only now it was as if the room had been moved slightly out of phase with the current dimension. Adam had never been in a space this secure before.

He stopped just inside the doorway. Over 20 beings were sitting in a circle at designated spots. Adam's designated place was next to the door. He looked around. Those in attendance were all different types of beings. They were family and much older than him. He was the youngest. He recognized some of them and others he had never seen before. They were all different, but he knew that they were all family. They didn't say anything. They were waiting.

(*This is serious. This kind of meeting only happens on the rarest and most serious occasions. Once through many lifetimes. A meeting with these family members in a location this secure. This is serious.*)

The door opened and a tall being entered. Adam was standing facing the being, his head reaching the being's chest. It was an ancient guardian with many battle scars. One of the founders. They never attended meetings. This was serious.

(*It's looking into me. Evaluating me.*)

Adam left himself open to the being. Let it explore everything about him. He wasn't afraid. He only had respect and gratitude for everything the being had done. Adam was honored to be in its presence. It turned and stood to the other side of the door. Watching the proceedings.

The older man who Adam was replacing spoke first. He described what happened. The stealing of the gift by family members. A shock rippled through those listening. Then, they began whispering to each other.

"Something similar happened to us. Members of that same family line stole an object from us that was being used to help others. It caused chaos for a short time, but eventually, things returned to normal."

"We also had an incident with that family line. They lied to several of our family members, stirring up trouble. Eventually, it was settled."

The other attendees began speaking and telling their stories. They were similar. This one family line causes problems for everyone else. Problems that seemed small individually but very large when combined. The minor difficulties connected like pieces of a puzzle. The larger puzzle leads to chaos and war.

"This is serious. Much more serious than we first thought. We must act now. Are we in agreement that this family line must be ended? We must end it now!"

"Yes," the group said in unison. Everyone except Adam and the tall being next to him at the door. It wasn't their place to vote. They were there to act on the decision which had been made. They stood and began walking to the edge of the secured area. It would dissolve as soon as they touched it.

"Wait," Adam said. "I'm not to participate in these decisions unless it involves me. A gift was stolen from me. I'm involved and would like to speak."

The beings stopped and turned. They showed no emotion but would listen. Adam had never attended one of these meetings but he knew it wasn't just about the spoken word. Ideas and concepts would be exchanged. He had to be honest. They would see if he wasn't.

Adam spoke. "I understand the decision. I will help carry out the decision that is made. But I wanted you to know that I received a much bigger gift. A bigger gift because that little gift was stolen. All of you are coming together wanting to help. But the bigger gift is meeting all of you. Seeing all my family for the first time."

Adam was speaking the truth. He was overwhelmed with love for them. He would do anything to protect them. They were his family.

They smiled. They would not terminate that family line. The secure area vanished. The beings left except for the much older one next to Adam. They turned to face each other. The guardian was smiling at Adam.

Adam woke, remembering everything.

(*Was that a dream? It felt real. As real as anything that has happened to me. It didn't feel like a dream. It felt real. I spoke the truth. They saw the truth. I will do anything to protect my family. Wait. Those decisions are final. They didn't go through with it. I'm missing something. Oh wow. I think that was a test. I had no idea. I think all of it was a test. Did I pass? They smiled at me. I think I passed.*)

He performed his morning rituals of brushing his teeth, making hot tea, and feeding the cats. He also checked for texts and emails.

"Tara, do you remember that Zoom meeting I attended called **Visitors To A Small Planet**? This guy named John was the speaker and I got so excited I videoed a reaction."

"Yes. You sent John an email wanting to be included in his mentorship program if he ever had an opening."

"He sent me an email. One of his students had to drop out due to family obligations. John accepted me into the program. That's crazy. I will have to tell him that he is working with a blank slate. I don't know anything from anything. It's so weird how things work out sometimes. All these coincidences. Things are moving so fast. I hope I don't hit a brick wall or something."

"When do you start?"

"This Sunday. We are going to meet through Zoom calls on Sunday evenings."

# # #

(*At my Zoom meeting with John last week, we completed a technique that was supposed to reveal a personal symbol. The symbol that appeared to me instantly was the same silver sword that occurred when I was a teenager. It's always been there. I can't tell him it came to me when I was a teenager. He will think I'm crazy because a sword is a weapon, not a symbol.*

We've been doing these meetings weekly for months, and I still can't tell him that I've been recording videos of my experiences. How can I tell him that I recorded a video telling how I linked my heart to the Earth long before he went over that technique? How can I tell him I was creating bubbles of light around myself long before he told me about that technique? He will think I'm arrogant. I don't want to fall into that arrogance trap again. I wish he knew just how much I understand what he is saying.)

Adam opened his tablet and logged into the meeting with his mentor.

"Hello, John."

"Hello, Adam. How are you?"

"Everything is good here."

"Last week we did that technique where you were supposed to get a personal symbol. Did you receive an image or guidance leading you to your symbol? You don't have to tell me your symbol. I was just curious if anything happened."

"I don't mind telling you, although you are going to think I'm crazy. It's a silver sword. It came inside me, point facing downward with the hilt through my shoulders and head. I know it's a sword but it's not a weapon."

John was excited. "What? A silver sword."

"Yes, but it's not a weapon."

"Right. It's a symbol. It's not a weapon. That's one of the techniques we have not gone over yet."

"You're not serious. Your joking, right."

"No. I'm serious. You know all that material I had you print out. It's in the big binder of techniques. I know you are not jumping ahead but I want you to jump ahead with three techniques this time. Open it and look."

Adam pulled the binder off the bookshelf. He never opened it. He preferred to let John go over the material. After the mentorship, Adam could use the binder as a reference. He never jumped forward.

"You're right. There it is. In black and white. The technique with a silver sword. It says something about comfort."

"Yes. That symbol is used when visualizing comfort for yourself or another. I've noticed that about you when doing these techniques. You really understand the material. It's second nature to you."

(*Oh my God. It's real. This is another thing that is real. I want to deny it, but I can't. How is this all real? If this is real, does that mean every crazy thing in my life is real? Stop it. Focus.*)

"What are we doing tonight?"

"We are going to work on a higher plane of existence. We will be using the heart chakra as some points during the technique. You may feel energy cover your body. You may see this energy as sparkling green crystals around you with some silver interlaced between them."

"Wait. Sparkling green crystals with silver. This happened to me a while back during a drive to the pink house. I even recorded a video talking about this exact thing. I'll send you a link to the video."

"Ok. I'll check it out."

(*Cat's out of the bag. I told him about the videos. I don't think he believes me. Maybe he shouldn't believe me. I'm even having a hard time believing it.*)

"A lot is dealing with emerald green, like the Emerald Tablets of Thoth. The author of **The Wizard of Oz** also knew some of this information. Did you know the ruby slippers were silver in the original books? Silver slippers on their way to the Emerald City. They were changed because color in movies had been introduced and ruby slippers would make a bigger impact on the screen. There is also something I heard in a presentation about a group of beings related to the emerald color that gave a gift to humans but were betrayed by one of their own kind. The gift was stolen. I'm getting off track again. Let's get back to the technique for today."

(*That dream from last night that wasn't a dream. That's it. It felt real. It was real. Everything in my life is pointing to this. I'm confirming it to myself through video documentation. I'm a new guardian. It goes beyond being human. Beyond space and time. It can't be real, yet I know it is real.*)

Adam's session with John ended. This time was different. John had confirmed much of what had already happened to Adam. It was there in the techniques they were covering. It was there in ancient writings. Adam's crazy little world was real. It was all real.

He woke around three in the morning as usual. Images and concepts flowed through his head. People only saw a reflection when they looked at him. They see a reflection of the physical world but he was so much more than that. They were so much more than their human reflection. They were family. Just as the beings he saw were members of their non-human families. The human and non-human families were pieces of the family puzzle. They were all family.

They were all connected to this universal waveform Adam had seen. All are related to universal consciousness. A small piece of the whole. A living expression of universal consciousness here to have the experience.

(That's the truth that needs to be protected. We are all part of that universal consciousness. The dark and the light. That's funny. That religious saying. I am that, I am. But that's just it, isn't it? You are everything you see, YOU ARE. If only other people could say those words out loud to themselves.)

"It's all just me."

"Jusme."

EPILOGUE

Don said "Tara, I finished the book. Can you believe it? I don't know how that happened in two months. I still have a lot of editing to do, but it's done."

"That seems pretty fast to me."

"I need to get a few people like our friends and family to help edit. I changed their names in the book. I hope they like the ones I gave them. I left your name the same but changed mine to Adam. I also had to move timelines and change a few things to make the story flow better. The experiences are real, though. People aren't going to believe it."

"It's ok. You said you were not writing the book to make money. That you had to do it."

"That's true. I guess it does not matter. I still have to create a cover. Maybe I'll just take a photo of me walking down the road in front of the pink house. I could make it a black and white photo. I mean, that is the whole book. Walking black and white paths. This thing about being a guardian feels real but I'm still not sure what kind. I guess something will happen to help me figure it out. It always does," Don said.

"Now that you have finished the book, do you think you will have more time to help around the house?"

"Yes. I'll be happy to help after all this sitting and writing. I'll also start staying overnight again at the pink house. Get more done."

"So, are you happy overall with the book?" Tara asked.

"Yeah. It's my crazy little world in five parts. It probably sounds disjointed and narcissistic but it's my first time writing. I don't know what I'm doing. I don't even know how to end it because strange stuff happens daily. Like right now, I'm feeling these pulses of energy. I've been feeling them all week like chills that run from one side of your body to the other. Then they come from the other side. It's like my body is changing or something. It's probably just old age."

"We are getting older. When are you going to the pink house next?"

"I don't know. A couple of weeks."

"At least you have all those albums you downloaded you can listen to during the drive."

"Yeah. I downloaded all but one of those albums related to the protecting songs I mentioned in the book."

"Which one did you not get?"

"The one for the first song that showed up was called **The Protector Prepares**."

"You got all the others. You should get that album as well. You can probably find it online."

"I don't know. I'll look it up, though. You are not going to believe this. I just said a bit ago that I didn't know what kind of guardian I am. The name of this album is **Dark Guardian**. What is that supposed to mean? Is it a guardian that is in the dark? Is it a guardian that protects against the dark? Is it a guardian of the dark? I don't know. I guess I'll find out."

You are more than the reflection people see.

Take another step and keep moving forward.

You are not alone.

Find me at www.bitchute.com/donhudnall

THE END

ABOUT THE AUTHOR

Don Hudnall was born in central Louisiana. His home has been in Louisiana except for the 20 years spent in the DFW Texas area during his professional career. He graduated college with a Bachler of Science in Toxicology. The art and science of poisons. Personality tests highlighted his scientific and creative sides.

His science side lead him to investigating uncontrolled hazardous waste sites and working in the Safety Department for Bell Helicopter Textron. After that he took jobs to satisfy his creative side. He started a pottery business then became the sole owner/operator of a vending business stocking soda, chips and candy. He also held jobs stocking nights at a hobby store and at the local NBC/FOX television station.

Throughout his life he remained involved in various organizations. He became Secretary of the Louisiana Teenagers Librarian Association for the State of Louisiana during high school. He was also Newsletter Editor, Secretary and President for the North Texas Section American Industrial Hygiene Association as well as the Newsletter Editor, Secretary and President of a local art gallery.

His primary hobby is gardening. He loves working in the dirt and watching things grow.

Made in the USA
Columbia, SC
24 June 2023

18861366R00183